T0204722

Mysterious Ways

Mysterious Ways

A NOVEL BY

Terry Davis

The Viking Press   New York

Copyright © 1980, 1984 by Terry Davis
All rights reserved
First published in 1984 by The Viking Press
40 West 23rd Street, New York, N.Y. 10010
Published simultaneously in Canada by
Penguin Books Canada Limited

A portion of this book appeared originally in *Spokane* magazine.

Library of Congress Cataloging in Publication Data
Davis, Terry.
Mysterious ways.
I. Title.
PS3554.A93777M9   1984   813'.54   83-40227
ISBN 0-670-50224-3

Grateful acknowledgment is made to the following for permission to reprint copyrighted material:

Chappell/Intersong Music Group, U.S.A.: Portions of lyrics from "Adieu Tristesse (A Felicidade)," original lyrics by Vincius DeMoraes, original music by Antonio Carlos Jobim. Copyright © 1959 by Editions Musicales France Verdettes. Published in the United States of America by Intersong–U.S.A., Inc., and United Artists Music. All rights controlled by Chappell & Co., Inc. International copyright secured. All rights reserved.

J. M. Dent and Sons, Ltd.: An excerpt from *The Inferno*, by Dante, translated by Carlyle-Okey-Wicksteed.

Farrar, Straus and Giroux, Inc.: A selection from *One Day in the Life of Ivan Denisovich*, by Alexander Solzhenitsyn, translated by Thomas P. Whitney. Copyright © Group W–Leontes–Norskfilm, 1970. Revisions © Gillon Aitken, 1971.

Slow Dancing Music, Inc. (BMI): Portions of lyrics from "Caterpillar," by Peter Albin. Copyright © MCMLXVII by Slow Dancing Music, Inc. (BMI), 515 Madison Avenue, New York, N.Y. 10022. All rights reserved.

Printed in the United States of America
Set in Electra
Designed by Roger Lax

À Mariette

Men must endure their going hence,
even as their coming hither...

King Lear

Part I

THE COMING HITHER

Sunday night, March 24, 1968,
11:30 p.m.

My name is Karl Russell and I'm an optimist.

Sometimes I feel like finding someone to confess to. Hello there. My name is Karl Russell and I'm some weird kind of optimist. In spite of how hard life tries to show me otherwise, I still have the feeling everything is going to turn out all right. I'm always starting over, always believing—with absolutely no evidence—that I can do better.

I think the reason I'd like to tell somebody is to see if they'd think I'm stupid. Sometimes I think it's a good quality in me, and other times it just seems pathetic. Sometimes I think it makes me unique, then other times I say, No way: if we all didn't start over, again and again, really believing we could change, what would keep us from blowing our brains out or degenerating into insanity?

When your family isn't alive anymore, all you can do is guess at how well you're growing up. Nobody will tell you how you're doing. Maybe nobody but your family knows you well enough, or maybe nobody else has a big enough stake in you to care.

I remember back in freshman composition we were talking about freedom one day, and this guy who was one of the top students said, "A man can't be completely free until his father dies." And I—deeply entrenched in the middle ranks—said, "Yeah? Well, who wants to be completely free?"

So here I am exercising a small degree of my freedom and starting over again in a few small ways.

This is my first night in the fraternity house, and already I can feel how different it is from the dorm. It's a big old two-story wooden house that reminds me of the house I grew up in. With only twelve guys and the housemother living here, it feels like a real home with a real family in it.

I'm resolved to be more social and to dress a little nicer, like these guys do. And I'm also resolved to study harder.

What it comes down to is that I've realized it's time I took a little greater control of my life. I'll be twenty-one years old in four months. I'm a junior in college. I should probably decide what I'm going to major in, at least.

It's for this purpose of greater control that I've decided to start another journal. Taking note of what you accomplished during the day is an excellent way to see how much time you wasted. The thing I like most about keeping a journal, though, is that it makes you feel like talking to yourself is not only respectable, but—if you're careful about it—even literary.

We had to keep a journal for freshman comp, and I enjoyed it and wish I still had mine.

The teacher's name was Sam Ochs and he had a baby girl he brought with him to class sometimes. He was reading my journal one night and holding her against his chest when—in what he called "the definitive critical act"—she shit all over it. I didn't mind then because he was so embarrassed he gave me an A for the course. But now I kind of wish I had that journal. Mom would have gotten an enormous kick out of me being literary. My compositions did survive, though, and sometimes I read them over and wonder if she'd think they were okay.

Tuesday, March 26, 1968, 1:20 a.m.

I was in a good mood all day, and I couldn't figure out why until I sat down here to write. Today was an early spring baseball day: one of those March days that's a little drier and a little warmer than the ones before, and full of the smell of spring grass. When you're a kid, you take a couple giant sniffs of that air and it's in your body about two seconds before it rearranges your chemistry and you can see into the future with perfect knowledge. Yeah, you say, school really is gonna let out in June and I'll be playing ball from morning till night right through to September.

God, it's amazing: I'll be twenty-one years old this summer, and this is the first spring I haven't played organized ball in twelve years. That's over half my life.

Today was also the first day of classes, and although I think I'm going to like all mine, classes are definitely not what got me so charged up. Here's my schedule:

Spring Quarter 1968

English 410:	Literature of the Camps	M–Th	8:40
Humanities 210:	World Masterpieces	M–Th	9:40
History 310:	Europe in the Middle Ages	M–Th	11:40
Spanish 303:	Spanish 9	M–F	3:40

I should get over to the registrar soon and make out a declaration-of-major form. I suppose P.E. is how I should go, since I've got the most credits there. But I'm not all that sure I want to coach anymore. My heart was set on it for a while, but now I don't know.

I do know one thing, though: It's a good thing I can't get drafted. If I weren't 4-F, I'd be so goddamned committed to a teaching career, nobody would believe it. If I weren't 4-F, I'd consider getting a teaching job a matter of life and death.

Life's lesson in regard to this is not lost on me. For years the only thing I even think about doing as a career is playing major-league ball. Then I tear up my arm, and baseball dreams are down the toilet. But if I hadn't gotten hurt I'd be draftable now, and I'd probably get sent to Vietnam and killed. Or worse. The lesson isn't lost on me just because I don't know exactly what it is. Maybe it's just that good luck and bad luck sometimes travel together.

I translated all my Spanish and got through the fall of the Roman Empire in History. They say the Middle Ages begin after the fall of Rome. What a relief it is to learn Rome didn't fall simply because the kids were growing their hair long, listening to psychedelic music, smoking pot, and practicing free love, like you hear downtown in the barber shop. The United States is going to have to expand its empire a lot, fill its armed forces with mercenaries, suffer a big decline in trade, create a huge civil service and boost taxes to support it, then get invaded by Goths, Huns, and Vandals all at the same time before we start to fall. I'd like to let the old guys down at the barber shop know we're safer than they think, but I'm staying out of barber shops till the end of the decade.

Mac McAdams, one of the other pledges, the only longhair in the house and the guy I feel most comfortable with here so far, thinks I look like a model for Nazi recruiting posters. So I'm letting my hair grow out.

After I finished History I got about thirty pages into the *Inferno* for World Masterpieces before I began to fade, and quit to write my entry here. I'm getting a kick out of Dante. I like the passage where he meets Virgil:

"Art thou then that Virgil, and that fountain which pours abroad so rich a stream of speech?"...

"O glory and light of other poets! May the long zeal avail me, and the great love that made me search thy volume."

Dante tells him about the she-wolf that scared him off the mountain. "See the beast from which I turned back; help me from her, thou famous sage; for she makes my veins and pulses tremble."

"Thou must take another road," Virgil replies, "if thou desirest to escape from this wild place."

I remember when I was small enough to sit on Mom's lap and she'd read me *The Iliad* and *The Odyssey*. In my senior year of high school I tried *The Aeneid*, but it wasn't the same without her voice. And I remember reciting "The Highwayman" to Jesse. I must have recited it a hundred times. I'll bet anything the little turdburger knew it by heart, but I could never get him to recite it back to me.

Wednesday morning, March 27, 1968,

6:20 a.m.

I've spent more peaceful nights than last night.

I took a shower after I finished writing here, and as I was toweling off I found a colony of warts growing on my wrist where I wear my watch. My wrist had been itching like crazy the past few days, but I'd taken my watch off and hadn't seen anything there. The warts are the size of BB shot and the same color as skin. The tops are getting darker this morning and they're beginning to harden like calluses. Last night they were just barely above the skin like tiny blisters. Seventeen of the little fuckers. I've counted them a whole bunch of times.

I've never had a wart in my life, but I have had a very creepy feeling about them since I was a kid.

I guess I was eight years old. It was the Fourth of July, and the first time Mom and Dad ever let me take the bus alone into downtown Spokane. My excuse for going was to see the parade, but I wasn't as interested in that as I was in the adventure of going the five or six miles from the city limits into the center of the city alone. A kid always expects and maybe hopes for some scary stuff on an adventure, but I wasn't expecting anything like the scare I got.

I remember dropping my dime down the coin chute and listening to the machine click as we pulled out, and I waved to Mom where she sat with Jesse on her lap behind the wheel of Dad's pickup.

I'd taken that ride a hundred times with Mom and Dad in the car, but by myself on the bus it was an adventure. I looked at the houses and yards and apartments and stores and at the Spokane River and the falls, as if I were a tourist coming into town for the first time.

I jumped off the bus in the middle of town and walked through the crowds to where the parade was forming. The cowboys and cowgirls and Indian men and women were having a hard time keeping their horses steady with people throwing firecrackers and the bands beating their drums. Some of the horses would rear up when the waves of Air Force jets flew over. At the roar of the jets everybody would cover their heads and duck, then we'd look up at the sky and get blinded by the bright sun, then lower our heads again and rub our eyes.

When the parade began and all the people marched and rode out of the staging area, I lost interest and started to explore. I had it in mind to find a good spot to get a hamburger and milk shake with the buck Dad gave me that morning before he left for work.

I'd just passed a place I judged a little too fancy for me and my dollar when I heard the sound of trash cans banging in the alley. I took a look and saw a bum bending deep into one of three or four big aluminum cans in back of the restaurant. I stood a few seconds watching the guy paw around in the can until he stopped and slowly rose up to look at me.

I wasn't so much scared as awestruck at the sight of the guy's face. Huge warts the size of noses grew on his forehead, cheeks, and chin, and smaller ones bubbled up out of his skin everywhere the big ones didn't. The guy's face just boiled with warts.

He growled deep in his throat and flipped his hand at me to go away. The hand was dirty with crap from the trash can and so covered with warts it looked like a toadstool patch. He stayed facing me, but I couldn't see his eyes for all the warts dripping off his forehead. Still, he was staring right into my soul. Then he turned and walked farther back into the alley and leaned over into another can.

I walked through the streets feeling numb. I couldn't see anything in my mind but the wartman's face. It was horrible, but it was fascinating too. I wondered if the wartman's gaze carried wartmanism, the way the wolfman's bite made you into a werewolf.

I didn't have much to say about my day in town when Mom picked me up at the bus stop. I never told her about the wartman, and I've never told anyone. I dreamed about him—not about *him*, really, just about his face—for years after that. I quit seeing his face in my dreams when Mom and Dad and Jesse got killed. I can't even remember thinking about him again until last night.

I didn't dream about him last night, but I don't think I slept either. Maybe if I'd told Mom about the wartman the day I saw him, he wouldn't have terrorized me all those years and he wouldn't be back now. Maybe if I told somebody now it might get his face out of my mind. I've got to talk more with people. I'm not alone in the world, even though I do feel that way a lot.

It's funny: I never realized before that I saw the wartman on the same day of the year that Mom and Dad and Jesse got killed. The same day, but seven years earlier. It's just a funny coincidence, but it makes a guy think.

THREE COMPOSITIONS

I

Composition I
Karl Russell
November 6, 1965
Topic: The Worst Thing That Has Ever Happened to Me

In the evening of the Fourth of July, 1963, in the second game of an American Legion double-header, I had just run from first to third on a bloop single by Franny Hallowell, when I saw a state patrol car roll into the park and pull up behind the backstop. Time was out, and as I stood by the bag getting my breath I watched the trooper walk over to our bench and talk to Coach. Mom and Dad and my little brother Jesse had gone to the drag races at Deer Park that afternoon, and the thought that they had been in an accident in that crazy traffic on the two-lane highway swept through me. But the ump called time in, and my thoughts went back to the game. Randy Riggins flew to right on the next pitch, and I tagged up and scored sliding.

No one was standing by the plate to shake my hand when I got up. Coach and all the guys stood by our bench like they were frozen. I took a step and Coach took a step. His face was as white as the lime that marked the foul lines. I knew it was my folks.

Coach walked up and put his arm around me. He walked me past the bench and bleachers, out of the light and into the long shadows in the park.

"Your mother and father were killed in an accident, Karl," Coach said. "Your little brother's alive, but the trooper says it'd be better if we didn't even hope."

The sprinklers were sweeping around in circles, and I registered the *tic-tic-tic* they made and the silver arcs they cut through the blue dusk. In my mind I saw myself standing there. Then I forgot myself. I turned and ran for the trooper and begged him to get me to my brother. It was just me and Jesse left in all the world.

The trooper drove me to the hospital in Deer Park as fast as he could, siren wailing, through the heavy traffic. He didn't look at me when we passed the spot where it happened. The cars were gone, but a couple flares were still burning. As we flew past I saw that sand had been spread over both lanes for about thirty yards, and across the road I caught sight of small pieces of red and white Fiberglas from Dad's '61 Corvette. I thought of Jesse, of how dumb he threw a ball and how he'd dive for the ground when I'd pretend I was going to throw him back a hard one.

The emergency room was empty when we got to the hospital, so we walked through it into a hall where we found the doctor who told us Jesse was dead.

My mother hated drag racing because of all the noise, but she would go to the races at Deer Park because she liked the little city park there. We would drop her off at the park with the picnic lunch, and she would read in peace until Dad and I and Jesse got tired of the races and came back to eat. I hadn't gone with them that day because of the ball game, and they hadn't come to watch me play because they had watched me play another double-header earlier in the week.

On the way back to town with the trooper and for a long time afterwards, I thought of how it could have been different: Dad could have driven the station wagon instead of the Corvette; the races could have been in Airway Heights instead of Deer Park; I could have gone with them; the guy who hit them could have died a slow death from burns so I wouldn't have spent so much time thinking of killing him.

I turned sixteen the next day. It wouldn't have been a big deal, except that we had always waited until that night to shoot off our fireworks. We always had a lot of fun, especially the first few years Jesse got to shoot his fireworks himself. All my birthdays up to then had been full of life and noise and color, and thinking of that made things seem dead quiet and gray.

I lived my last two years of high school with my baseball coach and his wife. In my senior year I met my girlfriend, and I'm still going with her. It's not that I don't have friends and people to love and who love me. But when Mom and Dad and Jesse died, it was like the world changed. I felt separated so far from life that I thought I'd never get joined to it again. I hardly ever feel that separate anymore, but sometimes I do.

II

Composition I
Karl Russell
September 10, 1965
Topic: My Favorite Inanimate Object

My dad was service manager for Northside Chevrolet in Spokane and my mom was the librarian at the one-room library in Nine Mile Falls, nine miles downstream from Spokane. We lived in a two-story wooden house a quarter mile north of Nine Mile, as everyone calls it, and a couple hundred yards off the west bank of the river.

We had a three-car shop that Dad had made from an old barn before I was born. The shop was where I spent the time I wasn't in school or playing baseball. Jesse, my little brother, used to love to come watch us do stuff. He especially liked to watch us weld or grind because of the sparks. Sometimes, when Dad had time, he'd give Jesse a piece of stock, put the full-face hat on him and the big gloves, and let him grind the stock down to a nub.

Dad would buy a lot of the older trade-ins with low resale value, and we would clean them up inside and rub out and wax the paint, and maybe put on a water pump or seal the radiator or something, and sell them.

The spring I was fifteen Dad drove home a 1951 Ford Custom two-door sedan a farmer from Colville had traded in. I washed it off before the sun went down and drove it inside and vacuumed out the dirt. Then I got some rubbing compound and rubbed out the hood to see if there was any paint left or if it was all just oxidation. That old blue Ford looked brand-new after about fifteen minutes. I walked back up to the house to tell Dad how well it had rubbed out and to get him to come see. He told me the Ford was mine and that I'd better take good care of it because it would be the last car he'd ever buy me.

For a few minutes Jesse was more excited than I was. He ran back down to the shop with me and rubbed out about two and a half hubcaps before he fell asleep on the back seat.

Mom came down about eleven to look at my car. We listened to the end of a Spokane Indians game on the car radio, then she woke Jesse, and she and I walked back to the house with me pushing Jesse in the wheelbarrow.

Mom and Dad and Jesse got killed in a car wreck a few months later on the day before my sixteenth birthday. I got my license the day after the funeral and put a lot of miles on the Ford through the fall. That was five years ago, and it's still as sanitary a stock '51 as you'll ever see around here. Even now it's only got 89,000 miles on it.

I'm the kind of guy who likes inanimate objects a lot. I would say, for example, that I almost love my Rawlings baseball glove and my Ford. I like Dad's tools, I like the little trailer he built to carry his tools and welding outfit, and his motorcycle, a 1955 Harley-Davidson, which I also would have to say I just about love. But the '51 is my favorite. The other stuff was Dad's and passed to me when he died, but the Ford he gave me himself.

III

Composition I
Karl Russell
December 2, 1965
Topic: Extra Credit—Choice of Topic

I lived my last two years of high school in Spokane across the street from Evergreen High with Tony and Andrea Commellini. Tony had been my baseball coach since sixth grade. He helped me get the insurance money after my folks were killed and talked me into suing the guy at fault in the accident for a bundle. I paid them sixty dollars a month room and board and fixed their cars and the stuff in the house that broke down.

I wasn't thinking straight when Coach suggested I sell our house. I should have kept the shop, or at least the welder and machines, and bought a place of my own. As it was, I kept Dad's tools, the little trailer he built, and his Harley. I even let all Mom's books go. Some people from California bought the place and turned the shop into a painting studio. I do have three of Dad's shop coats the guys at the garage gave me. They're white and they say Russ Russell, Service Mgr. in blue over the left breast pocket.

I drove my Ford out along the river a lot that fall and winter just to sit and look at the house. I could see the four of us there easily if I wanted to. The wind would blow little chunks of frozen snow along the road and they would rattle into the side of the car like bird shot. The freight trains would roll by along the river without any hoboes for Jesse to wave to. One day I decided I'd just have to start my life over and be happy.

The second worst thing that has ever happened to me—so far—turned out to be dislocating the elbow in my throwing arm. Coach wanted me to get thinking about something besides my folks and my brother, so after Christmas he put me on a weight program.

I noticed the difference in my strength after about three weeks. I liked the way it made me feel. My arms kept getting lighter and lighter until a bat was hardly any weight at all in my hands. Four afternoons a week I worked out hard and ran the cross-country course through the snow. Spring came finally, and practice started and things went well for me and I wound up having the best school and Legion season I'd ever had. I began getting feelers from colleges. Both Arizona State and U.S.C. wrote me, and I was pretty excited about it because playing for those schools is like playing Triple-A ball.

I skipped football my senior year so I could work more on my baseball skills. I worked out like a fiend with the weights and took batting practice with the pitching machine four nights a week in the gym.

One afternoon in February I was alone in the weight room doing tricep curls—it's an exercise where you lie on your back on a flat bench and, with your hands close together on the bar, lower the bar behind your head, then pull it back up to full arm's length above your chest—when something gave way in my right elbow. It felt like my arm had come apart, which I found out later was pretty much what happened. The bar fell on my chest and rolled back onto my throat, and about half choked me. I'd been working with eighty pounds and I couldn't get it off me with only one arm. All I could do was roll my head to the side and keep pushing with my left arm until the bar got so far off balance one end crashed to the floor. Pete Peterson, the basketball manager, came running out of the training room when he heard it.

We put ice on my elbow right away, but in a few minutes it had swelled to about the size of a cantaloupe. It hurt so bad I had to lie down to keep from fainting. Pete ran upstairs and got the basketball coach, who drove me to the hospital. I did faint dead away when the doctor bent my arm to get it in the X-ray machine.

Both lower arm bones had pulled out of the elbow. They tore the ligaments away and (as it was explained to me) scraped off the cartilage as they pulled out of the joint. I had an operation after the swelling went down a little. My arm was in a shoulder-to-wrist cast until school let out. Georgie, my girlfriend, had graduated the year before and was enrolled here at Eastern. She would take the bus to Spokane on weekends and drive us around in my Ford. My arm was perfectly formed for hanging out the window, where I could keep a beer cool in the evening breeze.

By the end of June, after the cast was off and I'd been in therapy for weeks, my right arm was still so much smaller than my left, they looked like a before-and-after ad for bodybuilding.

By the end of July, the therapist said I could throw.

I threw like a foreigner. I threw like a girl, with my elbow all stuck out ahead of the ball. And it hurt. Coach and I played catch after supper until I got to where I could throw the width of the backyard, which wasn't even ninety feet. Then I started practicing with the Legion team. Coach moved me from third to second so I'd have the short throw.

It wasn't short enough. No throw was short enough when I had to get the ball there fast. Coach was hitting infield, and I was gobbling up the balls. But my throws were hitting the dirt about six feet in front of first. Larry Constable, our first baseman, was getting so he wouldn't even stretch for my throws; he'd just break down like he was fielding grounders.

I felt fine. My arm hardly hurt at all by that time. I just couldn't throw. Coach hit me another one and I moved to my left, gobbled it, and in a fluid motion winged it into the dirt about fifteen feet away.

I turned around and walked out through the grass. I walked out to center and sat down with my back to the short cyclone fence. I watched the outfielders working over in right, and I looked in at the guys taking infield. Swanson had gone back to second and Jim Collins had come in to play third. I listened to the crack of the bat and watched the puff of dust the ball kicked up when it hit and listened to the throws whack into all the different gloves. Tears came to my eyes, and I cried hard. I think everybody heard me, but I didn't care.

All my scholarship offers had been withdrawn by then, but Coach talked to Coach Bell out here and he said if I could still hit they would take a look at me. I could still hit and I wanted the chance to play ball. So I said to myself, Okay. Start over. Be a pinch hitter.

The warts don't seem to have grown and there's no more itching. It was a pretty hectic day, with all my classes and my long shift at work in the Student Union Cafeteria, and I forgot about the warts until near closing, when I got so hot behind the grill I could hardly stand it and looked down and remembered I'd put on long sleeves that morning so nobody'd see them.

Talked a little with Bolão, my Brazilian roommate, tonight. Got a good feel for the guy. His real name's Carlos Henrique Porto, but he likes Bolão, which he said means "cake." His folks named him that because he was a cake-monster as a kid. I've seen him running tapes for people in the language lab and I figured I wouldn't like him because he's kind of "pretty" looking and is always so well turned out. Not only is it time for me to stop holding people's appearances against them, but it's also time for me to start wearing something besides T-shirts and jeans.

I was looking through the catalogue, trying to fill in my declaration-of-major form, grumbling about having taken all this Spanish and not being able to use it for anything, when Bolão asked me what I was doing and I told him. He said Spanish would be a great foundation for learning Portuguese, and then he got all in a frenzy telling me about Rio de Janeiro and putting Brazilian music on the stereo and showing me his posters that he hadn't put up yet, and assuring me that if I came to Rio to visit him this summer he'd have me speaking fluent Portuguese by August.

It's a thought. From the looks of the girls in his poster of Ipanema beach, I'd have a hard-on all summer, though, and I don't know if a guy can learn a language with all his blood flowing to his cock instead of his brain. But it's a thought.

We put the beach poster above his desk and the Christ the Redeemer poster above mine. It's this huge statue, hundreds of feet high, that stands on one of the huge rock mountains in and around Rio de Janeiro. Christ is stretching his arms out level with his shoulders so he's in the form of a giant cross. He's looking over the city and out to sea, and you get the feeling that he's inviting people to come sailing in off the South Atlantic and settle there under his blessing. We were going to put Christ above Crookshank's desk, since Crookshank contends they're personal friends, but we decided against it because we didn't want to get off on the wrong foot with the guy.

Bolão wants me to see the Brazilian movie *Orfeo Negro* that the foreign-language club is showing tomorrow night. He says it'll give me a chance to find out how much Portuguese I already know just from knowing some Spanish. I might ask Georgie if she feels like a dose of culture.

Bolão got recharged again telling me about the movie and he grabbed his guitar and sang some songs from it, and then some other Brazilian songs. We thought everybody had either gone to sleep or out for a beer, but when he began to sing guys started drifting in. He plays and sings like a pro.

After an hour or so I had to call a halt so I could do the rest of my studying for tomorrow. I wanted to write about it now because I'm kind of charged up myself. Got to pull myself together, though. Got to read some in Elie Wiesel's *Night*. It's a short book and I'm highly energized, so if I can get Brazil out of my head, maybe I can push through to the end tonight.

Friday, March 29, 1968, 7:10 a.m.

Up early to get a head start on the day with a shower, some work here at the desk, then a good breakfast with Georgie. Only got about four hours of sleep, but I feel good. I feel completely cleaned out after last night. It's like they say to women in the old movies: "There, there, dear. Have a good cry. Get it all out. You'll feel better."

I finished *Night* this morning around two-thirty. It's only 115 pages long and didn't even take two hours to read. I read the last line, then turned back to the front and read the dedication: "In memory of my parents and of my little sister, Tzipora." Then I put my head down on the desk and cried. The stuff that happens in that book is sad beyond any dreams of sadness I can imagine, but I cried for myself mostly, I know, not for the Wiesel family.

They get off the train at Auschwitz and immediately Wiesel loses his mother and his little sister. Forever.

Nobody knows, until it's happened in their lives, the blackness of the night that death brings. It's the only figure of speech I can come up with that even half describes how I felt when Mom and Dad and Jesse vanished from this life. I mean, I could physically feel the black emptiness seep into my bones like dry rot in a timber. And I knew that my house was weaker and my song had grown fainter, as the Indians used to say.

Anyway, what started my crying was the empathy I felt for Wiesel when he writes, "I saw them disappear into the distance." I marked all the important passages and I went right on from there, like a glutton for heartache, from that one to the one about his father's death.

Wiesel and his dad and the other male Jews from the train are being marched toward a ditch where something is burning. A German truck comes up and dumps a load of babies into the flames, so Wiesel knows they're walking toward their death. And he says, "In the depths of my heart, I bade farewell to my father, to the whole universe." Even though the Germans turned them away from the ditch and marched them into barracks, I cried harder.

Mr. Wiesel is sick and crying for Elie to bring him water, and the German officer yells for him to be quiet. Mr. Wiesel keeps calling Elie, and the German officer comes up and bashes him on the head with his club. And Elie says, "I did not move. I was afraid. My body was afraid of also receiving a blow.

"Then my father made a rattling noise and it was my name: Eliezer.

"His last word was my name," Elie says. "A summons, to which I did not respond."

And it was just then, when I was crying so hard it actually felt good, that Crookshank got home from his job parking cars at a hotel in Spokane. I tried to quit in the next breath, but of course I couldn't.

Crookshank closed the door and walked over to me, put his hand on my shoulder, and said, "Good Lord, Karl, what's wrong?"

I was too low to get any of the contempt I have for him worked to the surface, so I just said—and I was still crying—"I was reading a sad book and it made me think of my folks and my brother."

Crooks gave my shoulder a squeeze and a pat. There was none of that electric smile he flashes when he testifies about Jesus being his personal savior, and none of the condescending tone his voice takes on when he explains to you how simply life really works. "I might know a little how you feel. I've been blessed in my life, but even so I lose my faith sometimes. But we have to realize," he said, "that the Lord works in mysterious ways, that we aren't always able to understand the plan He has for our life."

He looked as if he might be ready to break down himself. Then he put on his pajamas and brushed his teeth. He was walking out the door headed for bed when he turned back to me. "'Night, brother." he said. "Lord bless ya."

"'Night, Gordon," I replied. "God bless you too."

It's hard for me not to like and respect someone who treats me with kindness. One of the many things I've got to shape up about myself is this business of judging people for how they look or what they believe.

Friday, March 29, 1968, 8:50 p.m.

Decided not to go see *Black Orpheus*. Georgie had to fill in for somebody at the hospital and I felt like putting in some work here at the desk to stay ahead. Bolão said he'd run the film for me in the lab Sunday night if I wanted to see it. Going to be hard to turn down a private showing.

Bolão got all upset tonight after dinner when Tommy Boreson, the sergeant at arms, jumped on him for trying to leave the house when there were still dirty dishes in the kitchen. Bolão is used to maids doing the housework where he's lived, so he's not quick to catch on to this "pledge-duty" business. And I think the idea of men doing housework offends him.

Boreson is "a good soul," as Mom used to say, but he doesn't have much self-confidence—probably because he's fat—so he pushes a little too hard to get his respect.

Bolão said a funny thing when they were yelling at each other. He said it about four times, and when I first heard it I thought he was saying "horseshit." But what he says is "whore shit"—*"puta merda."* That's one I've got to incorporate into my lexicon of profanity.

Had a good time with Georgie at breakfast this morning. We haven't been seeing each other much with me moved in here and her working so much in Spokane. I showed her the warts and asked her to find out how they get rid of them at the hospital. She didn't seem put off by them. But they're not on her, they're on me. They give me the fucking creeps!

I walked her to her Dart and listened to the poor, afflicted thing. The little slant six needs doctoring. I told her I'd trade her a tune-up for a wart job. I got a tune-up kit at Western Auto on my way home this afternoon, and I'll put it in tomorrow while dinner cooks.

Before I sat down here tonight I Lysoled the shower in case that's maybe where the warts came from. Anything could be growing there the way Bolão cleans it. And I threw away my old leather watchband and I'm buying a new metal one tomorrow. Right now it's onward into Español, Europe in the Middle Ages, and maybe some *Inferno*, then to bed and sound asleep by one o'clock before the drunks get home.

Sunday morning, March 31, 1968,

8:45 a.m.

Did a very stupid thing last night.

Georgie told me sometime during the evening that she'd talked to a guy in Dermatology who said the doctors there got rid of warts either by burning them out with an electric needle or by cutting. And I remembered Dad telling me about when he was a high school kid with bad eczema on his face, and how he couldn't get rid of it, so one night he took his straight razor and just shaved it off. It bled a lot, he said, but he kept putting cold towels on it and that stopped the bleeding, and the eczema never came back.

We had a good dinner, the nursing-school dance was fun, and Georgie's Dart ran great on the way to the party, where I drank too much of this incredibly strong punch that didn't smell or taste like booze. Everybody probably drank a little too much of that punch, but I might have been a little drunker than some people. I went around interviewing the nursing students to see who had the sharpest pair of manicure scissors in her purse and who had the steadiest hand to do wart surgery on me. I got so drunk I don't even remember how we got back to Georgie's. I'm sure I couldn't have made love, but I did wake up with my pants around my ankles, so I might have tried. I woke up peeing in the sink over the dirty dishes, so I think I have cause to worry about how I might have behaved. Georgie was asleep in her robe on the davenport.

I drove home in the beautiful purple dawn, still drunk. I stumbled upstairs and clipped off each of the warts with my fingernail clipper, then shaved my wrist smooth with my safety razor. It hardly hurt at all, but they bled like crazy for almost an hour. I was fascinated by the craters they left. They kept filling up with blood individually, like little blood volcanoes, then they'd overflow and blood would run all down my arm. I wrapped my wrist good in gauze, but it kept soaking through.

Mac woke me up at 8:30 to see if I wanted to go to church with him. There's blood on my sheets and a little trail of blood from my bunk to the bathroom sink, which was filthy with blood and wart chunks. I just finished cleaning the sink and putting on more gauze and wiping the blood off the floor, and now I'm headed back to bed. I'll change the sheets later.

None of this might have happened if we hadn't had such a great time Saturday at the house workday. I got to know some of the guys better, and I kept gaining altitude through the afternoon and into the evening until I finally entered orbit.

After Mac and I painted the porch floor he spent the rest of Saturday morning arguing with Crookshank over Crooks's literal interpretation of Genesis. Mac's dad is a Unitarian minister and Mac thinks of himself as a Christian. But Crooks says if he doesn't believe God's word, it doesn't matter what he thinks he is, because he isn't "saved."

Mac was scornful. "I can't believe this," he'd say. "I'm absolutely stunned. I find it incredible that someone with almost three-fourths of a college education, someone apparently not retarded and on the threshold of adulthood, actually believes horseshit such as talking snakes." And Crooks would come back calmly with Scripture: "'The statutes of the Lord are right, rejoicing the heart.'" And they'd go on like that as they trimmed the grass and spaded up the flower beds.

They started in again after lunch, but Leo Portella, the president of the house, had me put my stereo speakers out the window and turn up the volume. We drowned them out with Bob Dylan's *Blonde on Blonde* album.

Later on, after the work was done, we climbed up to the garage loft and drank the beer Boreson had put on ice there. All the R.O.T.C. guys were in the loft, and that's how I wound up talking to Charley and Gary. Six of them will be in Vietnam by Christmas. In spite of the sobering nature of our discussion, we all got drunk. Pericles, the basset hound that's the house mascot, fell out of the loft and broke his leg. Charley's girlfriend came looking for him. She stood in a shaft of sunlight as she looked up at us asking where her soldier boy was. The dust motes floated around her head and her blond hair shone like gold. I was so captivated by her I was lucky I didn't fall off and break my leg too.

I'm surprised how much I've gotten to like writing here. Sometimes it's hard to stop. But it's real easy to stop now. I feel awful, and I'm headed back to my bloodstained sheets.

Monday evening, April 1, 1968, 7:05 p.m.

After seeing *Orfeo Negro* last night, I'm really tempted to drop Spanish and add Portuguese, and I'm also thinking about quitting work. If I did quit, I'd have twenty-five more hours in the week. I could use fifteen of them to study and the other ten for attending some of the things offered on campus for a change. Mac, for example, left a note on my desk this afternoon asking me to meet him at the Christian Student Center at four to hear some Vietnamese minister talk about the war. I'm afraid Mac's going to give up on me if I don't accept one of his invites pretty soon.

Bolão woke me yesterday afternoon at three, saying the sorority girls were coming at four. I'd forgotten all about the picnic. He told me the guys figured that as a professional hamburger chef, I should be in charge of the grill. My head ached so bad I couldn't stand up straight.

I know the term "hangover" means that the effects of the drinking hang over into the next day. But in my case it might as well mean that the victim's body will hang over in excruciating, hair-to-toenail pain. God: I swear I'll never drink that much again! I took a shower, and by the time I put new gauze on my wrist I was able to open my eyes all the way and to stand up fairly straight.

Rudy Waller, another pledge, had the charcoal already burning in the fireplace in the back corner of the yard. As we stood there pressing burgers, I realized the severe limits of my liberalism. Rudy was wearing an ascot. He was wearing a fucking ascot! If you're David Niven or Roddy McDowall, maybe you can wear an ascot and not seem like a pretentious asshole. I fell into a funk for a while thinking how hopeless it is for me to even try to expand my mind when my heart's all shot through with these picky little bigotries.

When the girls arrived, our pledge class had to meet their pledge class. We lined up like football teams before a championship game and shook hands as the two pledge masters read off our names to all assembled. They seemed like nice girls, and didn't use as much hair spray as I would have expected.

Everything went okay, I got no complaints about the burgers, but I was still in my funk until after everyone had finished eating and Leo asked Bolão to sing.

The guy is wonderful. He had everyone captivated. He sang just enough songs in Portuguese to sort of intrigue people. In between the Brazilian songs he sang Beatles, Lovin' Spoonful, Zombies, and Dylan's "Just Like a Woman."

It was beginning to get dark and the air was feeling cool and damp when Bolão said, "Here's a song from the movie *Black Orpheus* that was filmed in Rio de Janeiro, the city where I live in Brazil." He told everyone he'd be showing it in the language lab in half an hour and invited us all to come see it. Then he said, "I dedicate the song to my roommate Karl Roosell" (he doesn't always pronounce everything right, but still he speaks great English) "who will maybe come to visit me this summer."

I was embarrassed because he pointed me out and everybody turned to look at me where I was sitting on the rear bumper of Thorville Anderson's '37 Chevy coupe. I still had the spatula in my hand, so I brought it up to the crown of my chef's hat in a little salute.

Nobody showed up at the language lab with us. I couldn't believe it! Well, almost nobody showed up. Bolão was hustling a girl named Laurie, and she and her friend Rhonda drove us up to the lab in Laurie's new yellow Camaro convertible.

Bolão put on the film, turned the sound way up, then disappeared with Laurie into the room where the tapes are stored. I sat on the floor right in front of the screen, elbows on my knees and chin in my hands like a kid, and Rhonda sat at the control table and smoked. I don't think she realized it was going to be in a foreign language. I only recognized about three words myself, but still I think I got the whole story.

Orfeo Negro is an allegory about how nobody—not even great and devoted lovers—beats death. It's taken from the Greek myth about Orpheus and Eurydice.

In *Orfeo Negro* everybody is black and poor, and Eurydice is a girl from a small town who takes the ferry across Guanabara Bay to Rio for *Carnavál* and meets Orfeo, who is the best male samba dancer in his *escola de samba,* which means "samba school."

Orfeo and Eurydice fall in love at first sight. He takes her home, tells his girlfriend he has to practice his guitar and get some rest for the big parade the next night, and he and Eurydice wind up in the sack.

Orfeo gets up before Eurydice and stands at the edge of the mountaintop where the *favela*—the slum they all live in—is located. He's playing his guitar and singing, and as the sun burns away the mist and you see the city and the bay and then the South Atlantic all spread out below, you think maybe it's not so awful to be poor in Rio if you can live in Orfeo's neighborhood. Just as he finishes his song two little boys and a little girl walk up. It's the first day of *Carnavál*, and they're too excited to stay in bed. They've never been up this early before, and they ask Orfeo if his song is what wakes up the sun.

Orfeo tells them it sure is, then he hands his guitar to one of the boys, who starts right in working on Orfeo's song.

That night all the *escolas de samba* are dancing down the street in the big parade and Eurydice is walking along watching Orfeo, when a guy in a skeleton costume slips out of the crowd and begins following her. Eurydice feels a supernatural fear, like the guy really *is* Death. Orfeo sees what's going on, but he's his samba school's big gun, and he can't leave the parade. When they finally come to the end of the street, Orfeo takes off looking for Eurydice. He finds her, and he and Death fight it out. Orfeo gets the worst of it, and when he wakes up, both Eurydice and Death are gone. He looks all the rest of the night for her, and finally finds her in the lowest level of the basement of the city morgue.

It's nearly dawn when Orfeo comes walking up the steep path along the edge of the mountain cliff to the *favela* carrying the body of Eurydice. His girlfriend has been waiting up all night for him, and when she sees him carrying Eurydice she freaks out and flings a rock at him. Orfeo's not even looking her way because his eyes are locked on Eurydice's beautiful dead face, and the rock hits him in the forehead. He staggers and slips and his body and the body of Eurydice bump and scrape all the way down the straight black mountainside and wind up cradled in the leaves of a huge plant at the bottom.

The three little kids are looking for Orfeo. They've got his guitar and they're after him to wake up the sun with his song. The little girl tells the kid with the guitar that he'd better do the job himself if the sun's going to come up on time. So the little guy starts playing and singing and the other two start dancing the samba. And there they are, these three little black kids, one playing and two dancing to this beautiful samba song as the sun breaks over the horizon and brings into full light the green hills around Rio, the rock mountains jutting up everywhere, the gray buildings of the city below, and the blue waters of the bay. And the kid keeps playing and singing and his two friends keep dancing, and pretty soon the song is louder and louder and coming from everywhere. And that's how it ends.

Bolão and Laurie came out when the film started flapping in the projector. I walked home alone, singing words I not only didn't know the meaning of but couldn't pronounce and trying to dance the samba, trying—like Bolão says white people have to—to keep my back concave and my ass high in the air as though I were impaled on a stock of sugarcane. I stayed up listening to Bolão's records through the headphones until the sun came up.

Monday, 11:15 p.m.

Just called Georgie, and she was cold as ice. Said she had to study and hung up. I must have done something really terrible Saturday night. Maybe she was mad that I didn't call her yesterday. I want to call her back, but I know I'd better not. Her voice just cut me to ribbons.

Tuesday, April 2, 6:50 a.m.

Had the worst dream of my life last night. A hundred times worse than the nuke dream. I was a wartman and I was falling off that mountain in Rio where Orfeo and Eurydice fell, scraping the solid rock cliff all the way down. I could hear the scraping sounds and feel the warts tearing away. I could feel the rush of air all cool and full of moisture, and the smell of rich vegetation was all around me. I just fell and fell and fell.

I've fallen in dreams before, and I've had my teeth knocked out and lost them to strange diseases in dreams, and I've dreamed I was naked in class and couldn't control myself and shit and peed in front of everybody. But in all the times I've fallen, I've never landed until last night.

I landed in that big plant where Orfeo and Eurydice land in the movie. I could feel the smoothness of the huge leaves and I smelled a beautiful, clean, green smell. While I was falling and while I lay in the plant, I wasn't scared at all.

The fear came when I woke up. I lay flat on my back on my bottom bunk next to the window and breathed the rainy air in deep, slow breaths. I crossed my hands on my chest and kept my eyes closed and concentrated on breathing. It scared me that such a thing could come out of my mind and that the feelings and sounds and colors could be so real.

I lay there and thought about warts until it started to get light. I can't understand why I'm so fascinated by something that scares the shit out of me like this. But I was the same way with the first dead animal I ever saw up close.

One of our neighbor's barn cats got hit by a car in front of our place, and it ran behind the shop to die. Its head was amazingly flat and blood flowed from its nose and mouth. I wondered how anything hurt so bad could get through a fence and go a hundred feet or so. I'd squat down on my haunches and look at it and think what a beautiful thing a live cat was and try to figure out what it was about this thing that made it nothing like a cat anymore. Although I never touched it with my hands, it didn't *feel* like a cat. I'd kick it under the lumber pile, then come back the next day and hook it out with a stick and look at it some more. I did that until something carried off the bones one night and left just a rag of fur.

We didn't have any cats of our own, but we had dogs, and when they'd come in smelling terrible, if it wasn't skunk, Dad would say, "Bozo's been rolling in something dead," or "Red Rider's been into dead meat." I'd wonder then, and I still wonder now, why a dog or any living creature would roll in something dead.

I had that same fascination about the wartman. I'd lie in bed and throw his face up like a movie on the backs of my closed eyelids. I'd concentrate on his eyes one night and wonder if he could see around all those warts. Then another night I'd stare at his mouth and wonder if he ever kissed anyone. I wasn't scared; it was pure fascination. I was just awestruck that a person like that could exist.

THE PAPER BOMBS

Composition I
Karl Russell
October 1, 1965
Topic: A Frightening Experience

It was the summer of 1956 in the era of the home bomb shelter. I was nine. My two main pursuits in life were baseball and fishing, but I liked playing war too. I dug foxholes in the garden patch and flung rocks and apples that fell from the trees at "Russian" bottles and cans I set up on the dirt bank across the road. Digging the foxholes in the rich, composted soil kept me in fishing worms, and I told myself that the popping up, throwing hard at the small targets, then ducking right back down again helped my throwing speed and accuracy.

One day, after my dad and I had used up about all the worms we had on hand, I was just a few feet down into a fresh hole when I realized that if I dug deep enough and wide enough I could collect worms enough to last us the rest of the summer, and that in the process we would have a home bomb shelter.

With shovel and mattock I dug myself out of sight. To be in a hole in rich earth is a secure feeling. The air there is moist and smells of growing things. You throw a shovelful skyward, and it spreads like water and the sun shines the colors of the rainbow through it.

I'd gotten down six or seven feet, so deep that each shovelful of dirt I threw up left me with about half a shovelful in my crew cut. I'd sat down on the floor of the hole and hunkered back against the dirt wall, and was calculating how I'd tunnel under the lawn and into the basement of the house, when the sky went dark for a second. I thought it was the shadow of Bozo, our black Lab. But when I looked up to say hello to him, he wasn't there. All I saw was gray sky, the color it is just before dawn, and then the gray turned into tiny shadows I thought I could hear fluttering down toward me.

The paper bombs were what I heard. Seven landed in the hole with me. They were black bombs stamped on two-inch-wide white paper strips the length of a legal fish. On the body of the black bomb, printed in white, was ATOM BOMB, and across the tail fins was THIS COULD BE REAL. In a corner of the white part, printed in tiny black letters, was the frequency of the civil-defense radio station.

I stacked the seven paper bombs carefully, folded the stack, and slid it into the back pocket of my jeans. Then I cut some steps up the wall of the hole and climbed out.

Hundreds, maybe thousands of paper bombs littered the garden patch and yard. They clung to the pines and spotted the yellow cheatgrass like salt and pepper. I grabbed a handful of the paper bombs and ran in the house to show my mother.

I banged through the screen door just in time to catch a TV broadcast where an officer from Fairchild Air Force Base explained that the paper bombs were part of a Strategic Air Command–Civil Defense exercise, and urged citizens to participate by constructing home bomb shelters or by storing food, water, and first-aid supplies in their basements.

Mom came outside with me, carrying my little brother Jesse on her hip, and looked at the paper bombs all around. I ran back in the kitchen and filled two milk jugs with water, then ran back out and joined them at the edge of the garden. We turned a circle, and everywhere we looked—on the roof of the house, in the shrubs, in the driveway, all over down around Dad's shop, in the fields, and in the pines where the woods began—the paper bombs flapped and fluttered in the steady breeze. Mom looked down into her hand where she held the paper bombs I'd given her, then she doubled her fist and squinched up her face like she was mad. She threw down the paper bombs and marched back into the house with little Jesse bouncing up and down on her hip.

Later in the afternoon I sat in the bomb shelter waiting for Dad to come home from work and take me fishing. I thought of the paper bombs and wondered if more would fall. I looked up through the cool shadow to the blue sky. I laid my head on my arms and closed my eyes and listened for the dim roar of a jet bomber. I remembered then that I hadn't heard the plane, only the flutter of the paper bombs falling. I looked up again and spotted a single tiny thread of cloud, thin as a strand of spiderweb, that might have been the bomber's vapor trail. Then I remembered we'd need food and first aid as well as water. So I climbed out of the hole and ran in the house again and grabbed a box of vanilla wafers and a couple plastic bread sacks from the kitchen and my Cub Scout first-aid kit from my fishing bag that sat with my pole next to the kitchen door. I ducked back down the hole and took the paper bombs from my jeans pocket and stuck them between the gauze pads at the bottom of the kit. I'd just begun to stuff the cookie box into a bread sack to make it waterproof when I heard my Dad calling for fishermen.

The Spokane River ran not more than a hundred yards from our house—just across the road and down the rocky bank—but my folks wouldn't let me fish there because it was too swift. So every Friday afternoon Dad drove me out to Marshall Creek, a few miles southwest of Spokane, where only kids were allowed to fish.

All along the path from the road to the creek, through the open fields and through the woods, we kicked up paper bombs. The wind would blow and paper bombs would fall from the trees and bushes like big flakes of dry snow. Bozo would leap in the air, twisting like a gigantic black trout after a fly, and catch them in his mouth.

"They must have dropped a zillion of these goddamned things," Dad said.

We stopped where the trail began its slope down to the grassy banks of the little creek. Paper bombs nested in the willows and birches like flocks of magpies and floated in the water, some backing up against rocks and tree roots, making shadows where I knew fish would hide. When we walked down to the water, in the shade of the trees with the sun gone down behind the hills and the breeze blowing over the water, I felt the same cool sensation on my skin as when I'd been back sitting in the bomb shelter, looking up at the sky.

"How 'bout a worm, son?" Dad said.

I dug into the metal box I carried on my belt and handed him a night crawler as big around as his fingers. As I gave Dad the worm I got a big whiff of the dirt on my fingers, and it made me think of the bomb shelter and of the paper bombs.

"Dad," I said, "if there's a war I hope the siren blows when we're all at home."

"There's not going to be any war, son," Dad replied.

I dug out a worm for myself and threaded it on the single hook of my Colorado spinner.

"But if there is," I said, "and I'm at school or playing ball, I'll run home. You don't come get me—okay?"

"That's quite a ways," Dad said.

"I know," I said. "But I can run it faster than you could drive. All the traffic's got to go north and you'd have to come south."

"If the siren blows, we'll be comin' to get our boy," Dad replied. "But don't worry about there being any war, Karl. You worry about base hits. Worry about catchin' a fish!"

Dad walked downstream to where the water ran fast, leaving me and Bozo to fish the dark water that swirled deep in under the bank and now and then sucked one of the floating paper bombs out of sight.

I caught a fifteen-inch rainbow there and two ten-inch eastern brook, all on pieces of the same big worm from the bomb shelter.

It was almost dark when we got home. I cleaned our fish at the garden spigot and was just hanging the guts on the fence for the crows when Mom called me to dinner.

That night I dreamed the nuke dream for the first time. I'm at school when the siren blows. I don't know what day it is, but it's not noon Wednesday, so we know it's a real air raid. My stomach falls— like when a curve doesn't break, only a thousand times worse—and I look over at my friend Tom Sears. Tom's face is white and his eyes are big and his mouth is open. Nobody says anything. We all turn and look at each other. I see the faces clearly: Tommy, Pat Henshaw, Loreen Sanderson. Every mouth hangs open and all eyes are big. All heads turn towards Mrs. Wiener, and we see that she looks just like us.

I explode into tears and run out the back door of the classroom and across the playground. I pump my legs but they only float. Each step propels me higher in the air than it carries me forward. I see little Jesse's face in my mind, all red and contorted like when he's crying for all he's worth. But it's not Jesse's face, it's mine. I put my head down and pump my legs and arms, but each step only floats me in the air.

Then all of a sudden I'm out on the highway, standing on the white line. Cars inch past me northward in both lanes. The cars of all the kids in school pass me. Donna Reed and her TV family go by. I grab onto the tailgate of a pickup and swing up to a standing position on the bumper. My legs are so heavy it's like I have polio. I ride that way in the stream of cars until we reach our road, where I jump off and fall into the gravel.

The dream is just like life. The sky is as blue as it really is and the clouds are as white and gentle looking and the gravel stings the palms of my hands exactly as it does in real life, so that when I bring my hands up to my face I see little pieces of gravel still sticking in them and the red indentations where other pieces stuck and then fell out.

My legs are even heavier now, but our house is in sight and I just want to make it home before the bomb drops. Living or dying doesn't matter. All I care about is making it home to be with Mom and Dad and Jesse. So with both hands I lift one leg and then the other in a swinging motion, and make pretty good time up the road. I can't see our car, but that's all right, I tell myself, because Dad almost always parks behind the house. Bozo's not in flight across the field to greet me, but he's probably inside, I think. They're all probably inside—my mother, my father, my little brother, my dog—all waiting for me in our house.

When I'm up the steps and in the front door, I start crying again because I'm so happy to be home. But no one answers my yell.

I can walk normally once I'm through the door, and I run to the kitchen and look out the back for the car. It's not there.

A feeling rises up in me that says the bomb's about to go off. In my mind I see the white flash from the newsreels, then the wind ripping through the clapboard houses, the windows exploding, blowing pellets of glass in slow motion across the Nevada desert. I run down to the basement and into the bathroom, where there are no windows. I sit down on the small oval rug and lean back against the toilet bowl. I've got my head down between my legs and my arms over my head like they teach us in school. I listen for the sound of a door opening upstairs and Mom and Dad calling my name. But the sound never comes. The bomb never comes, either. The dream ends with no sound and only the sight of the darkness and the empty feeling of being alone.

I got up the next morning still scared. I hung around Dad until he drove off to work, then I hung around Mom and Jesse in the kitchen, savoring Mom's little songs to Jesse and his burbles in reply until Mom sent me out to play.

It rained late in the night I first dreamed the nuke dream, and as I walked slowly through the grass to the garden patch the next morning I watched the wet blades leave shiny stripes on the toes of my tennis shoes. In the hole I'd dug as a bomb shelter but hadn't even thought of going to in my dream, I found the vanilla wafers, damp but edible, and the metal first-aid kit with the seven paper bombs in it already rusting. I ate the vanilla wafers as I filled in the hole, mixing grass clippings in with the dirt for the next generation of worms to grow fat on.

I must have dreamed the nuke dream once a week for the rest of that summer. I don't remember thinking all that often about the paper bombs, but lots of other things made it hard to forget the possibility of atomic war. I built models of some of our warplanes— the B-36, the Flying Wing, and the Sabre jet—and missiles like the Snark and the Nike, which today seem as old as a Henry J car or a Diamond T truck. I followed the news of bomb testing in the South Pacific and Nevada, and I listened to the grownups talk on the subject. I remember wishing we'd cleaned up on the Russians after beating Germany in World War II. In my rock wars with the bottles and cans, after I took care of the Rooskies I always pressed on and wiped out China.

But the single thing that kept the fear of nuclear war—and the nuke dream—most alive in me was the air-raid siren. Every Wednesday noon it would go off, and whether I was in town playing ball or home, my stomach would fall from the fear that wail produced in me. My legs would want to run, but at the same time they'd begin to lighten and I'd feel them floating out of control. Instantly I'd ask myself the day and time, and I'd always wonder if the Russians were smart enough to time their strike at noon on a Wednesday, when we'd never know until it was too late that *this* siren meant the real thing.

I dreamed the nuke dream steadily but with less frequency up through the fall of 1962, when I entered high school and didn't concern myself with much except baseball and girls. I still loved those great old horror movies, though, like *The Day the World Ended*, where the survivors of nuclear war mutate into monsters and eat each other. Then there was the Cuban missile crisis to remind all of us that we could be vaporized any time two of the world's tough guys believed they had to go head to head. And there was always the air-raid siren blowing every Wednesday noon from high on its tower next to the fire station.

Then, in the summer of 1963, my parents and my little brother were killed in a car wreck, and I stopped dreaming the nuke dream.

Bozo and I moved into town with my baseball coach and his wife, and I never slept another night in our house. I drove out to the old place a lot that summer and fall. Bozo would be sitting in the seat beside me, and I'd look at him and think how old he'd gotten. I hadn't paid much attention to him after I hit my teens and he'd become pretty much Jesse's dog. Bozo was fifteen or sixteen then, and most of his teeth had fallen out. The two of us would sit in my '51 Ford on the county road in front of the garden patch and just look down at the house and the shop and the yard getting brown.

I didn't get involved much in school that fall and winter, but when spring came and baseball started, it helped me live more in the present than in memories. When fishing opened in late April, Bozo and I hit all the local creeks on the weekends.

I sold our house that June to some people from California. With that money and Dad's insurance and the money from the lawsuit against the guy who hit them, I might have been the richest kid in school.

One morning after school had closed for the summer and Legion ball had begun, I got up early for practice and found Bozo dead on the bedroom floor. I wrapped him in a tarp and took him to the animal shelter and paid to have him cremated. I cried hard as I drove home. I knew it wasn't for Bozo, as good a friend as he'd been all my seventeen years, but for everything I missed so bad and would never have again except as memories.

I drove out to the old place and sat and looked. The new owners were gone, and I stole our mailbox because our name was still on it.

I kept on driving out the county road, feeling absolutely alone in all the world. I thought of the nuke dream and that feeling in it of facing the bomb alone. I remembered the day the paper bombs fell and the way Mom carried Jesse on her hip out to see them and how Dad had told me at the creek that if the siren blew he and Mom would be coming to get their boy.

I was passing the county dump where the new owners had said they were going to take the stuff from the shop that they hadn't sold and I didn't want. I remembered folding those seven paper bombs and putting them in my first-aid kit, and I wanted in the worst way to find them again and hold them in my hand. I knew the old kit had been in a junk box on the storage shelves.

I parked the '51 at the side of the road and walked through the yellow cheatgrass to the sand and the mounds of trash. I walked around until I found some stuff I recognized.

I dug with my hands through old cans of paint and rubbing compound, petrified paintbrushes, jars of fruit and tomatoes Mom had canned and that were probably still good, frayed fan belts, seatless campstools, an apple box full of car generators, and some terrycloth seat covers.

I'd dug myself nearly out of sight below the level of the trash all around me when I spotted some tiny flecks of blue and gold. There was the old Cub Scout first-aid kit sitting upside down in a rusty baby-moon hubcap. The lid was rusted through in places, and what hadn't rusted through was rusted thin as a leaf. The lid folded and broke when I forced it open with my thumbs. Inside I found the little bottle of water-purifying tablets and the rubber suction cup and rusted razorblade for snakebite lying in a bed of mold. I scratched through the layer of spongy white with my thumbnail, but all I hit was the rusty bottom of the kit. The paper bombs had molded away to nothing. All that remained was a fuzzy culture the color of cloud, dotted with spores as blue as sky.

Wednesday afternoon, April 3, 1968,

5:30 p.m.

About four strokes into shaving this morning, I realized I hadn't cleaned my razor after shaving the warts off my wrist on Sunday. I washed the shaving cream off and then washed my face with the hottest water I could stand. Then I washed again with Listerine. I thought about boiling my razor in a pot on the stove to sterilize it, but I threw it away instead and used Bolão's electric.

The feeling haunted me all morning. It only went away because I stopped thinking about it when I saw Georgie coming out of the science building. I almost had to beg her to talk to me, and I did have to beg her to tell me what was wrong.

It turns out she was just pretending to be asleep and saw me peeing in the sink. She said she needs a few days away from me to get over it. She said she just couldn't believe I was capable of doing anything so "filthy." I could see the softness coming back into her face, though, so I don't think I've lost her.

Georgie saw the gauze on my wrist and asked what happened. I told her she wasn't my only victim that night, that I'd attacked myself and shaved the warts off. She told me I was stupid, that they'll only spread, and that shaving them off won't work anyway because they have roots. I told her I might be stupid, but not so stupid that I didn't know warts had roots. That was when the feeling came back.

When I got home I checked under the gauze, but seventeen tiny scabs was all I found. I don't know what I was expecting.

The book we were supposed to start with in Literature of the Camps, *The Origins of Totalitarianism* by Hannah Arendt, was finally in the bookstore today. It's about fifty times longer than *Night*, and the print is small. I looked the book over for about thirty seconds, then walked into the cafeteria and quit my job. Seeing all those pages of small print was just what I needed to be absolutely sure I can use more hours in the week for my studies. It'll probably take all my extra time in the next week just to get this one book read. And I've got to decide soon about dropping Spanish and taking Portuguese.

Thursday, April 4, 1968, midnight

Martin Luther King got shot in Memphis today, but I didn't hear about it till tonight when I got back from Spokane and from having a couple experiences that about stopped my heart.

It was a beautiful afternoon and I didn't have dinner duty at the house, so I rode the Harley into Spokane. I stopped at the Viking Tavern more or less on a lark, but by a minor miracle (God, that's a pun!!) nobody asked for my I.D., so I drank three beers and ate a turkey sandwich for my supper.

The first thing happened at the Viking. There was this guy across the room sitting with his back to me. His hair was black and he was wearing a white shop coat with blue trim, and the instant I saw him I thought of Dad. He was about the same width across the shoulders as Dad.

As I opened my mouth to take my first bite of sandwich, I looked in the guy's direction and saw him pick up his napkin in one hand and each piece of silverware in the other and begin to wipe them off. I froze there with my mouth gaping and my sandwich stuck in my face, because that was exactly—*exactly*—what Dad used to do with his silverware when he ate out. It was like being back at the Coach House on a night Dad had to work and walking in and finding him all alone with his back to the door, wiping off his silverware with his napkin.

I breathed deep a few times and took a long pull on my beer. Then I bit a hunk out of my sandwich and chewed until my heart stopped pounding. I finished half the sandwich, then got up and walked past the guy to the bathroom and washed the glaze off my eyes. Then I walked out and looked down at the guy's face as I passed. He didn't look anything like Dad from the front. He was fat and too young and he had a Mexican-bandit moustache. It was just a funny coincidence to have seen him from the back when I did.

The second thing happened on the way home. I took the Fish Lake road and ran the Harley in fourth gear and didn't let off in the curves. There wasn't any traffic, so I just leaned deep and floated across the center line now and then through the sharpest bends. The moon was nearly full and it was white and cold and wet-looking when it came out from behind the clouds.

I was having a great time, when all of a sudden my headlight blinked once and went out. The moon had gone behind the clouds and it was so dark I couldn't see my front fender. I braked and geared down and started looking for the faded white line.

I found what was left of it and followed it slowly like an old trail. When I rounded a curve and saw the lighted entrance to the little cemetery up ahead, I said to myself, What a break! I lose my light right where I can see to fix it. Then when I rolled under the entrance arch my headlight came back on. Oh, Christ, I said as I drove by the graves toward the exit, it's a short. No use looking for a short out here tonight. I'll just try to make it home.

I switched on my high beam and it caught the tops of the tall polished gravestones and made them glow. And then the moon came out and they shone in its moist light like chunks of ice.

A lot of the grave markers were the small, rectangular stones about four inches high with just a name and two dates, like the ones Mom and Dad and Jesse have. I thought how I liked it that Mom and Dad are side by side, with Jesse between them and above. I don't know how it was they were laid to rest in this pyramid shape, but it makes me think of Mom and Dad supporting Jesse, and of him growing out of them.

I was thinking this stuff when I turned onto the highway and my headlight went out again. I stopped and gave the housing a couple whacks with my hand, but that didn't do it. The moon was behind the clouds again and now, about fifty yards from the lights at the cemetery entrance, it was dark as the interior of a lump of coal. I kicked down the sidestand and turned off the ignition. Before I could climb off the bike, the kind of chill that says you're being watched began its way up my back. It got so intense I began to shake. I breathed deep and turned to face it. Of course there wasn't anything there. There never is. The feeling went right away.

But then the moon slipped out from behind the clouds again and the entrance arch appeared down the way like the ghost of a circle on the blackboard in geometry class. The longer the moonlight flowed, the stronger and colder the chill came back. Now it was in my stomach and climbing for my heart.

Over the cemetery, against the deep black where the trees began, gray pyramids hovered in the air. They made me think of the faces of dead people. I knew the pyramids were the tops of the tall gravestones catching and reflecting the moonlight, but still they were scary, moving and growing brighter, then fainter, as the clouds blew and changed the light.

I started breathing heavily through my mouth until I heard Dad's voice say, "We're by you, son. Don't be afraid." That stunned the fear out of me.

I turned my back on the cemetery, hit the ignition switch, and kicked down on the pedal. She caught right away. I was going to get home as fast as I could, headlight or no, but I took the time to jiggle the light switch and the light came on again. I felt stupid for being afraid then, so I made a U-turn and rode back through the cemetery. When the beam of my light hit the pyramids, it burned them away like mist burnt away by the sun.

I got back about 8:30 and tiptoed upstairs. I looked through the Hannah Arendt book, but couldn't get into it. Couldn't get into the Middle Ages either. Bill Bagby, the pledge master, peeked in on his way to the bathroom and asked me what I thought of Martin Luther King being shot. Before I could answer he said, "Boy, the shit is really gonna hit the fan with black people now." I yelled after him that I hadn't heard about it, then I changed into my sweats and took off for the dorm to see if Donnie wanted to go running. I thought of how Donnie used to tell me Martin Luther King made him proud to be black.

We ran to the railroad tracks and headed west, like we used to when we were roommates. It's always black as hell out there because of the way the tracks cut so deep through the hilly wheat fields and the banks block out the lights of town. But tonight when the moon came out, it shone on the tracks and they glistened like ice a long way into the distance.

I told Donnie I'd had supper in Spokane and didn't know a thing about what happened.

"It's been all over TV," Donnie said. "They shot him with a thirty-ought-six. Hollow point. The hole in his face was three inches across. And that was the entrance hole. How big you suppose the exit hole in the back of his head was?"

"Jesus," I said. "Who did it?"

"'They' did," Don said. "The same solid citizens who bomb Sunday schools and kill little girls, the same ones who set dogs on people who just want to swim in the ocean or eat in a restaurant or go to college. We'll never know exactly who was behind it, but they all killed him."

It's hard to run on the tracks in daylight, because some of the ties stick up out of the gravel and some are buried a couple inches down into it. But at night it's hard *and* dangerous. Even so, Donnie was keeping a fast, steady pace, lifting his legs real high.

"He was staying in a motel," Donnie said. "Motels are for guys like us, Russ. Martin Luther King, Jr., was one of the greatest men in the world, and some redneck motherfuck shot him in a fucking motel."

I don't know much about King or much about black stuff except what I picked up living with Don, but the idea of a man like that who really was great and who put his life on the line every day in a country full of haters like ours, the idea of him getting shot with a deer rifle in a motel made me want to cry. I wondered if he had a family.

We climbed the bank where the tracks cut under the freeway and ran back to school against what little traffic there was.

In the dorm parking lot Donnie told me there's going to be a memorial service in Spokane tomorrow, and I said I'd go. Then he told me thanks for the run and went in and took the stairs. I knew from having done it with him hundreds of times that he'd run them by twos all the way to the top.

I'm back now after a shower, just sitting here at the desk and thinking.

All the while Don and I were running I couldn't get Dad's voice out of my head, and I couldn't shake the feeling of safety—of being watched over—that was with me on the ride home from the cemetery and is with me now. Usually out there on the tracks at night I'm looking in all directions and thinking about nothing but psychos with shotguns or wild dogs or flying saucers and breaking my ankle. And I feel safe now. I feel them outside the window now—Mom and Dad and Jesse—standing in the sky.

I'm not crazy. It's not that I think I'll see them if I walk over and look out. But I think I feel them.

It's a little difficult not to wonder what the fuck is going on with me. I grow a few warts, and it's like they bring all this other shit with them. I start thinking stuff I haven't thought since I was a kid, I have crazy dreams and see things, I hear Dad's voice plain as if he were sitting behind me on the Harley.

It seems like there's so much death around tonight.

I've got this safe, protected feeling, but it's hard not to wonder what I'm feeling protected from.

I've begun to really *need* to write this stuff down, and I don't like the feeling. I like the idea of talking about it to anyone even less, though.

Friday afternoon, April 5, 1968, 5:20 p.m.

What an afternoon I had!

Rode the Harley into Spokane at two for the memorial service for Dr. King. It was held at the Temple of Light Baptist church and attended by more black people than I've ever seen in person in my life. I didn't know there were that many black people living around here. Some of the guys wore black leather coats, black gloves, and black berets, and were not pleased to see the few white faces among the mourners. Mac and some of the rest of the Committee for Peace in Vietnam were there, along with Reverend Gardner from the Christian Student Center, and that was all the people I knew, except for Donnie and the other black guys in the Black Student Union.

I stood in back with some older black ladies. A black coffin sat on sawhorses in front of the preacher. The preacher said that Dr. King would ask all his brothers and sisters to pray that the darkness be lifted from the benighted soul of the killer and from the benighted souls of all the people whose hatred and fear he was the instrument of.

The preacher was a huge guy who reminded me of Rosey Grier. When he spread his arms out over the coffin, they stretched the length of it, and you could hear the swoosh his black robe made all the way back where I was. He had his arms spread over the coffin and he said, "The Reverend Dr. Martin Luther King told us not to satisfy our thirst for freedom by drinking from the cup of bitterness and hatred. 'We must ever conduct our struggle,' Dr. King reminded us, 'on the high plane of dignity and discipline.'" Then we held hands and sang "We Shall Overcome."

I was getting nervous about how I could slip out and avoid the march, and as I stood there with my arms crossed over my chest like everybody else, holding hands with the two black ladies beside me, I realized it was the first time I'd ever touched a black person aside from shaking hands with black athletes and wrestling around with Donnie. It gave me a funny feeling to stand there in the packed black church, singing and swaying with people who were my countrymen but seemed more foreign to me than someone like Bolão.

Six of the guys in black, one of whom was Donnie's new roommate, picked up the coffin and carried it down the aisle and outside, and right after them other guys in black began ushering people out. I had to fall in with everybody else, and pretty soon I was outside with my hands clasped to two other black people, this time an old lady with yellow-white hair and a little girl wearing a black dress and white patent-leather shoes. We were four abreast and singing "We Shall Overcome" again, marching down the middle of an arterial street in a line led by the coffin and flanked by the guys in berets.

Quite a few white people stood at the curb looking at us. Nobody yelled anything nasty, or anything at all. I was feeling excited and self-conscious to be there. I was thinking that I was taking part in history, when a white guy in a suit shoved a Q-6 News microphone in my face and walked in the little girl's way as he asked me if I represented Eastern Washington State College. I thought, What?

Then I looked down at my chest and realized I was wearing my letter jacket.

"I represent Russ, Norma, Jesse, and Karl Russell of Nine Mile Falls," I said. When I looked the guy in the face I saw another guy behind him with a videotape camera.

I started singing again, and after a few seconds the reporter went to talk to someone else. It was a windy day and the little girl was wearing only the short-sleeved black dress, so I asked her if she'd like my jacket, but she shook her head no.

We came to a little park, and they put the coffin on a plywood platform and some older black people took seats at folding chairs behind it. The guys in black surrounded the platform. The crowd spread out to listen to the speakers, and I got my chance to slip away. As I walked through the people an enormous black lady gave me a piece of paper that had Dr. King's "I Have a Dream" speech on it.

I'd planned to blaze right back to school in time to catch Señor Gonsalves and drop Spanish, but I looked at the first line of the speech and couldn't quit reading. I read one line over and over. "Continue to work with the faith that unearned suffering is redemptive," King told black people.

I wonder where a guy gets the kind of faith and strength it takes to wait for justice when he's being treated like shit and doesn't deserve it. Maybe you're supposed to wait for some afterlife to get the treatment you deserve. But how do you keep from getting bitter and hateful while you're waiting?

One thing is clear to me: There'd better be an afterlife if Martin Luther King is going to get the redemption he deserves, because he sure as hell didn't get it here.

I've packed a lot of living and maybe even some learning into the past eighteen hours. I started studying right after dinner last night and only took one break before I hit the rack at two. Donnie called to say he'd seen me on the six o'clock news, so I went down to the basement at eleven to see if they'd rerun me. And, by God, there I was, looking dumbfounded, my mouth hanging open catching flies before I finally spoke up. It was embarrassing because quite a few of the guys were there. But most of them were drunk, and they cheered for me.

I studied some more this morning, then in the afternoon I finally accepted one of Mac's invitations and went to the Christian Student Center with him and heard his hero, the Reverend ("call me Phil") Gardner, talk on the subject of sin.

Sin, I learned, is not so much a matter of how we act as it is the emotion out of which we act. When we don't act out of love is when we're sinning.

If you're going to believe in a God that puts down rules, it seems to me like you should either believe those rules—like Crookshank does—or find yourself a God whose rules you do believe.

One of the things that frosts me most about college is that you're supposed to realize, once you're here awhile, that traditional or conventional beliefs are all bullshit. That God is only "a metaphor," that the guys who run your country are all a bunch of devious assholes, that because Thomas Jefferson owned slaves, the Declaration of Independence is a racist document, that because you're white and not poor, everything bad in the world is your fault, that communists are the real humanitarians, that to be truly sensitive you've got to become a Buddhist vegetarian and do yoga, that you're a secret homosexual if you like guns, and that competition is evil and athletes are either stupid or fascists or both. I wonder if it's possible to get educated without becoming a fucking creep.

But it's funny: I don't have any respect for Crookshank's total submission to authority and rules and tradition either. Oh, help! I'm lost! I'm a man without conviction!

Gardner actually seemed like a nice guy, and I'm not sure why I reacted so violently to him. Probably because he was wearing Hush Puppy shoes and had his glasses sitting on top of his head and his sweater hanging over his shoulders and tied around his neck by the arms.

I'm such an asshole!! I've got to quit judging people by their styles. But how else do you judge people? Maybe you try not to judge them. Maybe you just let them be until they try to make you act like them, then you do something about it.

Boy, could I use a load of this *agape* Gardner talked about. He said it's usually defined as "love," better defined as "charity," but really means "an ethical devotion to one's fellow man."

After his talk was finished I'd slipped into the kitchen and was putting down their incredibly good, huge cinnamon rolls as fast as I could, when Gardner walked up and called me by name and introduced himself. He said he'd seen me play ball last year and asked why I wasn't on the team anymore. I told him about my arm. He asked if I missed playing, and I said I'd gotten interested in school for a change and didn't mind that part of my life being over.

"The cliché notwithstanding, Karl," he said, "the Lord really does work in mysterious ways. Maybe he works in our lives every day, or maybe he set the ripples going in the beginning and pulled back to watch us swim for it. Maybe you were meant to be something other than a ballplayer."

"I doubt it," I said.

Gardner is about five eleven and a hundred fifty pounds. He looks like he's constructed out of knotted rope and he shakes hands like one of those new trash compactors. But he puts out this big feeling of softness. His Ivy-League brown hair is soft, his eyes are brown and soft, his cotton tattersall shirts are soft, his suntan pants are soft, his Hush Puppies are soft, and his voice is soft. I don't think Gardner is going to be a very comfortable guy for me to be around; he makes me feel like he's an actor playing the part of a campus minister.

He touched my arm and kind of led me from the kitchen through the crowd into the big living room. We came to a bookcase and he grabbed a fat paperback and handed it to me.

"Here," he said. "This is the Dartmouth Bible. It's heavily anno-
tated, and I guarantee you'll get sucked in. It's a great story."

I scratched my head. "Seems to me I've heard of it," I said. "Wasn't
there a movie?"

I was edging toward the door and Gardner could see it. "Come
back and see us any time," he said.

I was feeling good as I walked away and I was close to Georgie's
apartment, so I thought I'd take a chance. I knocked on her door,
and when she answered I said, "Georgie, if you'll come get a Coke
with me I'll promise to never again pee in your kitchen."

She frowned and turned to look at the kitchen sink. Then she
stepped out onto the porch and closed the door behind her.

We split a small Coke in the Union, and Georgie sat across from
me and took off her boot and snuggled her foot in my crotch. All is
well with us again!

She's got to work tonight, but tomorrow night we're going to see
Our Man Flint at the drive-in.

Thinking about tomorrow night after the movie puts me in the
perfect frame of mind and body to contemplate the subject of sin, so
maybe I'll read a chapter in my new Bible before I go to sleep.

Monday morning, April 8, 1968, 2:20 a.m.

I'm about out of my fucking skull. I've got to go to a doctor and
find out what the fuck is happening to me.

On the way back to Georgie's from the movie she whispered in my
ear that she'd like to go to the wheat fields instead of to her place.
So I wheeled the Ford around in the next intersection and barreled
us out of town.

We parked on a rise where we could see the glow of the lights of
Spokane. We drank a few more beers and listened to the radio and
cuddled under the blankets. Then, after she took the last drink of the
last bottle of the half-case, Georgie whipped off her clothes, grabbed
the blankets away from me, and bailed into the back, yelling "Ger-

onimo!" as she went. I took off my clothes and followed her.

Georgie'd been teasing me all night about my hair getting longer, and as we lay there with me on the bottom she reached both hands under my shoulders to the top of my head and started messing with my hair. Then all of a sudden she stopped and said, "Jesus, Karl, you've got to wash your hair more often. There's sand all in it."

I'd washed my hair right after supper and I knew there wasn't any sand in it. So I sat up and felt my scalp with both hands, and I could feel the tiny warts all over. I lost the buzz I'd had and started to feel cold, then I began to shake. I wanted to scream and I was afraid I was going to start crying.

"That's all right," Georgie giggled. "We Indians have been screwed by dirty white men for two hundred years." She was three-quarters drunk and in the best mood I'd seen her in since Christmas.

I told her I didn't feel so good.

"I'm sorry, hon," she said. "I didn't mean anything."

I was sober as a highway patrolman and freezing and shaking. "I'm just cold, George," I said. "And I don't feel so good."

Georgie said she had to pee.

We were parked on this hill at the edge of the wheat where a farm road dead-ended. The night was clear and bright with the cold, white light of the full spring moon. Georgie walked naked, kind of tiptoeing in her bare feet and holding her arms around her shoulders with the cold, a little way from the car. She squatted down to where the winter wheat just brushed her butt. It was so quiet I could hear the whizz of her peeing.

I was looking at Georgie silhouetted there on the crest of the field against the gun-blue night sky, but I was thinking about myself and still on the edge of crying with wondering what the holy fuck was happening to me.

Georgie giggled, and the sound crinkled across the night like wadding up cellophane in your fist. I'd crawled over the seat and had my pants on when she opened the door. "The wheat tickles your bottom," Georgie said.

We got our clothes on and Georgie snuggled over by me and put her arm on my shoulder. She reached for my head and was starting to say something. But I didn't want her to touch my hair again, and I flinched with the shiver that ran through me. It made Georgie jump.

"Please, George," I said. "I'm getting sick. I'd better get back to the house. I'm sorry," I said, firing up the Ford and backing into the field and spraying young winter wheat shafts and dirt into the air as I headed us back to the highway. "I'm sorry, Georgie," I said again. "I'm embarrassed to be dirty is all. And I'm really not feeling very good."

I ran six miles hard as I could when I got home. When I showered and washed my hair the warts on my scalp felt like the eyes that grow on potatoes. It's hard to keep from touching them. I sat down here to try to write some of the fear away, but that doesn't work any better than running. Maybe I should try sleeping. Maybe in the morning they'll be gone.

GEORGETTA LAMEDEER

Composition II
Karl Russell
February 6, 1966
Topic: A Friend of the Opposite Sex

American Indians are round people. If on TV or in the movies you see an American Indian—a man or a woman—with a well-defined build, you can bet that person doesn't have much Indian blood.

I'm not saying Indians are fat. It's just that even the strongest, most in-shape Indians I've ever seen have had this roundness rather than angularity to their features. Jim Thorpe, the famous Indian athlete whom King Gustaf V of Sweden in 1912 called "the greatest athlete in the world," is a good example.

Georgetta Lamedeer was a big girl a grade ahead of me when she transferred into Evergreen Junior High. We had never actually met, but I knew who she was. Because she was big and had this Indian roundness about her, I wasn't particularly attracted to her. I didn't do much with girls when I was that age, but if I had, I would have liked to do it with a little blonde cheerleader.

I'd grown up a lot by the summer before my junior year of high school when my folks and my little brother were killed in a car wreck. I went out with girls as often as I could, for example. But when school started that fall, my senses were so dulled I wasn't interested in anything.

One afternoon in October I was driving out of Spokane headed for Nine Mile Falls and another "last look" at the house where I'd lived with my family, when I saw Georgie walking on the shoulder of the road. I pulled over and asked her if she wanted a ride.

Georgie was carrying two armfuls of books and a gym bag, and when she left the door open while she set her stuff in back, a gust of wind blew the feeling and smell of fall into the car. It was the first I'd noticed the change in the air, and the feeling on my skin and inside my nose as I breathed it made me happy. I introduced myself and Georgie introduced herself and said she already knew me, or she wouldn't have accepted the ride. I said if I hadn't already known her, too, I'd have passed her right by.

I glanced over at her as we drove and said to myself that Georgetta Lamedeer had really shaped up since junior high. What had really happened, I think, is that I'd grown up a lot.

When we came in sight of an old trailer and some outbuildings, Georgie pointed and said that was where she lived. I was embarrassed for her, because if the Northwest had a Tobacco Road, her place would have been on it. I was surprised, too, because I'd never seen Georgie when she wasn't as well turned out and clean and neat as the girls in school whose families had a lot of money.

We'd gotten about two car lengths up Georgie's road when I stopped and asked if I could treat her to a burger. Georgie touched my leg with her little finger and said, "Turn this car around!"

We went to the Panda Drive-In, a hot-rod hangout with excellent fries. We both called home to say where we were, then we ate and sat in the car and talked till eleven.

Georgie was coming here to Eastern the next year to study nursing. The people she lived with were her foster parents, who got money from the state and the federal government for keeping her. She never knew her natural mother, and her father died from alcoholism in the Veterans' Hospital when she was seven. Before he died, he cried and told her she'd been born in a 1937 Kaiser on the Fort Peck Reservation in Montana, that she was a full-blood—part Assiniboin and part Crow—and that she should always be proud about it.

It is my opinion that medical science will find out one day that there's something in the physiology of Indians that makes them more intolerant of alcohol than other races. You don't need to do any scientific research to see that Indians don't have problems with alcohol because of something reasonable like a lack of will power or an awareness of the disintegration of their heritage. All you have to do is pay a little bit of attention to see the problem is in the blood.

Georgie had lived in an orphanage for five years until a foster family in Coeur d'Alene took her. That didn't work out. (She told me later that the reason was her foster father raped her. He also cut off a finger on each of her hands, one before he raped her to scare her into doing it, then one after to scare her into not telling.) She said the people she was living with now were real nice.

I felt three major emotions as Georgie and I sat talking. The first was shame for thinking I had such a tough life when she'd had a *really* tough one; the second was a combination of surprise and relief to find out I could feel happy again; and the third was your basic romantic interest.

Georgie has such a shine to her that she almost looks polished. That evening her brown eyes were shining, her black hair was shining, and her brown skin shone like she'd gone over herself with a buffer. All the roundnesses of her—her eyes and her cheeks, her mouth, her shoulders and her breasts too—made me want to reach over and touch her.

She told me she'd cried when she heard about my folks and my brother. She said she knew I'd be fine and grow up all the stronger, and she sounded like she knew what she was talking about.

We got to be friends after that. I did a lot of work on my car that fall and winter, and Georgie and I spent many Sunday nights in the Northside Chevrolet garage, where the guys let me use one of their bays because my dad had been service manager. We'd listen to the radio and Georgie would study sometimes and sometimes work with me. Her foster parents really were nice people, I found out after I met them, and one Sunday night Georgie borrowed their '49 Studebaker pickup and we did a ring job on it as an anniversary present to them.

Georgie is still one of my best friends.

Monday, April 8, 1968, 5 p.m.

Called a dermatologist in Spokane this morning and got an appointment for Thursday to have the warts removed. It made me feel better to have taken some sensible action. I should have had it done as soon as they showed up. He'll burn the fucking things out, and that will be that. I guess he'll probably have to cut my hair.

The warts on my wrist have all grown back and I can't keep my hands off the ones on my head.

Today was my first day of Português (that's how they spell it), and it was pretty bad. I didn't understand a single word of what the professor, Dona Leila, said. Dona Leila had told me she was sure I wouldn't have any trouble because of all my Spanish. But I mean I did not understand one single fucking word!! After class she told me to spend extra time listening to the tapes in the lab, and if I hadn't begun to distinguish the words by the end of the week, she'd tutor me. I'm sure I can get some help from Bolão, too, and I'm going to listen to his records through the headphones, which will be the same as lab work.

Dona Leila is in her early or middle thirties, I'd say, and I wouldn't be surprised if she hasn't got some Brazilian Indian blood in her. She's a lot darker than Georgie and her hair springs out thick all over her head in these long, floppy curls. She's real attractive. She wore jeans today, and one of those long, loose African shirts a lot of blacks are starting to wear. And it did not look like she was wearing a bra. I'm going to be in desperate trouble if you can't learn Português with a hard-on.

I was real, real scared last night. I was so scared I prayed and asked God to keep me from becoming a wartperson. It's funny: I don't even believe in a God who answers prayers. But who else do you talk to about stuff like that? I couldn't sleep, so I lay in my bottom bunk with my eyes open, just barely able to make out the springs of Portella's bunk above me. Then I thought of the pyramids I saw in the cemetery, and I thought of Dad's voice telling me he and Mom and Jesse were by me. And I thought of Mom's voice. And in my mind I could hear both their voices. I felt a lot better then, and fell asleep not long after.

Thursday, April 11, 1968, 10:50 p.m.

The warts are history now. All that's left of them are little burn holes with tiny, jagged black lips like the edges of steel cut with a torch. The doctor did it with an instrument that looked like an electric ice pick. He'd burn down through the wartmeat into real flesh, then he'd swirl around in the hole till he burned out the sides. The blood would boil for part of a second, then it would be all burnt up.

The shots hurt a little, the burning tissue stank some, and I'm not crazy about having a bald spot on top of my head. But the hardest thing to endure about it all was the doctor's running commentary.

His name was Havermeyer, and he looked as young as I am. His hair was longer than mine, which, thank heaven, is long enough to cover my new bald spot. He worked fast, and he talked as fast as he worked.

First he gave me about half a dozen shots all around the wartpatch on my wrist, then he plugged in the burner and held it up in my face.

"We burn 'em out," he said. "Just like the cattlemen and the homesteaders. We," he said, "are the cattlemen."

I was sitting on the examination table in my T-shirt with my forearm resting on my thigh. He bent down and touched the point of the burner to a wart. There was just the faintest sizzling sound, then a tiny bubble of blood, then a little black hole he began to scour.

"When we talk about our nature's wonders," Havermeyer said, "one of the wonders we'd better talk about is warts. Absolutely fascinating little buggers. More than fascinating." He looked up at me, and I could see tiny black specks on his thick glasses. He bent down again. "More than fascinating," he said. And he burned more warts. "Their secrets are manifold and prodigious, Russell." He straightened up and shook the burner in my face. "I am talking manifold and prodigious," he said, before he bent back down. "The little guys are so neat I hate to do them in like this," he said. "But they'll sprout right up again."

"What!" I said. "What are we doing this for, then?"

"Oh, we're probably intimidating these guys sufficiently," he said. "I mean the virus will manifest itself on some other carrier. Might pop up on the family dog or cat, for example. Cat catches a mouse, bats it around with a warty paw, scratches the wart open, keeps on batting the mouse: mouse winds up with warts. Miss Mouse steps out with Mr. Toad, they do the Funky Broadway at the side of the road"— I thought the crazy fucker was going to start dancing!—"the mouse opens up a wart on the lip of a tin can, and pretty soon toad finds himself with a real wart along with all those venom glands that look like warts."

Havermeyer glanced up at me. "You can get warts from toads, you know," he said, before he looked back down.

"Kid comes along, picks up the toad, and sets it on the crest of the fender fin of a '58 Caddy. The toad teeters, loses his balance. His little toad fingers stretch over the peak of the fin. Between those fingers lurks the real wart. His back legs flail, struggle for purchase. The waxy surface of the metal militates against adhesion, and the toad falls. The jagged edge of a tiny scratch on the side of the fin catches the wart as the toad descends.

"Toad is just a Cadillac memory when the junior high coed rests her arm on the Caddy fin as her boyfriend suggests they do their social studies together in his parents' rec room that night and maybe tune in 'The Man from U.N.C.L.E.,' if they finish early. In a couple days the young lady is in her bath when we hear, 'Oooh, Mom! I got a big ugly wart under my arm!'"

Havermeyer had moved around so that he was squatting on his haunches beside me, getting a straight shot at the warts on the side of my wrist.

"And it's not like they need to be passed from carrier to carrier," he said. "They'll just pop up. On a foot, a tongue, on a penis, in a vagina. You ought to get you an eyeful of venereal warts sometime.

They look amazingly like baby cauliflower."

"I really ought to see some," I said. "Everybody ought to."

"We talk about warts as a virus," Havermeyer said as he worked away, "but they aren't actually viruses themselves. They're the media through which the virus reproduces, launches its satellites, establishes its turf. Warts are how the virus tells us hello." He looked up at me with a satisfied smile.

"Tells us hello?" I said.

"That's right," Havermeyer replied. He bent his head back to his work. "Communication. At least, it could be communication," he said. "I'm saying maybe, but I'm thinking probably."

I said I wasn't interested in hearing any more from the wart virus.

"Number sev...en...teen!" Havermeyer exclaimed, as he scoured the last wart.

He straightened up, hooked a stool with his foot, and pulled it over to us. I sat on it and he sat above me on the table with his legs hanging down over my shoulders. As his scissors clicked and hair dropped on my shoulders, he told me he was cutting a circle I could cover nicely with a yarmulke if I wanted to.

I looked it up tonight and found out a yarmulke is that skullcap male Orthodox Jews wear.

Havermeyer wrapped his legs around my chest and then gave me the shots in my scalp. I flinched every time the needle went in, but he held me pretty still. He unwrapped his legs and poked my bare scalp with his fingernail until I told him I couldn't feel it. Then he started with the burner.

"Consider this, Russell," he said. "You can reason with warts. You can entreat them. You can maybe even fool them. Ever heard the folk-medicine stories where the local shaman gets the carrier to draw a picture of his warts, then burn the picture or send it out to sea in a bottle or bury it or get rid of it some other way?"

"No," I replied.

"Eighty percent of the time the warts go away," Havermeyer said. "Hyponosis works too."

"How do you hypnotize a wart?" I asked.

"'How do you hypnotize a wart?'" he repeated. "I love it. You don't hypnotize the wart, Russell," he said. "You hypnotize the carrier and tell him his warts will be gone in a certain length of time. And in eight out of ten cases, they are."

"What if they aren't?" I asked.

"Then we get a bunch of the boys and we burn 'em out," he replied. "But eight out of ten times you tell 'em to go away, and they go. What do you suppose that suggests?"

How the fuck do I know what it suggests? I thought. I said I didn't know.

He lowered the burner to the level of my shoulder and the smoke curling off the tip went right up my nose.

"Consider this," he said. "What has to happen in the body for tissue to just go away? It probably has to die. But how's it going to die, or how are we going to kill it? Not so hard: identify all the precapillary arterioles in the neighborhood, shut down the blood flow, and glaah...glaah—" Havermeyer made strangling noises—"no blood, no oxygen, et cetera, et cetera: no tissue life.

"But feature this," he said. "Say your shaman or your shamanette gets you to draw just six of your twenty-nine warts on the paper. Say your warts are real whoppers and your paper is small. Eighty percent of the time, the six pictured warts go away and the twenty-three others stick around for another sitting."

He paused for a response, and I told him I didn't think I got the point.

"The point," he said, "is, how the hell did your body cut off the blood to those six warts and not the others? And what mechanism was it in your body—or in your mind, of course—that read the images, identified the wart on the tip of your index finger, did it in, and left you the fingertip as original, as smooth, as if it had never suffered an invasion of anything? So smooth, your postwart fingerprints are identical to your prewart?

"What we're talking about here is either a superintelligent mechanism in the body that we can somehow reach through both conscious and subconscious suggestion in the presence of the wart virus. Or some external intelligence—and this is *my* theory—that understands we've taken offense at its overtures, and therefore says 'bye-bye' as mysteriously, as mischievously, maybe, as it said hello. Mother Nature works in mysterious ways, my boy.

"Now, the internal mechanism," Havermeyer went on lecturing as he continued rooting out my warts. "The internal-mechanism idea offers potential fully in the realm of miracle. Say we found out how to get in touch with this mechanism at will, and in the presence of *all* invasionary cells, not just warts. Among other things"—and he reached down over my head and snapped his fingers in my face— "we could cure cancer like that! We could just say, 'Get on outa here, melanoma!' and melanoma would hit the road.

"But," he went on, "but...but! What if warts *are* the communication of an external intelligence, a nonbiological intelligence, maybe? And what if we could get on good terms with it? What if something as immensely complex as cell rejection were child's play to this entity? No only could we cure cancer and birth defects with its cooperation, we could wipe out flatulence, tooth decay, and bunions as well. I'm being facetious with these last two examples," he said, taking time out from burning warts to laugh. Getting back to work, he said dreamily, "We could submit any biological proposal to arbitration. It would change the universe for us."

I felt pressure on my scalp twice more, then Havermeyer lifted a leg over my head and hopped down off the table.

"That'll do it," he said. "Nineteen of 'em. A full baker's dozen plus six. A grand total of thirty-six warts. At two grand a unit, you owe me $72,000. I hope you're heavily covered by virus insurance, my friend." He laughed and slapped me on the shoulder and started taping gauze on my wrist.

I asked him what it was really going to cost me, and he said thirty bucks. "Less than a buck a wart—cheap at twice the price," he said.

"What'd you do to the warts on your wrist?" he asked as he started taping gauze over my bald spot.

"I shaved 'em off one time," I replied.

"Do not do that!" Havermeyer said. "Do not ever do that! That's the one sure way to spread warts. The ones on your wrist were more calloused and more deeply entrenched than the ones on your head because you messed with them. Amateurs in the wart business," he said, "should not perform surgery on themselves. You've got to be subtle with warts. Either that, or you've got to burn 'em right down through the roots. Warts don't have a whole lot of respect for half-measures."

I thanked him and told him I'd remember.

Getting the warts off made me feel better than I've felt in weeks, and I sang on the way home on the Fish Lake road, weaving through the dotted white line for miles. When I got back to Cheney, I steam-cleaned the Harley at the Texaco station, and that made me feel even better.

At the house I found my typewriter out in the middle of my desk with a sheet of paper in it. Who's been typing on my typewriter? I said to myself. I looked closer and discovered it was a passport application. Bolão walked over, took the headphones off, and said, "Type it up right now. Do not procrastinate."

I could hear that great Brazilian music beating faintly from the headphones.

"Sit down," Bolão said.

I sat down, and he put the headphones over my ears. That samba rhythm jumped through my head and flowed right to my ass and nailed me to the chair. I think I "heard the call," as Crookshank would say in a much different context. So I typed out the form as I danced a little samba in my chair.

I'm excited about going to Rio, but I'm not out of control about it. It's a long time yet till the end of school. And just because a guy gets a passport doesn't mean he's got to go anywhere.

God, it's amazing how things can turn around. I was down and scared and about half-crazy all week, and now I've got my girl back, my skin has been returned to its smooth condition, and my mind eased. Who says this life is just a big shit sandwich! Who says it's a vale of tears!

Sunday night, April 14, 1968

Who says there's no justice in the world! We learn here in college that life is "absurd," that things don't make sense. Bullshit!! Some things make all kinds of sense. If I didn't get justice done to me this weekend, there isn't any such thing as justice.

Friday afternoon in front of the language lab, I mentioned to Leila that I was riding my motorcycle to Seattle after class, and she said, "And why don't you take me also?" I was amazed and flattered, and when I saw the look on her face and the way she held her body and touched my wrist with her fingertips, I realized I could be in for the adventure of my life. I immediately began to feel guilty for wanting to betray Georgie, but that didn't stop me from doing it.

As I left class and walked outside across the lawn with the sky all blue and the green buds of spring pushing out everywhere and the air so exhilarating it felt like the pure oxygen we used to sneak from the training room, I wondered if the people I passed could read my face. I had to concentrate to keep my legs from moving faster by themselves. I wanted to skip like a school kid. And then I thought, God, what if I run into Georgie?

Leila was sitting on her apartment steps when I pulled up. She was wearing so many clothes, she looked like somebody had pumped her up with air. She had a long green-striped scarf around her neck and half a dozen or so sweaters underneath her blue overalls. You could see she was psyched for the trip. She had a glow on her skin like the shine on a chestnut, and it was in her brown eyes too. All the curls of her black hair bounced as she walked down the sidewalk. I stuffed her big straw purse in the empty saddlebag, and we were off.

When we hit the freeway and I turned us up to about seventy-five, Leila began to bounce around behind me and squeal and shout, "*O meu deus!* Oh my God, this is fun!" until she about knocked us over.

We were at Moses Lake before the sun was down and it started getting cold. The wind came up out of all that desolation in the middle of the state, and I began to wish I hadn't taken off the windshield. Leila tightened her arms around me and burrowed her face into the fur collar of my jacket. Spring wasn't anywhere out there in the dark. Tumbleweeds blew across the freeway in bunches, scuttling like quail, looking eerie coming out of the darkness and across the headlight beam, and sounding eerie, too, as they scraped over the road. I cut the speed down to sixty, and it wasn't so cold. We whipped through the little wide spot in the road called George, Washington, then we were winding down the steep curves where the Columbia River cuts through the land.

We pulled into the little town of Vantage on the west bank of the river and fueled up. Leila hooked her arm through mine as we walked into the cafe by the service station.

"*Está muito frio. Nãoé*, Karl?" she said. And she smiled a smile all blushed from the cold.

"It's cold as shit out there, all right," I replied. And Leila laughed, and repeated in her accent that I was beginning to get a kick out of, "It's cold as shit!"

I said I'd like us to make it to Cle Elum, a little town at the foot of the Cascades over halfway to Seattle, before we stopped. Leila smiled and said, "You are the captain of the ship, Karl."

We didn't make Cle Elum. The wind and cold were burning through my gloves like they weren't even there, and my fingertips were hurting so bad I could hardly control my hands. So I pulled off on the Ellensburg ramp and into the first motel. For miles I'd been thinking about how'd we sleep, but when we got to our rooms I was so fucking cold I didn't care. I peeled off my jacket and ran to the bathroom and stuck my hands under the cold water. I had my eyes closed and was still gritting my teeth with the pain when Leila brushed by me, saying, "I'll make us a hot bathtub."

I opened my eyes, and she was stark naked. She looked like a big, strong native woman from *National Geographic*. Feeling was coming back to my hands, so I turned on the hot water a little and plugged the sink. Steam began to rise from the tub and coat the mirror.

Leila got in the tub and lay back. She had more pubic hair than I'd ever seen on a person in my life, and wet, black hair curled against her breasts from under her arms. I was surprised how sexy she looked with all that hair.

"Come in here and get yourself warm with me," Leila said.

I stepped into the other room and got out of my clothes. I was still cold enough to be shaky and my dick was shriveled up to nothing. The poor little thing could have crawled into a thimble, turned around twice, and gone to sleep.

The tub overflowed a little when I got in. It was hard not to focus on Leila's breasts because the water, when we stayed still, hit her just exactly in the middle of her nipples, and when we moved it rose and dropped, magnifying them a little, then leaving them shiny-wet and beaded. I began to get hard just looking at her, and in a minute the head of my cock poked above the water like a stupid floating plum. Leila smiled the same mischievous smile she'd been smiling since that afternoon and bent forward and kissed it. Then she began to soap her breasts, and I leaned back and closed my eyes.

Georgie never entered my mind when Leila and I toweled each other off and then made love on the bed. I didn't think of anything but what we were doing. Leila made me do things. She'd push me down or turn me over or pull my hand where she wanted it, or just hold me still and do stuff to me. It felt neat to be done to, and it made me think that might be how girls feel.

I thought of Georgie when we quit, though, and when we walked out to get a bite to eat. Leila smoked and talked about her *brasileira* friend in Seattle and how deep "into the Movement" she was. What I wanted to do was to call Georgie. I'd never made love with anyone but Georgie. And I'd never slept with anyone but Georgie either, so sleeping with Leila was pretty hard. Even after all the love we'd made, I still wasn't tired enough to overcome the strangeness of sleeping with somebody I didn't know.

Leila wanted to make love again in the morning, so we did.

The sky was clear when we got on the road, and there was no wind. You could see the greenness coming up everywhere now that it was day, so it felt like spring again. We rolled past Cle Elum and started to climb Snoqualmie Pass. Up ahead the Cascades were all covered with snow.

The road was bare and wet as we climbed, and water was falling everywhere down the mountainsides from the melting snow. On the summit the snow was piled up to the cabin roofs and all filthy and pithy, but there wasn't any snow on the road, thank God. When we started down the other side, the mist from some of the waterfalls floated over us and woke Leila, who'd been sleeping behind me.

"O *meu deus!*" she yelled in my ear. "Karl, you aren't much a captain to let me miss all these beauties."

I was about to yell back when we dropped down onto the flat where the vista opened up. And there was Mt. Rainier, incredibly huge and crystal-clear against the cloudless sky. Leila went to squealing and squirreling and pointing and about knocked us over again.

We fueled up in North Bend, barreled through Issaquah, then rattled over the grating on the floating bridge and we were in Seattle. I looked up at the Space Needle and thought of the last time I saw it in the summer of '62 when Mom and Dad and Jesse and I drove to the World's Fair in Dad's new Impala wagon. It was the last trip the four of us ever took together.

Leila's friend was named Eliana and she was just twenty-two, but she taught Latin American politics at the college. She was blonde and had blue eyes and looked like me, except that she had very short hair. She lived with a bunch of people in a big old house near the University of Washington. After we were introduced Eliana told me I looked tired. She took me to her bed, which was a little mattress on the floor of a room with books everywhere. The only place there weren't books was a spot on the wall facing me where there was a poster of Che Guevara in black with his fist raised against a red background.

Leila woke me later with little kisses all over my face. Behind her Eliana was changing clothes. She didn't have anything on top and she was wearing those tiny little panties like the bottoms of a bikini swimsuit. When she heard me speak to Leila, she turned so I couldn't see her breasts.

"Tonight we are going to the house of some some friends for a big *festa*," Leila said. "And we are going to eat *feijoada* and drink *pinga* and *falar muito português com os nossos amigos* and have a big time generally."

It was dark when the big troop of us hit the street. I was ready for a night of adventure. Eliana was walking in the lead with an older black guy who wore a full beard. He was my height but outweighed me by thirty or forty pounds. He was pretty formidable-looking, with his beard and his build and his Afro and his black leather coat over a black turtleneck. I asked Leila who he was, and she said he was Eliana's "man" who had just gotten out of prison in California.

We made quite a parade down the sidewalk. One of us wore a long white robe and rope belt and rope sandals, another looked like someone from a South American rodeo with his leather hat with the wide brim curled up front and back and his leather chaps and vest, another wearing a World War II GI helmet liner, one in a cheap old third-

or fourth-hand fur coat that dragged on the sidewalk, and Leila in her overalls with nothing underneath but a thin white cotton T-shirt you could see her breasts through. Then there was me in my leather aviator's cap and my goggles pulled down over my eyes because Leila wanted me to look like the captain. And then came two more large black guys dressed in black bringing up the rear.

We arrived at another big old house not far away, where I met people from Chile, Argentina, Venezuela, Ecuador, Cuba, and one of those little countries around Panama, plus a big contingent of Brazilians, who were all dark like Bolão but not Indian-looking like Leila.

It was a good-natured madhouse. Brazilian music was playing on the stereo and a Brazilian guy named Cassiano had a table set up with a blender, ice, fruit, sugar, and an enormous number of bottles of the Brazilian liquor *pinga*. He was making drinks called *batidas* as fast as he could blend them up. In the kitchen three big pots of black beans with pork were cooking and a huge kettle of rice was steaming.

None of the women were wearing bras, so nobody paid any special attention to Leila, whose nipples you could see now and then through her T-shirt under her overalls. I was playing special attention to *all* the women, however. I was self-conscious about it, but still I couldn't keep staring from nipple-bulge to nipple-bulge.

In the dining room another Che Guevara poster hung on a wall under a long red banner that said in black *¡VENCEREMOS!*, which means "We will conquer!" The people clustered around the table were the Movement people, I guessed. They were dressed pretty normally, and they didn't seem bent on getting drunk like the rest of us.

Eliana seemed to be in charge. She was talking about how the "fascist" government of Brazil had just crushed the "Front," the only above-ground political opposition. And I thought, Fascists! I know about fascists. I'm gonna sit here and listen. So I sat down on the floor and leaned against an old console radio and sipped my *batida*. Eliana's boyfriend looked down at me and I smiled back up at him, but he didn't respond.

Eliana went on about a Brazilian priest from Recife who was coming to the university to talk about the CIA teaching torture techniques to the Brazilian police. And I piped up, "Ah, come on. The CIA wouldn't do that in Brazil, for God's sake. It's probably just propaganda that they do it in Vietnam, and we're not even at war with anybody in Brazil."

Everybody turned to look at me. Then Eliana's boyfriend said, "This is a closed meeting."

And I said, "Huh?"

And the black guy at the other end of the table said, "Closed, Chuck. This is a *private* meeting."

Chuck? I thought. And I said, "Oh, sorry." As I went back to the living room I was thinking, I'm gonna talk to Eliana about this CIA stuff.

I stood and talked to Cassiano awhile and drank one pineapple and one coconut *batida* and read the label of a *pinga* bottle and learned they make the stuff out of sugarcane. Then Leila and the other women came dancing out of the kitchen carrying dinner. They broke up the political meeting and everyone yelled at everyone else for a few minutes fairly good-naturedly, except for the black guys, who were sullen and getting scarier to me all the time, and who left before supper.

The *feijoada* was great. We heaped rice on our plates and then ladled beans and pork and juice over it. I was the one to jump up and change the records and I felt part of things, even though I was only getting about one-eighth of what was being said in Portuguese and Spanish. Leila was putting down banana *batidas* like there was going to be a world-wide banana blight the next day, and towards the end of the meal she began to sing along with the music and rock back and forth in her chair with her eyes closed.

Cassiano and I and a Cuban guy cleared the table and did the dishes and danced at the kitchen counter in our wash-rinse-and-dry line. Somebody'd turned the music up, and it was the kind of samba music that I remembered from *Orfeo Negro*, and I was thinking of what Bolão had told me about the samba, that you did it with your ass stuck all up in the air like you were impaled on a stalk of sugarcane. Then Leila and Eliana came dancing into the kitchen singing along with the music.

Eliana told us everybody was going out to the Robin to drink beer. Then another song came on, and Leila moved in front of me and turned her back and grabbed my hands and put them on her hips. In a second everybody in the kitchen was in a line behind us with their hands on the hips of the person in front, and we were all dancing in this long line that moved into the dining room, then to the living room, then to a bedroom where the coats were piled. I thought I was going to die of erotica from watching Leila's ass move. And when we got to the bedroom and people peeled off to get their coats, she held my hands at her hips and moved back into me as she kept dancing. I missed coming in my pants by a fraction of a second as the record ended. It immobilized me for a while, and I was the last one out the door to the cars.

When my eyes got adjusted to the darkness in the Robin, I could see that aside from Eliana I had the shortest hair in the place. It was a small old tavern, and militantly unfestive. There weren't any beer signs behind the bar, where something that looked like one of those long-haired, pig-nosed Himalayan bears was drawing beers. The only colored lights in the place came from the jukebox and the cigarette machine.

We sat down at a row of picnic tables near the three black guys, who'd left before supper. Cassiano brought pitchers of beer from the bar and the Cuban guy brought glasses. Cassiano asked Eliana's boyfriend who he thought shot Martin Luther King.

"An American," the guy said.

Cassiano said that bigotry and cruelty were elements of human nature in general, and not just limited to Americans and other capitalist whites. He went on to tell a story about how in the forties, fifties, and even up into the sixties, in Rio and São Paulo and some of the bigger cities of Brazil, poor people would maim their children or sell them to people who would maim them so that when they were put on the streets to beg, they'd arouse more attention and sympathy. "They would put blocks of wood on a baby's ears," he said, "then wind rope around the baby's head against the blocks so that the skull grew into a cone shape."

"This is very true," Leila said. "I remember my mother taking me shopping in Copacabana, and when we would see these little pinheaded kids, five, six years old like me, and ones with their arms and legs broken into the shapes of Z's and little ones with their heads flattened, she would say, 'Leilinha, be happy you have a mother and father who love you.'"

And the Cubano—as all the Brazilians were calling him—said,

"Be happy you had a mother and father with money."

Cassiano said that right up to the revolution of '64 you could still see these people, most of them grown into adults, begging on the streets. "They were such an eyesore for the tourists coming for *Carnavál* and such an irony to Brazilian *'ordem e progresso'* that finally the army got rid of them."

And Leila said, "There was a story that *os mudados*—"

Cassiano broke in. "That means the altered," he said, looking at me.

"There was a story that these altered people, they banded together and lived in an old fallen-down subway," said Leila.

I got up for more beer about then and, as I tried to navigate to the bar, found out how destroyed by the *batidas* I was. The Himalayan bear-guy didn't ask for any I.D., so I bought two pitchers. And all the time I was thinking of little kids like Jesse living with ropes squeezing their heads and their little arms and legs broken into Z's.

"You can also look at it like this," Cassiano said. "The *favelados* probably didn't *like* selling their babies. And the bourgeoisie probably doesn't *like* it that their neighbor's son disappears one night and comes home three weeks later with his testicles looking like a rat run over by a car. The *favelados* were probably just too hungry in those days, and the bourgeoisie too scared today. But the *polícia brasileira*, who smash the kid's nuts with the rubber mallets"—and here he looked over at Eliana—"these police, they *like* it," he said.

"These pigs, they *do* enjoy it," Leila said. "And these CIA who show them the things more sophisticated than hammers, those pigs, they enjoy it even more."

"Will you guys stop with the 'pig CIA' stuff!" I said. "Individual Americans might be as cruel and hateful as bad people in any country. But the United States government is not gonna send Americans to teach Brazilians to torture other Brazilians. Especially kids, for God's sake! If you guys had grown up in this country you'd know that," I said. And I looked at Eliana's boyfriend.

"Shit," he said, as he got up and left the table.

"You are such a boy, Karl," Leila said. "You are such the all-American boy." She and Eliana and a few others got up and left too.

Nobody said anything for a minute, then the Cubano said, "You ought to read a little more broadly, man."

"And watch less television," said Cassiano.

I got up and peed, and as I was coming out of the bathroom I came face to face with Eliana. She pushed me back against the sink and closed the door. Then she pulled her T-shirt up to her chin and said, "Look, Karl."

My vision was spinning and I couldn't focus very well on her face. I didn't want to look down.

"Look at my breasts, Karl," Eliana said. "It won't hurt you."

I looked down at her little breasts. At first I thought she'd made X's across her nipples with a black felt marker.

"Look," she said.

I bent my head and saw that the black lines were scars, deep and jagged, and that they went right through her nipples. She didn't have any nipples.

Somebody rattled the door, but Eliana had it locked. "The police do this, Karl," she said. "They use electricity. There is an American in the room, and when you don't answer the questions he nods his head. He wears gray slacks and a navy blue sportcoat over a light-blue cotton button-down shirt. He wears brown-framed glasses, a red-black-and-gray striped tie, and those kind of slip-on shoes people put coins in."

Someone rattled the door again. "Eliana!" It was her boyfriend.

"Just a minute, Leon," Eliana replied. "What they wanted to know from me wasn't important," she said. "The people they asked about were already safe in France, and they knew it. I answered their questions, but they kept burning my breasts. They had the wires in my cunt"—she kind of spit the word and a bead of saliva hit my cheek. "They had the wires in my cunt and they were ready to crank the handle on the little box when the American shook his head. You *are* very naive, Karl," Eliana said, and dropped her shirt.

I wasn't thinking about anything political and I wasn't even thinking about Eliana. I was thinking of Georgie and how her first foster father had raped her and cut off two of her fingers. And I was thinking of how much pressure you'd have to put on to cut through a finger bone. I almost started to cry, I wanted to be with Georgie so bad.

That night I dreamed I was a wartman again. I looked the same as in the falling dream. But in this dream, instead of dying, I was living with the altered people Cassiano and Leila had talked about. I was sitting against a cool tiled wall. Neither my scalp nor the skin on my back and shoulders could touch the wall because of the warts. The sound of dripping water was everywhere, along with the smell of water and moss and wet dirt. Things in the shapes of mushrooms moved around me in the darkness. I knew these shapes were the *mudados*. They seemed to like me and want me to not be scared. But I was scared, and I heard myself start to scream.

I woke up in my clothes on a pink blanket on Eliana's living-room floor. Eliana was kneeling by me in a flannel shirt that was huge on her. "Karl, Karl," she said. "You're okay."

I had a terrible headache and worse nausea, and I wished I was back in Cheney with Georgie. I looked around and didn't see Leila among the other people sleeping on the floor, some of whom now rose up on one arm to look at me. "Where's Leila?" I asked.

"She wasn't feeling well," Eliana said. "She went to the Cubano's where she could sleep in a bed."

Leon's voice came from the bedroom. "Baby," he said softly, "come on back to bed."

I found my coat and cap and goggles and got Leila's phone number and wrote it on my hand, then I walked out to the bike all bent over with my hangover headache.

The moist night air made me feel a little better, and I sat on the Harley for a minute or so and breathed through my mouth. She started on the second kick, and in the light from the speedometer I looked at my watch and saw it was 4:30. I turned at the first arterial street I came to, turned from there onto the freeway, and before I'd gone a mile I found a Holiday Inn.

I called Georgie as soon as I got to the room. I let it ring fifty times but she wouldn't wake up. I knelt at the toilet and stuck my finger down my throat and threw up until I couldn't throw up anymore, then I slid out of my clothes and lay on the cool linoleum floor until I stopped sweating.

I got up and called Georgie again and let it ring a hundred times. I began to wonder if she wasn't home, if she could be working all night at the hospital or if she'd been in an accident or if she was at a late party.

I didn't dream anymore that night. I woke up about 9:30, turned on the TV and switched through the salivating preachers until I found cartoons. My head still ached, but I was feeling better. I called Georgie again. She still wasn't home, and I really started to worry. I called the friend she rides to the hospital with, and she said she would have heard if Georgie'd been in an accident. She was real short with me, and it made me feel funny.

On TV Bugs Bunny had gone back in time and was being chased by Elmer Fudd dressed as a caveman. I thought of sitting up with Georgie on a Saturday or Sunday morning watching cartoons and eating chocolate pinwheel cookies, and a scared feeling started in my stomach as I began to wonder if she was in bed with somebody else, watching the same cartoons as me.

Once the feeling started it came on like battery acid. It burned right up my stomach into my chest and fanned out at the bottom of my throat. I drank about half a dozen plastic cups of plastic-tasting water, showered, dressed, and left without even trying to get hold of Leila.

The rain started as I went through the yellow light by the A&W in North Bend, and it turned to snow as the road began its climb up the pass. I had to drop my speed to fifty because of the curves and because the wet snow was sticking to my goggles and I couldn't see.

It must have been snowing a long time up there, because it was packed over ice on the summit and the cars were backed up God knows how far. But the bad thing was that the rain and wet snow had soaked me and I was freezing.

Snow was beginning to cake up on my legs when I started down the leeward slope. The snow turned back into rain before I'd gone very far downhill. My pants thawed out, but the slush kicked up by the cars in front and the passing trucks was getting down the neck of my jacket and making me even colder. Big globs of it would spatter my goggles so bad that I'd have to pull over and take them off, unzip my jacket, and clean them with my shirt.

I was soaked through everywhere and shaking so bad I couldn't hold still. My teeth were chattering so hard I couldn't keep my mouth closed, and the slush would get in my mouth and I'd taste the oily road film and the gravel and I'd spit it out and just let it dribble down my front. There wasn't anything I could do but keep going until I hit Cle Elum and found a motel.

Trying to make it over the pass alive had pushed thoughts of Georgie to the back of my mind and made that acid feeling through my chest fade. But lying there thawing out in the bathtub of the Evergreen Motel made me think of having been with Leila, and that brought Georgie right back to the front of my mind and the sick, scared feeling back to my heart. I thought of how Georgie'd soap me when we took baths together, and in my mind I saw her holding someone else's cock and soaping it until it disappeared in lather.

I hung my long johns and socks on a hanger and hooked it through the grate of the wall heater and turned it up full, then I hung my pants and shirt over the back of a chair and set it in front. I wrung the water out of my jacket and cap in the bathtub and hung them from the shower-curtain rod.

I was exhausted, but I couldn't sleep. I pulled the covers up to my nose and breathed deep and tried to relax there in the dark with the rap of the rain on the windows. But there was no way in hell I could relax. Over the crisp fragrance of the new bedclothes I thought I could smell Leila and me, and I began to see Georgie doing with someone all the things I'd done with Leila. I put my wet clothes back on and hit the road again.

I blew through the desert like a fucking hydroplane. I could feel Georgie's hands on my bare back, the way her fingers would tap to the Beach Boys album we'd put on when we made love. And I could feel the tiny time-lapse where the one finger on each of her hands was missing.

I fueled up in Moses Lake just to be sure I'd make it and so I could pee. I'd peed in my pants on the pass to get warm for a few seconds, and because I'd been so wet it didn't matter anyway.

I didn't think I could get more worried but I did, the closer I got to Cheney. And by the time I turned onto Georgie's street my heart was pounding in my head like a diesel. Georgie's Dart was there, and a red '66 Mustang convertible with a black top was parked behind it.

Georgie answered the door, and her eyes got big for a second when she saw it was me, but then she kind of set her face.

"I've been calling," I said. "I was worried."

"I thought you were in Seattle," Georgie said. "I can't talk right now."

There wasn't any Georgie in her voice. It was like we'd never known each other.

"You can't talk?" I said.

"Someone's here," she said.

I looked at her for a second. "A guy?" I said.

"Yes," Georgie said. She blinked, then lowered her eyes. "I'm sorry," she said. When she looked up her face was set again. "You should get those wet clothes off, Karl," she said. "I'll be talking to you."

Thursday morning, April 25, 1968,

1:10 a.m.

Sergio Mendes and Brazil '66 on the stereo and I'm here at the desk clamped into the headphones. *Fool on the Hill* album playing for about the fifth time.

It's been ten days now, and Georgie hasn't called. Every day and every night last week I drove by her apartment. Sometimes the Mustang convertible was there. I missed a lot of classes, I didn't run, I didn't read, I didn't write here in the journal, and I didn't even feel like listening to music. I walked around campus and drove by Georgie's and slept more than a healthy person should.

I heard her voice perfectly in my mind. I could smell her smells and I could feel her skin. I thought how good she'd been to me for almost four years, and I knew I'd never find anyone else who'd get to know me that well and still love me. As clear as if I were looking at a movie I saw her naked, wearing my boxer shorts on her head like a chef's hat as she fried rice and eggs and onions on the stove in her little kitchen. And I wondered if she were wearing Mustang's shorts on her head now, and I wondered if she pulled the covers up and held them over his head when he farted in bed. I couldn't keep sights and thoughts like that out of my head.

But this morning when I was up on campus some other sights worked their way into my mind and changed my attitude a little. I saw a bunch of very good looking girls, and I realized that for the first time since I've been in college I'm unattached.

It's an interesting feeling. A feeling of vast potential. It's like standing on the west bank of the Mississippi River in the early 1800s and looking out over the frontier and thinking, I can have almost anything out there I want. But you keep on squinting into the falling sun and you maybe have some second thoughts. Jesus, you think, there's Injuns out there movin' among them shadows. There's bear, poisonous snake, and mountain lion. But still it's a wonderful feeling to know you can have a piece of it if you've got the nerve to take it. The nerve and a little luck.

So I'm feeling a little better about life in the spring of 1968. A little better. There may be better adventures ahead of me. I didn't do so well with my last one.

I'm way behind in all my classes, but I'll catch up.

Read like a fiend tonight. Got up through page 50 in *One Day in the Life of Ivan Denisovich* for Literature of the Camps.

I think my favorite class for the next couple weeks is going to be World Masterpieces because we're into *Paradise Lost*, an epic poem in which John Milton tries to "justify the ways of God to men." I call that a fairly tall order, so I'm wishing him luck—I'd like to learn the justice in God's ways!!—and I'm going to watch close to see if he does it. If I were Dr. Hazelton, that's one question I'd ask on the test: "John Milton wrote *Paradise Lost* to justify the ways of God to men. How'd he do?"

I like the sound of Milton's words even when I'm not understanding all of them. It's a feeling that I'm reading one of the most important things a human being ever wrote. It's more than that, though. It's like I'm right there with Milton, looking over the edge of hell at "Th' infernal serpent" with his "horrid crew" in their "dungeon horrible on all sides round / As one great furnace flamed."

It starts out like this with the traditional invocation to the muse:

> Of man's first disobedience, and the fruit
> Of that forbidden tree whose mortal taste
> Brought death into the world, and all our woe,
> With loss of Eden, till one greater Man
> Restore us, and regain the blissful seat,
> Sing, Heavenly Muse...

Then a few lines later Milton asks the muse for help with his "adventurous song" because he's writing about "things unattempted yet in prose or rhyme."

Mom never told me the story of *Paradise Lost*, but I bet she read it herself. When I hit a tough passage I read it aloud to see if that helps. And when I do, I think of Mom and how she used to tell me that she knew one day I'd read the classics myself.

Thursday night, 11:30 p.m.

Got a letter from the registrar today saying they had to notify my draft board that I was no longer a full-time student. Withdrawing from Portuguese left me with eleven credits, and you have to be taking twelve to be full time.

"Ha, ha, and fuck you, folks!" I said to the letter. "I ain't about to be drafted. I'm 4-F!!"

But it made me think about the guys who have to drop a class for some real good reason, and then three months later wind up in Vietnam. Who knows why things happen? Fucking up my arm destroyed my chance to go all the way as a ballplayer. But with a good arm, maybe I'd have gotten drafted and killed or blasted into something somebody got paid to feed and clean.

It's funny to think this, but in spite of the bad luck I've had in my twenty years, I feel real lucky. I say the bad luck *I've* had, but it was my folks and my brother who got killed, and I should probably say the bad luck *they* had. I *am* fortunate. I act like a total asshole zombie for the past two weeks, and instead of treating me like I deserve, which would be either to thump shit out of me or ignore me, the guys all ask me do I need dough, are my classes going okay, am I sick, do I want to resign my pledgeship? I felt like I could have told almost anyone in the house and not had my troubles taken lightly.

I had to talk to Bolão about dropping Portuguese because he knows Leila and would have heard about it anyway, and because he got me to take the class in the first place. "She does one or two guys in every class," he told me, which made me feel stupid for having thought there was something special about me.

April 26

It's Friday night, ten o'clock. I've put in a good three hours studying for the fourth night in a row, and now I'm about to splash some cold water on my face and head for a party at Perry Lantz's apartment. My plan is to drink large volumes of beer.

Just finished *One Day in the Life of Ivan Denisovich*, thankful as always for short books, especially short good books like this one and *Night*.

Denisovich is minding his own business as he finishes his soup, when a tall old man sits down across from him. He's heard the old guy's been sitting in camps and prisons "for years without end."

> Among all the stooped backs in camp the old man's was notable for its straightness. At the table he sat so tall it seemed he was sitting on something. . . . He ate his thin soup slowly with a worn-down wooden spoon. He did not bend to the bowl like the others but carried his spoon high up to his mouth. . . . There was something in him that refused to compromise. He didn't put his ten ounces of bread on the dirty splotched table as the others did. He put it on a clean-washed piece of cloth.

I guess if you don't compromise they never let you out of the camp. I can't imagine the guts it takes to stick to your standards under conditions like that. I don't understand these guys who are going to jail or to Canada to protest or evade the draft. I understand the ones who go to Canada least because those guys can *never* come back. Never again in their lives will they be able to set foot in the houses where they grew up.

I'd like to be the kind of man who refuses to compromise. I don't know if the war in Vietnam is right or wrong, so I can't set standards about it. But in a camp you know absolutely that what's being done to you is wrong, so you keep your back straight and refuse to bend. I'd like to be the kind of man who refuses to compromise, but I hope a mortal challenge never comes along to test me.

Sunday, April 28, 1968, 6:05 p.m.

Of how I was drunk Saturday morning around three
Wobbling under the spring stars
Along the sidewalk by the fir trees on Showalter lawn
When I heard ferocious sobbing under the fragrant branches
And took a gander thereunder to find
A girl not unknown to me, beautiful
And stricken with the grief of having been dumped
By the studliest of my fraternity brothers,
Sing, O Muse of Eastern Washington State College, Sing!

I was having a great time Friday night until about 2:30 when the party broke up and I looked around and realized I was the only guy there who didn't have a date. Everybody was with somebody. Even Boreson. Everybody had somebody but me.

I was on foot because the party was close by and because I'd gone there to get drunk as a skunk. The night was dark and drizzly, perfect for drunkenness and self-pity. Lights were blazing in the house when I turned our corner, and since I didn't want to see any happy people I walked on by.

I'd only walked a few yards down the shiny asphalt sidewalk crossing Showalter lawn when I heard what sounded like a girl's laughter coming from the line of fir trees up ahead. I cursed the happy couple I imagined making out under cover of those soft, good-smelling branches when I realized what I was hearing wasn't laughter at all but hard crying. I spread the branches where the sound seemed to be coming from and saw the dark form of a long-haired girl. She was sitting and heaving back and forth so hard with her crying that her hair would spread out on the dirt when she bent over, then her head would crack back against the tree trunk when she came up. I stuck my head through the branches and said, "Hey!"

The girl looked up at me and let out a scream that shocked me so bad I fell back on the sidewalk. I got up on my hands and knees. "Don't be scared," I said. "I heard you crying and wanted to see if you were okay. I'm coming in. Don't be scared."

I crawled through the branches and sat down facing her on the dry ground under the tree. In the little light that filtered through the branches I could see that it was Jennifer Haskell, Charley Hildebrand's girlfriend.

"You're Jennifer Haskell," I said. "You go with Charley, one of my fraternity brothers. My name's Karl Russell."

She peered at me through her tangled hair. There were sticks in it. "I go with shit," Jennifer said. She looked like she had two black eyes.

"Did you get beat up?" I asked.

"Oh, Jesus," she said. Then she got control of her crying. "I know you, Karl," she said. "You ride a Harley. My dad rides a Harley." She sniffed. "I'm not hurt," she said. A string of snot dropped from her nose and she tried to sniff it back, but it was too long. She got it with the sleeve of Charley's letter jacket she was wearing. "I'm just upset," Jennifer said. "Charley broke up with me tonight and I'm not taking it like a good soldier. But I'm going home now." She crawled past me through the branches and out into the rain.

I crawled out after her and got to my feet beside her. She ran her hands through her hair, then shook her head and twirled her hair, making the little sticks and things fly out of it. She walked up the sidewalk, and I walked beside her.

"I'm sorry you guys broke up," I said. "I broke up with my girl a couple weeks ago—she broke up with me, I should say. I know it doesn't feel good."

"It was nice of you to check on somebody you thought was in trouble," Jennifer said.

We were under the streetlight then, and she stopped and I could see she didn't have two black eyes at all. It was just her eye makeup that had run. She looked like a raccoon.

"There's my truck," she said. She pointed to a '66 Ford three-quarter-ton pickup sitting in front of the library. "'Night, Karl," Jennifer said as she crossed the street.

"'Night, Jennifer," I said. "It's gonna get better!" I hollered after her.

"Thanks, Karl," I heard her say quietly.

I stayed there watching the orange running lights on the roof of her rig until she turned out of sight.

I got up around noon the next day, free from hangover but suffering from love. I spent the afternoon in the library with my nose in *Paradise Lost* and Jennifer Haskell on my mind. It was tough getting a clear picture of "bottomless perdition" with its "adamantine chains and penal fire" when shots of Jennifer kept breaking through the flames. In my mind I saw her face red and puffy from crying, looking like the world's most beautiful and sexiest raccoon.

And then on my way home I was walking with my head down, thinking of the terrible grades I'm going to earn on my mid-terms Tuesday, when I reached the house and lifted my head and saw Jennifer for real right in front of me on the porch steps handing Charley his letter jacket on a hanger in a plastic cleaners' bag. Her light-brown hair was all combed and shiny, her eyes were clear, and her face was full of enthusiasm. I stood where I was on the sidewalk and pretended not to be straining to hear what she was saying. Charley held the hanger and bent down to kiss her where she stood on the step below him.

Jennifer put her hands on his shoulders, threw her head back, and said, louder than before, "Oh, no you don't, soldier!" She turned and walked fast up the sidewalk toward me.

"Hi, Karl Russell," she said as she passed me.

"Hello, Jennifer Haskell," I said to her back.

I studied hard after dinner till eleven o'clock, when I took a break to watch the news. I'd thought some of Jennifer, but I was mostly bearing down for mid-terms and I made it all the way through *Paradise*

Lost. It ends in the twelfth book with Adam and Eve kicked out of Eden.

> Some natural tears they dropped, but wiped them soon:
> The world was all before them, where to choose
> Their place of rest, and Providence their guide.
> They, hand in hand, with wandering steps and slow,
> Through Eden took their solitary way.

I'd been concentrating so hard I'd lost my awareness of the life around me, and when I walked down to the basement to watch the news I was surprised to find myself alone in the house. All alone on a Saturday night, I thought. Who says college life ain't fun?

I watched the Columbia University students taking over some campus buildings. Now there's kids that know how to have fun at college, I thought. Maybe if I join Students for a Democratic Society, I thought. I'd date girls who wore a lot of black and said "fuck." We'd storm buildings together and spit down on cops from upper-story windows.

Being alone in the big old house was giving me the creeps, so I turned off the news and went out for some air. As I walked up to campus I teased myself with the idea that Jennifer might be at the tree. It was so corny I was embarrassed even to think it. But I walked there anyway, and peeked through the branches. And there was Jennifer Haskell sitting with her arms around her knees and her back against the tree trunk.

She turned her head at the sound the branches made. She had her hair in a long braid. "Is that you, Karl?" she asked.

"It's me," I replied. "Okay if I come in?"

"Come on," she said.

Although I couldn't see her well, there was enough light to see she didn't have her enthusiasm on, but she didn't look like she'd been crying either. "I can't believe you're here," I said. "I was hoping you would be."

"I was hoping *you* would be," she said.

"I saw you this afternoon at the house," I said.

"I remember," she said.

We were quiet for a while. I was going nuts inside, though. I really couldn't believe what was happening to me.

"Want to walk?" Jennifer asked. She got to her feet and walked through the branches, and I followed. She walked close to the trees, brushing them all with her shoulder. I was afraid to try to take her hand. When we cleared the trees Jennifer turned toward the library, and I saw her rig parked there.

"Walk me to my truck?" she said.

"Sure," I said. A little panic went through me and I thought, Shit, a fifty-yard walk is all there is to it? I was afraid, but I felt like I had to make some kind of move or lose my big chance. "Like to go for a Coke someplace?" I said.

She didn't reply right away, and I knew I'd blown it.

"I don't feel like it tonight," Jennifer said.

Oh, shit, I thought. I am such a dork.

"But I'd like to see you," she said. "I drove into town because I hoped you'd be at the tree again."

"I'd like to see you too," I said. "There's a good movie at the Union tomorrow night. It's called *Fantastic Voyage*. It's about some people who get miniaturized and go inside a living human body. Feel like seeing it together?" All of a sudden it sounded like the dumbest movie in the world, and I sounded like the dumbest guy.

But Jennifer Haskell said, "Let's do."

And in fifteen minutes I'm meeting her in front of the Union.

Tuesday morning, April 30, 1968,

6:00 a.m.

In about three hours I take the first of three mid-terms today, and I'm not ready for any of them. I feel like I should care, but I don't. The only thing I've been able to care about since Sunday night is Jen.

Sunday night was warm, and I didn't wear a jacket. But Jen was waiting on the steps of the Union in a hunting coat. I thought a wool hunting coat was mildly inappropriate until we got in the movie and she pulled out a big sack of popcorn from the game pocket in back, two cans of Mountain Dew from the flap pockets in front, and two boxes of licorice Nibs from the breast pockets when we finished the popcorn.

When we got to her rig after the movie she leaned back against the driver's door, and with a smile I took to be one of genuine shyness, she said, "My dad put a tape player in the truck for my birthday." Then she looked down for a second, hooked her thumbs in her front belt loops, brought her eyes up again, and asked, "Feel like riding and listening to some music?"

I kind of savored it a second or two before I told her, "Sure."

We drove to the house and I got five beers out of the Ford. I whipped into the garage and got a bucket and put the beers in it, then we drove to Safeway and I bought some ice. We set the bucket on the seat between us and let the beers get cold as we drove.

Jen headed us west out of town toward the freeway, then turned south on a little blacktop road she said went to Badger Lake. We bounced over the railroad tracks and she handed me her tape box from off the floor between her legs and switched on the dome light. "You're in charge of the music," she said.

She has great tapes: Beatles, Stones, Jefferson Airplane, Big Brother and the Holding Company, Simon and Garfunkel, the Fifth Dimension, the Doors, some old Beach Boys, Vanilla Fudge. I grabbed *Rubber Soul* and popped it in. When the music started four little red lights began blinking in time.

Jen wanted to roll down the windows so we could smell the spring air, so we rolled them down and she turned on the heater and put the blower on high. We drank slow and I opened the new beers, since I was also in charge of the bar.

Jen said she grew up on a horse ranch near the little town of Chewelah about fifty miles north of Spokane. She has two of her own horses, which is why she lives in a rented farmhouse.

I told her about my folks, about why I was at Eastern instead of a bigger school playing ball, and about Georgie, but not about Leila. And I had the urge to tell her about seeing the wartman back when I was a kid and starting to get warts now myself and being afraid and about the dreams. But I held off on that, and told her instead that we were down to one beer. Jen said she was having such a good time she was moved to make a beer run to Spokane. I reminded her that neither of us was twenty-one, and she said I looked a lot older and that if people wouldn't sell us beer she'd cry and tell them it wasn't for us, that it was for our three small children at home fenced in the kitchen, crying for their Sunday night beer.

"Let's us head for Spokane," I said.

Jen turned off onto a bumpy dirt road that cut through the scrub pines and the house-sized basalt formations that rose up all over in the sweep of her headlights. She said this road would take us east to the Fish Lake road and the back way into Spokane. That three-quarter-ton Ford was flying over those bumps like an unlimited hydroplane over a light chop. I was already feeling a weight lifted off me because I was about to begin telling her the story of the wartman and the stuff that was scaring me, when all of a sudden the headlights didn't seem to be cutting through the dark anymore and Jen nailed the brake pedal to the floor. When I threw my arms out to keep from hitting the windshield, I let go of the beer and it cracked against the dash and threw foam all over the cab.

"God, Karl, look at him!" Jen said.

I sat back in the seat and looked out at the biggest, blackest Angus bull I'd ever seen in real life or pictures. Steam was rising off him like atmosphere around a small planet; his nose was torn between the nostrils, and frothy blood and saliva covered his nose and mouth.

"He was just there," Jen said. "I was paying attention, but all at once he was just there."

"He must have pulled the ring out of his nose," I said. "Look at the blood. If we'd have hit that thing it would have been all over."

"For us, at least," Jen said. She let out her breath. "All right, you big honker," she said to the bull. "Out of the way! Go out and reason with him, Karl."

I opened the door slowly and backed on the running board a few steps until I could hop into the truck bed. I grabbed an empty bottle and cocked my worthless throwing arm, leaned over, and said into Jen's window, "I hope you've got this rig fully insured."

That bull was the biggest animal I've ever seen. I've never see an elephant and I've never seen a whale, but I've seen moose and big elk and lots of cattle and draft horses and Brahma bulls and grizzly bears in Glacier Park, and that Angus bull was the biggest animal I've ever seen in real life. The top of his head was level with the top of the pickup.

I flung the bottle and hit him square between the eyes. I can't throw far, but I'm still fairly accurate. The bull didn't even blink. Then I thought, hit him in the nose, his nose must be tender.

"Jen," I said down into her window, "turn off your lights and we'll see what that does. And hold onto the wheel. I'm gonna see if I can't whack him one in the nose."

Jen cut her lights and I picked up another bottle. The sky was full of stars and seemed curved like the ceiling of a cathedral. The bull was only about eight feet in front of me, but I couldn't see him to save my soul. There was this dense black out there where he was, blacker than the other night around us.

"If you were a cowboy you'd go out there and bite down on his ear and walk him out of the way like a big dog," Jen whispered.

"I ain't no cowboy," I said. "But I used to be a baseball player. Here goes."

I flung the bottle. There was the lightest thud, then the clank of the bottle hitting the hard-packed dirt. I grabbed another bottle. "Here goes again," I said. Another dull thud, like throwing your books down on the davenport. I picked up another bottle, took two steps back in the truck bed, and let fly. The bottle hit Jen's chrome horse hood ornament and shattered in a zillion pieces.

"God, Karl," Jen yelled up out of the cab. "You said you used to be a baseball player."

I started laughing and couldn't stop. I fell back in the bed and laughed more. Jen got out of the cab, walked back on the running board, climbed in the bed, and kicked me lightly.

"Get up and save me from this animal," she said. "This is a beer run, not 'Wild Kingdom.'"

I quit laughing and stood up and rubbed my arm. "Arm's had it," I said. "You try the last one."

"Okay," she said. She walked back to the tailgate, took three quick steps forward, and threw. We didn't hear a thing. We looked at each other in the little bit of light from the stars.

"Maybe he just absorbed it," I said. "Like the blob."

"Get in," Jen said. "Let's push him out of the way and go to Spokane."

So we got in and I put the Doors into the tape player. Jen turned on her lights. The Doors were playing "Break on Through to the Other Side" and Jen turned it up all the way. She dropped the lever into D and crept forward.

The bull didn't move. The chrome horse rearing on its hind legs on Jen's hood passed under the bull's chin and Jen stopped. She turned on the dome light and we could see the blood falling from the bull's nose into pools the size of silver dollars on the hood. Jen put her thumbs in her ears and made a face at the bull. We could see his black eyes, and he didn't blink.

"Here goes," Jen said. She shut off the dome light and let her foot off the brake.

"I don't think he can hurt us," I said. "But he can sure as hell do some damage to your truck."

"It's really my dad's truck," Jen said. She smiled and took her foot off the brake again. We didn't move and she gave it a little gas, then more gas. The right rear wheel began to throw gravel and Jen romped it.

The bull bellowed and jumped sideways. One of his forelegs banged the front of the truck hard, and then he was trotting down the road in front of us, not even limping.

The Doors were deafening us, so I turned them down. "I can't believe it," I said. "A bull on this tiny road in the middle of nowhere at eleven o'clock at night—and we almost hit him! A fucking bull!" And I said to myself, Oh, no. I've shown my true crude colors now.

Jen turned toward me, and in the green light from the dash she looked very serious. "A *big* fucking bull," she said. And both of us laughed.

We hit the Fish Lake road and passed the cemetery. I thought of Mom and Dad and Jesse, especially Mom, because Mom would have understood best what a good time I was having.

I had no trouble buying a half-case of cold Oly at a little IGA at two minutes to midnight, two minutes before the guy closed. Jen and I drove and drank our beer and listened to music until a light blue line started showing at the bottom of the eastern sky. She drove me back to the house and walked me to the door. We stood where I'd seen her and Charley standing a couple days before. She kissed me for a long time, but she didn't touch me with anything but her lips. I kissed back, trying to make her feel what I was feeling.

I slept through all my classes Monday, and after I woke up all I did was walk around with a goofy look on my face. I didn't even try to study. I've been afraid to call her because I don't want to push it.

Thursday night, May 2, 1968, 11:40 p.m.

My passport came in the mail today and I sat here at the desk and looked at it and held it and felt sophisticated. I've never seen a passport before, and I've never known anyone personally who had one. I don't even know if I'll use it. But it's still a neat feeling knowing you can go to any country on the planet if you want. Any country except Cuba, North Korea, and North Vietnam, that is. And who—besides McAdams—would want to go there?

Mac got all exasperated when a bunch of us were watching the student riots in Paris on the news a few minutes ago. "In Berkeley they're marching for free speech," he said. "In New York City, Columbia students are holding university buildings. In Paris kids are out in the streets trying to bring down the whole fucking government, for Christ's sake!" He got up from the davenport and addressed us all. "And what are we doing here in Cheney, Washington? We elect beauty queens and dress 'em up like Indians. We put beds on wheels and push 'em around campus. We chug beer as fast as we can, then see how far we can piss and throw up. Shit!" Mac said, and he headed out the door.

The door didn't latch, so it swung back open slowly and let in the rainy air. Boreson got up to close it and leaned out. "Hey, McAdams!" he yelled. "Why doncha transfer to a college in Vietnam?"

And we could all hear Mac yell back, "I might. But it'll be *North* Vietnam if I do!"

Got my Europe in the Middle Ages mid-term back today and was amazed to find a B− on it. It was all multiple-choice, machine-corrected, and graded on a curve. There must be a load of numbskulls in the class to create the curve I got a B− on.

No word from Jen. It's probably my place to call her, but I'm going to try to hold off until Saturday or Sunday. I'm going to be very casual. I'm not going to be the one looking and feeling like a dope if nothing comes of this.

Friday, May 3, 1968, 4:30 p.m.

Boy, did this day change course in the middle!

I'm reading through the first act of *Hamlet* again, resolved to blast right through to the end, when I hit Laertes telling Ophelia not to give in to a tumble with Hamlet because it wouldn't be satisfying down the line and because it couldn't lead to anything, since, being Prince of Denmark, Hamlet's got to marry the best match for the state rather than for himself personally.

> For Hamlet and the trifling of his favour,
> Hold it a fashion and a toy in blood,
> A violet in the youth of primy nature,
> Forward, not permanent, sweet, not lasting,
> The perfume and suppliance of a minute...

I can't concentrate because all I can think of is "the perfume and suppliance of a minute" with Jen. I get this terrible urge to call her. She's a cowgirl, she probably gets up early, it might be okay, I think. But I don't want to call her because I want to be cool.

So I push on in *Hamlet*, and I come to where Ophelia admonishes Laertes to take his own advice and keep it in his pants when he gets back to France.

> ... good my brother,
> Do not, as some ungracious pastors do,

> Show me the steep and thorny way to heaven;
> Whiles, like a puff'd and reckless libertine,
> Himself the primrose path of dalliance treads...

And all I can think of is dalliance with Jen. So I call her and she's not home. I let it ring and ring. I think she's feeding the horses, but I let it ring long enough for her to grow and harvest the oats. She's not home.

I walk back to my desk, telling myself what an asshole I am all the way. But I can't concentrate. So I give up, whip downstairs and out the door, jump in the Ford, and drive around the countryside like an idiot looking for a place with two horses like Jen described.

The sun got higher and higher. I might have driven by her place, but I wouldn't have known if I did. I stopped in the Union for a burger and couldn't eat it when it came. That's how wrought up I was. And how sick is that? But when I got back to the house, there on my desk was a letter with a return address from a p.o. box in Chewelah. Jen's from Chewelah!

In the envelope was a card with a comic drawing of a bull mounted on a cow, both of them all smiles. Above the drawing it said, "Sure had a nice time," and below, "And that's no bull!" And Jen had written across the bottom: "Had to go home for a horse sale. Be back Sunday afternoon. Call me!!!" A P.S. added, "In spite of our not having had quite this nice a time, the card was too appropriate not to send. XXX, Jen."

I was suddenly hungry as a bear and studious as a monk, although nowhere near as abstention-minded. So I grabbed *Hamlet* and took off for Pizza Pandemonium to read and eat a poorboy.

I'm back now with my belly full of food and my head full of Shakespeare and thoughts of Sunday evening.

The past twenty-four hours have been riddled with successes. And all I had on the negative side was one bad dream and one bizarre vision. Somebody up there must like me!

I called Jen yesterday afternoon, and as soon as she heard my voice she said, "If you get right out here on that Harley-Davidson and take me for a ride, I'll fix you supper." I told her I was on my way, and she gave me directions and told me to get a move on.

I changed into my black Frisco jeans and my engineer boots, swabbed out my ears with a Q-tip and Old Spice and brushed my teeth till my gums bled. Then I hit it. I flew over those little dirt roads with the chunks of basalt sticking out of them everywhere like a motocross rider on a fat yak. "Harley-Davidson," I said, "don't fail me now."

I dropped down a steep hill and there was Jen standing at the side of the road waving me into her yard. "Hi, Karl Russell," she said.

She led me through the living room and into the spotless kitchen, then out back to the corral where she introduced me to Smokey, her stallion, and to a quarter-horse gelding her father had named Eugene McCarthy.

We turned our backs on the horses and leaned against the corral fence. Yellow tulips and purple irises bloomed in the flower beds around the basalt foundation of the little white house, and robins made noise in the two apple trees. At the side of the house a black-and-white cat walked into the sunlight and stretched.

"Sylvester the cat," Jen said.

I looked past Sylvester and down through the coulee I now realized we were in. The basalt walls on both sides were perfectly vertical where thousands or millions of years ago water had eroded this trench through the lava flow. Across the road where the coulee floor was wall-to-wall marsh, a red-winged blackbird perched on a cattail.

"Beautiful place to live," I said.

Jen grabbed my jacket sleeve and pulled me toward the bike. "Come on," she said. She picked up Sylvester. "Mind if we take this cat for a ride?" she asked. "Sylvester's an old hand at riding in a saddlebag." I unhinged the top from one of the bags and made a sweeping gesture with my arm. "Come on aboard, cat," I said.

Jen set him in the bag and he peeked over the edge and looked around.

The Harley fired over on the first kick, and off we went, up and down like a roller coaster on that lousy little road. The sun was setting and we were riding parallel to a horizon so neon pink you could almost hear it sizzle. Big yellow buttercups bloomed in the grass all over and moss grew deep green next to patches of flat-white lichen on the gray basalt formations all around, and whenever we'd dip down there'd be alder and birch trees growing near the road, their leaves fluttering in the light breeze like banners strung around a used-car lot. The smell of spring water was thick in those low places. It was an excellent ride in spite of the condition of the road. When we hit a level spot Jen yelled in my ear, "Screw back on that throttle! I was *raised* on one of these things!" So I turned up the wick a bit and we neared takeoff speed.

And, Jesus, did we take off. We dipped into a shallow spot and when we rose out of it the ground just dropped away and we were airborne.

"Whoooooa!" I yelled. And in my mind I heard Dad say, "Hold 'er, Newt! She's rearin for the barn!"

And above Dad's voice Jen yelled out, startled but happy, *"Eeiiii!"*

And out of the corner of my eye I saw Sylvester the cat fly up out of the saddlebag like a flushed mutant grouse.

When we landed, Jen's yell changed to a scream of pain. I hit the binders and we slid to a stop.

"You goddamn cat!" Jen was yelling. She'd bailed off the bike and was standing in the road slowly turning a circle, trying different holds on Sylvester. He was wrapped around her shoulders like a skunk stole, his claws clamped into her shirt front and back. "You fucking cat!" Jen yelled. *Aghhhhhh!"* she screamed. "That's my tit!"

She had him by the throat and the back legs. She let his back legs go, got hold of his front legs, and slowly worked down to his paws. Sucking in a deep breath and hunching her shoulders forward, she yanked. *"Aghhhhh!"* she screamed again. She held Sylvester in the air at arm's length as though she were going to dedicate him to something. "You goddamn cat," she said into Sylvester's pinched little face. She choked him a few seconds, then tossed him into the sparse grass at the side of the road.

I got off the bike, laughing. Jen unbuttoned her shirt and pulled up her bra. "Oh, ouch," she said, squinching her face into a grimace. "That stupid cat really got me." Tiny beads of blood shone like jewels on her beautiful breast. She saw me staring and turned away.

"I'll make the sacrifice," I said. "I'll suck out the poison."

"You wish," Jen said. She walked through the grass and knelt at the edge of some standing water and washed her breast. I picked up Sylvester.

"Shall we leave this cat for the coyotes?" I yelled over to her.

Jen walked back and grabbed him and continued over to the bike. "There any air in these bags when you close the lids?" she asked.

"Yeah," I replied. "They've got little holes in the bottoms, and the lids don't fit all that tight anyway." "That's too bad," Jen said. Then she stuck Sylvester in the bag with the lid and closed it.

We rode home through the dusk at a slower pace. I pulled up beside the house and Jen got off and let Sylvester out. "Come on, you stupid cat," she said. "Go play in the road!" she yelled after him as he hightailed it for the barn.

Jen carried two buckets of oats out of the barn and I followed with a bale of hay. I heard her cooing to Smokey as she spread the oats in the trough. I saw that she'd worked her way back to his flanks. Her head lay on the point of his hip and she was saying, "Oh, you big old Smokey. You're the nicest big old horse." And Smokey began to loll his head. His eyes rolled, and he looked like he'd rounded the corner past ecstasy. When I looked around Eugene McCarthy, I could see why: Jen was rubbing his nuts. "You big old horse!" I heard her say. She gave him three or four solid smacks on his rump, then sang out, "Eat your supper now! You're a good old horse!" Then she walked over and peered around Eugene's rump. She raised her eyebrows and smiled provocatively. She took Eugene's tail and held it in front of her face like a veil and raised her eyebrows again. Then she let the tail fall almost hair by hair and said, through the whisper sound it made, "Time for stallions to eat their suppers, Karl." Then she laughed and took my arm and we walked to the house.

Jen was quiet while we fixed supper. We listened to FM radio and she scrubbed the spuds so we could eat the skins while I cut up green onions. We were almost shoulder to shoulder at the sink, and I could smell her. She smelled a little like horse and a little like feminine sweat and a little like a baby. Her golden hair seemed more gold in the soft white light from above the sink and her face was tan and her skin shone like gold too. I couldn't help taking side looks down at the rise beneath the breast pocket of her flannel shirt.

We ate in front of Jen's big old-time radio and listened to music. Jen was drinking more wine than I was, but I was the one getting drunk. I began carrying on about how great Big Brother and the Holding Company and their singer Janis Joplin were, and I spread my arms out and twirled around on the seat of my pants a couple times, then flung myself on my back and scootched across the floor to where Jen was sitting cross-legged.

"'I'm a caterpillar,'" I sang as I lifted my head. "'I'm a caterpillar crawlin' for your love, crawlin' for your lo-ve.'" And when I got up to Jen's lap I dropped my head back to the floor and raised my arms in a finale. But my head didn't hit the floor, it hit something warm and squishy, and I heard Jen try to stifle a laugh. The fragrance of sour cream and green onions rose up around me and I didn't have to reach back to know I'd landed in her potato. Jen was pointing to her mouth and trying not to laugh, but as she burst out in a big cackle she sprayed me with a mouthful of wine.

"Oh, God, Karl," she said. "I'm sorry. I peed my pants."

I don't know if she was sorry about me being in her potato or her having spit wine on me or having peed her pants. "I'll be right back," Jen said. As she whipped up the stairs two by two I could see that her jeans were all wet.

She came back down wearing a sweatshirt and sweatpants, with shampoo and a huge towel in her hand. She popped into the kitchen and returned with some paper towels and knelt beside me.

"Sorry," I said. "I got carried away by rock and roll."

"I spit on you," Jen said. "I can't believe it. I'm so sorry."

"That's okay," I said. As she bent over me I could see the beautiful soft breasty look in her sweatshirt that meant she'd taken off her bra. "The truth is, it felt kinda sexy," I said.

"*Oughh ick!*" Jen said.

"You know," I said, "kinda sexy, but not *real* sexy."

She cleaned me off with the paper towels, then led me to the kitchen like an invalid. On the radio Jimi Hendrix hit the first notes of "All Along the Watchtower" and Jen and I both made guitar sounds.

"Bend over," Jen said and pushed my head under the faucet. Nobody'd ever washed my hair except Mom, and that was a long time ago. It felt great. Jen took a long time with my hair. She talked about how much she liked long hair on guys, *really* long hair. When she was home she saw an old high-school friend who had a ponytail, and she said it looked "luscious" on him.

Thinking of a guy with a ponytail reminded me of all the hippy people I'd seen in Seattle with Leila. I didn't want to think about that, and had turned my thoughts to the way the word "luscious" had rolled off Jen's tongue when I felt pressure on my hip. Very lightly I felt Jen's thighs close on me. And very, very lightly I pressed back.

"Got to rinse it till it squeaks," Jen said—exactly like Mom. She took bunches of my hair and squeezed them out like socks. Sounds rose from my head like the squeals of tires at a drag strip. She asked about my patch of short hair, and I told her I'd had some stitches taken.

"I guess that does it," Jen said. She slapped me on the butt. "Take off your shirt," she said. "It's all wet. And go in and light the lamps. I'll make us a fire in the stove."

I went in and lit her two kerosene lamps and sat in front of the wood stove. A load of blankets landed on me. "Wrap up in these," Jen said as she sailed past. She was back in a minute with a few sticks of kindling and larch logs. I watched as she made the fire. "One sec," she said, closing the door of the stove. She popped up and turned off the lights. Two big pillows hit me from the side and knocked me over, then Jen was beside me saying, "Give me some room under these blankets!"

The only light came from the kerosene lamps in the corners of the room and the peach-colored glow of the radio dial and some flickers of fire through the little mica windows in the stove. Jen had unbraided her hair, and there was so much of it I felt like it had sort of attacked me. Jen's hair is thick and coarse and smells like herb tea. I think she felt the effect it had on me because when I put my arms around her and slipped my leg between hers and moved into her she had a little convulsion into me too, and made a startled sound between a yelp and a moan—an erotic whimper was what it was. And I said to myself right there, Okay, settle down, have patience. Just let go thinking you have to take this move all the way.

Jen started to move and kiss and whimper her little erotic whimper, and I responded and responded and responded. She never quite hit my erotic ground zero, though she flew low over it a lot of times, so I never touched hers. And yet it was very sexy.

We were both beat from putting out all that energy and from holding back all that energy—at least, I'd been holding back—and we were both relaxed enough to blend into the weave of Jen's wool blankets. So when José Feliciano finished a beautiful version of the Doors' "Light My Fire" and the breathy FM deejay signed off as though midnight were just too momentous an event for him to handle in his total hipness and deep sensitivity, we took it for time out.

"I feel so good I don't wanna move," Jen said. "Can you stay?"

"I can stay," I said.

"Well, if you want to sleep with me," Jen said, "you're gonna have to sleep right here."

"I like it here," I said. "Right here is fine."

And she turned her back to me and took my hand and put it on her breast and snuggled her butt into my crotch. "Have sweet dreams, Karl," Jen said. And she was asleep in no time.

I thought of getting up to turn off the radio and blow out the lamps, but I didn't want to move. As soon as my hard-on went away I fell asleep.

I didn't have sweet dreams. I dreamed again that I was a wartman living underground with those altered people in Rio. I sat in exactly the same position as before, my butt on mossy ground, my back against a smooth tiled wall. Water was dripping everywhere and the air smelled like mushrooms, like the holes I used to dig in the composted soil in the garden patch when I was a kid. I felt the weight of the warts on my skin and I felt the warts on my back and shoulders and the back of my head against the cool tile and on my butt and legs against the ground. I could see the shapes of the altered people moving in the darkness and I could hear them talking. I couldn't hear what they were saying, though, or even make out the language.

The different thing about the dream this time was that the bull we had almost hit was there. A few feet in front of me in the darkness, with the mumbling shapes moving low to the ground around it, was a mass blacker than the rest of the darkness. I could hear him breathe like an idling diesel—it shook the ground—and I could hear the blood bubble where his nostril was ripped, and right at the height where his nose would be was a shiny black spot I knew was blood.

What I felt in the dream was beyond fear. It was desolation. I could feel *me*—the me I'd known all my years—inside that wartskin, and I *knew* I'd be in there forever, alone in the world, except for the things that moved around me in the darkness.

And then the bull started to move. I heard his hooves strike rock and I felt the rumble of his breathing move through me from the ground. The shiny black spot led the black shape toward me. I could hear the bubbles of blood burst with each breath. Then the drops were splattering me. I touched myself where the first ones landed. And at the same instant I felt the slickness and realized it was blood, I also felt my wartskin and I screamed out every terror I'd ever imagined.

The scream broke the dream, but the scream itself didn't stop. I woke up sitting in the dim light of the one lamp still burning, screaming my lungs out at the dark shape of Jen's wood stove. Jen had me around the shoulders and she was yelling in my ear. "Karl, Karl, Karl!" she yelled. "It's all right. You were dreaming, is all."

Her voice got through my own voice ringing in my head, and I shut up. I felt the pressure of her hands on my shoulders and realized I was rocking back and forth like babies and retarded people do. I took some slow breaths. I closed my fists on the coarse wool blanket and thought carefully, Now, that's not moss. And I took in a long breath through my nose and smelled the warm smells of our bodies and a little shampoo smell from my hair and a whiff of kerosene in the room and I said to myself. These aren't cave smells. And then I started to feel really stupid, worthless and stupid and unmanly.

I didn't turn my head when I spoke. "Sorry I woke ya, Jen," I said. I got up and walked across the room and stood at a window. It was a bright night full of moonlight.I heard Jen get up and the floor creaking softly as she walked toward me. I heard crickets outside and frogs from the marsh across the road. Her arms went around me and she laid her head on my shoulder. She began to knead the muscles of my back.

I looked at the stars and wondered what the fuck made me dream that shit. And in half a second I said to myself, Sure! You got the letter from Havermeyer the Dermatologist today, you stupid butthole. It was just a form letter saying Havermeyer had gotten a biochemistry fellowship at Stanford for further study into "viral communications" and that his brother, the elder Dr. Havermeyer, would be taking over his practice. The letter must have been what did it, I thought. And being with Jen must have brought back seeing the bull.

Everything was quiet except for the faint chirp of crickets and frogs from outside. Then Jen said softly, "Oh, God, Karl! Look!"

She was pointing out the window high into the night sky, where three white shafts of light were pulsing. With each pulse they got a little brighter and a little bluer.

"Whaddaya think it is?" I asked. I started getting scared again.

"It's the northern lights," Jen said. "Come on! Let's get outside before they fade."

We stood in the yard and looked straight up. The shafts of light stretched all the way from the northern horizon past the middle of the sky. God knows how many thousands of miles of sky they covered with each pulsation. I've seen the northern lights plenty, but never like that. Jen was behind me with her chin on my shoulder and her thumbs hooked into the waistband of my boxers. "God, Karl, just look at 'em," she said. "I've never seen them blaze like this."

And then all at once they began to shrink. They retreated and retreated right before our eyes until they were just three faint peaks of white making a pyramid way out there in the dark where it looks like everything ends.

I had begun to shake so hard Jen couldn't hold me still.

"You're freezing," she said. "Come get in bed with me." She led me inside, grabbed a lamp, turned up the wick, then took my hand again and led me upstairs. She set the lamp on her chest of drawers, where it was reflected in the mirror.

I walked to the window as Jen began to undress. The pyramid still shone faintly, and a warm feeling rose in me and I stopped shivering. I felt Mom and Dad's love the way I'd felt it in the cemetery and the way I'd felt it back at the house that night.

Jen put her arms around me. "Come to bed, Karl," she said. She left one hand on my chest and with the other reached down and began to play gently with my balls. I thought of her with her stallion. It was real sexy and I got hard right away. I wanted to say something, but I was afraid to open my mouth because the way she was making me feel, I might have sounded like a horse.

"Let's pull the shade so the sun won't wake us up," Jen said. So she drew the shade and led me to bed.

And that is only the carnal realm of good stuff that's happened! I also scored big in the realm of the intellect. I got A's on both my World Masterpieces and Literature of the Camps mid-terms!

Thursday, May 9, 1968, midnight

I think I've just lived through something like a "debauch." This might make my college experience complete before it's over. It's a good thing I don't have classes tomorrow, or I'd probably miss them a fourth day in a row.

It started Tuesday just before lunch as I was sitting in the '51 listening to the Vanilla Fudge sing "People Get Ready" on my new tape deck when I heard McAdams yelling from the porch.

"His name is Ali!" Mac shouted. "It's *Ali*, for fuck sakes! He's a Muslim. He adopted a new religion. Come on, Boreson. Religious freedom's one of the things you R.O.T.C. guys wanna die for so bad, ain't it?"

"Clay's a Muslim 'cause he thinks it'll keep him outa Vietnam," Tommy says. "If he wants to live in America and enjoy our freedoms, he can defend the country like everybody else."

Mac spun around in a circle and his hair whirled into the shape of an umbrella. "Oh, I get, it," he said. "Ali isn't just a heretic, commie, nigger. He's also chickenshit. You'd hit 'im in the big toe and he'd go down for the count, right, Tommy?"

I fired up the Ford and backed to the corner just as Mac stepped off the curb. He laid his forearms on the window molding and leaned in. "This fucking country makes me so sick I could shit on the sidewalk," he said.

"Jump in," I said. "I just recently wired for total sound here. Rock and roll'll cure what ails ya. And I'll buy ya a burger."

"All right!" Mac said, jumping in. "Drive by Safeway and I'll get some beers." He sat back and shrugged. "I never know how to react to stupidity that deep," he said. "All I ever do is be stupid right back." I turned up the volume, pulled the lever into first, and rolled us smoothly toward the Safeway store.

I hadn't been paying a whole lot of attention to the news lately, so I hadn't heard that Ali's appeal of his draft-evasion conviction had been denied. Mac filled me in on this, and as we walked through Safeway I told him about my mid-term grades. "All right!" he yelled out, and turned to the checker and asked for her church key. She handed it over and Mac popped us two beers right there.

"Congratulations, Karl," Mac said, handing me a beer. He raised his. "To the biker-scholar. Long may he lurk in our libraries and haunt our highways."

"You kids can't drink in here!" the lady said.

"'Kids,'" Mac yelled, and waved his false I.D. "'Kids!'" He addressed the store generally. "That's right, America," he said. "Send us to die in Vietnam, but for heaven's sake don't let us drink in your grocery stores!"

"Sorry," I said to the lady. "We're on our way."

At the A&W we sat in the car and listened to the Lovin' Spoonful while we ate. I told Mac how psyched I was that we were into Shakespeare in World Masterpieces, and through a mouthful of teenburger he says, "'Like flies to wanton boys, are we to the gods. They kill us for their sport.' Yeah. The old Bard of Avon, ya gotta love 'im."

"You takin' a Shakespeare course?" I asked. It irritated me that Mac knew about Shakespeare and could quote him from memory.

"No chance," Mac replied. "I get all the Shakespeare I can handle when I'm home. My dad's a Shakespeare freak."

"I thought your dad was a minister," I said.

"He is," Mac said. "But when he says he's quoting from the Big B he only means the Bible about half the time. The rest of the time he's quoting the Bard."

Suddenly Mac's frizzy-haired friend Felicity leaned down and stuck her head in Mac's window. Her cigarette breath shot across the car and knocked me back against the door. I turned my head and took some deep gulps of air out the window.

Felicity is so skinny it's fair to call her "skeletal." Technically, I suppose, you've got to say she has tits. But all you see protruding in her purplish tie-dyed T-shirt are nipples that look like mini-marshmallows under there. She's got great hair, though. It's clean and shiny and frizzes way out past her shoulders. It filled the whole window as she stood there talking to Mac. All that black hair makes her doughy little face look like a new potato set in obsidian.

Her little black eyes zeroed in on the beer in Mac's hand. "If you guys were to take me for a ride and force me to drink beer, I'd probably divulge all my secrets," she said with a big grin.

Your tits are a secret, I thought. "We're just headed back to study," I said.

"Russell aced two mid-terms, and it's altered his perspective on the true purpose of higher education in America," Mac said.

"So what is it you have to study on an afternoon as beautiful as this?" Felicity asked me. She pulled her head out the window, spread her arms wide, and craned her neck straight up at the clear blue sky.

"Shakespeare," I said.

"Shakespeare!" Felicity shrieked. She stuck her face back in the window. "Shakespeare!"

"Well, Shakespeare and some other stuff," I said.

"Let me in, McAdams," Felicity said. "I'll tell Karl all about Shakespeare. I played Gonorrhelia in *King Lear*."

Gonorrhelia? I thought. Mac was out of the car and Felicity had slid in next to me before I could protest. She smelled like a bus-station waiting room, but she was pretty funny, so I tolerated the seating arrangement. On the way to Safeway to buy more beers Felicity told us that back in high school she'd had the clap when she played Cordelia in *King Lear*, and everybody'd called her Gonorrhelia.

Then we headed northwest into the wheat fields and onto one of the little roads that run through the wheat until they finally just disappear. The wheat was deep green and about two feet high all around us. It grew the same height between the brown-dirt tire tracks that the road had become, and it made a shushing sound as the Ford's undercarriage swept over it. When we dropped down between the hills, all we could see around us was wheat.

"God," Feliocity said, "it's like being inside a wheat kaleidoscope."

"I feel like I've been ingested by a giant herbivore," Mac said.

"God," Felicity said, "what if we were stoned?"

And then when we crested a hill we could look out in every direction and see nothing but green wheat below us and blue sky above. We were at the top of the highest hill around, so I stopped, pulled out the Association, who had replaced Dylan, and said, "Let's get out and sit in the wheat and see how it feels."

"God," said Felicity, "what a trippy idea."

So the three of us got out and walked a ways from the car and sat down together in the waving wheat, with the green wheat tops just level with our eyes. I took a pull on about my sixth beer and looked over at my dark blue Ford against the light-blue sky.

Felicity fell back slowly until she disappeared in wheat. Her voice was muffled by the wind moving all around us, but I heard her say, "This is too much. This *requires* being stoned." She shot to her feet and jogged off to the car. In half a minute she was back standing between Mac and me, a baggie about an eighth full of old alfalfa-looking stuff in her bony little fist. I'll bet that's marijuana, I said to myself.

We walked through the wheat to the edge of the hill and sat just where the slope started down. I don't have any idea how far we actually could see, but for one hell of a long way west the green hills rolled into the golden sunset. A few smoky clouds lay over part of the sun, and through them red-gold streaks shot up until they faded into blue.

Then a smell like burning rope, a good, rich, sweet smell, broke through the spell. I turned, and there, a few inches from my face, pinched between Felicity's yellow-brown stained fingers, was a thin, hand-rolled cigarette. I took it. But not only had I never smoked marijuana before—or ever even *seen* it—I'd never smoked a cigarette. "So how do you do it?" I asked Felicity. "I've never smoked before."

"Just like a cigarette," she replied. "Only hold the smoke in longer."

"No help to me," I said. "Cigarettes are what I've never smoked before."

"You've never smoked a cigarette?" Felicity said. "And you're how old?"

"Almost twenty-one," I said. "It just never appealed to me."

Mac tilted his head and looked over at me. "Suck the smoke down and hold it," he said.

The thought of putting my lips around something that had been in Felicity's mouth and between those fingers of hers didn't thrill me, but I puckered and sucked hard on the tiny end of the cigarette. The smoke went down easy. In a couple seconds it hit and the burning started. I began to cough. I coughed and coughed. I did major-league coughing.

"Take a drink of beer," Mac said.

I couldn't talk. With my left hand I held up my empty bottle. "I'm dry," I managed to say between coughs.

Mac jumped up and was gone. In a few seconds he was back and set a beer on my stomach. I sat up, drank about half, and quit coughing. "I'll get the hang of it," I said.

We sat and smoked three more joints as we watched the light fade. I told Felicity that all the land out there was called the Palouse and that it was the richest wheat country on the face of the earth except for an area in Russia near Odessa, where the same geologic thing had happened, with the glaciers melting and dropping all the rich topsoil they'd scraped off the land on their way down from the north. "I don't know why it's called the Palouse, though," I said.

"'Pelouse' is the French word for 'lawn,'" Felicity said.

I just once would like to be the one who knew the French word for something.

"Well, that makes sense," I said. "When the French explorers got here, they probably stood on this very hill and looked out at all the grass and said, 'Zat's ah mightee nizz palouse.'" And all of a sudden I started to laugh. It was the funniest thing I'd ever heard. I fell back into the wheat, and Mac and Felicity started to giggle. Then they began to laugh and they both fell over.

I pulled up a bunch of wheat stalks and stuffed them down the collar of my shirt. They stuck up all around my head, front and back. I got to my hands and knees and crawled over to Mac. "Look," I said, "I'm a wheat person. Attack of the wheat people!" I began yelling. "Attack of the wheat people!"

I crawled over to Felicity. But before I could say anything she shrieked, "Oh, no! A wheat person! God, it's the attack of the wheat people!" She pulled up a handful of wheat and stuck it down the front of her shirt. I pulled up some more and stuck it down the back. Then we both crawled over to Mac, yelling, "Attack of the wheat people! Attack of the wheat people!" We pulled up wheat and threw it on him till he was covered.

Suddenly I was overcome by a raging hunger for tacos. I quit playing around and stood on my knees. "God, you guys," I said. "I might not make it if I don't get a taco soon. Let's pick up a friend of mine. We can take her some wheat and she can be a wheat person too."

"We're a roving band of wheat people!" Felicity yelled. And Mac and I joined in.

By the time we got to Jen's it was pretty dark and her porch light was on. As we started across the lawn we could see her sitting hunched over her study table. I grabbed the screen-door handle and rattled it hard. Jen jumped and turned in her chair.

"Attack of the wheat people!" I hollered.

"Wheat people attack!" Mac screamed. And Felicity yelled, "Wheat people rule!"

Jen looked at us for about a second, then she grabbed a lever-action carbine I hadn't noticed leaning against the wall. She stood, leveled the rifle, and began walking toward us.

"Whoooooa!" yelled Mac, as he fell backwards off the porch.

"Jesus Christ!" screamed Felicity, as she streaked for the car.

"Jen!" I yelled. "It's me. It's Russ! Karl Russell!"

Just then Sylvester brushed against my ankle. I grabbed him, got one hand around his throat, and held him against my chest with the other. "One more step, lady," I said, "and it's one less life for the furbag here. Put down the gun."

Jen kept coming and poked the barrel of her Winchester Model 70 against the screen. She peered out at me. "Karl," she said, "is that you?"

"We came to take you on a taco scarf," I said. "And to make you a wheat person."

Jen lowered the gun. "Do I have to dress up like somebody's lawn?" she asked.

"You don't have to," I replied. "But you'd be surprised how much fun it is." I whipped back to the car, holding Sylvester tight against my chest. "Jen doesn't feel like being a wheat person," I told Mac and Felicity. "But Sylvester wants to be a wheat cat."

We threaded wheat through Sylvester's flea collar until he looked like a big bunch of parsley.

When Jen got in we were all giggling, Sylvester was prowling the top of the front seat, and the Doors were into "Soul Kitchen." Jen looked us over. "I think I'm a beer or two behind," she said as I dropped the clutch.

"We'll remedy that," Mac said, handing her a beer.

Jen kept looking behind her at the strange plant life.

"The one with the higher voice is Felicity," I said. "And the other one is Mac. Mac and Felicity," I said, "this is Jen."

Jen grabbed Sylvester from where he was curled behind my neck. "What have you three done to my cat?" she said.

"He wanted to be a wheat cat," I said.

Mac and Felicity began to giggle. The Doors broke into "Light My Fire" about then, and Felicity said, "Speaking of fire, why don't we fire up another number!"

Oh, shit, I thought. What's Jen gonna think? I pretended I hadn't heard.

Then Mac said, "I think about another toke and a half would put just the right edge on our appetites."

Oh, shit, I thought.

Jen turned around. "You guys been smoking marijuana?" she asked.

"You don't think we got this whacked just drinking beer, do you?" Felicity replied.

Jen looked at Mac and Felicity sitting in the dark back seat, now and then lifting beer bottles to their mouths hidden behind the wheat stalks covering their entire heads. She glanced down at Sylvester, who had sought refuge in her lap. "Can I try some?" she said.

"It would be a pleasure to turn you on," replied Felicity.

I was amazed. Not only was Jen not shocked, she wanted to try it. It made me feel funny.

The joint passed from Felicity to Mac to Jen to me. I was handing it back to Jen to give to Felicity, so Jen was getting an extra turn every time. She wasn't coughing at all.

"Great work," Felicity was telling Jen. "You're a natural doper. You need that extra hit on every pass to catch up."

"Pass me up some wheat," Jen said after a few minutes. "I'm feeling like an alien up here."

When we got to the Taco Time on North Monroe in Spokane, Jen had herself fixed up like a standard wheat person. "Attack of the wheat people!" she yelled as she strode to the door. The face of the high-school girl behind the counter went blank when she saw us. "Don't worry," Jen said. "We're just wheat people. Keep us full of tacos and we're docile as your average plant folk."

We'd been digging into our tacos for a while when I looked up. There we were reflected in the window: four people with long shafts of wheat growing out of their collars. The sight struck me as totally hilarious. Jen looked at me, and I pointed to the window. "God, look at us!" she said.

"Here's to the wheat people!" Felicity said, raising a taco. "We ain't afraid to go against the grain!"

Jen was laughing so hard she couldn't speak. Finally I saw that it wasn't our reflection she was looking at. The Ford was spotlighted perfectly, and framed in the front passenger window Sylvester peered out at us from inside his tube of wheat. You could see his little black and white face so forlorn. He looked like the stuffing in a giant green manicotti.

We stumbled out of the Taco Time still laughing. Jen opened her door and grabbed Sylvester and began pulling the wheat out of his collar. The rest of us defoliated ourselves, then we took care of Jen. "What a night!" Jen said as she hugged Sylvester to her flannel shirt between her breasts. "Felicity," she said as we pulled out, "hand me up some makings. I roll cigarettes for my dad all the time."

I began to lose control of my extremities as we smoked the four perfectly symmetrical joints Jen rolled. I took the Fish Lake road and lost feeling in my hands about the time we passed the cemetery, then my legs and feet went as we cruised into Cheney. I just pointed us where I was directed.

Mac and Felicity got out at the big old house she shared with some incredible number of people and animals. "The drama department's putting on the Eighth of May kegger tomorrow," she said. "Attendance is mandatory for you two. Meet us here at one."

I was so blissed out that we were almost to Jen's before it occurred to me to inquire about the significance of the eighth of May.

"It's the day the outdoor intercourse season opens," Jen said.

"Oh," I said. "Sure."

"We're gonna have to brush our teeth for hours," Jen said as we climbed the stairs at her place. And it did seem like we brushed our teeth a long, long time.

Jen opened all the windows and put two extra blankets and her sleeping bag on the bed. I liked the soft weight of all those covers, and the room was flooded with the good smells of the corral and the pines and the marsh. I was barely conscious, but I remember how cool and smooth and good Jen's skin felt as she curled her back into me and brought my hand around to her breast.

Friday afternoon, May 10, 1968

On the afternoon of May 8, the street in front of Felicity's house was clogged with cars, mostly VW bugs with peace symbols in the back windows. Jen and I rode up the sidewalk and parked the bike on the lawn. "Sergeant Pepper" was blasting from two big cabinet speakers in the open back of a '49 Chevy sedan-delivery. An old VW bus with a cargo of four kegs in big rubber garbage cans overflowing with ice was parked beside it.

Lots of people were milling around. I had the shortest hair of anybody in the group. "We're strangers in a strange land," I said quietly.

"You're not kiddin'," Jen replied.

Just then Felicity skipped out her door and down the walk. She was wearing purple painter's pants and a thin white sleeveless man's undershirt through which her nipples protruded like raisins in tapioca. She must have had her hair recharged, because it was about three times frizzier and more voluminous than the day before. She looked like a famous historical figure with her hair that way, and I racked my brain about it all the way out to the deserted farm where the kegger was held.

Jen and I rode up to the partially collapsed barn and parked the bike in the shade. The sun was hot and the sky was holding clear.

All the colors—the flat-white lichen on the basalt, the dark-green moss, the medium-green cattail stocks and their dark-brown tops, the dark-green alfalfa in the field beyond the ditch where the cattails grew, and the yellow buttercups everywhere—all the colors shone so sharp and distinct in the spring air, it was like they glowed. You could smell the alfalfa and the pines and the water in the ditch, along with car exhaust, and cigarette and marijuana smoke.

We walked to the kegs, where a man in his forties with long, curly salt-and-pepper hair and a big beard to match asked us for two bucks apiece. "Pretty cheap for all the beer you can drink," he said. On his sweatshirt he wore a white button with McCARTHY on it in blue. He pointed to an upside-down red felt hunting hat next to the keg on the floor of the VW bus and told us we could contribute if we wanted.

We stepped over to the hat and read the typed note pinned to it:

> Help send members of the EWSC Committee for Peace in Vietnam to the Democratic convention in Chicago this summer. We must make these people listen to what they don't want to hear.
>
> EWSC–CPVN

I looked at Jen. "I don't think I'll contribute," I said.

She took a folded dollar bill out of the breast pocket of her overalls and dropped it in the hat. "You bought the beer," she said. "I'll stop the war."

Mac, Felicity, Bolão, and a blonde who looked like she'd been abducted from a shampoo commercial walked up then. I asked Bolão if he'd brought his guitar, and he said, "You bet your shoes, man."

"That's 'boots,'" Jen said. "You bet your boots."

"Whatever's right," Bolão replied. I believe he'd drunk one or two on the road.

Everybody got beers—Mac and Felicity each dropped in some change—and we all walked out in the sun and sat on the spongy ground and leaned back against a big chunk of basalt. The rock was round, so we sat like spokes on a wheel and couldn't look one another in the face. But everybody had their eyes closed anyway, and their faces turned up to the sun.

"It won't be long, Karl," Bolão said, "until you are drinking a cold *cerveja* on the Praia de Montenegro."

Jen leaned her head by mine. "Where won't it be long before you're drinking a what?"

"A beer," I said. "I guess the Praia de Montenegro is a beach in Rio."

"The little golden beer tears will fall down your plastic cup in the hot sun," Bolão crooned. "And you will look around at all the girls from Ipanema and Leblon sunning beside you, and you will believe you are died and gone in heaven."

Jen looked me in the face. "Died, maybe," she said. "But not gone to heaven." She got to her feet. "Who needs a beer?" she asked. "I'm making the trip."

Why should I feel bad about going to Rio for the summer? I thought. I would have talked to Jen about it.

Bolão stood and belched. "Karl," he said, "let's go bleed our rats together."

We walked quite a way up into the trees, where we peed and looked down on the gathering. There was getting to be quite a crowd. Felicity was dancing alone on top of the rock we'd been sitting around. She had her arms raised above her head and her fingertips pressed together like a harem dancer. I noticed my old comp. teacher, Sam Ochs, and his family get out of a white Saab. I turned to Bolão, who was looking out over the crowd and peeing on his black penny loafers. "If you were me," I said, "would you go to Rio?"

"Absolutely," he said. He had his shorts caught in his zipper. "Most assuredly. You will have the time of your life. I'll see to it personally. We'll dance Carnavál every night. I'll see to it personally."

We walked back down and got another beer. The money was really piling up in the hat. I stopped in the beer line and shook hands with Ochs. "Hi, Mr. Ochs," I said. "I'm Karl Russell. I was in your composition class."

"I remember you, Karl," he said. "It hasn't been that long. Still got that old Ford you wrote about?"

"Still got it," I said. "But I'm mounted on two wheels today. Riding my Harley-Davidson."

"A Harley-Davidson," Ochs said. His little daughter was perched on his shoulders and he pulled her off balance and looked her in the face. "This big boy might take us for a motorcycle ride later. What do you think of that, you funny kid?" The little girl let out a series of squeals and banged him on the head with her fistful of buttercups.

"I'd be happy to take you two for a ride," I said.

Ochs introduced me to his wife and the two kids, and we said we'd see each other later. Mrs. Ochs dropped a five-dollar bill in the hat. I wondered why a guy would bring his family to a kegger.

Mac walked by on his way to the keg just then and I fell in with him. He had his shirt off and looked a lot less intellectually formidable with his soft, white belly exposed. I suddenly felt a great affection for him. I threw my arm over his shoulder and filled his empty cup from my quart.

Felicity was passing the CPVN hat through the crowd and I stopped and pointed Mac in her direction and asked him what famous historical woman she looked like.

"She looks like a feral child," Mac said. "But I love her anyway."

"No," I said. "She looks like some real historical person. Goddamn! It's drivin' me nuts!"

One of Felicity's scuzziest friends, a guy a few years older than us who never seemed to shave but never really grew a beard either and who smelled like an old wet dog, was taking money at the keg. He's a surly guy with black, oily hair and an oily olive complexion who makes me want to shower and scrub down with a vegetable brush every time I run into him. He's supposed to be an artist, and last year he spread a canvas over half the floor in the field house and climbed into the rafters and dropped balloons filled with paint on it. He was scraping paint off the floor half the spring term. He's one of those people who make you think being an asshole is a prerequisite for being an artist. His first name—incredibly—is Lasch.

"Laschorino!" I said. "You big whipper!" I held up a clenched fist. "Right arm!" I said.

Mac giggled. "That's 'right on,'" he said.

I knew it was.

"You guys pay?" asked Lasch.

"We paid," Mac said as he filled his cup. Mac isn't one of the Whipper's biggest fans. I think they compete for leadership in various radical organizations, and for girls.

I didn't have my cup anymore, and Lasch wanted me to pay for another one. "You can shake loose another buck," he said. "They pay you jocks to go to school. The rest of us hafta pay them." He curled his lip at me. Even his teeth were black and oily.

"Tell you what, Whip," I said. "Why don't I shake loose a few of your molars?"

Whip's reply was a vicious scowl.

I took a cup, filled it, threw my arm around Mac again, and off we walked to find Felicity.

We found her passing the CPVN hat around a circle of people sitting in the grass in the shade of the barn. Included in this group were the Reverend Gardner, my World Masterpieces prof, Dr. Hazelton, Ochs, his wife, their two kids—the older of whom was taking a snooze in his mom's lap—the curly-haired guy who'd been taking money at first, and some graduate-student types you can usually identify by the signs of early aging around the guys' eyes and the long brown hair pulled back so tight on the heads of the girls that their eyes are stretched open wide in a look of constant astonishment. I was suddenly struck by the vast number of people in the world— Christ, in this tiny college town!—who are so, so different from me.

"Sit in with us, Karl," Gardner said. "We're about to start something you'll enjoy." He began to clap his hands. "All right, people," he called out. "Get a comfortable spot in the circle. It's time to turn all this conviviality just slightly toward the educational."

"Categories!" shouted Mac, as he dived for a place in the circle. "Categories," he said again, rubbing his hands together like a mad scientist. "I get to start." He was sitting just at the edge of the shadow cast by the barn roof. He had a sly smile on his face as he started the clapping sequence.

Felicity grabbed the hat from Gardner, who had dropped in a five. "I'm outa here," she said. "Categories is the most senseless activity I've ever encountered."

I slipped into her spot and started clapping along. Playing categories is one of my very most favorite things to do while drinking beer. You not only have a great time getting drunk, but there's a chance you can get educated if you're playing with the right people. You clap twice, slap your thighs twice, stomp your feet twice, then you speak. If it's your turn to name something in the category and you blow it, you have to chug your beer as fast as you can.

After Mac had stomped his feet he sang out, "Members of the Bloomsbury Group!"

Oh, shit, I thought. I'm in trouble already. I don't know any of the new bands.

The girl next to Mac clapped, slapped her thighs, stomped her feet, and said sedately, "Virginia Woolf."

It's not a band! It's British writers! I figured I'd just say Dickens or Kipling and avoid looking totally stupid when it came around to me. But the young guy next to the girl couldn't come up with a name, so we all yelled for him to drink and I was saved.

That guy must not have been a literary type because he called out, "Bones in the human body!"

There were plenty of bones left when it got around to me. I could have named plenty, but I chose one of my two least favorite—the ulna.

Dr. Hazelton's turn came, and he clapped and slapped and stomped and called out, "Sinners in Dante's Hell!"

Foolish guy, I said to myself. He must have forgotten I read the *Inferno* in his class. But then I wondered if maybe he wasn't trying to help me out.

I did my clapping, slapping, and stomping: "Blas-pheemers!" I screamed, and turned and smiled big at Gardner.

"Sowers of discord!" Gardner called out, and smiled back at me.

"Perverts!" the girl next to him said.

"Alchemists!" said her boyfriend.

"People who commit treachery against guests and hosts!" said a lady professor wearing a serape.

Mac clapped, slapped, and stomped for all he was worth, then screamed out, "Republicans!" He started drinking before anybody had a chance to call him on it.

I was doing fine until the lady in the serape nailed me with "Keats's great odes." I didn't have a clue. But I kept the clapping sequence and with supreme confidence yelled out, "Ode Lang Syne!"

"Not quite!" shouted Mac, who had just come back dragging Felicity, who was dragging Lasch. "Ode Lang Syne!" Mac shouted. "Buffoonery! Here's to Russell," he chanted, and everyone joined in. "Here's to Russell, he's true blue. He's a horse's ass through and through. Drink, chug-a-lug, drink!" I drank.

Two lovely arms reached around me as I downed the last swallow, and Jen leaned down and smiled. Everybody cheered, and I stood and signaled time-out. "Headed for more beer," I said. "Be right back."

Jen took my arm and we walked toward the keg. "I was gonna tell you I might go to Rio this summer," I said. "I just hadn't gotten around to it yet."

"Well," Jen said, "I didn't get around to telling you I'll be wrangling horses on a dude ranch in B.C. this summer, either. I was kind of hoping you'd make it up for a visit," she said. "But British Columbia's a little far from Brazil."

"I haven't decided if I'm going," I said.

"Of course you're going," Jen said. "How many of us have friends who'll show us around places like Rio de Janeiro?"

We'd reached the kegs, and when we looked up to get our beers we were greeted by a girl with no shirt on. And no bra. She was holding the CPVN hat between her breasts. I couldn't help staring. Jen took the cup out of my hand and began to draw our beers.

"You guys chip in yet?" the girl asked.

"Yes, we did," I said.

"Well, thank you very much," the girl said. Her breasts swayed and my eyes followed them.

Jen stuck a cup in my face and broke my line of vision. "Let's get back to the game," she said. "I want to play."

We settled in between Hazelton and Gardner and I introduced Jen. Mac, Lasch, and Felicity were sitting across from us on the log. The sun had moved so that it covered just the part of the log where Felicity sat. Spotlighted like that, she resembled perfectly the famous historical figure whose name I couldn't think of to save my soul. It was her hair, the way it fell straight from the top of her head, then frizzed out past her shoulders in the shape of a Christmas tree made out of coal. Her face hung there like a popcorn ball.

I was feeling the beer start to get hold of me and telling myself how much I didn't want to act like a drunk kid around Mr. and Mrs. Ochs and Gardner and Hazelton, when Gardner called, "Plays by William Shakespeare."

The lady next to him said in an even voice, "*Antony and Cleopatra.*"

There it was.

"Yesssssss!" I yowled. I stood up and rushed toward Felicity. "Cleopatra!!!" I screamed in her face. "Cle-o-pat-raaaa!" She fell back off the log and pulled Lasch and Mac with her. Beer flew everywhere. I got right down in her face. "Cleo-fucking-patra!" I screamed. "That's who you look like. Cleopatra!"

Felicity started to laugh. "Jesus Christ, Karl," she said. "You scared me so bad I almost shit my pants." Her thin little shirt was soaked with beer and you could see her nipples plainly.

I turned to the group. "Don't you guys think she looks just like Cleopatra?" I said.

"She needs some heavy blue eye shadow," Mrs. Ochs said. "With heavy blue eye shadow she'd look a lot like Elizabeth Taylor in the face." I think Mrs. Ochs was getting drunk. She was letting her beer spill into her little boy's ear.

Then Lasch jumped up and swung at me. He hit me in the side of the head, and it spun me half around. But he swung from across the log and his momentum brought him forward and he tripped and fell facefirst into the beer in my right hand.

I was a lot more embarrassed than hurt or mad, and I tried to help him up. His hair was dripping beer. "Sorry, Whip," I said. "I got excited 'cause I'd been trying all day to think who Felicity looked like."

He slapped my hand away and came up swinging. Mac, Felicity, and Gardner grabbed him and Gardner took a shot in the jaw. Everybody was standing and yelling and people came running from all over.

"How 'bout we take that motorcycle ride now, Karl?" Ochs said.

"Sure," I said.

"We're off on a trash-food run!" Ochs announced to the group. "We're taking orders now."

"And I'm buying!" I chimed in.

Ochs grabbed his little girl and listened to what people wanted to eat. Lasch had taken off his shirt and walked away, and Mac and Felicity were laughing and trying to brush the grass and twigs and beer mud off her.

I'd settled into the big white leather seat of the Harley and Ochs had settled in behind me with his daughter on his lap when Jen came hustling up.

She got close and looked me over. "You okay?" she asked.

"I'm fine," I said. "We're just headed to town for eats. What can we bring ya?"

"Shoestring potatoes," Jen replied. "And for Godsakes, be careful!"

"Shoestring potatoes it shall be," said Ochs.

The little girl put her arms around my waist and I felt her head loll against my back.

The sun was down when we got back. The sky above the pines was a violet gray and streaks of neon pink were shooting through the few clouds that had blown up with the warm evening breeze. The Young Rascals were turned up so loud I had to yell for Ochs to hear me when we bounced past the old Chevy sedan-delivery with the speakers on top, and through all the dancing people.

I was telling him I had to do a final paper for World Masterpieces and was thinking of doing it on *King Lear*. I guess I was still talking a little loud when we pulled up by the barn where it was quieter and away from the general blast of the music. When I turned off the switch I asked him if he remembered this quote: "'Like flies to wanton boys are—'"

But Felicity's voice interrupted me, and Ochs and I turned.

"Wanton boys *and girls*," Felicity said, as she and Mac walked by hand in hand, stark naked. Physically they were a pretty sorry sight. There were about as sexy, for example, as tub-and-tile caulk squirted into the shape of people. But something about the look on their faces and the way it made me feel just for a sec there caused my heart to fill up with affection for them.

"It's 'As,'" Ochs said.

"What?" I said.

We were both still staring after Felicity and Mac.

"It's 'As,'" he said. "The quote from *Lear*. 'As flies to wanton boys, are we to the gods,'" he said. "'They kill us for their sport.'"

"Oh, yeah," I said. "Thanks. But the gods ain't gettin' many licks in on us today. I'm havin' a hellava good time."

"Me too," Ochs replied. He got off the bike with his little girl in his arms. "We thank you for the ride," he said.

I carried the eats and handed them out when we reached the categories players, all of whom were taking a break. Ochs's little boy was awake. He was naked, standing by his mom, putting buttercups in her hair. His little dong appeared to be dangling in her beer cup. It looked like she was taking a urine sample.

"Naked kid!" Ochs hollered to his boy.

"Daddy!" the kid yelled as he ran and jumped into Ochs's free arm.

"Violence, nudity, beer drinking, and general good times reach epidemic proportions in Cheney-Spokane area," I announced to the group.

The whole bunch of us headed for the kegs then. After I drew my beer I took off looking for Jen, the beer in one hand and a big can of shoestring potatoes in the other. I started shaking the can of shoestring potatoes and calling, "Here, Jen! Here, Jennie-Jen!" I was thinking of how Mom used to go outside after her dumb cats. The only way she could get the stupid things in the house was to bribe them with food. She'd go out with a bag of cat food and rattle it, calling, "Here, kitties, kitties, kitties! Here, kitty-kits!" Then if the dry food didn't work, she'd open one of those smelly cans of fish and go banging on it with a fork. Sometimes there would be three or four cats keeping Mom company in her reading chair after a roundup like that.

I was about halfway to the fire when Jen, Bolão, and Lady Clairol walked out of the darkness right in front of me. They each had an armload of firewood. Jen made me carry her wood. She gave me a kiss and a drink of my beer, then she popped the lid on the can and all I heard out of her was munching until we reached the fire.

As we tossed our wood on the pile, Mac walked up—still naked except for his hiking boots—and asked Bolão to play some tunes.

"I can't play naked," Bolão said. "People's attention would be diverted to my baton."

"Your baton?" said Lady Clairol. "I used to twirl in high school!"

"Maybe you two could have a twirl-off," said Jen.

"You don't have to get naked," Mac said. "But you do have to play some tunes. So go get your guitar!"

As we were watching Mac's white butt disappear into the darkness, Donnie walked by in the direction of the keg. I hadn't seen him since the memorial service for Dr. King. I grabbed him away from his friends, took him by both arms, and stood him in front of Jen.

"Jen," I said, "this is the famous fleet-footed Donnie Davis, my old roommate from the dorm. Donnie," I said, "this is Jennifer Haskell."

"Hi, Donnie," Jen said, offering him some shoestring potatoes.

"Pleased to meet you," Donnie said, as he dipped his big hand into the can and got it stuck for a few seconds.

"Come sit with us," Jen said. "A friend of ours is gonna sing."

"Okay," Donnie said. And off he went.

People were talking and sloshing beer around and tossing wood on the fire, but Bolão blasted right into it and everybody got quiet. He's so good, and he makes so much noise on his nylon-stringed guitar, that he stuns you at first. Even drunk, he's a great entertainer. He'd sung a couple songs in Portuguese and was into another when out of nowhere the sweet notes of a flute joined him. The night got stone quiet, except for Bolão's guitar and the beautiful, almost haunting flute notes that came out so clean and distinct, then just melted into the dark like the sparks from the fire.

Nobody made any noise, but we all looked around to see who it was. Jen pulled me close and whispered, "Over there—it's your teacher."

It was Dr. Hazelton, sitting with the Ochs family and Reverend Gardner at the edge of the firelight across from us. He rocked a little with the music and played like he and Bolão had been a duo all their lives.

They were into the José Feliciano version of "Light My Fire" when Jen said she had to get home and study. We were walking out of the circle of firelight and had almost reached the bike when Bolão began another tune.

I recognized it by the third note. It was *A Felicidade*," the song from *Orfeo Negro*. He played and sang it slowly, pronouncing all the words distinctly. Jen moved in front of me and set my beer on the ground. Then she took my hands and held them on her breasts.

"'Happiness is like a feather,'" Bolão sang in Portuguese, "'that the wind carries off through the air. It flies so lightly, but it's got a short life. Its flight ends when the wind stops blowing.'"

"It's a beautiful song," Jen whispered. She held my hands tight to her breasts. "It seems so sad," she said.

"It is," I said.

"We gotta go," Jen said.

We got the bike and pushed it down the road so we wouldn't spoil the song. As Bolão began the last verse I kicked the sidestand down and we stopped and turned to listen. We could see the dark shapes of the people around the fire and the black line of trees on one side of the light and the black shape of the barn on the other. I thought

I could make out Bolão's silhouette through the fire.

"Tell me what it says," Jen said.

"'Happiness is like a drop of dew on a petal of a flower,'" I whispered in her hair. "'It shines quietly, then it trembles lightly. Then it falls like a tear, falls like a tear, falls like a tear,'" I repeated slowly with Bolão, "'falls like a tear of love.'"

"And '*a felicidade*' means happiness?" Jen asked.

"'A *felicidade*' means happiness," I replied.

"Don't even shut it off," Jen said in my ear when we pulled up in front of her place. "I'll just run right in." She got off the bike and gave me a soft kiss, then pulled back and looked at me with the sweetest look in our history together. "You be careful tonight!" she yelled over her shoulder as she ran to the door.

"I will!" I yelled back. I stayed till she got inside and turned on the lights, then I powered it on in a neat half doughnut, spraying gravel against the corral fence, and wailed off in the direction of more beer and music.

As I came out of the trees onto the straight stretch that leads to the farm, a string of cars passed me. It looked like things were breaking up, but I thought I'd stay a minute to see if anyone I knew was hanging in. The little road was clogged with cars going out, so I pulled into the field and found a flat rock to set the sidestand on and parked and started walking toward the fire. In a few steps I met Donnie coming toward me.

"I thought I'd stick around," he said. "To let you know there might be some ill will waiting here for ya."

"Ill will?" I said. "Against me?"

Donnie pulled me out of the stream of light from the cars bumping slowly past us. "I don't know these people," Donnie said. "But the shit hit the fan after you left. Some fat fuck with a headband came running up to the fire in the middle of one of your friend's songs, yelling that some money had been stolen. People jumped up and started screaming at one another, then your friend McAdams punched the guy I heard took a swing at you earlier. They wrestled around a little, then McAdams cut his back on a rock. The Brazilian guy and the girl with no tits were walking him past us, and I heard him say the guy named Lasch said you probably stole the money, since you'd just split."

"I might need their fucking money," I said. "Come on," I said to Don as I started for the fire.

People think because Don's big and black and strong that he's also tough and mean. He is tough on the football field, and he'd be tough anywhere if he had to be. But Donnie's no tough black kid from the ghetto. He grew up on the south side of Spokane and his dad had a successful landscaping business.

"Whatcha gonna do?" Donnie asked.

"I just wanna find the guy who advises the Committee and tell him I didn't take their dough," I said.

"Oh," Donnie said. We stopped at the kegs. They'd tapped the last one and left it unattended. "You *look* like you could beat somebody up with one arm," Donnie said as I handed him a beer. "Maybe we could intimidate a few folks."

"Outstanding idea," I said. "Let's go intimidate some people." As we turned, we saw flames start up the barn wall. "Oh, shit!" I said. "Look at that!" Flames were scaling the wall, and soon the barn went up with a swoosh and then a roar. People started hooting and clapping and pointing at the flames leaping high up into the darkness.

"You know, Russ," Donnie said, "I think this is getting to be a good place to get the fuck out of. On second thought, let's *not* go intimidate any folks."

"I just gotta find this one guy," I said. We walked up the hill through the bright firelight that now flooded all the cleared land and even reached a little way through the trees. We found the professor with the salt-and-pepper beard sitting with Felicity and the guy in the headband. I went up to him and got down on my haunches so I could look him in the face. "I'm Karl Russell," I said. "I heard you might think I took your money. I didn't."

"Of course you didn't," the guy said.

"We know who took it," said Felicity. "Or at least we're pretty sure. He was here to drop something off, he stayed for a beer, then went back to Spokane."

"We know the fucker ripped us off," said Headband. He raised his cup to Donnie.

Felicity looked at me, then at Donnie. "You guys feel like helping us get our money back?" she asked.

"Call the police, Felicity," I said. "That's what they're for."

"The police are exactly who we don't want involved with this particular guy," the professor said. He was looking down at his feet and dancing his toes out the ends of his sandals.

"It'll just take a minute," Felicity said. She was looking up at Donnie. "We just need to confront him a little on it."

"'Confront him a little'?" I said. "Felicity, people who 'confront' dope pushers—"

"He's not a pusher," she said. "He just deals, and he's so whacked-out anyway he probably already forgot he took the money. All we'll probably have to do is remind him. You guys won't have to say a word," she said as she looked up at Don. "All we want you to do is stand there."

"And we'll buy you breakfast," the professor said. "It'll be on the Committee."

"I could use a bite," Donnie said.

"Right on!" shouted Headband, raising his fist.

"Just follow us," said the professor.

"People get hurt doin' shit like this!" I yelled back to Donnie as we followed the professor's VW Bug to the freeway.

"I ain't gonna do nothin' but stand there!" Donnie yelled in my ear. "And then I'm gonna get fed!"

"Yeah, you'll get fed," I replied. "The way Felicity was looking at you, you're gonna get fed all right."

"Ain't she a scrawny little thing," Donnie said.

Two Cheney fire trucks screamed by headed for the red glow in the sky behind us.

We followed the Bug into the old neighborhood west of downtown Spokane called Peaceful Valley. It was dark as the inside of a cave down there along the river because the river cliffs blocked out the city lights and two of every three streetlights were out. We made one last turn that put us on the dirt street closest to the river. The Bug's taillights stopped moving, then went out a couple blocks down the street. We parked the bike behind a huge lilac bush. The neighborhood didn't even have sidewalks, so we walked in the street.

"Man," Donnie said, "this place is low, low rent."

In a minute we ran into Felicity, Headband, and the professor walking toward us.

The professor walked up to the door and we fanned out around him on the porch. The shades were all drawn, but yellow light seeped around their edges and we could hear a baby coughing and crying and the sound of TV.

A girl who could have been anywhere from thirteen to twenty-five years old opened the door. She was more wasted than Felicity, but through her thin cotton T-shirt shone a stunning set of breasts. Even through her shirt you could see the gray-blue veins stretch around them like the great rivers of the world from space.

"We need to talk to Johnny for a minute," the professor said.

"He's right in here," the girl said. She smiled, and you could see where a couple teeth were missing.

The place was real clean. An old Penncrest stereo sat on an apple crate on the wood floor and in the crate sat a few albums. There was a davenport with a pink cotton blanket tucked neatly around the cushions and an old blue rocker. On the other side of the room was a dining table covered with marijuana about two inches thick. The coughing, crying baby hung over the tray of its high chair and played in the marijuana, and below it on the floor on a mechanic's creeper covered with a towel that said Y.M.C.A. lay a tiny baby in a clean white gown. Johnny appeared in the kitchen doorway. The guy was a snake.

As he leaned his arm on top of the rusty refrigerator you could see about every muscle he had. He looked made out of braided leather. His eyes set on me, then moved to each of us. He bristled when he came to Donnie and you could see the muscles twitch in his stomach where his denim jacket with the cut-off sleeves hung open. The twitch went up his stomach, up his arms, up his neck, and into his face. Long brown hair hung to his shoulders and he wore the CPVN's red hunting hat tilted back on his head.

"What's happenin', Blood?" he said to Donnie.

The professor had his eyes fixed on the hat. "We think we had a mix-up earlier this evening," he said.

"A mix-up?" Johnny said. "That's too bad. You all seemed highly organized to me." As he walked into the room he dropped his cigarette butt on the floor. The girl picked it up and took it to an ashtray. Then she took the crying baby out of its high chair and into the kitchen.

"Let me show you all the place," Johnny said.

We bunched up in the tiny hall and Johnny held out his hand. "Here's the kitchen," he said. On his forearm was a poorly done tattoo of a marijuana leaf. In the tiny kitchen the girl was washing away the baby's tears with a dish towel she'd dipped under the faucet. Johnny turned, took one step, and held out his other hand. "This is the bedroom," he said.

We filed into the tiny bedroom. One wall was completely covered by a red flag with a gold star in the center. In a corner sat a little carbine with a long, curved clip sticking out of it. On the apple crate they used for a night table lay a .45. In the middle of the mattress on the floor, with an American flag for a bedspread, sat a healthy pile of money.

"It's not much of a place," Johnny said. "But it'll do us until we can put something together."

"I'm sorry it's so messy," the girl said from the doorway. She'd begun to nurse the older baby, who was sucking so hard you could hear it all over the house. "I want you all to see Johnny's medals," the girl said, raising her skinny arm up to a glass case on the wall above the bed.

In the case were sergeant's stripes, a gold shoulder patch with AIR-BORNE across the top, a purple heart with a gold star on the ribbon, and in a little case of its own a beautiful silver star with a tiny white star in the center hanging from a red, white, and blue ribbon. I took a peek at two plaques next to the case. One was a high-school diploma from Missouri that said Johnny White had graduated in 1965. The other was a certificate saying he'd been all-state in football.

"We're pretty tired," Johnny was saying as I stepped into the living room. "And the babies got to have their sleep. Let me show you all the outside," he said.

He led us to the door, and we all saw the survival knife hanging from his belt in back.

Felicity looked up at me. "We are getting the fuck *out*," I whispered to her before she could speak.

But when we went outside Felicity stayed behind, holding the tiny baby and talking to the girl, who was still holding the older baby to her breast. The girl walked into the bedroom. Then Johnny spoke and I turned.

"Not much of a yard," he said, as his arm swept around. "But we got the river around behind." He walked into the total darkness around the side of the house. You could hear the river boiling back there. "Come on, Blood!" he yelled to Donnie. "Take a look at this ol' river roll!"

Donnie took a step and I grabbed his arm. "This guy could beat us both to death," I whispered. "Head for the bike, Don. I'll be right along."

"Hey!" Johnny yelled above the rumble of the river.

Just then Felicity bounced down the steps holding a paper sack. "I got it!" she whispered with a big grin on her face. Both Headband and the professor perked right up.

"Hey, you all!" called Johnny.

"Let's split!" whispered Headband, and off toward the Bug he ran.

"Hey!" Johnny yelled. We could hear him walking toward us. Felicity and the professor took off running.

"Hey, man!" Johnny called from the darkness. "Come take a look at this ol' river roll!"

Then I took off too. The bike needed about three kicks before it would fire over, and I was listening for footsteps every second. When she finally started I really poured it to her, with Donnie clamped onto me like a sea creature to a rock.

"He's gonna beat that little girl till there ain't nothin' left," I heard Don say above the roar of the engine.

Neither Donnnie nor I could eat much of our breakfast at first. But the three assholes who'd been lucky to escape that situation with all their vital organs still in their bodies were giddy and gleesome about getting back their dough in such a slick way. I have to admit the good cheer was infectious after a while—especially for Don, as Felicity played with him under the table. In the parking lot she hung onto him like a spider monkey on an orangutan and begged me to take them both back to Cheney on the bike.

"Three grown-up people on one motorcycle!" I screamed at her. "Sure, Felicity. The cops'll think that's cute. They'll tell the judge to sentence us to a circus." But while I was yelling at her, the professor and Headband took off.

"So what're we gonna do, Russ?" Donnie said. He looked at me with a sly smile as Felicity continued winding herself around him like a pernicious vine.

We rode okay for a while. But after we passed the cemetery I began to feel a vibration.

"You guys feel anything back there?" I yelled.

All I got in response was giggling from Felicity, who was on the seat behind me with Donnie on the carrier behind her. Then Felicity lunged forward and about put us all on the pavement.

"What the fuck is goin' on back there?" I screamed. "We could get killed!"

"Sorry, Karl," Felicity gasped in my ear. She had her chin dug into my shoulder. "I had to change positions," she said. Then she let out this great shudder like she was being flash-frozen. Pretty soon the vibration started up again. Then Felicity's chin began a rhythmic battering on my shoulder and she began to pant, then moan.

Goddamn, I thought, Felicity sounds like she's—And then Donnie started to groan and the vibration got worse.

"YOU GUYS ARE FUCKING!!!" I screamed. "YOU'RE FUCK-ING ON MY DAD'S MOTORCYCLE!"

"We're about finished," Felicity gasped. Then she shrieked and Donnie let out this horrendous groan. Then they both collapsed forward and knocked me up on the tank. I was ready, though, and hung on. I'd dropped our speed down to fifteen miles an hour by then.

"GET THE FUCK OFFA ME, YOU TWO!!!" I screamed. I felt the weight leave my back, and got settled on the seat again and turned up the gas. I wanted to get home and scrub down.

"Karl!" Felicity yelled blithely in my ear. "You didn't really think Don and I were fucking, did you?"

"You are two sick people!" I yelled back.

"It was just acting," Felicity said. "We were playing a joke on you."

"Yeah, Russ!" Donnie yelled. "Not bad, huh!"

"Nice try, you two scuzzballs!" I yelled back. "I *smelled* it!"

We crossed the railroad tracks, then pulled onto the main road, and in two minutes we were in front of Felicity's. They got off slowly, spent some time doing something behind me, then walked arm in arm to her door. Donnie kissed her good night. I could have puked!

I didn't talk to him till we pulled into the dorm parking lot. A thin band of gray-blue light lay on the eastern horizon.

"God, Russ," Donnie said as he got off the bike, "you sure know how to show a guy a good time."

"I can't believe it," I said. "I can't believe you did that. What if I catch something off the seat? I can feel it soaking through my jeans."

"Oh, come on, man," Donnie said. "It was a joke. I wouldn't have fucked that woman with your dick. Take care, Russ," he said, as he turned and sprinted for the door.

"'Night, Don!" I yelled after him.

I breathed the good early-morning air in deep as I putted slowly back to the house.

Wednesday afternoon, May 15, 1968

Spent Friday and Saturday nights at Jen's. Would have spent the whole weekend there if I hadn't needed to put in some time here at the house getting my pledge duties done and spending some time with the guys. Initiation is coming up Saturday the 25th, and it's supposed to be a serious and dignified ceremony, not a bunch of crazy shit like people think fraternities do. The guys vote on us the night of the 24th. If they vote us in and we do okay in the ceremony— and we still want to be members—then we're in.

I'm going to stick around the house more. Not because I'm afraid the guys will blackball me, but because I want them to know I like and respect them.

Met with Dr. Hazelton yesterday to tell him I'd decided to write my final paper on God's character in the Book of Job. I'm going to discuss Him just like He was an ordinary literary character. He said it sounded "intriguing." He asked me what I was majoring in. I told him I hadn't quite decided yet, but I thought probably P.E. He told me I "seem to have some affection for ideas," and then asked if I knew what "liberal arts" meant.

I told him I didn't know the literal definition, but that in terms of the behavior of the people involved it meant you smoked a pipe, wore leather patches on your coat-sleeves, found it difficult to agree with the government on anything, couldn't bear to ever fire a gun, and had an affinity for European cars.

He laughed, and I laughed too. He said stuff like that was just a style some people picked up. The real meaning of "liberal arts," he said—what it meant to the Greeks—was "the arts a free man pursues," the arts of mind as opposed to the manual arts that slaves practiced, like masonry and carpentry. The point, he said, was to pursue the life you love. If you love sports, he said, give your life to sports. But if you love ideas, he said, you shouldn't be ashamed to give your life to their pursuit.

What I was thinking was that I loved sports *and* ideas and that I felt like pursuing *everything*. But what I told him was I loved his flute-playing at the kegger, and he seemd to appreciate that.

We finish *Scroll of Agony, The Warsaw Diary of Chaim A. Kaplan* in Literature of the Camps today, and I'm going to be there with one big question: How could the Jews ever have let themselves and their children get put on those trains when they all knew what was at the end of the line?

Very early in the book it's clear to Kaplan that the Nazis are going to exterminate every Jew they can. Yet nowhere in all 321 pages— that's *three years* of evidence that the Nazis are eventually going to kill him—does Kaplan think of taking any action, let alone of fighting back somehow. It wouldn't have done any good. They'd just have killed him, and he was an old guy anyway, and fighting wasn't exactly up his alley. But he didn't even *think* about taking at least one of them out with him. He doesn't even call them assholes or cocksuckers or pricks or shiteaters. He calls them things like "oppressors" and "conquerors" and "killers" and "murderers," terms I consider way too dignified for such total scum.

I can't even begin to understand a man like Kaplan. We could be from different planets. I understand the fucking Nazis better than I understand Kaplan.

First, I don't understand this idea of being part of a Jewish "nation" and the whole nation being judged by God. If God really does judge people, He ought to judge them individually, by their actions. I wouldn't love any God who judged people on the basis of their being part of a group they were born into. We say prejudice is a bad quality in people, and it seems to me it's a really shitty quality in a god.

Kaplan says he's grateful to his father for leaving him with a spiritual legacy that would stay with him and sustain him forever. My dad left me with a kind of spiritual legacy too. Dad made it clear to me that you didn't let yourself be treated in a way you knew you didn't deserve. He told me that anybody who was going to hurt me or Jesse for no reason was giving up his rights to be treated with the respect we were supposed to show everyone, and that I should find a way to hurt him bad before Jesse or I got hurt. This makes perfect sense to me, but I suppose everybody's principles make perfect sense to them.

I'd like to live my life like the straight-backed old man in Solzhenitsyn's *One Day in the Life of Ivan Denisovich*. He couldn't beat the power of the Soviet Union, and he didn't do anything futile that would get him killed. But he also didn't compromise totally: he kept his back straight and he set his bread on a napkin instead of the dirty table. He saved his spirit.

Sunday morning, May 19, 1968

At Jen's

Jen was a little late Friday evening, and I sat in her old overstuffed porch chair reading *King Lear* and rubbing the fur off Sylvester till she came riding up through the purple twilight on Eugene McCarthy. They must have ridden hard because they were both all sweaty. Jen smelled wonderful. I stood by and helped a little as she unsaddled and put stuff away.

"I need a bath," Jen said as we walked to the house.

"Okay," I said. "I'll inculturate you while you're in the tub."

Jen turned her key in the door and pushed through. "Karl," she said over her shoulder, "I'm afraid people only do it in water in the movies." She must have been tired.

"No," I said. I waved my book at her as she turned. "I'm gonna read you *King Lear*."

"God, Russ," she said. "I thought we were friends."

Jen had the kerosene lamps lighted and she was lying back in the big old claw-footed tub under a great froth of bubblebath when I walked into the bathroom. "Okay, Jen," I said, as I sat down on the toilet seat. "Now just relax. Keep all your channels open and just let the language wash over you. This is the Bard of Avon talking to us here."

Jen rolled her eyes and sank a little deeper through the suds. The more I read, the lower Jen sank. The bubbles looked like gold mesh in the yellow glow of the lamp above her head. By the time I got halfway through the second scene Jen had sunk out of sight.

I got up and knelt at the edge of the tub and stuck my face down in the suds. "Ya don't like it," I said, about where I thought her ear would be. "Just a couple more lines. Some great stuff's coming up here. It's contemporary," I said. "It's about astrology."

Jen raised her head a little. She was all golden with bubbles. "Astrology is a crock of shit," she said.

"Of course it is," I said. "Shakespeare thinks so too. Just listen." I got back on the toilet seat and began to read.

> This is the excellent foppery of the world, that, when we are sick in fortune,—often the surfeit of our own behavior,—we make guilty of our disasters the sun, the moon, and the stars: as if we were villains by necessity, fools by heavenly compulsion, knaves, thieves, and teachers, by spherical predominance, drunkards, liars, and adulterers by an enforced obedience of planetary influence; and all that we are evil in by a divine thrusting-on: an admirable evasion of whoremaster man, to lay his goatish disposition to the charge of a star.

Jen sat up and looked at me. Her breasts were beaded with gold. "What?" she said.

"He says it's foolish," I said, "foolish and really typical of people, especially when things are going bad—and usually when the stuff is totally our fault—to say all our problems are the result of heavenly forces. He says it's evading responsibility to say we are what we are because a divine power thrust it on us."

Jen's expression didn't change. "The only thing that interests me there is the divine thrusting," she said. Her face softened then, and she smiled. "Come on and get in with me," she said. "I think I've had all the inculturation I can handle."

I peeled off my clothes and got into the tub slowly so it wouldn't overflow. We faced each other and she held me lightly around the calves and I held her just underneath her knees. She must have been really beat, because she dropped off to sleep with her head pillowed against the tub edge.

I dried her slowly with a regular towel, then wrapped her in her big brown towel like a monk's robe with a hood, carried her into the bedroom, and put her in bed. She opened her eyes, but closed them again right away. I'd never felt sexier for her. I covered her, then dried myself with the robe, then hung it over my cock. "Look, Jen," I whispered. "I'm all ready for divine thrusting."

She didn't even stir.

"I guess the thrill is gone," I whispered. But I knew it wasn't. In just a few seconds the robe fell to the floor. Since I wasn't sleepy, I went downstairs to finish *King Lear*.

We got up early Saturday morning and made love. We watched cartoons and ate toast and jelly, then I went back to the house to study, do the lunch dishes, and generally put in an appearance.

At lunch Bolão and I talked about when I should fly to Rio. He's leaving on June 6 and wants a couple days to get squared away before I show up. So I called a travel agent in Spokane and got a flight on Monday, June 10. Bolão promises he'll be at the airport to meet me.

I can't believe I'm going. I especially can't believe I'm going in an airplane. I've never flown before.

Jen and I put on our good clothes and drove to Spokane to pick up the ticket. We had an early supper in the restaurant on top of the Ridpath Hotel, then came home and studied. We went to bed early and cuddled. Jen said it was practice in case we ever got to be old people together. It was fine with me.

This morning, though, something potentially disastrous happened.

I was sitting here at the kitchen table—where I am right now—and I'd just finished my journal entry when Jen came up and asked what all the papers were. I told her they were my journal—"all the secrets about me," I said. She asked if she could read it, and without considering all the stuff she'd encounter, I said sure. She grabbed it up and went over to the davenport by the window, and she's been there ever since—over two hours now—and all she's said is, "Bring me another coffee, please, Russ."

She just said something else. She said, "Russ, is all this stuff true?"

"Christ, Jen," I said. "It's a journal. You don't lie to your own journal."

She just looked at me, then went on reading.

It made me nervous, so I went out for a run. As I ran I wondered what Jen would think about Leila and Georgie. I worried about that, but mostly I worried about what she'd think of the warts. I wondered if she'd think I was crazy for being afraid they'd go all over me, or for having dreams and seeing lights in the sky and thinking they were signs from my folks.

I ran until I got too tired to think. When I made my loop and came in sight of Jen's place again, she was out in her porch chair.

She turned when she heard me and met me at the gate. She took my hand and walked me across the road into the grass and the wild flowers. We walked a ways to where the trees began and the basalt formations were as big as Jen's little house. Sweat was running down my arm and all over her hand. She took off her T-shirt and wiped her hand, then she wiped off both my arms. Then she told me to bend down.

We were in the shadow of a big rock where moss covered the ground. When I got down on my knees I could feel myself sinking in a little. Jen wasn't wearing a bra and as she wiped my face with her shirt her breasts would brush my cheek. She pulled me to her and held my head between her breasts. "Oh, Russ," she said. "There's nothing wrong with you. Everybody thinks something terrible's going to happen to them. Ever since my mom got cancer and had a breast removed, I've just *known* I'd get breast cancer. *Everybody* thinks stuff like that.

"And *everybody* gets warts and stuff on their skin. In junior high I got plantar warts from the swimming pool in Chewelah. I had them all over my feet. Our doctor cut them out, and that was that. Oh, honey," Jen said as she rubbed the back of my neck, "there's nothing wrong with you. When I read you wanted to tell me and then didn't, it made me want to cry."

Nobody but Mom had ever called me "honey." Nobody but her has seen inside me and known what I was thinking. I was the one who cried. I guess maybe the real reason I let Jen read the journal was so she'd find out what I hadn't been able to tell her. I mean, I really cried. I sobbed and shook—somebody driving by in a diesel tractor would have heard me over his engine. I tried to talk, but I couldn't.

Jen got me up and walked me the few steps to the rock. She sat me down and leaned back against the rock, holding my head in her lap, and dried my tears and my nose and her breasts with her shirt. I cried and cried, and cried some more. After a while I started feeling better. It was like finally, after years of being afraid—ever since I'd seen the wartman in Spokane when I was a little kid—I was free of it at last.

Jen wiped my face one last time, then looked down at the shirt in her hands. It was soaked with sweat and tears and you could see the smeared snot glistening here and there. "*Glaaaah!*" she said, holding the shirt out away from her with two fingers. "I'm not gonna put this thing on again."

We were both starved, so after Jen put on a clean shirt we headed straight for the kitchen. I washed my face at the sink and Jen made us fried-egg sandwiches and asked me questions. She asked about Mom and Dad and Jesse, about baseball, about what it was like to live with a family you weren't related to, about Georgie. We talked for hours, and then we went to bed and she asked the final question of the night. "Aren't you afraid Johnny might be dangerous?" she said.

Johnny? I thought. Johnny? Who the hell is—and then I remembered. "Yeah," I said. "The guy *is* dangerous. But to Felicity and her asshole friends, I think, a lot more than to me and Donnie."

"And his poor wife," Jen said. "Even just reading about that guy made me wanna leave the state." She turned to face me. "I'm so glad you found me sitting under that tree."

"Me too," I replied.

We kissed, then Jen turned over. Soon her breathing evened out and little twitches began to go through her. I couldn't sleep, though, so I got out of bed and tiptoed down here to the kitchen table to write.

Thursday night, May 23, 1968

At Jen's

I was taking a shower yesterday morning, scrubbing my head with Jen's little shampoo brush, when she said something I didn't hear. I opened my eyes, pulled back the curtain, stuck my head out, and asked her what she'd said. She looked at me and screamed.

In the mirror behind her I saw the blood all over me. My head was covered with bloody lather and bright blood dripped down my face and neck.

"Jesus, Russ!" Jen said. "What is it?"

"I don't know," I said. "I don't feel anything."

I closed the curtain and got back under the spray. I flicked the brush off my hand and felt my head as I rinsed the soap off. I couldn't feel anything there, and I didn't feel any pain. I turned off the water, asked Jen to get an old towel, and pulled the curtain all the way open.

I looked in the mirror and didn't see any blood. Jen looked me over and didn't see any either. "Turn around," she said.

I started to turn and we both saw the bright blood matting the back of my head and starting down my neck.

"Sit down on the edge of the tub," Jen said. She folded the towel across my shoulders and bent to look. I could feel her fingers moving my hair out of the way. I asked what she saw and she said she didn't see a thing. Then her fingers stopped.

"What is it?" I asked. But I knew what it was.

"Well...," Jen said.

"It's warts," I said. "That's where I had them before."

"I guess they are," Jen said.

She took me into the bedroom, sat me on a chair, wiped the blood, and dried the rest of me with the clean part of the towel. Then she bent my head down. "Just stay this way a minute, hon," she said. "They've about stopped bleeding."

Out of the corner of my eye I saw her take her watch off the dresser. "Doctors' offices open in fifteen minutes," she said as she stepped into her jeans. "I'm calling your dermatologist and we're getting these things off as soon as we can."

I couldn't taste my coffee as we sat at the kitchen table. I could feel it hot in my mouth, but it didn't have any taste. I watched Jen talk on the phone and thought how the warts had grown overnight. I knew they hadn't been there yesterday afternoon because Jen would have felt them as she held my head and stroked my hair when I was crying. The fucking things had grown in about six hours!

"Our appointment's at three-thirty tomorrow afternoon," Jen said as she sat down. "By four-thirty they'll be gone."

I nodded my head and tried to smile at her for the way she was treating me. But all I could think of was how the warts had grown overnight.

My spirits didn't pick up much when Jen and I got to Spokane this afternoon. Havermeyer's brother looks exactly like Havermeyer and inspires as much confidence. I asked if they were twins.

"Not on your life," he said. "Bernie's just a punk kid. He's eleven months younger. That's why he's so competitive. He develops theories like this 'viral communications' shtick just to distract me, then he takes a Ph.D. in some other field and lords it over me that he's becoming a Renaissance man. 'Viral communications'! Can you believe it! I guess Stanford'll award a fellowship to anybody. They think he's gonna talk warts into curing cancer! What the little fart's probably doing is sitting on the beach, writing a children's book about an elephant seal who yearns to dance ballet.

"Two years ago Bernie told me he was taking the Schawlow-Townes

Fellowship at Harvard—my old Alma Mammie, by the way—and you know what he did there?"

"What?" I said. I really wasn't in the mood.

"We have an appointment to get warts removed," Jen said.

"Sure," Havermeyer said. "But you'll love this. Bernie had the fellowship all right, but what he mostly spent his time on was taking a Ph.D. in art history and turning his dissertation into a coffee-table book on *Epidermal Anomalies as Illustrated in Flemish Portraiture.* He's a sick kid, but you really hafta appreciate his breadth of quirkiness."

Jen stepped up to him. "Look, Doctor," she said, "we'd like to get these things taken off, then we'd like to be on our way."

Havermeyer looked Jen over, then centered his eyes on her breasts. "Well," he said, "whatever you say. But personally I think they look fine on you." He shook his head. "Your time for the hundred will go way down," he said. "But I bet you both end up missing them."

"Oh, Christ," Jen said. She shook her head and walked to the window and looked out.

"Come on, Doctor Havermeyer," I said. "The warts are on my head. Start burnin', please."

"Okay," Havermeyer said. "Just a little derm humor." He had me take off my shirt and sit up on the table. Jen came over. "You might want to wait outside," Havermeyer said to her. "There are funner things to look at than wart-burnings. You could read my brother's book."

"I'm gonna stay," Jen said. "I'll be fine."

Havermeyer looked through my hair, found the warts, and snipped a clear spot around them. "You say my brother did these about a month ago?" he asked.

"That's right," I said.

"Well, the kid didn't go deep enough," he said. "But they're gone for good this time. Mark 'er down," he said. "And we'll send the bill to Dr. Viral Communications in care of Stanford University."

He gave me the shots, then got up on a stool and started burning. Jen held my hand. You could hear them sizzle and Jen turned her head away from the smoke. "Nasty, ain't it!" Havermeyer said. "Just imagine what a whole burning person smells like."

He got them all, he said. Then, as I stood to put on my shirt, he stopped me. "Hold on a second," he said. "Let's take a gander at these here."

"At what?" Jen and I both said.

"At this," Havermeyer said. He took my arms and had me bend over the exam table. He told Jen to step over to my left side. I could feel his hands where people give you kidney punches. I bent around, but couldn't see. He held a mirror for me, and then I could see a couple of them. They looked like calluses—like the ones I'd had on my wrist—but these were as big around as nickels.

"You guys wanna leave this patch?" he asked. "You grow attached to them or something?" He snickered a little.

"Karl," Jen said, "you didn't have these yesterday, did you?"

"No," I said. Oh, Christ! I thought. "I don't think so."

"Well, whaddaya say we excise these little babies?" Havermeyer said.

"How many are there?" I asked.

"Six," Jen said.

"Do it," I said.

Havermeyer said he was going to make sure he got all the roots. He told me to lie on my stomach, that he was going to cut them out, and that he had to give me a shot that might hurt.

It did hurt. When I couldn't feel him pinch me anymore, he started cutting. I could feel the pressure, but that was all. Jen had moved to the head of the table and taken my hand. I felt a lot of pressure and heard Havermeyer grunting. Jen was looking back with her jaw set. Then all of a sudden I felt the cutting and I let out a yell. The pain stopped as soon as Havermeyer did, but I'd already broken out in sweat all over.

Havermeyer whipped around the table and got into his cabinet. "They're deeper than I thought," he said, as he worked with his back to us. "I didn't go deep enough with the shot. I'm sorry, Russell."

"It's okay," I said. I started to breathe hard and feel a little sick.

Jen got down on her knees and whispered to me. "It's okay, hon. A few minutes more and they'll all be gone."

Havermeyer walked back with a syringe in his hand that had a needle on it three or four inches long. I flinched every time he put it in, but after a minute or so I couldn't feel anything below my nipples.

It wasn't long before Havermeyer exhaled a great "Whew!" "That's it!" he said. "All stitched up." He moved in front of me and held out a stainless steel dish. "We got 'em," he said. "And are they whoppers!"

Jen stood up, and when Havermeyer showed her what was in the dish her face went white. "I've grown horseradishes that never got this big," he said.

"Let's see," I said.

Havermeyer lowered the dish. Six bloody white things that did look like horseradishes with the stalks cut off lay in the film of blood that covered the bottom of the dish. One of them was longer than the needle he'd shot me with the second time.

"I put a good thick pad on you," Havermeyer said, going to the cabinet again. He turned back with two small boxes and handed them to Jen. He had to poke her with them to get her attention. "They'll probably seep a little tonight," he said. "Just keep putting on pads till it stops."

He walked to the window and turned and leaned against the radiator. "Russell," he said, "I want you to lie here awhile until you feel like walking. And I want you to leave your phone number at the desk. I'm going to send these to the lab. Just to make sure we don't have any funny tissue here. And I *will* call and tell you what they say."

He grabbed a towel out of his cabinet and gave it to me. Then he took Jen's arm and my hand. "There's no charge for this, kids," he said. "We bill this one to Brother Bernie." He walked out.

Jen dried the sweat off me, then she pulled up a chair and laid her head by mine for a second or two. It was a little hard to move my left arm and Jen had to help me with my shirt. We left both our numbers at the desk.

As we were going into J.C. Penney's we looked at our reflection in the window. Jen fluffed my hair a little around the bandage on my head, then threw up her hands. "I'm so dumb!" she said. "I almost forgot!"

She reached into the canvas book bag she carries for a purse, pulled out a brown cotton beanie with a white C on it, and set it on my head over the bandage. Then she took some bobby pins out of the bag and pinned it to my hair.

"There you go, Russ," she said. "Consider yourself an honorary Chewelah High freshman."

"Thanks, Jen," I said. What I looked like was a big, blond Jew in his yarmulke.

I don't know quite what to think. I'm not scared, especially. I just feel sort of dull, like the anesthetic was still hanging on and had worked its way all through me.

Wednesday afternoon, May 22, 1968

I got up early and fried spuds, took Jen some coffee when I woke her up, then scrambled eggs with green onions when she came downstairs. I served it all up with toast and V-8 juice and managed to have everything hot at the same time. I was wearing my Chewelah beanie, and I thanked Jen for going through that ordeal with me.

It's gotten real hard to act natural around Jen. No matter how good a friend she's become, I just can't stand for her to know those fucking things grow on me. I can't stand for her to have seen them. A few days ago she was making me feel like I was beautiful. I'd get out of the shower and towel off in the doorway, and she'd tell me how good-looking I was and how she couldn't wait to have me inside her. But I feel ugly now.

Those warts kind of looked like horseradishes, all right. But what they mostly looked like was little skinned animals. Their flesh was white, but it wasn't cold and firm like vegetable flesh. They looked warm and porous, like meat. You could see the blood seep out of them.

I don't see how Jen can stand to touch me. That's one way I'm feeling. Then I'm also scared about what Havermeyer's going to tell me when he calls. I'm thinking so much about myself, it's like I'm living outside my body, watching myself be afraid.

After being so quiet last night Jen was all full of life this morning. We planned a camping trip for Memorial Day weekend.

On my way back to the house in the Ford, the radio was full of news about squads of Vietcong having infiltrated Saigon. I came in through the basement and sat with Mac and Boreson as they watched the morning news. They were both excited about it. Not only were they not arguing, they were united in their absorption in the fighting. GIs who looked our age and younger were crouched behind a little masonry wall firing into a building across the street. Some of the guys just held their rifles up over the wall and fired without looking. I doubt I'd have the guts to do that even on my bravest day. Now and then automatic rifle fire would pop and you'd see puffs of smoke across the street as bullets raked the wall and our guys flattened out.

It's hard not to realize I have it pretty good compared to our guys in Vietnam, but that doesn't make me feel any more fortunate in my stomach. In my stomach I feel afraid.

Havermeyer just called. He said he went to the lab himself and eyeballed the stuff and couldn't find a single cell he wouldn't have been proud to take home to his mother. He said I didn't have a thing to worry about "dermwise." But he advised me that if I ever got any more warts I might consider adopting a more hospitable attitude toward them. Welcome them just like somebody new to the neighborhood, he said, and see if that didn't cut their hostility a little. He said it had been an angry bunch of warts he'd cut out of me.

This news makes my day a lot better.

I called Jen, and she told me I was a big dummy for even having been worried about it. She said I was too handsome to have anything wrong with me.

Initiation didn't turn out to be the sedate affair we were led to expect.

After our formal dinner last night, they took us to one of the downstairs study rooms and left us for at least—and I mean *at least*—six hours. Charley and Gary came in with four white robes. They didn't say a word as they helped us get into them. It was pitch dark and hot, and it got real close real fast. At first Leo, as house president, had given us our instructions and told us not to make a sound. But Bolão started grousing right away. "*Puta merda!*" he'd whisper. "Whore shit, man! If I'd wanted to go to college and be tortured I'd have stayed in Brazil." He was fairly lighthearted and funny at first, but after an hour or so he began to seethe. You could hear him breathing hard, gnashing his teeth and cussing in Portuguese.

I was fairly comfortable in a corner by a dresser with my back against the rock foundation. The rocks kept my back cool when the rest of me was roasting. If I turned my face to the rocks I could almost smell the cool earth on the other side. I could feel moss when I rubbed my face over the rocks.

Mac was the most verbal, and he didn't whisper. "You know," he'd say, "it's 19-fucking-68 and it's a little difficult to believe an organization like this, supposedly dedicated to the development of excellence in a young man's character, doesn't have better things to do than play early Christians in the fucking catacombs!"

In a few minutes music began blasting down out of the ceiling. It was so loud we couldn't have heard each other if we'd shouted. I didn't mind how loud the music was, and I leaned back against the wall and tried to relax. I stretched my legs out and turned my head and breathed as close to the rocks as I could get my nose. We waited and waited and waited for somebody to come get us, but nobody came. Finally, in spite of the music, I fell asleep.

I dreamed that dream where I'm a wartman living in the cave in Rio with *os mudados*, the altered people. This time the music was in the dream—I found out later it was Ravel's *Bolero*—and the shapes that hovered a few feet from me in the darkness swayed to it as it boomed and echoed off the rock walls.

I knew I was dreaming and that the mossy, earthy smell on the rocks where my head was resting came from the walls of a basement study room in the Alpha Zeta fraternity house in Cheney, Washington, and not from a cave or a collapsed subway tunnel or whatever it was supposed to be in Rio, and I knew the bodies I could feel around me in the darkness were just regular guys. But I couldn't get myself to know those things well enough not to be afraid. Slowly I lost everything I knew and felt myself slipping away. And then I *was* a wartman. I was a wartman and I was in a cave and the shapes swaying in the darkness around me were more hideous than a hundred bad dreams, and I knew I was one of them.

I screamed and screamed and just kept on screaming. The music stopped, Grigsby got up and turned on the light, and everybody asked me what was wrong. Before I had a chance to say anything Boreson and Thorv Anderson burst in. Tommy took me out and Thorv got the other guys settled back down on the floor. Tommy pulled the hood of the robe over my head and it came down so far over my face I couldn't see a thing. Then they led me upstairs.

I knew they'd led me into the chapter room because I could feel the carpet on my bare feet. I could feel bodies very near me, but nothing touched me. Then someone directly in front of me began to speak.

"'Rejoice, O young man, in thy youth,'" Crookshank was saying, "'and let thy heart cheer thee in the days of thy youth. And walk in the ways of thine heart, and in the sight of thine eyes. But know thou, that for all these things God will bring thee into judgement.'"

And then someone lifted my hood.

In a semicircle around me, five robed and hooded figures stood swaying to the faint music. Light came from big candles on the mantel. For a second it made me think the dream had come true, and I fell back a little and sucked in a breath. Hands caught me and held me till I stood steady. God, what a pussy those guys must think I am!

"'Remember now thy creator in the days of thy youth,'" one of the figures said—I couldn't get the voice—"'while the evil days come not, nor the years draw nigh.'"

"'He that diggeth a pit shall fall into it,'" another voice said—it was Charley—"'and whoso breaketh a hedge, a serpent shall bite him.'"

"'Whoso removeth stones shall be hurt therewith, and he that cleaveth wood shall be endangered thereby,'" Leo said from beneath a dark hood.

The central figure turned and moved to the mantel, took something, then moved to one of the candles. When he turned he was holding a golden lamp, the kind a genie would live in. A flame was burning bright at the end of the lamp's long, curved neck. He walked toward me, the sleeves of his robe covering him so well I couldn't see any hands, and it looked like the lamp was floating in the dark.

"'Take ye thy light and thy salvation,'" Crookshank said.

I took the lamp, and a new voice spoke. "'Ask, and it shall be given you,'" the voice said. "'Seek, and ye shall find. Knock and it shall be opened unto you. For every one that asketh receiveth, and he that seeketh findeth, and to him that knocketh it shall be opened.'"

Then Leo spoke up. "'A friend loveth at all times,'" he said, "'and a brother is born for adversity. A man that hath friends must show himself friendly, and there is a friend that sticketh closer than a brother.'" Then he stretched out his arms. "Bring me the lamp," he said.

So I stepped over and set the lamp in Leo's hands, and immediately everything went dark. Everybody started yelling. Then it seemed like every light in the first floor went on. The robed guys had their hoods pulled back. Most of the yelling was directed at Leo. I had screwed up, but they were saying it was his fault.

"What'd you take the lamp for, Leo?" Whitz yelled. "Now what're we supposed to do?"

"He gave it to me," Leo said. "I had to take it. I was afraid he was gonna drop the fucking thing." Leo looked at me then. "Man, Karl, I'm sorry," he said.

"It's my fault," I said. "I was kinda tired. I wasn't paying enough attention."

Gary pushed Bagby off the arm of the davenport. "It's not Russell's fault!" he yelled. "It's Bagby's fault. He's the fucking pledge master! He's supposed to get the pledges ready for this!"

I'd never seen any of the guys act like that with each other. Bags jumped up and went after Gary. "Hold it, you guys," I said. "I'm taking responsibility for this. Just somebody tell me what to do and I'll do it." I sat back down on the davenport and closed my eyes. There it is, I said to myself. I'm out of the fraternity. Dog shit. I can't believe it.

Crookshank and Whitz got me up and walked me back to where I'd stood before. The five robed guys got in their semicircle and all the rest of the guys stood close around me. But everybody was smiling like goons. I mean *everyone* was wearing this giant shit-eating grin— even Crookshank.

They're glad I'm going, I thought. They never wanted me in the fraternity in the first place.

The lights were still up and the robed guys had their hoods off.

"'All things come alike to all,'" Crooks said. "'There is one event to the righteous and to the wicked, to the good and to the clean and to the unclean, to him that sacrificeth and to him that sacrificeth not. The Lord maketh his sun to rise on the evil and on the good, and sendeth rain on the just and the unjust. Yet,'" he went on, "'to him that is joined to all the living there is hope.'"

And everybody who wasn't dressed in a robe started cheering. I didn't have a clue.

"'How oft shall my brother sin against me, and I forgive him?'" Crooks continued. "'Till seven times? Not until seven times, but until seventy times seven.'"

More cheers and whoops erupted from the guys. Crookshank spread his arms like a minister and everybody got quiet. "'Go thy way,'" he said. "'Eat thy bread with joy, and drink thy wine with a merry heart, for God now accepteth thy works.'"

And then everybody was cheering and jumping all over me and trying to shake my hand and yelling congratulations at me. "You're in!" Leo yelled in my ear. "You're in! Everybody fucks up. That's the way it works. Somebody always puts out the lamp!"

Everybody laughed. Boreson walked me upstairs then, and I washed my face and put on some clothes. Then Tommy and I sat quietly on the steps and watched the others go through the ceremony.

When Gary went down to get Bolão, he came back *following* Bolão, who charged down the hall and up the stairs in his sweat-soaked robe. All the lights came on then, and Leo and Crookshank whipped up the stairs after him. They were up there quite awhile. When Bolão came down the stairs, he had his clothes on and his suitcase in his hand. He stood beside me on the bottom step as he addressed the group.

"I've enjoyed myself here," he said, with sadness in his voice. "But I'm leaving now. People in my family don't allow themselves to be treated like this. I hope there aren't any hard feelings. I just have to go now."

I think the guys were dumbfounded. I thought it was going a little far, but Bolão really brought it off. I was proud of him, in a way. He looked down at me and asked if I'd drive him to a motel, and I said sure, and followed him out the door.

At the Shady Knoll motel, I gave him Jen's number and told him to get hold of me there if I wasn't at the house. He was sorry we weren't going to be roommates anymore, he said, but I told him we'd dance *Carnavál* every night when I got to Rio. "You bet your shoes, man," Bolão said.

The lights were out when I got back to the house. I wanted to know what was going on, so I walked quietly up the steps and sat on the porch under the chapter-room windows and put my ear to the wall. I heard Mac's voice. "'A city that is set on a hill cannot be hid,'" he said.

Oh, Christ, I thought. How are they gonna handle this?

"'Neither do men light a candle, and put it under a bushel, but on a candlestick,'" Mac went on. "'And it giveth light unto *all* that are in the house.'"

Silence. Jesus, I thought, this is the sort of mystical shit Mac can really get into. I bet the guys didn't bargain for this.

Then Mac spoke again. "'Let your light so shine before men, that they may see your good works.' I give the lamp to *all* my brothers," he said.

Then I heard gasps and commotion and shouts of, "Hey, what's goin' on?" I got up and knocked on the door and Grigsby let me in. "The shit just hit the fan," he whispered. "He gave the lamp to

Crookshank. Crooks didn't know what to do. Finally he just took it and put it out."

All of a sudden Mac was shouting. "You mean it was a fucking trick?" he screamed. "You leave us down there for hours roasting and listening to Ravel until we're half nuts, then you fucking trick us!"

Everybody was quiet.

"It's not a trick, McAdams," Crookshank said. "It's a parable, an illustration of transgression and forgiveness."

"I know what a parable is, you stupid fuck!" Mac said. Then he nailed Crooks with a looping right to his hairline.

It didn't sound like a fist on bone at all. What it sounded like—before Mac's scream drowned it out—was a stadium full of old professional wrestlers all cracking their knuckles at the same time.

Crooks stumbled back, but Mac went down like he was shot. Nobody jumped in, because it was all over. Mac was curled around his broken hand. He was white and breathing like he was about to pass out. "You're all done here, McAdams," Leo said. "We don't want a fucking thing to do with you."

"Hold it," Crookshank said. A purple knob had already begun rising on his forehead. "Are we going to just talk about forgiveness or are we going to forgive when we get a chance? Maybe Mac had higher expectations of the ceremony than we were prepared to meet," he said. It was the first time I'd ever heard him call Mac by his nickname. He bent down and helped Mac to his feet. The room was silent as Crooks and the other robed guys formed their semicircle.

"'How oft shall my brother sin against me, and I forgive him?'" Crooks said. "'Till seven times? Not until seven times, but until seventy times seven.'" He looked at Mac. Mac's hand was already the size of a softball. Poor Mac was about out.

"'Go thy way,'" Crooks said, real fast. "'Eat thy bread with joy, and drink thy wine with a merry heart, for God now accepteth thy works.'"

Mac slumped and Leo caught him and lifted him in his arms like a baby. Everybody drew back. I opened the door and Charley and Gary sprinted out for their pickup, then Leo followed with Mac.

At Jen's

Last week was pretty hectic, what with studying and visiting Mac in the hospital and bringing him home and getting Bolão and his stuff moved over to Felicity's. But it was a good week, and Jen and I ended it perfectly. We got up at 4:30 Friday, hitched the trailer to Jen's pickup, loaded the horses, and were on the road to her folks' ranch before sunup.

There's something exciting about being on the road early like that. You've got the whole world to yourself—yourself and the tractor-trailer rigs—and you're headed out through the dark on a great adventure. We were slightly wired on the strong coffee and honey Jen had filled the thermos with. She was at the wheel and I was in charge of coffee and music. José Feliciano sang quietly on the tape player as we rolled through Spokane and headed north.

The sun was just rising over the mountains to the east as we crossed the Little Spokane River on 395 and climbed the hill that takes you out onto Wildrose Prairie. As the sky got lighter and everything came into focus, the patches of forest and fields of alfalfa and the farms and finally the mountains that surrounded us in the distance all became distinct. We drove past the little town of Deer Park and the tiny town of Clayton and began to climb. Trees grew thick right down to the ditches at the sides of the highway.

Jen warned me again that even though it had been two years since her brother got killed, her dad still broke down about it sometimes. I told her that of the few things in the world I thought I understood really well, I understood best of all crying about people you loved who'd died.

We climbed a steep, rocky ridge and finally crested it.

"Well," Jen said, "there it is: the Chewelah Valley." She turned her head and yelled out the window. "Smokey, Eugene! We're almost home, you guys!"

Below us the road ran straight through green fields to a little town in the distance, then into the mountains that closed in tight all around. Blue-gray smoke rose from a mill in a thin cloud, like a piece of slate, that covered the whole valley like a lid.

"It's always the same," Jen said, as she rode the brake a little down the grade. "It always looks the same, it always feels the same, and it always smells the same. A little more alfalfa smell in spring, cut hay in summer, a little more wood smoke in fall, and you can kinda smell the snow in winter. But it's always the same."

We passed the mill, slowed down at the Reduce Speed sign, then turned at the blinking traffic light, the only one in town. "There's Chewelah High," Jen said, tilting her head at an old three-story brick building coming up on my side of the road.

"Old Chewelah High," I said. "I'm an honorary member of the freshman class, you know."

"I know you are," Jen said. "I've seen your beanie." We passed a few farmhouses and Jen called out the people's names.

We climbed and turned and dipped and then we were in a tiny grassy valley. A stream ran down out of the woods under a little wooden bridge. The house at the valley's head was modest, a two-story wooden house with a tin roof, like a lot of the farmhouses we'd passed. Next to the barn was a big corral.

"Here we are," Jen said as we bounced over the bridge, then over the cattle guard and through the open gate. She walked Smokey and Eugene out of the trailer, and they kicked up their heels and ran into the woods. She pointed to where I should back the trailer, and as I was looking around a stumpy cowboy walked toward us from the house. I backed till I felt the trailer nudge the fence, then I popped out and extended my hand to Jen's dad. He was the classic cowboy—big chest, bowed legs, an open face weathered and wrinkled from the sun.

"I'm Karl Russell," I said.

"Hello, Russ," he said as we shook. "I'm Sam Haskell."

"Hi, Daddy!" Jen said, giving Sam a hug.

"Hello, Jennie," Sam said, as he gave her a couple pats on the back exactly like I'd watched Jen pat her horses.

Barbara, Jen's mom, was fixing breakfast. While Jen helped her and Sam listened to the radio news, I wandered around the first floor.

I looked at photos of Jen and her brother on the wall of the living room. Sam Jr. looked like a younger version of his dad. He had that big, smiling, open face and his hair cut was right down to his skull.

After breakfast I walked out with Sam to look at the new little horses. "We've only had two bad ones this spring," Sam said, as we stopped at the stall of a foal that looked fine to me. "We'll sell little Hubert Humphrey here come summer. And this one here," he said at the next stall, "we'll be getting rid of him too."

"What's his name?" I asked.

"We just call him Blackie," Sam said. "I was gonna call 'im Bobby Kennedy, but I decided I'd have to reserve judgment there. Bobby may not be all style like his brother was."

"I don't know," I said. "I've been kinda busy with school and I haven't followed the primaries."

"You play tennis, I guess," Sam said.

"No," I said. "That was Charley, the other boyfriend. I was a baseball player. Before I hurt my arm."

There were a few seconds of awkward silence.

Later I was standing by the fridge peeling carrots onto a newspaper when I noticed a note on the fridge under a magnetic red-winged blackbird. It said, "Jennie and Karl for breakfast Friday." It struck me as so sweet, and just the kind of thing a real family would do, the kind of thing my mom would have done. All of a sudden I was overcome with the knowledge that I wasn't part of a real family. Living with a bunch of guys was fine, but it wasn't anything like a real family.

I lifted my head and saw Jen looking at me. She walked over and asked what was wrong. I pointed to the note and Jen smiled at it before she took it down, crumpled it up, and dropped it in the cold firebox of the woodburner.

After lunch Sam and I went out for a ride. He was patient as he showed me how to saddle my horse, whose name was General Eisenhower. When I finally swung up in the saddle and we got the stirrups adjusted, Sam looked up at me and said, "Old Ike's not gonna have any surprises for ya. You just hang on an' get the feel of it. You could fall asleep up there, an' old Ike'd bring ya home."

Ike and I both did okay as we rode slowly up out of the valley. He put his feet in all the right places. It was real steep in spots, and I had to grab the saddlehorn to stay on. I got whacked in the side of the head with a branch once, but that was the extent of the trauma. I rode a little behind Sam's shoulder. There was nothing to see in any direction but trees, mountains, and sky.

Sam told me that both Jen and Sam Jr. had ridden before they could walk. "They'd yell and bawl and holler when you'd take 'em out of the saddle," he said. "Sometimes they'd go to sleep and fall off. We got to tyin' 'em to the saddle then."

I told him Dad used to tie me behind him on the Harley.

We got to a low spot where a spring came up. The horses' feet made sucking sounds as they popped out of the mud. Ike bent down to eat some bright green grass, and I couldn't get his head back up. Sam rode back and grabbed his mane and jerked him up, and we were off again.

"My boy was real good with horses," Sam said. "He got to rodeoin' and turned professional when he was still in high school." His face was shaded under his gray, sweat-stained hat. He looked okay.

"I lost my folks when I was fifteen," I said. "And my little brother. They were driving that stretch between Deer Park and Spokane and a drunk hit 'em."

"Bull killed Sam," he said. "A bull won't usually fall, but this bull fell on Sam. Crushed his chest."

We rode along up a little hill. In the meadow below us lay a tumbledown house and barn with rows of apple trees behind them. Grass grew tall everywhere. We rode down by the house. It was just old gray, weathered boards in a heap. There was a little of the roof left. Sam pulled up. "I was born in this house," he said. "My mother planted those trees."

He gave his horse a little kick and we moved out slowly through the grass. "Ya know," Sam said as he looked straight ahead, "a guy loves his folks and he never forgets 'em. But they fade in your memory after a while. I'll always love my wife, and I'll always love my daughters. But I'll see my boy's face just like it was till the day I die."

I couldn't imagine Mom and Dad and Jesse ever fading from my memory.

We got back in time to see Jen get bucked off a squatty, chestnut-colored horse with either fear or meanness in his eyes. Jen got up, rubbed her side, walked over to the horse, held him still by his mane, and punched him right above the nostrils with her fist. "Goddamn you, horse!" she said.

"Jennie's got a way with animals," Sam said as he walked by me to the house.

Jen swung slowly into the saddle, her mom holding the horse's head. Nothing happened for a second or two after her mom let go. But then he kicked his back legs out and started to run and kick. He didn't buck like a bucking bronco in a rodeo, just ran around and kicked and dipped his head and kind of twisted like he was nuts or scared. He stumbled and went down on his side, and my heart jumped. But Jen pushed off as he was falling and landed easy on her side. She was up before the horse and kicked him in the rear. "You are the stupidest horse I've ever seen!" she yelled.

Jen and her mom both held his head this time, and Jen rubbed his nose and whispered something to him. He was a little less crazy when Mrs. Haskell let him go. Jen stayed on until about all he did was dip his head and kick his back legs a little. She rode him over to where I sat on the fence.

"You're great!" I said.

"I'm not so great," Jen replied. "I've been getting on and off this horse since right after you and Daddy left."

She got down and took off the saddle and dropped it in the dirt. As she took off the bridle the horse went running and kicking around the corral. Jen climbed the fence and sat beside me. "I'm sad," she said. "I wanted you to see me do what I do best."

"Jesus, Jen," I said, "you did beautiful. I was especially impressed with your right cross."

"That goddamn horse," Jen said.

In the evening Jen was helping her mom in the kitchen and I was watching the TV news with Sam. One of our nuclear subs was missing in the South Atlantic, the UN voted to blockade Rhodesia, and we still hadn't cleared the Vietcong out of Saigon. Robert Kennedy was going to debate Eugene McCarthy in California after losing to him in the Oregon primary.

Sam lifted his hat and ran his hand over his eighth-inch of gray hair. "Good God, boy," he said. "How'd ya like to raise children in this world today? I'm glad Jennie's about grown up."

"I don't remember the fifties being all that peaceful, Sam," I said. "I still have dreams about the Russians bombing us."

"Goddamn Russians still *might* bomb us!" Sam said. "*And* the Chinese *and* the Vietcong *and* the Black Panthers—"

"And the hippies, Daddy!" Jen yelled from the kitchen. "Don't forget the hippies."

"*And* the hippies!" Sam said. He put his hat back on and smiled at the TV.

Jen and I walked along the creek after supper, then when it got dark we sat in the porch swing. We heard crickets and frogs and night birds from out in the dark and Carol Burnett from the TV in the living room.

"We won't be able to make love tonight," Jen said. "We'd have to sneak, and I'd hate to do that."

"We don't have to make love tonight," I said.

"As soon as we get out of sight in the morning we'll find a spot to pull off and you can have me in the woods!" she whispered in my ear.

I didn't get to have Jen in the woods. I didn't get to have her anywhere—at least not that morning—because I fell asleep. I fell asleep, and woke up at a Canadian border crossing.

I listened to the border guard and looked around. When we pulled out I focused my most dumbfounded expression on Jen.

"Don't be mad, Russ!" she said. "I got to thinking how long we're gonna be apart and I wanted you to see where I'd be working so you'd know where to think of me. I didn't want to wake you. Don't be mad!"

"I'm not mad," I said. The country was beautiful. High, rugged mountains rose all around us and in the distance to the north lay even higher ones with a rim of snow. We were headed for the heart of the Canadian Rockies. We followed the Bull River to Fort Steele. A couple miles northeast of Fort Steele, Jen pulled off the road.

"This is it," she said. She pointed across the road where a big wooden sign above a huge country mailbox said TOP OF THE WORLD RANCH. "This is where I'll be from next Thursday till the end of August. I'll be leading pack trips into those mountains, rounding up cattle and horses, branding, breaking, teaching kids to ride." She swung her hand at the alfalfa fields on both sides of the road. "And if I'm really unlucky," she said, "I'll be putting up this hay when they cut it."

We spent two nights in British Columbia camp grounds and had a great time. We made love in a hot spring, proving to Jen that it can, in fact, be done in water. The drive home, though, wasn't barrels of fun. Nothing bad happened; it was just that we'd both realized this was the last weekend we'd have together for a long time. It settled on us like bad weather, and neither of us said much. Every few miles I'd look over at Jen, and she'd be looking at me too.

We pulled in here to Jen's this afternoon about one. I wanted to turn things around a little for us, so I dropped her off, drove to the house, and got the Rio poster and book of photographs Bolão had given me and made it back before Jen had finished unpacking.

I held up the rolled poster and the little book. "Now I'm gonna show you where I'll be this summer," I said.

We walked out to the porch and I sat in the big chair and Jen sat on my lap. We went through the photos in the Rio de Janeiro book. We saw Guanabara Bay, just a little deeper blue than the sky, with all the green mountains in the misty distance, the old colonial build-ings in downtown Rio right next to modern skyscrapers, the wide beach sidewalks made of little colored rocks set in swirl patterns, and the Yacht Club.

"I refuse to think of you going out on any yachts," Jen said.

"I'm not goin' out on any yachts," I replied.

We saw Sugarloaf, the gigantic rock mountain that surges up out of the bay. We saw the Botanical Gardens and the beautiful girls sunning on Ipanema beach. We saw dancers from the samba school dressed in their costumes—men and women all about three-quarters naked—dancing down the street during *Carnavál*.

"That looks like fun," Jen said.

"No need to imagine me there," I said. "*Carnavál*'s in February, and I'll be home in August."

And then I unrolled my poster of Christ the Redeemer, the statue that stands hundreds of feet tall on Corcovado mountain above the city.

"Looks like you'll be in good hands down there," Jen said.

I did feel like Christ was welcoming me with His kind face and His arms stretched wide.

Jen put her head on my shoulder and gave me a little kiss on the neck. "I *will* be thinking of you in Rio," she said.

It was cool in that shady corner of the porch and both Jen and I were comfortable in the mildewy old chair. We sat there a long time before we finally got up and went to bed.

Wednesday afternoon, June 5, 1968

In spite of how good things are looking—A— on my World Masterpieces paper, A on my Lit. of the Camps final, and doing pretty well in the Masterpieces final this morning—I'm not feeling so hot. Jen left about a half-hour ago, and there's this hole in my life I can feel getting bigger by the minute.

We had lunch in the truck at the A&W. We didn't say much, and neither of us finished our burgers. Jen had told me before that she didn't want any big sentimental good-byes, just a casual good-bye like she was going back to her place and me to the house on a night I wasn't staying with her.

We looked at each other and down at our unfinished burgers and Jen said, "Well, I guess this is about it."

I gathered up the trash and got out of the truck and walked over to her side. She said she'd drive me by the house, but I said I'd rather walk.

"So long," I said as I turned away. "See ya in three months."

"Come here, you turd," Jen said. "I don't want *that* casual a good-bye."

I stepped back to the window and Jen kissed me a quick one on the mouth. "So long, Russ," she said. "I'll be thinking of ya."

She hung her arm out the window and waved just her fingers until she rounded the curve and passed out of sight behind the motel.

I know how to fix holes in your life—you fill them up with action. But I can't get myself to do anything. I don't even feel like running. I don't even feel like writing anymore about how shitty I feel.

I just watched Robert Kennedy get shot. I can't believe it.

I feel like talking to somebody, but I'm the only one in the house. I turned on TV, and there was Kennedy giving his victory speech. I have contempt for most politicians because they never seem capable of acting naturally. Everything most of those assholes do is in order to make themselves seem perfect in the eyes of people so stupid it shouldn't matter what they think. But Kennedy didn't seem like that. He acted like somebody you might be friends with. He gave his little speech, he walked through the kitchen, and some asshole shot him.

They haven't said he's dead, but it's hard to believe he'll pull through. John Kennedy, Martin Luther King, and now Robert Kennedy—this hasn't been a decade where the good guys make it.

Friday evening, June 7, 1968

I got straight A's this quarter!!! Me! A FOUR-POINT-OH!!! I checked my grade on the History final this afternoon, and I got a 98.

I was amazed I'd done that well, because I stayed up almost the whole night before. Mac came back to the house right after he saw Kennedy get shot. We watched TV until they said Kennedy was dead, then we went out and ran until we couldn't run anymore.

I miss Jen, but I can already feel the hole in my life closing. I'm not going to let it close completely, but I am going to fill it with a lot of new experiences. I want to stay the same, but I plan to change in a lot of ways too. I'm coming back from Rio speaking fluent Portugese, I'm going to change my major to History, and I'm going to try to get straight A's again fall quarter.

When I saw that A beside my name on the grade sheet taped to the door of the History classroom, I felt like running and kicking up my heels, like Smokey and Eugene McCarthy when Jen let them loose. I started walking, and when I got to the stadium and saw all that green wheat behind it making the world look like nothing but green wheat and blue sky, I took off my tennies and my shirt and walked out in it. I walked and walked and didn't hear a sound but the wind through the wheat. On a big, rounded hill I lay on my back and looked up. It was just the green stalks of wheat and the blue sky, not even a white cloud.

Then I began hearing a far-off rumble. It got louder and louder until the ground began to shake. I'd never felt an earthquake, and I wondered if that was what it was.

Then I saw it. It was a B-52 bomber painted flat black, flying on a line right between my eyes, making its approach to Fairchild Air Force Base. I knew it was hundreds of feet off the ground and couldn't hurt me. But the goddamn thing was so loud and so awesome and it shook the ground so hard that I fell back into the wheat. As it flew over me I could make out the little spots where the black had flaked off and the silver showed through, and I could feel the blast of heat from the engines.

I lay there quite a while after the heat went away and the ground stopped shaking and the roar finally died in the distance. I thought of the guys who flew the bomber and dropped the bombs, and the Vietcong guys they dropped the bombs on, and I was glad I wasn't any of them.

Part II

THE GOING HENCE

Early morning, Tuesday, June 11, 1968

Out my window I'm watching the sunrise, and it's an awesome sight. The ocean is gray and the sky is gray except high in the east, where it's pale blue above black clouds piled like mountains on the horizon. The jagged tops of the clouds are outlined in violet-blues and reds so fierce and hot they're sizzling. They're burning like an acetylene flame when you run the oxygen to it. It looks like somebody's welding something behind that huge, black bank of clouds.

I'm on what they call a "stretched" 727—it's stretched so they can get more passengers on these overseas flights, I guess—and my seat's so narrow I have to keep my shoulders shrugged and my arms folded in my lap just to fit it. There's a group of Brazilian kids on the plane headed home after a trip to Disneyland, and for the first few hours I felt like a prisoner of the Mickey Mouse Club. They were running up the aisles with their ears on, climbing over seats, singing, throwing stuff. They settled down when the stewardesses brought dinner, which I refused because I was afraid food would be all it would take to make me sick.

As everybody was eating and I was looking out the window watching the sky get dark, I thought of the Jews in the boxcars on their way to the camps, packed in with no ventilation in the cold of winter and the heat of summer, holding their kids up so they wouldn't have to wade in the shit and pee all over the floor, watching the old and the sick die and slip down out of sight, hoping the ordeal would be over when they got where they were going, but probably knowing that would be when the final ordeal really started. What a pussy you are, I said to myself. You haven't got a clue about discomfort. I told myself I should be ashamed.

I slept quite a while, and when I woke up I washed my face and brushed my teeth and felt fine. It was a little eerie walking through the dark plane full of silent, curled shapes. I sat down and looked out the window at the stars. You didn't have to look up to see them. You could just look straight out and see plenty. It felt like we were closer to the stars than we were to the earth. I looked for groups of three stars in pyramid shapes and saw a load of them. I looked at the stars until the darkness started fading into gray. Then I began this journal entry.

The stewardesses just now turned on the lights and about everyone is up. The kids are subdued. I'm feeling great but starved. I see the breakfast cart headed down the aisle, so I'll close now and pull down my tray.

Tuesday midnight

I'm sitting on the patio of the Copacabana Palace Hotel. Even though it's late, quite a few people are out around the pool and walking on the sidewalk that parallels the beach. I've already been told by the guys at the desk not to go out on the beach at night. I went for a walk on the sidewalk, though. It's funny: those mosaic sidewalks that are so beautiful in the posters are smeared with dog shit in real life.

The ocean's a long way out there across the sand in this part of town. When there was a lull in the traffic on Avenida Atlantica, I could just barely hear the surf breaking out in the dark like a distant naval barrage in an old war movie.

Avenida Atlantica is three lanes in both directions with a grassy stretch between. You've got to run maybe thirty yards to make the grass, and I barely made it through the crazy Brazilian drivers. I believe they actually tried to run me down.

I may not be in the best of humors tonight. Bolão never showed up at the airport. I couldn't have missed him, because the Rio airport is smaller than Spokane's—it's only got three gates—and I stuck around for over two hours. He'd told me one of his friends or someone in his family would pick me up if he couldn't, so I never got his phone number or his address and I couldn't call his house. Jesus, was that stupid! I tried to look his father up in the phone book, but there are hundreds of Portos in Rio. Porto here makes Smith seem exotic back home.

Bolão told me he lived near the American School, and I just now got hold of a city map and found out from the guys at the desk where it is. The map's on one side of me and my notebook's on the other. I'm situated under good light, and if the fucking insects don't devour me first—after I get another *Cuba Libre,* which is what they call rum and Coke here—I'm going to start taking down street names in the neighborhood of the American School and matching them to Portos.

Actually, I'm kind of having fun. This hotel is expensive, but I've got plenty of dough and my return ticket, so I can just go home if it looks like I'm going to be here all alone for some reason.

Wednesday night, June 12, 1968

What a day! If I'd read this day in a book, I'd say the author was stretching things. It's the same feeling I had when Mom and Dad and Jesse died, only less intense. You know it happened, but it doesn't *feel* like it could have.

Bolão's dead. I was all happy to have found his house so easily, then I learned he was dead. His parents got the call from the States last night. He and Felicity were shot to death. Somebody found them in a car in the woods outside Cheney.

I knew who did it the second his sister Márcia told me. She led me to her dad, who was sitting in his den on the second floor looking out a big window into the lush, green forest in back of their house.

Márcia introduced us, and I said I was sorry to interrupt him. He was gracious and told me Carlos Henrique (I'd almost forgotten Bolão's real name) had talked about me in his letters and that they'd looked forward to my visit. I said I was sure I knew who shot Bolão and asked if he would help me make a call to Spokane.

He got me the operator for the States and I got Donnie's folks' number and the number of the Spokane police.

It was around 4 a.m. in Spokane, and Mrs. Davis answered the phone. When she said Donnie was still out in Cheney, my heart started to jump. Donnie's dad came on and I told him where I was and how I'd found out about Bolão and Felicity. I said I was sure I knew who did it, and that there was a chance the guy could be looking for Don. I told him he'd better get hold of Donnie as fast as he could and tell him what had happened and have him tell the police about the crazy guy with the guns who lives down by the river in Peaceful Valley. He said he'd call Donnie in the dorm, then get right out there.

The operator got me the police then, and I told a detective everything I could think of. It sounded pretty crazy, me being in Brazil. I told him where I was staying and gave him the Portos' number too. I told him I thought Johnny was really, really dangerous, and he thanked me.

Senhor Porto asked me to stay for lunch, but I declined. He told me he wanted me to feel like a son in his house. I thanked him and said I'd come back.

Márcia told me not to feel alone in Rio, that she'd call at the hotel soon and introduce me to the city. Then she shook my hand and hurried back up the path.

As I was turning to leave I saw a little boy, maybe ten, standing, maybe hiding, in the bushes near the swimming pool. He was slim and dark, and as beautiful a physical specimen as Bolão and Márcia. He wore a red, green, and black striped soccer shirt with a club patch on the breast like one Bolão had. I waved to him. "*Eu sou dos Estados Unidos,*" I said. "*Sou amigo de seu irmão.*"

The glazed expression never left his face. He just sank back a little farther into the bushes.

I wasn't sure how to use the past tense, so "I'm a friend of your brother" was the only way I could say it. As I walked away down the street, I wished I hadn't said anything at all.

The Portos live back against the forested mountains in the mostly rich, mostly residential southwestern section of the city. And it was only as I walked through the streets of the neighborhood where Bolão had grown up that I thought directly of him, and how he'd never sing another song or say, "You bet your shoes, man!" He'd never flex his fingers around the steering wheel of a car, never lose himself in a good book and forget about the world. Never again would he hear the voices of people he loved call his name. I wondered how scared Bolão had been, and I wondered if it hurt or if it was just like having your light turned out with a little click. If I were looking at a guy about to shoot me, I'd be scared. I'd try to go out like the straight-backed old man, but I'd be terrified. I wondered if Bolão'd been fucking Felicity in the woods or if she'd been taking him to the airport when Johnny waylaid them. None of it mattered—I just wondered, was all.

I looked at the people I passed, and at the buildings and into the store windows and up at the signs and all around at the cars, but I didn't register much. I walked east through Gávea into Leblon along a canal with a couple feet of filthy water in it until I wound up where the beach meets the rock mountains rising up out of the ocean. I crossed the street and walked north on the sidewalk next to the sand through Leblon and into Ipanema.

I walked through Ipanema into Copacabana, where the little houses end and the high-rise apartments begin, then to the end of Copacabana beach, where I climbed the rocks and sat awhile and watched the surfers. Bolão had said they'd be there, and they were.

I knew I needed a plan, but I didn't feel like making one.

Back at the hotel I took a shower, then a nap, and slept through suppertime. I'd been writing this stuff and was about to quit and take another shower and go out looking for an open restaurant when Márcia called just now and said she was on her way and for me not to eat one bite of anything.

It's clear that the Portos feel responsible for me being here. And it's clear that the thing for me to do is let them off that hook, since they've got a lot more important things than me to think about. I should head back home.

I've got a plan now, thanks to the very gracious Márcia Porto.

Márcia walked into the lobby a few minutes to eleven last night. She asked me what I felt like eating, and I looked out the open doors in the direction of the ocean and told her I wouldn't be surprised if they had decent seafood somewhere in the neighborhood.

"I know for a fact they do," Márcia replied, in English I think is going to prove better than mine.

We walked south along Avenida Atlantica towards Ipanema until we came to a restaurant where quite a few people were sitting outside at umbrella tables. All the umbrellas were green and had "Chopp Antarctica" written on them in white. I asked Márcia if that meant people were supposed to go to Antarctica to shop, and she told me "Antarctica" was a brand name and "chopp" was draft beer.

"Bolão wrote us you were a joker," Márcia said. "He said you were the quintessential American."

"Quintessential?" I said. (I looked it up the minute I got back to the hotel.)

We took a table and sat across from one another. People wear their clothes funny here. Everything looks way too small, but still it fits in the right places. Márcia's T-shirt, for example. It looked too small in the sleeves and it was so short at the bottom you could see her belly button every time she raised her shoulders. She had the three neck buttons undone and you could see down her front to below the level of her nipples. But you couldn't see any tan line. I resolved not to stare at her, but it was tough, because Márcia's breasts are an anatomical wonder. I don't see how thin girls can have such big breasts.

I could only read about four words on the menu, so Márcia helped me order. She didn't know the English names of some of the fish, but she described one with big bones, so I ordered that and it tasted good and was easy to eat.

Her uncle, who's a lawyer in San Francisco, is bringing Bolão home, she said. The funeral will be Friday, and she asked me to attend. She asked if "the girl"—Felicity—had been Bolão's girlfriend, and I told her no, that she was just a friend. She asked about the guy who shot them, and I told her about Johnny.

"God, what a vicious fucking place the United States is," Márcia said. She put down her wine glass and shivered. "They kill everybody!" she said.

"We're a real bad-looking bunch to the rest of the world, I suppose," I said. "And we don't look all that great to me either. It's a huge country, Márcia. Plenty of room for lots of sickos with nothing to fill their lives but hatred."

A Brazilian girl who can call the U.S. "a vicious fucking country" knows her American English pretty well, so I asked Márcia where she learned hers and she said both she and her little brother Flavio went to the American School.

"You go to the American School?" I said. "I thought it was a high school."

"It is," Márcia said. "I'm a sophomore."

Good Lord, I said to myself. I'm not just in another country, I'm on another planet. I'd thought Márcia was older than I am.

"You look older to me," I said.

Márcia smiled.

As we ate our steamed fish and vegetables and drank our cold white wine, Márcia told me she and her dad had a proposal. They proposed, she said, that I spend my vacation in Rio as had been planned. That I come stay with them or, if I preferred, rent a little furnished apartment in Ipanema or Leblon. That I enroll in a Portuguese class and buy some Brazilian clothes and put my baggy American stuff back in my suitcase. That I ride the busses, attend *futebol* games, go to the beach in the mornings, have my *cafézinho* standing next to the people at the counter in my neighborhood bar, listen to the radio, get a Brazilian girlfriend and, above all, flee when I see anybody looking even slightly American coming in my direction.

"Well," Márcia asked when she'd finished, "what do you think, Karl?"

What I thought was, how amazingly gracious of these people at a time like this in their lives. "I accept all of it but the offer to stay at your place," I said. "I can't impose like that. But I will take some help finding an apartment. I can probably read the ads, but I don't think I can talk to the people."

"No problem," Márcia said. "There's an English-language newspaper called the *Brazil Herald* that has lots of apartment ads. If the people you call don't speak English, I'll translate."

"Great," I said. "Thank you very much."

"My father wants you to feel like a son in his house," Márcia said. Her composure was starting to go. You could see it draining from her face.

"This is very, very good of you and your family," I said.

Márcia wanted to pay, but I refused absolutely. As we walked to the curb I thanked her for her kindness and she thanked me for dinner. She said she'd call, then shook my hand and climbed into a little square VW taxi.

I thought about taking a bus back to the hotel—they run all night—but as I walked along I got to liking the feel of the sea air on my skin and the sound of Portuguese being spoken around me and the sensation of being just another *carioca* walking home after a late supper with a friend.

And I really liked the music that came from everywhere. From a little transistor a black girl held as she leaned on the fender of her boyfriend's taxi, from apartment windows above me, from guys tapping their hands on the roof of a car and singing. It wasn't all the same song, of course, but it was all Brazilian music—it all had that samba beat Bolão introduced me to.

As I walked and listened and looked around, I realized a lot of people were dancing. Right out on the streets. Not with each other so much—just men and women alone or in groups. The streets were *alive* with music. The whole night was alive with it.

I didn't know how to think of Bolão. I've had a lot of practice trying to create an attitude about death I can live with. Ha, ha. But I can't imagine a better place than this earth, and I can't imagine a better condition than being alive.

Friday night, June 14, 1968

It's a cool night in Rio and I'm back in my hotel room after what feels like a long day. It's winter here, which they say means rain, and I got my first taste of it this afternoon. The window's open right in front of me at the little desk here, and you can still smell the rain and feel it in the breeze.

I took a bus to Gávea and walked the mile or so up into the hills to the Portos'. The sky had been getting darker and heavier all day and I'd passed lots of guys sitting on their haunches selling umbrellas spread on blankets on the sidewalk beside them. But I guess I thought I was in paradise or someplace where it couldn't possibly rain on me.

I was about halfway up the mountain when the storm hit. The thunder scared me at first because it sounded like the treetops were exploding, and when I went to steady myself against the masonry wall that runs all along the sidewalk there, I could feel the vibrations go through it into my hand. The wind blew up then, and a shower of thick, waxy leaves and little branches fell a second or two before the rain swept in. It sliced down in diagonal waves, and the wind would bend the waves in arcs like a curtain blowing. It rained so hard it hurt you when it hit.

I was headed around to the Portos' back door when Márcia saw me trot by. She was dressed in black, with a lacy black scarf over her head. She got an umbrella and took me around through the kitchen and up to Bolão's room, where she told me to put on some dry clothes.

Bolão had plenty of stuff to wear, but all the shirts were too small and the pants too short and none of the coats would quite button. Bolão had his own bathroom and I was in it, standing in front of the mirror tying one of his ties when I heard the bedroom door open. In the mirror I saw his mom walk in. I recognized her from the photo he'd kept on his desk in our study room. She was dressed like Márcia and she looked like Márcia except for a hollowness in her face. I didn't want her to see me in her son's clothes.

I watched in the mirror as she walked over to the bed and picked up the pillow and pressed it to her face. You could see her chest expand with the deep breaths she was taking. She took one last sniff of the pillow, set it back at the head of the bed, and ran both hands across it until the white cotton pillowcase was perfectly smooth, then she walked out and closed the door behind her.

I waited a minute, then went downstairs through the houseful of people. The storm was still right on top of us. The thunder sounded like it was rolling across the roof. There was a little tinkling of glass coming from all over the house, and I couldn't imagine what it was until I looked up and saw the chandeliers swaying.

I followed a stream of people into a darkened room where hundreds of candles were burning. At the front of the room lay a closed casket and on top of it sat a gold-framed photo of Bolão. I was headed out the door when the Porto family moved into the doorway, so I walked to the back and took a seat.

It was real dark back where I was because most of the candles were up around the casket. I sat through it all back there in the dark. It looked like a primitive ritual in the flickering candlelight, with the silhouettes of the casket and the priest and the mourners seeming such a long way off. I thought about all of us there committing Bolão to eternity.

I tried to focus my thoughts on God and Jesus and heaven the way I'd learned in Sunday school when I was a kid. In the past few months I've read the Bible and thought more about those things than I ever have before in my life—even more than just after Mom and Dad and Jesse were killed—and it came as kind of a surprise to me as I sat there that I didn't believe a word of that old shit. It's not so much that I didn't believe it, as it just didn't mean anything. I couldn't get a clear image in my mind of anything comforting or a clear feeling anywhere inside me about those things. The glow of the candles and the black moving shadows and the voice of the priest in a language I didn't even understand were so much more real to me. I even think I felt something like comfort as I let it all wash over me.

They took Bolão to an old, old cemetery in Botafogo, the district just northwest of Copacabana. The cemetery is surrounded on three sides by apartments and on the fourth side a huge black rock mountain rises up. The people are buried inside concrete or stone vaults with the names of their families over doors that lead down into the ground. The place is full of old, blackened ironwork and blackened statues as well as bright, fresh flowers and literally thousands of burning candles.

The Porto family vault was one of those built right into the rock mountain, so as we watched Bolão's casket go down the steps and through the door, all we saw as background was old black rock. Not a snatch of blue sky, no cloud, none of the flowers that were all around in back of us to see if we only turned our heads a little. All you saw was that old black rock, so thick and so dense you didn't like thinking about it. It made you hope eternity wasn't like that.

When it was over, though, and we all turned to head for the cars, the mountain not too far in the distance in that direction shone like an island in the golden sunset. It was Corcovado, and there on top was the huge statue of Christ the Redeemer high up in the now cloudless sky with his arms outstretched and golden sunlight like a halo radiating all around him.

As we walked out people were pointing up there, and I could tell they were saying how beautiful it was. Some of them were probably saying it was a sign. I'm not going to say it wasn't. It was a beautiful sight, and it moved me.

I took off Bolão's tie as I walked home, and unbuttoned his shirt a couple buttons. I studied myself in the store windows as I walked by and thought I looked pretty Brazilian. Even for a Brazilian everything I was wearing was way too small, but at least it all had that tight look. Even my hair looked kind of Brazilian. It's curling over my collar now like Bolão's did.

Tomorrow, before I go to lunch at the Portos', I'm going to shop for clothes.

Here I am in my new apartment. It was the first one I looked at, but it was perfect, so I jumped at it. It's *completely* furnished—dishes, sheets, towels, even a radio. I've got two bedrooms, a big living room, a decent-sized kitchen, and a bathroom with a tub-shower combination and a bidet, which I've discovered is great for washing your butt when you don't want to take a whole shower. Since it's beginning to look like I'll have diarrhea for the duration of my stay here, a facility for quick butt washing will be a real boon.

I didn't even know what a bidet was until about two hours ago. The first one I ever saw in my life was the one in the bathroom at the hotel, and I thought it was a urinal or something to wash your feet in.

Senhor Porto didn't think the rent was too bad for Ipanema, even though I'm five blocks off the beach back against the mountain where the *favelados* walk up the hill to the *favela*. It's CR$2.000 a month, which works out to about 400 bucks. I think it's outrageous, but that's the going rate here. I said the *favelados* didn't bother me (they aren't all black, only about 98 percent) because I didn't feel any of the hatred I'd feel back home if I lived on the edge of a black ghetto. He said there *was* prejudice in Brazil, but not much hatred yet, though that would come if the poor ever realized a better life was possible for them. But just because the *favelados* didn't hate me, he said, didn't mean they wouldn't steal my money.

I've left all my American clothes, except my jeans and the EWSC T-shirts I brought to trade, in my suitcase under the single bed in the second bedroom. I hung up my new Brazilian-collared shirts and pants on wooden hangers in the big wooden standing closet my landlady, Senhora Schächter, called an *armoire*, and I've put my other new clothes in the chest of drawers.

None of the pants here—except the American jeans that cost about twenty-five bucks—have back pockets! This is a problem I'm going to have to solve in some way other than the Brazilian, because I'm not about to dangle a little purse from a strap around my wrist like the rest of the guys here. These guys go through a lot of what I consider degradation and physical discomfort just to present women with a smooth, tightly wrapped set of buns. I do look fetching, though, I have to admit it. I wish Jen could see me.

Tomorrow morning I'll take a bus downtown to the Federal University and see about a Portuguese class, and on the way back I'll stop at the bookstore I spotted just a couple blocks from here and see if they have any books in English so I can have something to read besides the Dartmouth Bible and my dictionary.

I think I'm going to be happy in my little place. My street—Rua Nascimento Silva—is lined with big trees and there's plenty of little kids and dogs. Out my living-room windows I see the mountains and out the bedroom windows I look down into the backyard of an autobody shop. At the north end of my block is Montenegro Street, and I can walk down it and be on the hippest beach in Rio in about five minutes.

I'm excited about being here, excited about all the things I can learn and take home with me.

Monday evening, June 17, 1968

Quite a number of surprises today.

Surprise No. 1: Had the alarm set for 5:30, but woke up before it rang. Had no idea what to expect when I turned on the radio hoping for some music that would get the day off to a flying start. It's an old tube radio, a Bosch, and it crackled a little, and then this unmistakably rock-jock voice booms out of it screaming, "Moon-dee-owwwwww!" On my way downtown later I saw a billboard advertising Mundial—Radio 91.

The first song the guy played was "Here Comes the Sun." He said something in Portuguese, then he said, "Da-Bee-tawls—'Ere Come dee Sun.'" Then he screamed, "Moon-dee-owwwww!" again.

I felt like I was home. I pulled on my shorts and my old Arizona State Baseball T-shirt, laced up my runners, hid my key on top of the door jamb, and started my run.

I ran down Montenegro past the bar A Garota de Ipanema to the beach. All the stores were still closed, the iron gratings pulled down over the windows and padlocked to hasps buried in the sidewalk. The little bar-restaurants were just opening up, though, and as I ran past them I was caught for a few yards in that beautiful first-coffee-of-the-morning smell. I ran by one guy who was pouring his big pitcher of boiling water over the bag of coffee in the huge stainless-steel coffee urn. I gave him a wave and he waved back and yelled something to me.

About three steps through the fine white beach sand made me realize my tennies would have to come off. I tied the laces together and draped them around my neck, ran to the edge of the water where the sand was wet and firm, then turned south. I ran all the way down to the rocks at the end of Leblon, then headed back north. It was a beautiful morning, clear and warm. If this is winter here, summer must really be something. A few guys fishing in the surf responded to my *"Bom dia"* with a nod or a verbal greeting. Back near Montenegro, since there was no one close enough to hear my childishness, I came out with a big "Moon-dee-owwwww!" as I sprinted across my imaginary finish line.

Surprise No. 2: In the side streets a few blocks south of Montenegro, I saw people unloading fruits and vegetables from old Chevy and International trucks and setting the stuff up in wooden stalls lining the street. It was a public market. The produce was luscious. The avocados were big as pineapples and some of the pineapples were big as watermelons. The bananas were tiny, though, fat little yellow things hanging in great bunches from the tops of the stalls.

On one block the stalls were all for seafood. Lying in the ice chips were fish that I'd only seen in books—sharks two feet long and big, ugly greenish-brown fish with barnacles all over them and mouths like nasty bulldogs' mouths. Men and women were skinning and filleting to beat the band.

I figured to buy some fruit and maybe some fish when I got back from school. I didn't make it in time, though. When I got back with my little nylon-net shopping bag like the other Brazilians, the vendors were tearing everything down. Leaves, peelings, smashed fruit, smashed vegetables, and a few small squished fish lay over the street mixing with the water from the melted ice—and making the best-smelling and probably the most nutritious garbage a guy could imagine. The stuff running in the gutters looked like a nutrition shake. If they kept the stuff cleaner, they could ship it to Biafra and get those poor people well again. Bodybuilders would fight to get at it. Guys in orange overalls wère scooping it up with big shovels and tossing it into Mercedes garbage trucks.

Surprise No. 3: Had myself squared away for a *"Português para Estrangeiros"* class to begin in two weeks and was walking back across the campus of the Federal University to catch the bus back to the South Zone when I came upon a black guy about my age standing on the raised edge of a concrete fountain addressing a crowd of maybe two hundred young people. He was a ragged-looking guy, and highly agitated. He'd yell and jab his fist in the air and his red T-shirt would ride up and show the ripped-out, fraying white lining of his old black pants. I couldn't understand a word he was saying, but I could see he was moving the people.

I was straining to make out at least a conjunction, and it must have shown in my face because from close to my ear came a quiet voice translating. "'They want to solve *their* inflation problem by closing down *our* university and putting an end to *our* education. It is one thing to devalue our money, but if they continue devaluing our education until we have no more university, they will have devalued our lives.'"

Quite a response erupted from the crowd then, and I turned to see what kind of girl belonged to the feminine voice. She was black. I don't mean black as in off-white or creamy-coffee or brown. When you talk about the color of Betinha's skin you are talking *black*, Jack! And in this case, black *is* beautiful. Betinha I would not call exactly beautiful, but her skin I would. She looks oiled and hand-rubbed. The way her veins stand out reminds you of the grain in wood.

The guy jumped down then, and the crowd began breaking up. The girl kept clapping after almost everyone else had stopped. When she finished I thanked her for translating for me. "You're an American!" she said in her strong Brazilian accent. She looked me up and down. "I thought you might be Argentine because of your clothes. You're of German descent, aren't you?"

"No, I'm not," I said. "My name's Karl Russell and my family came from Swedes, Scots, and Irish. Call me Russ." I looked her up and down. "Let me see..." I said. "I bet I can guess the continent your family came from."

She laughed. "I think you might guess right, Roose," she said. I got a kick out of the way she said my name. "My name is Betinha," she said as she shook my hand.

Betinha explained that the students were afraid the government was going to close down the university or make it private so they wouldn't have to support it anymore. I told her I hoped they didn't do it before I had a chance to learn Portuguese.

"I wouldn't mind speaking Portuguese with you if you would speak American English with me," she said.

"American English is the only English I know," I said. "But Jesus, how could you speak any better than you're speaking now?"

"I want to go to graduate school in the States," Betinha said. "In American literature. I want to know the slang, I want to know English as the Americans speak it. Jesus! Blasphemy too!"

It turned out she lived in Ipanema, so we rode the bus home together. I gave my first American English lesson on the way, and it was to tell her that saying "Jesus" wasn't blasphemy. That unless you were a real sicko on religion, you would just call that profanity. Then I had to explain "sicko."

I haven't gotten to the surprise part yet. It wasn't so much meeting Betinha as it was finding out where she lived. When we got off the bus, she walked past Nascimento Silva and up the path to the *favela* on the hill. It probably shouldn't have been so surprising, but she was so impeccably dressed and spoke such excellent English and seemed so well educated and was so self-possessed. A guy hates to admit he'd be surprised about stuff like that.

Surprise No. 4: Bought my little shopping bag on the way to the *feira* from a guy with no legs sitting on a padded piece of plywood with wheels on the bottom. He looked like a bust placed on a cheap stand. He looked like he was *growing* out of the Naugahyde. He was wearing a T-shirt and the top eight or ten inches of a nice pair of pants. I pointed to the stack of yellow nets, said, "*Uma como essa, por favor,*" and the guy wheeled down the line of colors by pushing off the sidewalk with his hands. I noticed then that he was wearing old black leather gloves. And when he held the little net up to me, I saw he had just a *huge* set of arms. A guy would get huge arms pushing himself around on a piece of plywood.

I gave the guy fifty centavos and walked away. It was hard to get the condition of his gloves out of my mind. They were all scuffed and full of holes, and what you could see of his hands through the holes was as scuffed as the gloves. It was hard not to wonder what life would be like pushing yourself around Rio with your hands.

But the guy wasn't the surprise. Later on, I was in the post office buying stamps, and I was thinking about him and what made him want to sell something to earn money instead of just begging like so many other people you see on the streets here. And I was shaking my head trying to get the pictures of him and all those beggars out of my mind when I bumped into somebody. I looked up to say "*Desculpe,*" but when I saw her I couldn't say anything.

It was a wartlady. She was wearing an old wool hat and a heavy coat pulled up to her chin and covering her arms all the way to the gloves on her hands. But her face wasn't covered, and I was looking right down into it. The warts just boiled out of her face. She had a wart that blossomed out between her eyes like a mushroom. She was the one to say "*Desculpe,*" then she lowered her head and scuffed toward the counter. I couldn't help staring after her. I was looking at the dark-brown old-fashioned nylons she was wearing and how the warts on her legs made them poke out all over like they were full of marbles. But a lot of the bumps in her stockings were bigger than marbles.

A nicely dressed woman whapped me on the arm with her purse, said something, then scowled at me. I managed to say "*Desculpe*" to her, but I went on gaping. The wartlady had her shoulders hunched and her head down, but over the collar of her coat you could see the warts hanging from her cheeks and her earlobe like some kind of sick fruit.

I got out on the sidewalk again, with the sun and the noise and the colors, but the only thing that could break through the wartlady's face in my mind was the face of the wartman I'd seen when I was a kid. I concentrated on putting one foot in front of the other so I'd get home. I walked right past the guy on the corner of Montenegro who makes candy by melting brown sugar and mixing it with peanuts in a pot over a charcoal burner. The stuff tastes wonderful and the good smell floats over the street. But all I could think of as I looked down at the nuts in the brown mixture was warts.

Surprise No. 5: Got home and found Senhora Schächter standing on a chair in the kitchen putting some dishes in the cupboard above the sink. She's small and bony and she wears her gray hair in a crew cut. She reminds me of an old boxing trainer. She moved slowly like she was in pain, but she acted cheerful as she told me she'd brought some dishes she thought I might need. Her sweater rode up her arm as she was reaching, and I saw the number tattooed there.

She got down from the chair and looked up into my face and asked if I was feeling well. I said I guessed I was just tired from running around all day. She said if I took a little nap I could run around all night. As she was leaving, she told me to call her Anna.

I did try to take a nap, but it was hopeless. When I closed my eyes I saw wartpeople. It feels a little better to be sitting here at the desk writing.

I just now checked for warts on my head and back for about the zillionth time. I haven't been able to feel anything there and I can't see anything when I hold up a little mirror and look back into the big mirror on the bathroom door. My head's perfectly smooth where the warts were, and all I've got on my side and back where they were are little scars from the stitches. My wrist where they were the first time is perfectly smooth too.

I've got to get out of here and take a little air.

Early Tuesday morning, June 18, 1968

I'm sitting at a table in the Bar Lisboa. This is going to be my bar. It's on Montenegro two blocks from the apartment. It just opened up for the day. The street's quiet and I can hear the coffee still dripping out of the grounds.

I ran the beach in the gray light before dawn. After I showered I couldn't stand the feeling of being alone in the apartment, so I came out and found this place opening up.

Last night I'd gone out walking to give the city a chance to break up my thoughts. I was afraid I'd dream, and I figured if I got really, really tired, maybe I wouldn't. So I started walking. But the more I walked the more I thought about warts and wartpeople. A guy will think some real stupid things when he's scared. I'd begun to wonder if there wasn't a family of wartpeople throughout the world with one member in each city and maybe more than one in big places like Rio and New York. I didn't think they came from space, but it was sort of like the movie *Invasion of the Body Snatchers.* It was *Invasion of the Wartpeople,* and they would look into the eyes of little kids and the kids would grow up and become wartpeople themselves.

In a bookstore I bought a copy of Hemingway's *As Aventuras de Nick Adams,* which at the rate I read Portuguese could take me the rest of my life to finish. And they had paperback copies of all Shakespeare's plays in English, so I bought *King Lear* because it looked like an old friend sitting there on the shelf.

I wandered through Ipanema into Copacabana and through the tunnel into Botafogo. It seemed like there were a million beggars and other down-and-outers, and I couldn't help looking to see if they were wartpeople. If somebody was back in the shadows I hung around a little to get a look, and if they didn't move I walked into the shadows to check them out. What a sick fucker I can become!

Of course I didn't see any wartpeople. Of course I didn't see any fucking wartpeople!!!

They've got Christ the Redeemer lighted at night, and no matter if you're someone like Crookshank who thinks he's got a personal relationship with Him and He's got a plan for your life or any of that shit or if you're someone like me, He's still a beautiful sight. So I walked to where I could get a shot right up into His face, and it brought me to the foot of the mountain by the cemetery where Bolão is. It's dark back there. And the closer I got to the cemetery and the good view of Christ, the more candles I saw burning along the curb. Beside some of them a little bowl of cooked rice would be sitting, or maybe there'd be a picture of a woman with a halo and the smile of a saint. I saw a bunch of candles burning in a circle around a black rooster with his throat cut and dripping blood into a tin can. People were out walking and you could hear music floating from the apartment windows.

Down by the cemetery gate where the light was bright, three figures sat on the sidewalk. The middle one was a *mudado* I'm sure. His arms, instead of bending forward at the elbows, bent backward. And his legs were bent in the middle of his thigh and his calf as well as normally at the knee. All he was wearing was shorts, so you could see the wonders of him in their totality. His face was flat and his head was elongated like he'd spent his early years with his face in a clamp. He reached his twisted arm out to me and his palm came up level with my knee.

I looked down at his hand and into his face. It looked ancient, but his body looked young in spite of how it had been treated. He could have been my age. The guy beside him, who was too young to have been his father, said something to me and reached out his hand too. Then the woman on his other side did the same.

I got out the ten-cruzeiro note I had folded in my change pocket and put it in the *mudado*'s hand. He pulled it back, kind of untwisting it, and rested it at his side again, his fingers pointing backward into the cemetery.

I just wanted to get the fuck out of there, but the man and woman still had their hands out and were all worked up about something. The guy got up, and I stepped back. He saw I was scared, and he reached forward slowly and turned me sideways by my shoulder. Then he pointed up to Christ looking down on us through the brilliant white light of the spotlights all around His base. The woman said something and I made out the word *"Deus."* All they were saying was "God bless you," I think. I felt like an asshole for being scared. *"Desculpe me, desculpe me,"* I said as I backed off. *"Não, não!"* the man and woman both said. *"Obrigada!"* the woman said over and over, calling me *"Senhor."* The guy said something with *"Deus"* in it again, then I turned and headed back for Ipanema.

It was after midnight when I got back to Montenegro, and I *had* succeeded in making myself good and tired. But the hillside all around the path to the *favela* was bright with patches of those candles, and I walked over to look. I think it was the smell of the moist earth where the springs run down and maybe looking up the cliff side of the mountain that ran straight and black up into the black sky that made me dream the dream. Although it could have been the samba music floating down from the *favela*.

I dreamed again that I was a wartman falling down that black mountain cliff. I felt the rush of air and heard it swooshing in my ears as I fell. And I felt the warts scraping the rock and tearing and pulling way down deep inside me at their roots before they gave up chunks of themselves. And as I fell and felt my body get lighter, I smelled that old smell of the holes I'd dig in the garden back home. It was all around me from the moss and the plants on the cliff. But it was also in my head, like I *was* home digging in the backyard with Mom in the house and Jesse crawling around stuck under a piece of furniture and Dad on his way home from the garage.

The thing about this dream is that it's both terrifying *and* comforting.

I'm on my third *café-média* here, and about to prove that foreign travel is often the shits. I feel intestinally bad, but my spirit is a hell of a lot better than when I sat down here an hour or so ago. I'm going to buy a *Brazil Herald* and take it home. When I finish reading it I'm going to sit a spell with Ernest Hemingway in Portuguese and see how far I can get through the woods of Michigan with Nick Adams.

If Betinha calls I might ask if she'd allow me to take her to an American movie.

Wednesday morning, June 19, 1968

As I was walking home yesterday, I listened to how people greet each other on the street. Young people will meet somebody and say, "*Tá legal?*" The "*tá*" is short for "*está,*" I'm sure. It's like "*Está bem?*"— "Is it good?" "Is it okay?" What they're saying is, "Is it legal?"

I was walking on Avenida Atlantica with the morning rush-hour traffic roaring by me, and I stuck my ass up in the air and got that little hitch in my back Bolão always said was the secret to both the samba and the *carioca* walk, and I said aloud to the cars shooting by, "*Bom dia, gente! Tudo legal?*" "Good morning, people! Everything legal?"

I'm learning! I'm not dumb!!!

The phone was ringing when I got back to the apartment. I unlocked the door as fast as I could and sprinted for it. I was hoping it was Betinha, but it was Bolão's mom inviting me for a *feijoada* that evening.

It was an excellent meal. I pretended I'd never eaten *feijoada* before, because everybody was having a good time telling me what was in it, grimacing about the pig snouts and intestines and stuff and explaining how it was a Brazilian institution.

"Beans and rice," Flavio said. "*Um, dois! Feijão, arroz!*" He got up and started marching around the dinner table. The words rhyme; it's "*Oom, doisch! Fay-zhow, ah-hoisch!*"

Flavio was having a great time marching around the table, lifting his legs high, chanting. His dad grabbed him finally and pulled him onto his lap, tickled him a little, then gave him a couple hugs.

"It's a rhyme, Karl," Senhor Porto said. "Brazilian soldiers used to march to it. What was it your colonial soldiers marched to?" he said. "'Hay foot, straw foot'?"

"That's right," I said. "'Hay foot, straw foot.'"

"I prefer 'One, two! Beans and rice!'" Flavio said. "But I prefer it in Portuguese."

It was hard for me to take my eyes off Flavio because I was thinking so much of Jesse. Flavio doesn't look anything like Jesse. It was just that ten-year-old look they both had of being ready to raise hell and having all the energy in the world to do it.

After dinner Flavio took a turn around the table, then lit out for the door, chanting *"Oom, doisch! Fay-zhow, ah-hoisch!"* I smiled again at Senhor Porto and Dona Regina, then took off myself, chanting, *"Oom, doisch! Fay-zhow, ah-hoisch!"* loud enough for Flavio to hear.

I caught up to him at the open front door. A soccer ball was sitting on the porch and we both went for it. Flavio hipped me out of the way and got to it first. He booted it out onto the lawn, then caught up to it and started running around the yard kicking it, keeping it just a foot or two in front of him and really controlling it well. The little fart was good—it was like he was dribbling a basketball. I chased him awhile, and finally had to finesse the ball away from him.

I grabbed him, picked him up, and tossed him over my shoulder, then I laid my foot into the ball. It bounced way back into the bushes, about the only place in the whole yard where the floodlights didn't reach. I held Flavio still. "Okay," I said. "We're even now. When I say 'go,' we'll race to the ball."

Flavio pounded on my back with his fists. "I didn't see where it went!" he yelled. "You are a big cheater sport, Karl!"

"I need a little advantage, kid," I said over my shoulder. "I don't know the game. And besides," I said, "I'm a guest in your house and in your country. You have to be nice to me." I put him in an airplane spin, whirled him three or four times, then set him carefully back on his feet. He wobbled around with his arms spread for balance, then I pushed him over with my foot and took off after the ball.

I got to it first, but Flavio was right behind me. I bent over to pick it up and he leaped on my back and grabbed me around the neck. I was about to let him know he was strangling me when, in the little bit of light that made it through the bushes, I spied a lizard on the white stucco wall. "Flavio," I said quietly. "Look at the lizard."

Flavio quit strangling me. "Where?" he whispered. His head was next to mine and I felt his breath on my cheek when he spoke.

"Right in front of your face on the wall," I whispered.

The lizard was about six inches from both our faces. He was about three inches long, and translucent. You couldn't exactly see through him, but you could see *into* him. You could see the gray shadow of his heart expanding and contracting as it beat. His eyes were shiny black like tiny jewels set in water, and his fingers had tiny suction cups on the ends that looked like gum rubber.

"Let's capture him!" Flavio whispered.

I told him to go get a jar and he snuck away like we were under fire. He was right back in half a minute with a net shopping bag, the holes of which were about six times bigger than the lizard. I held it in front of his face, stuck my finger through one of the holes at the lizard, who hadn't moved, and whispered, "Don't you think he might wiggle through these holes and escape?"

Flavio looked at my wiggling finger, then at the lizard. "We'll save this for the bigger ones," he whispered. Then he scrambled out through the bushes again.

The bigger ones? I thought. Christ, the bigger ones'll capture *us!*

Flavio was right back again with a huge jar like an American mason jar.

"Okay," I whispered. "You get him."

Flavio cupped his hand and reached out slowly. The tiny shadow inside the lizard speeded up its beating. He flicked his head back and forth, and Flavio lunged. But the lizard was gone, scurrying straight up the wall toward the vines. You could hear his fingers scratching lightly over the plastered surface. He made it to the vines and disappeared into the green and the shadows.

"We lost him," Flavio said.

"Maybe not," I said. I stood up slowly and put my eye to the spot I'd seen him enter the vines. I could just see part of him, the little gray lines running to the pumping gray shadow of his heart. I reached in with two fingers and brought him out.

"Ah-*ha!*" Flavio said as he held up the jar. I put the lizard inside, touched him to the jar wall, and he stuck. "Ah-*ha!*" Flavio said as he turned the jar to the light. He tucked the jar under his arm and said he was going to show his mom and dad but would come back soon with a *lanterna* and we'd catch a lot more.

What he came back with was a flashlight, and we did catch a lot more. It reminded me of how Jesse and I used to get fishing worms on summer nights. We'd crawl on our hands and knees through the grass we'd been watering all afternoon, Jesse holding the light. I was a lot younger then, and I didn't know what I know now, so we'd be in competition. He'd spot a worm and go to grab it, but I'd hold him down in the grass with my arm or foot and pluck up the worm myself and drop it in the can. I let Jesse have a few, but if I had it to do again I'd let him have them all. It wasn't only crawling around holding the light for Flavio that made me think of those times. It was also the smell of the grass and dirt. It was that moist-earth smell of the holes I'd dig in the backyard, the smell that comes in the dreams.

We had eight translucent lizards in the jar, one of them about six inches long, when Dona Regina called Flavio in. He and I walked up on the porch together, and Senhor Porto came out then too. Flavio held the jar up to the light, and we all took a look. The lizards were a strange sight. Held up to the light like that, you could see into them better. You could see the shadows of other organs, and the major vessels stood out sharply, running to their thumping hearts. In the glare of the porch light the lizards looked like they were clinging with their puckered little fingertips to nothing but air.

"Well, Flavio," I said, "now ya gotta eat 'em."

"I'm not going to eat them," Flavio said. He walked into the house then, but he turned around at the door. "When you come back again, Karl," he said, "we'll capture a lot more and *you* can eat them!"

"*Boa noite*, Flavio," I said. "Sleep good."

"*Boa noite*," he replied, as he disappeared with his lizards.

The night of the translucent lizards was a good night after the bad one the night before. The phone began to ring as I was putting my key in the lock back at the apartment, and I barely made it to the little phone table in the hall in time because my back was hurting so bad from trying to walk like a Brazilian most of the day and then crawling around through bushes most of the evening. But I did catch it before it quit ringing. It was Betinha, asking if I'd like to meet her for lunch tomorrow at school.

"*Tá legal*," I said.

In a few minutes I'll be on my way downtown to meet her.

Spent an excellent afternoon and evening with Betinha yesterday. We ate lunch at a little bar-restaurant a couple blocks from the university in the heart of the city. It was filled with students, taxi drivers, and city-crew guys in their orange work overalls. The students we were sharing the table with were getting more and more agitated and I was getting a little nervous. "What's going on with these folks?" I asked Betinha.

"There's a demonstration Friday," she said. "Some of them think it should be at the university, and others favor the Ministry of Education. It's already decided, though," she said. "We're holding it at the Ministry."

"I might fling my body into the gears of the oppressors' machine with you," I said. "Especially if we could go have a beer afterward."

"I'll note the degree to which you slow the machine," Betinha said. "If the government doesn't close down the university, I'll have a beer with you."

After lunch we walked all the way from downtown to Copacabana and saw *The Graduate*. What I liked best about it, I think, since I'd seen it before, was that an usher showed you to your seat with a little flashlight. It made me think of taking Jesse to see *Dumbo* and *Cinderella* way back when I could first ride the bus downtown alone and Jesse was so young you had to tie his shoes for him. I missed a lot of the movie just thinking about those days before they tore down the old Orpheum, when all the theaters in Spokane had ushers with flashlights. Jesse always wanted to hold the light, and he cried if the usher didn't let him. I thought of the time I was supposed to take him to *Bear Country*, but we went to *The Beast from 20,000 Fathoms* instead. He got so scared he wouldn't leave the theater, and I had to call Mom to come get us.

About a third of the way into the movie I guess Mrs. Robinson got me charged up or something, because I stopped thinking about Jesse and the old days and started thinking about Betinha. I wanted to touch her skin. You could look right down at her bare arm there on the cushion and not see it because it was so black. I did touch her when we came out. I gave her forearm a squeeze and told her how thoughtful it had been of her to tip the usher. I told her I'd pay her back by treating her to something in the way of dessert if she could think of something tasty and a place to get it. Betinha said there was a great ice-cream store in Ipanema.

We walked along the ocean and saw little piles of flowers at the water's edge and candles burning in hollows scooped in the sand. I told her about the rooster I'd seen with its throat cut. She said it was *macumba*, a religion that combined Catholicism and the African religions the slaves brought with them. She said it was like voodoo in the Caribbean countries. Her grandmother, mother, and one of her sisters were *macumbistas*, Betinha said.

The ice-cream store turned out to be just a block from the Bar Lisboa, so I told Betinha that dessert included a *cafézinho*, and we walked there with our paper cups of ice cream and our little flat wooden spoons.

We sat at the table where I'm writing this now and drank our coffee. The bar was packed, and it felt neat to be there with Betinha. I told her that was where I had my morning coffee. I also told her I felt lucky to have met her and that I wished we could do some other things together.

"Such as what, for example?" she said.

Her nipples had come up with the evening breeze, and even though she was wearing a bra under her red T-shirt, they still stood out distinctly. Distinctly *and* far. I experienced extreme difficulty keeping my eyes level with hers.

"How 'bout I go with you to the demonstration at the Ministry of Education?" I said.

"*Tá legal*," she replied. "Let's meet here at eleven Friday morning and ride the bus together."

I wanted to take a long, unrestrained look at Betinha's breasts. She was wearing one of those little carved wooden fists on a chain around her neck. You see a lot of them here. "Betinha," I said, "what's this you're wearing here?" I reached out slowly and held it in my fingers. It wasn't that her T-shirt was low-cut or anything, I just wanted a good look at the lovely, medium-sized roundnesses in the cloth.

Betinha took the little fist out of my fingers and held it at the level of her lips. "It's a *figa*," she said.

I had to look at it. I hadn't looked at one closely before and I noticed that it wasn't a regular fist. The thumb was stuck between the first and second fingers. It was undeniably suggestive.

"We call it a *figa*," Betinha said. "It's what Italians call a fig. You know," she said. "It's how they... how they..." She couldn't think of the words. She held up her middle finger.

"It's how they give the finger!" I said. Then I remembered. "It's a fig! I remember from Dante's *Inferno*. Do Italians *still* do that? They were doing that in the thirteenth century! There was this guy in the *Inferno*, down around the Eighth Circle, I think—he was one of the thieves—and he gave God the fig. Takes a hard guy to give God the fig," I said.

"Now *that* would be blasphemy," Betinha said. "For Brazilians a *figa* means good luck. Here we see it as a symbol of fecundity and good fortune."

I held Betinha's hand and pulled the *figa* closer and gave it another look. The thumb was poking between the first two fingers and looking every bit as symbolic of fecundity and good fortune as a guy could imagine. "It's beautiful," I said, and took my hand away.

As we hit the street I told Betinha that I lived just half a block away. I wanted to ask her over, but I knew it wasn't the right moment.

"I'd like to visit sometime, Karl," she said. "But now I have to get home and make dinner."

"Well, another time," I said.

"Let me walk you to your door," she said.

Betinha came through the gate with me and walked all the way back to where my stairs go up. It was dark back there because nobody had turned the porch light on yet. I wasn't about to turn it on.

"Well," I said. "This is where I live. Thanks for the great day, Betinha."

She took half a step toward me. I thought she was going to kiss me. Actually, I *hoped* she was going to kiss me. I wondered how her lips would feel. I'm wondering now as I write this how they'd feel. Betinha's lips are easily twice as thick as mine.

But she didn't kiss me. She took half a step forward, standing so close I could feel her breath on my neck, unhooked the chain her *figa* was hanging from, and put it around my neck. When she bent closer to fasten it, her short Afro brushed my nose and I felt how coarse her hair was and smelled how clean and good it smelled. I rested my hands just lightly at her hips. And all of a sudden, like that—with the good smell of her hair filling my nostrils and her body so close—I wondered if she hadn't kissed me because of *my* features. I wondered what she thought of my lips being so thin. I tried to let the thought go as I felt the weight of the *figa* settle on its chain.

"There," Betinha said, as she stepped away. "You might not want the fecundity in your life now," she said. "But we can always use good fortune."

Late Friday night, June 21, 1968

Jesus Christ, what a day Betinha and I had! We were lucky to make it back from downtown before the cops turned us into *mudados*.

Betinha met me at eleven at the Lisboa. She was dressed conservatively in black slacks and a white blouse with a big collar and lace down the front. I hadn't known what a gentleman wears to a demonstration in Rio, but I wanted to look Brazilian, so I was wearing my white flared pants and my black long-sleeved shirt and Bolão's black loafers that I hadn't returned with his other stuff.

I was astounded at how many people were gathered at the university. They completely flooded the open area by the fountain and overflowed between the buildings in one direction and into the street in the other. Police were everywhere around the crowd, but nowhere inside it. I saw hundreds of police today, and all but maybe five officers were black. There were a lot more whites among the protesters than blacks.

The guy who'd been speaking when I met Betinha was there, with the same ragged clothes and dirty hair matted in little tufts that made him look like he had a black sheep curled around his head. The woolly guy had a megaphone, and as he began speaking into it you could hear other people speaking into megaphones in different parts of the crowd. There was a lot of confusion as we got in our lines of eight abreast, but the atmosphere was full of excitement and good cheer. Betinha took my hand before everybody began linking hands or arms, and that heightened my sense of the moment.

It was quite a sensation to be part of a line of people that dense and long. On one side of me Betinha walked, very erect and dignified, and on my other side, with her arm through mine, walked a lady old enough to be my mom. She was dressed in a blue skirt and a loose white peasant blouse. She smiled at me and waved the sign she held in her other hand. I looked up at it, then smiled at her. It said in Portuguese, FREE EDUCATION FOR ALL. A lot of people carried signs, but more people carried the green Brazilian flag and plain red flags, and people were also holding a lot of banners that stretched the full width of the line.

Every other row or so there'd be a guy with a drum strapped over his shoulder, and it felt to me like these guys were all beating the same rhythm. It wasn't a march rhythm like you'd hear in a parade back home, but a samba rhythm like you hear in the Rio streets. And the people weren't marching, they were walking and swinging their hips—almost dancing—to that samba beat. Betinha was the only person I could see who wasn't caught up in that samba rhythm. She was smiling, though, and I could feel a little of that drumbeat in the way she swung my arm.

It was like *Carnavál* until we got to the ministry, then it got like a civil disturbance. We couldn't tell who started it, and we never got any idea what happened. We could see the huge ministry building up ahead, and we saw the line split and the people begin to move into what was supposed to be a gigantic circle around the building. But then we began hearing shouts, and we could see people breaking out of line and blue-uniformed cops breaking in. The crowd watching on the sidewalks could see better than we could, and those people began to scatter. The drums stopped. We heard popping sounds from near the ministry, and I looked up and saw dark little projectiles floating slowly through the air in high arcs, then falling into the collapsing line of marchers. It was tear gas, and as soon as it began to boil up, the cops lining our part of the street charged us.

It was a good thing Betinha and I were right in the middle of the line, because if we hadn't been we would have gotten our heads split for sure. I didn't know whether to shit or go blind. Everybody was pressing in on us, so we couldn't run. All we could do was watch the cops wade into the line, going for people's heads with their riot clubs. The gas had blown back to us then, and I grabbed Betinha and pulled her down to one knee with me. The cops had clubbed their way through to us by then too. The older lady had dropped her sign and was gagging from the gas. She held her hand out to the cop a step in front of her, but he swung his club and caught her in the side of the head. You could see the skin split and open up just for part of a second before the blood came.

I wanted to kill the guy. I wanted to take his stick away from him and beat the fucker until he looked like *feijoada*. I stood up and went for him, and in a millisecond got my eyes, nose, throat, and lungs so full of gas I couldn't do anything. Betinha grabbed me and started running, pulling me behind her into an alley, where we ran until I had to stop and throw up.

Tear gas is vicious stuff. It doesn't just make you cough, like in the movies. It burns your eyes and your nose and throat and feels like it's eating your lungs out. And it makes you sick.

I got up again and we ran until we came to an arterial. I could hardly see, just enough to tell it was like we'd arrived in another city. Betinha was waving for a taxi and asking me at the same time if I had the money to pay for it. I handed her my wallet and leaned against her, hanging my head over her shoulder. Betinha was the only thing keeping me from falling in the gutter. A taxi pulled up before any cops hit the street or any gas blew in. Betinha told the driver to take us to Ipanema by the beach route.

At the apartment I took my shower first, then got a pair of my jeans and an EWSC T-shirt for Betinha. Our clothes were ruined, at least the white ones. The gas smell might wash out, but the brownish-yellow stains didn't look like they would. I walked Betinha out to the street and told her to please keep the shirt. She thanked me and kissed me on both cheeks the way friends do here. I watched her walk down to Montenegro. She turned and waved, then started across the street toward the path up the hill. I turned away, but turned right back again when I heard the screech of air brakes. A dark-blue two-and-a-half-ton truck had pulled up at the end of the street. Cops with rifles and fixed bayonets were piling out the back of it and jogging up the path. When the last cop had climbed out of sight, Betinha turned and walked back to me.

"Karl," she said, "could I stay with you awhile? I can't go home right now."

I told her sure. We came back in and she told me that sometimes cops would sweep through the *favela* looking for common criminals, or sometimes sweep a park or blockade a movie house and check everybody's I.D. Sometimes it was obviously political, she said, and sometimes it didn't seem to be. This time she was afraid it had to do with the demonstration. The woolly guy with the megaphone was one of her neighbors, she said, and she was a member of the organizing committee, so she thought she'd better not go home.

On my way back from the store with stuff for supper, I saw cops leading people into a blue police van that had pulled up behind the truck. They were all about my age. Another cop, also about my age, stood guard over them with an old Thompson submachine gun. It was *real* scary, and there was absolutely *no* romance in being the little part of it I was.

Betinha telephoned a neighbor in the *favela* and heard that the police were taking all the *favelados* who were students at the Federal University. She was told she shouldn't come home that night. Things were scary enough that I didn't even smile when she said that.

I washed okra while Betinha turned the radio from station to station as the six o'clock news was broadcast. She translated the different versions, but they were were all the same story: a small group of leftist students had attacked police protecting the Ministry of Education this afternoon. Several police had been injured.

I yelled out from the kitchen that we really hadn't seen what went on at the head of the line, and Betinha yelled back that it was certainly obvious that the older lady beside us had been attacking that policeman when he smashed her head. She *really* yelled it. It was like she'd spit the words.

I shut up and cut the okra into pieces and unwrapped the hamburger. Then I didn't know what to do. I didn't feel like going into the living room and telling Betinha it was time for her to cook, even though she'd told me to let her know when I was done. I looked out the kitchen window at the two cops standing on the corner. Then two long, lean black hands slipped around my waist and Betinha leaned her forehead against my shoulder. *"Desculpe,* Karl," she said.

I turned around to say *I* was sorry and that I was stupid. But Betinha held her finger to my lips. She took it away and then she kissed me before I could speak. Her lips were wonderful. Then she told me to go listen to my "Moon-dee-owwwww."

The okra and hamburger fried together was good, and Radio Mundial was playing great songs.

After supper Betinha asked if I'd like to take the radio into the bedroom. I took it in while she cleaned the dinner table. Then she went into the bathroom, and when she came out she was wearing only her white bikini panties. The sight of her made it tough to get my breath, and it wasn't because I'd been gassed that afternoon. She turned off the light and lay down. I stripped to my shorts and lay down beside her.

We listened to the radio and kissed a long time. Sirens screamed all over Ipanema and Leblon, but we didn't give them a second thought. Eventually we were soaked with each other's sweat. We both still smelled a little of tear gas, but the smells of our bodies were driving it away.

Finally Betinha kissed me softly, then pulled away a little. "I can't have vaginal intercourse," she said. "I'm a virgin and I just can't do that until I marry."

A virgin? I thought. Jesus Christ! A twenty-year-old virgin in 1968! I've gotta get this girl to a museum! I let out a much bigger sigh than I'd meant to.

"But we can have anal intercourse," Betinha said.

Then I guess I was silent too long.

"You don't think that's dirty, do you, Karl?" she asked.

"Oh, no," I said. "'Course not." Actually, I wasn't sure what I thought about it. All I could see of her were the whites of her eyes and the faint gleaming of her teeth. I kissed her on the cheek with the sweetest kiss I had in me. "That's against the law in my country," I said. "What if they find out back home and extradite me and toss me in the clink? And besides, it's probably a sin everywhere."

"That's all right," Betinha said, as she slipped off her panties. "We'll do our penance."

I thought it would be difficult, but it wasn't. I think Betinha had done it before. I hadn't been sure I'd like it, but I liked it a lot.

The dream started out okay. Betinha and I were lying naked on a beach so white it didn't look like sand. It didn't feel like sand, either. I couldn't feel anything but Betinha's wet, smooth skin. It was like being on a beach of light. I looked down at her and watched her eyes go closed. I closed my eyes and kissed her. Her lips were big and thick and luscious and smooth, and I felt them all over my whole body.

But then I began to feel something else. Betinha's lips began to feel rough on mine, like they were chapped. And then the feeling moved down and all over my body, like the beach had turned from light to sand. But it got rougher and rougher, like lying on rocks, and Betinha had vanished. But I was still kissing her. I opened my eyes, and she was the wartlady.

I let out a scream that should have awakened the stones in the walls of the building. It did wake me, and it woke Betinha. At first I thought I was sitting up in bed listening to myself scream. But it was the sirens. They were far off, but still all around us. Betinha sat up with me and held me. She told me not to worry, that the sirens were a long way off and that nothing would harm me, that I'd only been dreaming. She pulled me down and turned over and cuddled back against me. I stayed in bed until I was sure she was asleep. The dream had frightened me, and having Betinha hold me like that had made me miss Jen.

So I came out here to write. I'm scared. Tonight I wish I'd never come to Rio.

Sunday night, June 23, 1968

It seems like a hundred years ago that I woke up to the smell of the *cafézinho* Betinha held under my nose Saturday morning. She'd wanted to get out. She said she'd be fine as long as she didn't go home, and that there was a crafts fair in the park down the street she wanted to take me to.

We walked south on Nascimento Silva so we wouldn't pass the cops on Montenegro. It was a bright, clear, cool morning with a little breeze. People were already on their way to the beach with their straw mats and umbrellas. When we got to the park the crafts people were setting up their stands. Most of them were young and lean and hippy-looking. The girls who weren't wearing jeans wore long skirts of light, bright-patterned cotton. The park was filled with rich colors, from the different complexions of the people, to their clothes, to the stuff they were selling. The guy making kites was the focal point of everything because of the bright orange, yellow, green, and blue bird kites sitting on his table and flying from strings tied to stakes in the ground.

Betinha went to talk to a black girl selling black rag dolls, and when I came across a guy with a whole table full of *figas* I bought her a little gold one to replace hers that she'd given me.

I saw her waving to me from a table of leather stuff, and walked over.

"Look at these *bolsas*," she said, pointing to some very nice shoulder bags.

"I'll try one on," I said.

Betinha set the strap on my shoulder. It looked a lilttle progressive for me—the only bag I've ever carried is a gym bag—but it didn't look too bizarre. Now I wouldn't have to carry my passport in one front pocket and my wallet in the other and destroy that sleek look Brazilian pants give your crotch.

"By God," I said, "this could just be the new Karl Russell!"

I paid for it and dropped in my notebook and dictionary and then when Betinha wasn't looking the little box with the *figa*. As we walked away I reached in.

"*Oopa!*" I said. "There's something in my new *bolsa!*" I held the *figa* up to her. "Here's a little fecundity and good fortune back to you, Betinha," I said. "So you won't forget me when I'm gone."

As I was fastening the chain around her neck, I saw behind her the first police van pull up across the park. I felt her stiffen. I turned and saw the van she had seen. We looked down to the north end of the park and saw the van there. We turned and saw the cops already storming out of the van on the south side. The park went absolutely silent for a couple seconds. All you could hear was the sharp rapping of the cops' boots on the asphalt and the sound of their pants' legs rubbing together like the surf running up on the beach. But when they began thumping across the hard-packed sand of the park, people got frantic. A few broke and ran, but there was no place to go: the cops had formed a giant square all around the park and they were walking toward the center holding their riot clubs in front of their chests with both hands.

Terror flooded Betinha's face. She bit her lip and looked down at the ground. But when she looked up at me the terror was gone. She took my arm and began walking me toward the statue in the center of the park.

"It's a police sweep," she said. "They'll check our identification and they might look for drugs. Maybe it's someone special they're looking for." She bit her lips again when she said that. "It'll be okay," she said. "Tell them right away that you're an American tourist."

We waited by the statue until the cops had forced all the people into a tight mass around us. So much dust had gotten kicked up, you could hardly see or breathe. Little kids were screaming and crying, and it was their little hysterical voices that almost pushed me over.

Way up ahead in the shade of a tree, a white guy in a dark suit sat at a little wooden table. Two cops would search each person, even mothers with little kids, as the white guy checked their I.D.'s. The line moved fast. Almost everybody walked off looking relieved, but the cops took a few people to the vans, one for men and one for women. Out of the corner of my eye I watched Betinha chew her lip.

The line got shorter and shorter and shorter. We were completely soaked with sweat. The drops stood out on Betinha's face, and the sun made colors through some of them.

Betinha walked up to the table in that dignified posture she'd had in the demonstration. The cops searched her, and she set her I.D. in front of the white guy. He picked it up but didn't even look at it, just gestured to the cop in charge, who gestured to two others, who took her away.

I still believed I'd be okay. I just couldn't see them taking me. I walked up and handed the guy my passport. "*Sou Americano,*" I said. "*Eu sou dos Estados Unidos.*"

The cops patted me down, then laid my wallet, notebook, dictionary, and bag on the table. The white guy didn't say a word. He popped my passport in his briefcase where he'd tossed Betinha's I.D., nodded to the cops, and they took me away.

I rode for what seemed like a couple hours in total darkness on the metal benches in the van. Not a sliver of light got through the big back doors, and I don't think any air did either. It got so hot after a while you could hardly breathe, but the air was so thick and bad you didn't want to. Two guys whose voices sounded young argued the whole time. I was incredulous. They might want these guys, I thought, and they might want Betinha. But they couldn't possibly want me.

For a long time it was stop and go, and you could hear traffic. Then for a long time there weren't any traffic sounds, just the drone of the van's wheels and the guys arguing. Then we slowed and turned and finally stopped. The doors banged open and light flooded in and blinded me for a few seconds. A voice told us to get out.

We were in a police compound on the water. There was a cyclone fence around white buildings. A blue police boat sat at a dock, and out in the bay was an island with more white buildings and a cyclone fence. The women from the other van walked out from between some buildings and down to the dock. Betinha was distinctive because of her height and her erect posture. We started down to the dock, but the white guy who'd taken my passport grabbed my arm and pulled me out of line. He had my bag slung over his shoulder. He took me inside and put me in a little white room with a table and two straight chairs and left me there without a word. There was a toilet in the corner, and finally being able to go to the bathroom gave me great relief, which seems stupid now.

Three guys came in eventually. One of them told me to take off my clothes. He didn't say anything else, so I didn't know what they were going to do. That was the most scared I got the whole time. As I took off my clothes I started to shake, I was so scared. The guy put on gloves made out of that same thin rubber that condoms are made of. He talked as he went over me. I didn't get much, but I did get the word *"drogas"* which I knew meant drugs. He was talking and acting very calm, but that didn't calm my fear. He turned me around and made me spread out over the table. He got down and looked at my butt, then, still talking, he stuck his finger way up inside me and moved it around. When he finished he grabbed my shirt with the hand he'd had up my ass and tossed it to me and told me to put on my clothes. He was taking off the gloves as the three of them walked out.

I don't know how long it was before Bolão's dad showed up. There weren't any windows, so I couldn't tell when the sun went down. I tried to sleep, but I couldn't. I guess I was too scared. The fear went dull and turned to dread. I got hungry and thirsty, but there was only the toilet to drink from. Finally there was a knock on the door and Senhor Porto stuck his head in. I was so relieved I felt like crying. He had my bag in his hand. He walked in and took me by the arm. "Come with me, my boy," he said. "I'll take you back to your apartment now."

It was dark when we got outside. I looked down at the dock, and the boat was gone. It was out at the dock on the island. The lights on the island were sort of peach colored. I wondered what was happening to Betinha, and a shiver went through me.

I sank back into the seat of Senhor Porto's Mercedes and listened to him talk. He said they called him when they found his name and number in my notebook.I asked him about Betinha and he said he didn't know a thing about her. He said I was still welcome as a son in his house, but that he thought I should consider going back to my country. He said it was common for the police to keep harassing people after they'd picked them up once.

He got out of the car with me when we got to my place, gave me a little hug, and kissed me on both cheeks. "I think you should go home soon, Karl," he said.

I told him I'd never be able to describe how good it was to see his face looking at me from around that door. Then we said our goodnights.

The safety of my own place felt wonderful. The warm shower felt wonderful too, and I closed my eyes and leaned back and let the water run over me. But I couldn't stop seeing the X scars where the police had burned Leila's friend's nipples into no nipples at all. I had to do something to help Betinha. Even if it was only getting word to her folks that she'd been picked up. I had to do *something*.

I stayed in the shower till the hot water ran out.

A new shift of two cops stood on the corner where the path went up to the *favela*. They're just grunt cops, I said to myself. They couldn't know anything about me. It was really dark in the *favela* for eleven o'clock on a Saturday night, and I didn't understand why until I saw kerosene lamps burning in the windows of the little tin-roofed houses and realized few of them had electricity. But radios were playing and quite a few people were out sitting on five-gallon cans in front of their houses or walking the wide dirt path. My only hope was to find the little store with the pay phone Betinha had told me was near her house.

On a side path up a little hill sat a low, dark building with a lighted Coca-Cola sign in the window, so I headed up there. It was a store, but I didn't see any phone. It was full of people and smoke and radio music. As I stuck my head in the low door a woman's laughter rose above the other voices. Two men and a girl sitting on a pop cooler looked at me and immediately shut up. It was real dark in there, and the people were real black. You couldn't see anything but the glowing tips of cigarettes back in there a ways, and they looked like eyes.

"*Com licença*," I said—it was the most polite way I knew to excuse myself. "*Com licença. Não falo bem português, mas é importante. Eu tenho uma amiga Betinha—*"

When I said Betinha's name two people shot out of the darkness at the back of the store like coal out of a cannon. A woman in a yellow tanktop grabbed both my arms and started yelling in my face. The guy with her pushed us outside. Everybody in the store had gotten up and the place had filled with voices.

The guy walked us down the path to the first house and opened the door. The woman rushed in ahead of us. She spoke fast to an older woman. They were all three built like Betinha and they were all the same deep black. Betinha's name was all I could understand of what they were saying to me.

I told them my name and tried to explain that Betinha was with the police. The younger woman began to wail then and the older one got down on her knees on the dirt floor and took my hands. The guy knelt on one knee and said something very slowly in French. I said I didn't speak French, and he said, "*Ah puta merda!*"

The mother took charge then. She explained slowly with big, slow gestures that she was Betinha's mother, the guy her brother Solono, the other woman her sister. She patted my thigh and told me to speak slowly and they would understand.

I explained the best I could about the march, the gas, seeing the cops coming to the *favela* and then Betinha spending the night. I told them we'd gone to the park that morning and the police had come and taken us to a place on the water. The sister began to wail again and Solono closed his eyes. The mother got up, turned, and walked to the other side of the tiny house.

I was afraid I was going to cry. I felt ashamed for not being able to help Betinha at all when she'd helped me so much. "*Por favor*," I said. "*Eu quero ajudar.*" I took out my notebook and wrote down my name, address, and phone number. There was no one to give it to because they were all looking away. Finally Solono looked up and took it.

If I got it right, Solono told me I could help, that sometimes the police just dropped people anywhere when they finished with them. If Betinha was hurt when they were done with her, she might not be able to call and we'd have to find her. He said he knew people who would have their eyes open.

We walked together down the path. I could see the lights above the gate to my building. Solono swept his arm out and around at all the lights of the city. You could see downtown, way out to the North Zone, the little towns along the beach to the south, and all the rest of the city that lay over the mountains to the west. Betinha could be anywhere out there, he said, and she might even be out there right now.

I stood for a minute or two before I started down. I looked out at the lights on Sugarloaf in the bay. You could see the lights of the little cable car that goes to the top climbing slowly through the darkness. I looked at the other lights in the bay. Unless you stood awhile, you couldn't tell what might be a ship and what might be an island. I thought of Betinha out there, and I thought of the story Leila's friend had told me and of what they'd done to her breasts.

Christ the Redeemer stood two mountaintops to the southwest. I watched His back for a breath or two, then I walked on down the hill. The cops were still on the corner.

I slept till two o'clock this afternoon and woke up frustrated, pissed off, and confused. I argued with myself as I showered. Christ, I said to myself, I came all this way. I might as well stay and at least learn some Portuguese. My class starts tomorrow. The cops aren't gonna harass me. They know I haven't done anything. And I told Solono I'd help him look for Betinha. Betinha and I hadn't said a word to each other after the cops got us rounded up like cattle, and I was ashamed that I'd let them scare me into pulling away from my friend. I told myself I had to make up for that somehow.

Also, my ass hurt from that guy sticking his finger up it. I washed and washed but I couldn't get feeling clean, and it hurt to touch myself with the washrag.

I got dressed and sat down at the desk with *As Aventuras de Nick Adams* and my dictionary, determined to get a few pages read before I went out for coffee. But my ass was feeling so weird I couldn't stand it after a few minutes. So I went into the bedroom, pulled down my pants and shorts, lay back on the bed, held my legs up, and looked between them into a mirror. There were warts growing all around my asshole.

The sight of them scared me so bad I almost got sick. I couldn't get my breath. I thought of how hard Havermeyer had pressed when he cut the ones off my back and remembering the feeling of it made my whole body contract.

I popped off the bed, pulled up my pants and started pacing and thinking. I wondered if the guy could have given them to me on purpose somehow when he was searching me for drugs. If that's what he'd been doing! I picked up the dictionary and found "wart." *Verruga* is the word in Portuguese. "*Verruga*," I said aloud. "*Verrugas...? Verrugas?*" The guy'd been talking to his buddies when he had his finger up me, but I don't think he'd used that word. But fuck, I thought, he had a glove on—nothing could have come off his finger. But what if he'd put something on the glove?

"Fuck!" I yelled, and I threw the dictionary against the wall as hard as I could. It was a feeble throw and it hurt my arm. Fuck it, I thought. This is the last fucking straw. I'm going home just as soon as I can get my ticket changed. If it hadn't been Sunday, I would have run to the nearest travel agency.

I was on my way out to try to walk off some of my near-insanity when Dona Regina and Flavio met me at the gate. Dona Regina hugged me, then kissed me on both cheeks. Flavio shook my hand and held up his jar of pretty sick looking lizards.

I told his mom I'd decided to leave.

"Oh, no, no, Karl!" she said. "I've made a phone call this morning. You'll have no more trouble with the police in Rio."

"It's not that," I said. "I need to get home to see a doctor." I knew I was in trouble the second I said that. I *knew* it. Dona Regina got all excited. She told me I didn't have to go home just to see a doctor. She said they had the finest doctors in the world in Rio.

I'd already put my foot in it. I said I needed to see a dermatologist about a skin condition that had flared up. She pulled me to the car, saying that she'd get me an appointment with the dermatologist who treated her children. She and I got in back and Flavio got in front beside their driver. Dona Regina spoke, and off we rode in the Mercedes like we were in a palace.

Dona Regina got me an appointment with their dermatologist for tomorrow afternoon, but I'll be gone tomorrow if I can get a flight.

Monday, June 24, 1968, 8 p.m.

The phone rang at 3:30 this morning. I was dead asleep. I heard it, but it didn't register somehow that anyone in Rio would be calling me that late. It was Solono. He said to meet him on the dark corner of Nascimento Silva. I put on my tennies, jeans, and a T-shirt, washed my face to wake up, and went out into the warm, humid night. I stood inside the gate and looked up and down the street. The corner where the cops stood was fully lighted, but the streetlight on the south corner was almost totally blocked out by trees. I stepped out and walked quietly down that way.

Solono was sitting on his haunches just around the corner. He got up slowly and shook my hand. As we walked to the bus stop I looked at our reflection in the store windows and thought of Bill Cosby and Robert Culp in *I Spy*. I was completely aware we weren't playing, but I couldn't help feeling a sense of adventure. I don't think I'd have felt that way if I hadn't known I'd be going home in a matter of hours.

We got on a Cosme Velho bus. When we sat down, Solono closed his eyes and didn't say anything till the bus stopped at the end of the line. We'd gone through a tunnel into a neighborhood that made you think of a little old mountain village. I hadn't been anyplace in town where the mountains were this thick. It was like we'd left Rio, even though Rio was all around us just over the mountains.

Solono started talking as soon as we hit the sidewalk. The streets here were deserted—no cars driving by, no people, no radios playing out the windows—and he spoke quietly. A black girl had been found. She'd been beaten and the *mudados* were—"

"The *mudados!*" I said.

He paused for a second trying to think how to explain.

"*Eu conheço,*" I said. "*Eu conheço.*" I knew what they were.

The *mudados* didn't know her. The people who'd called had to stay hidden from the police, so we were going to the *Estação dos Mudados* to see the girl. Solono said he didn't know if he wanted it to be Betinha or not.

We cut up a side street, and where it dead-ended we took a path that climbed through the thick trees. The sky was starting to get gray in the east. Soon the ground leveled out and began to feel funny. I looked down, scuffed away the moss and leaves, and realized we were on concrete. Solono turned and pulled me after him.

"The government tried to build a subway in the fifties," he said. "They began building it in different parts of the city. They were going to connect all the parts eventually. But the excavations kept falling in because of all the sand. They'd just begun building a station here in Cosme Velho inside the mountain—solid rock—when the government stopped the whole project. Some *mudados* and others moved in. It's better than the *favela*," he said. "The *Estação dos Mudados* has tiled bathrooms."

We climbed some mossy steps, then it seemed we'd come as far as we could. The mountain rose straight up in front of us, blacker than the sky. I turned to Solono, but he'd walked forward and was pulling at the vines. "Come on," he said. I went ahead with my hand out to feel what I was walking into. Solono held back the vines like a curtain. "Go ahead," he said.

The second I stepped into the cavern I smelled that wet, leafy smell and heard the dripping water and saw the shadows in the dim, yellow light up ahead, just like in the dream. No fucking way am I going down there, I told myself. But when Solono came up beside me and all I could see of him were his eyes and his teeth, I thought of lying next to Betinha in the dark. It seemed like another life ago.

My shoes squeaked on the smooth tile, and when we got near the lantern light I saw all the faces turned toward us. I followed Solono and stood behind him as he knelt beside the girl on the straw mat. Her face was partially covered by the wool blanket around her. It wasn't Betinha. Solono tried to hide his relief, but he didn't succeed.

I wouldn't have been able to tell if it was Betinha or not. I didn't think this girl's breasts looked like Betinha's, but she was the same height, wore her hair in that same short Afro, and had that same tight muscle tone. Her face was so bruised and swollen none of her features were distinguishable. Maybe it wasn't Betinha, but it was someone somebody loved. Then I knew who it was. I reached down and touched Solono's shoulder. "It's Betinha's friend from the park on Saturday," I said.

He nodded his head. He stood and talked to a white-haired man, then he told me he was going out to call a friend who owned a taxi and we were going to take the girl to the free hospital.

I did not want to be in that place with those people. The white-haired man motioned for me to sit, and I saw he didn't have any hands, just stumps at the ends of his wrists. Two of the three people sitting with the girl got up, and one led the other back to where more people lay asleep on the floor. I sat down and leaned back against the damp wall. A woman put another blanket around the girl. All the light came from old-fashioned kerosene lamps except for one brand-new Coleman lantern on a five-gallon can near the girl. My eyes wanted to close, but there was no way in hell I was going to let myself fall asleep there. I heard movements back where the people were sleeping and watched something black and mushroom-shaped come toward me out of the dark. It was a dwarf woman. She held a cup out to me and I smelled the coffee and felt the heat of it on my face.

"*Um café para o senhor*," she said. Tremors ran through the fat hanging off her arms.

A coffee for the gentleman. Jesus Christ, I thought. The cup began to shake and the coffee to spill over. I took it. "*Muito obrigado*," I said, as she moved through the light and out of it again. I drank the coffee slowly out of the big old white mug. It was real bracing without sugar. I kept my nose in the cup so I wouldn't smell the smell of the dream that was all around me.

The people sleeping had begun to stir. They started getting up and I could see the dark shapes of them back there. From all around light rose as people turned up the wicks on their lanterns. I did not want to watch these people troop by me on their way out to the world to start their day. So I kept my eyes on the entrance, and in a few minutes Solono pulled back the vines.

We held the edges of the straw mat like a stretcher and lifted the girl carefully. I'd grabbed the end that put my back to the people walking out from the sleeping area, and I didn't look back as we carried her out. An old black Checker taxi stood at the curb, and we laid the girl on the back seat. Solono sat back there on the floor and held her steady as we drove to a big old house they called the free hospital.

We left the girl there, then walked back to Ipanema and Solono stopped at the corner where we'd met. He told me he needed to go home the back way. Neither of us mentioned Betinha. I shook his hand and told him, "*Até logo*,"—"Be seeing you," even though I knew I wouldn't see him again. "*Até logo*, Karl," he said.

I took a shower and looked at the warts. I thought they were growing, but I didn't really know. I told myself it was my imagination. They hadn't been hurting.

A little before nine, I took a taxi to the Copacabana Palace and made the arrangements for my return ticket. I checked the desk just on the outside chance there was a letter for me, and it turned out there were two. I walked back and stopped at a little restaurant to have breakfast and read the letters—a sweet, beautiful one from Jen and one from Donnie. They haven't caught Johnny yet, he said, but they're sure he's long gone out of Spokane. I sat and ate my eggs and read Jen's letter a second time. I was so goddamn glad I was going home. I bought a bunch of souvenirs and a beautiful white cotton shirt with a lot of embroidery on it for Jen.

I'm all packed now. I couldn't get hold of Dona Anna, but I'll leave a note on the door and she'll get it when she comes to pick up the rent. I'm leaving her half the July rent, since I didn't give her any notice.

I'm so sleepy I can hardly keep my eyes open. I'm kind of afraid to go to sleep. I've been in front of the mirror with my pants down all evening looking at the warts, and they *are* getting bigger. There's no question. I'm calling Havermeyer from Miami and getting an appointment for Thursday morning. I've washed my face about a hundred times today and I still can't get that smell from the *Estação* out of my nose.

Friday, June 28, 1968, 4:20 a.m.

I'm still in Rio, and I've been crazy for most of the past three days. You can only cry so much, grind your teeth so much, walk so much, stay awake so much, and cry so much again. You can only allow yourself so much shock, hysteria, and self-pity (I fucking *deserve* self-pity!!!), and then you've got to do something that helps.

I fell asleep—Christ, when was it now? Monday night. I fell asleep and I was sleeping as sound and deep and sweet as I've ever slept in my life, when all of a sudden I woke up like somebody turned on a switch. I sat up in bed like a jack-in-the-box. My parents were in the apartment. I don't mean I thought they were in the apartment, or felt they were in the apartment. My folks were *in* the apartment. All I had to do to get to see them was to walk out in the living room. Jesse was there too.

But something else was out there. It was the monster that's always there in the dark when you're a kid. In the closet, under your bed, out the window. When you get up and crack the door or lean down and lift the bedspread or pull back the curtain, you never see it. It knew you were coming, and vanished. That monster was out there too. Shivers were running up my arms to my neck, and they're doing it now as I write about it. I was terrified, but I had to go out there and see the monster if I was going to get to see Mom and Dad and Jesse again.

I got out of bed and walked across the wood floor, through the doorway, and turned. Three balls of white light were floating in the black sky outside the open window. They flared and blinded me, and I turned my head. When I could see again, I was looking into the full-length mirror on the bathroom door, and the warts were all over me. I was the monster in the dark.

I gasped and couldn't breathe. I touched myself, and I could feel them. I let out some sound and turned to the balls of light. They pulsed and the room grew brighter, but then they began to fade. They faded and drew away. They'd become just tiny points of light a trillion miles away in the night sky—like ordinary stars—before they finally disappeared.

I turned on the hall light and looked at myself. The warts were everywhere. I ran my hand up my arm, and the same feeling came over me as in the dream when I was lying with Betinha and she turned into a wartlady. I looked closely at my face, and that's when I came apart. I gasped again and couldn't get enough air.

I marched from room to room just as fast as I could go, sobbing and gasping and kind of bellowing whenever I had enough air. God knows what the other people in the building thought was going on in my apartment. I kept stopping in front of the mirror.

I've got warts on my eyelids, warts in my nose, warts on my lips. None of them are as big and ugly as the wartman's in Spokane or the wartlady's here. But mine are big and ugly enough.

I've got warts on my cock.

I flopped down on the bed and cried till I didn't have any tears left and my tear ducts were raw and the sun was up.

I put on some clothes and sat. I got up and walked. I looked at my suitcase open on the bedroom floor. I got Jen's letter out and read it again. I didn't think I could cry anymore, but I could. At eleven o'clock I peeked out the door to see if anybody was around. Nobody was, and I took down the note to Dona Anna.

I had to think what to do, but I couldn't think straight. Missing this plane didn't mean I couldn't go home. My ticket would still be good, I thought. I called the travel agency in the Copacabana Palace, but the lady I got didn't speak English and the lady who did wasn't there and I couldn't make myself understood, and I started crying again. I smashed the phone down and flung myself back on the bed and cried and wondered how I'd ever get the guts to go out and get the ticket changed, if it was still good—or to go home at all, for that matter. I couldn't stand for anybody to look at me, especially anyone I cared about. Jen could never look at me. She could never touch me.

I lifted one eye and saw the clock. It was so clean and smooth, with its flawless white face and precise little numbers and perfect little arms like arrows with those sneaky, fucking little luminous veins waiting to shine in the dark. I grabbed it and threw it against the wall. I picked it up and threw it again and again and again until my worthless, piece-of-shit right arm wouldn't throw anymore and the clock was nothing but junk on the floor and a brown leather case in my hand.

I was exhausted, but I couldn't sleep. And I didn't want to sleep. Sleep is supposed to be a refuge, but sleep for me has gotten to be a trip to someplace I don't want to go. I sat in the big chair in the living room and looked out the window where the three balls of light had hung in the air. I watched the sky go from blue to smoky gray to black. The way I was feeling became a sentence in my mind. It was the sentence "I want my mother," and it rolled and rolled and rolled through my mind as strong and regular as waves breaking and flooding up the beach, getting pulled back to their source, then breaking again and flooding the beach again like arms open as wide as they can open. Mom would love me no matter what I looked like.

I didn't expect the balls of light to come again, but I hoped they would. Nothing came, not even any feelings. Eventually even the sentence wouldn't come anymore.

I woke to noise from the body shop behind the apartment and to a beautiful blue sky before my eyes. I got up and walked to the mirror. It hadn't been a dream. It was my life. I walked to the window in the little bedroom and looked down at a guy pounding a crease out of the front fender of a '47 Chrysler sedan. Back home, I thought, we'd pop that out of there with a dent-puller. I watched the guy swing his hammer, and every time he banged that old metal and the dirt dropped and the dust flew I let out a roar. He finished before I was ready to quit.

I banged around from room to room feeling the warts under my arms and on the insides of my thighs rubbing and getting more and more raw the longer I kept walking and the more I picked up the pace. There's a path through my apartment now where the varnish is worn off what they call the parquet floor. Sweat was pouring off me and there was a trail of it from room to room. I turned on the radio, but the Mundial DJ sounded so happy, so fucking charged up with a youthful zest for life, that if he'd been doing a broadcast from my bedroom I'd have beat him to death with his microphone.

I alternated from feeling furious to trying to send the desolation inside me out like a hate-ray to make everything ugly. It didn't work. The world outside remained beautiful. As the lights came on in the buildings all around, I aimed my hatred at the lighted windows and the free, happy, beautiful, smooth people living behind them. Then I decided I would, by God, get out there in that darkness. I looked at the roofs of the buildings where the clotheslines and the TV antennas had disappeared, and I realized how grateful certain of us should be that about a third of our life is darkness.

I walked away from Montenegro and kept to the side streets. I had to keep crossing to avoid meeting people, but that was easy. It was like normal life. I could have been anybody out for a little night air.

I was working my way to the beach when I got to Prudente de Morais and heard live samba music moving in my direction. As the music got louder I began to hear singing too. That's a well-lighted street with a lot of traffic, and I thought I'd just take a peek around the parked cars, then run for it. Close by, fifteen or twenty people with drums and whistles and woodblocks and tambourines were marching down the street. Two people at the front carried a banner that said A BANDA DE IPANEMA. About an equal number of people were dancing down the sidewalk beside the band, dancing and singing with them.

I retreated past some parked cars and leaned against a black Aero-Willys where a tree blocked the streetlight. I couldn't help smiling as the music got louder and they danced into view. They were really having fun. I could see them fine, but they couldn't have seen me even if they'd looked. Mostly they were people in their late twenties or early thirties, some of the girls maybe my age. My body had about given in to the samba when the band did a column-right and the whole bunch turned and started toward me.

I froze. The street was full of people, and so was the sidewalk. A guy scraping two pieces of wood together making a squeaky, raspy sound was about to collide with me head-on. I wanted to run, but there was nowhere to go. There was nothing I could do.

I smiled and leaned back harder into the Willys and the guy stepped around me. A lot of people danced by. None of them was really paying much attention, and none of them acted like my appearance was noteworthy in the slightest. And then they were past and I took a normal breath. But then I felt a hand on my shoulder.

It was a girl like a thousand girls in a thousand photos of Rio. Young, brown, tight-skinned, beautiful. She wore a thin piece of red ribbon tied around her forehead like a headband. She might have thought she recognized me from the back, she might just have been going to invite me to dance along. Her face was only inches from mine and the word she'd been about to say had left her with her mouth open. She wheezed, then stepped back. She blinked and closed her mouth. She turned her head away. *"Desculpe,"* she said as she ran to catch up with her friends. *"Desculpe,"* I heard her say again.

I was devastated by the horror I'd seen on the girl's face. Since the spring I'd kind of let myself feel beautiful. First Leila had made me feel that way, then Jen made me feel it more because, aside from enjoying making love to me, she knew all about me and liked me in spite of it. And even being with Betinha a short time had made me feel beautiful.

Looking in the mirror hadn't done my ego a lot of good, but I guess I'd seen through the warts to the old me and I guess way down deep some of that beautiful feeling had still been there. It took looking at myself through the eyes of that pretty girl to see the new me.

The devastation didn't take the form of sorrow—not then. First, I flipped out. The rest of the way to the beach, instead of avoiding people I walked across the street to face them. *"Boa noite,"* I'd say, and give them a big, warty smile. One girl with her boyfriend couldn't take her eyes off me. We met under a streetlight and her eyes followed me until she about twisted her head off. I watched her reflection in the windshield of a parked car and saw her stop. I turned and walked back so that I was center stage in the little theater of light. I gave her a big smile, puckered my lips, and sent her half a dozen big smackers. She screamed and buried her face in her boyfriend's shoulder. I blew them a kiss and went on my way.

I stood on the sidewalk facing the traffic streaming by. What a cityful of dumb fucks! I thought. They've got one street that runs by the beach and give it a different name in every neighborhood. A blue VW shot by almost on two wheels as he weaved between cars. I started screaming and sprinting after him. "Cocksucker!" I screamed. "You're cute! Kill somebody, maim somebody! Goafuckinghead, ass-hoooooole!"

A day or so of heavy weeping is hard on a guy's respiratory system. I'd only run about a block, but my wind was gone. I was bent over with my hands on my knees getting my breath when a tiny Fiat crammed full of people pulled up beside me, Dad at the wheel, Mom with a baby on her lap, four small kids all trying to stand up on the back seat so they could fly through the front window when Dad was hit from behind or had to stop fast. I guess the guy thought I was hurt or sick or something. He leaned across his wife to speak to me and I brought my head up. Mom gasped and Dad didn't have anything to say. I turned slightly to face the kids in back. One kid pointed at me. "*Olha!*" he said. "*Que coisa!*" "Look! What a thing!" Dad sat back in his seat, put the Fiat in gear, and dropped the clutch.

I spotted a break in the traffic, whipped out to the grass divider, and took on the northbound lane. I yelled at cars and shook my fist. Thinking back on it, I put myself in mind of a lean, mangy, half-rabid dog, chasing cars. I was especially effective with convertibles, I think. When a guy in a red Mustang with his girlfriend came by, I took off abreast of them. "Hey, you faggot fuck!" I yelled at the guy. "You two oughta try a flight through that windshield! Slide a block or two facedown on the pavement! Get rid of a little of that beauty!" The guy was slowing steadily. The cars ahead were backing up at a red light. Our pace slowed to a trot, then to a walk, then I was just standing there looking down at them in their splendid evening wear.

The girl said something, then pointed up at me. I was no more to them than one of the little *favelado* kids who run out with rags and wipe your windows for whatever change you'll flip them. "*Vai foder a sua mae, rapaz,*" I said. It was the only Portuguese insult I knew. "Go fuck your mother, man." The guy started to get out of the car, but people began honking their horns because the light had changed. I was hoping I could at least mess up his clothes a little, but the girl put her hand on his shoulder and told him to sit. The guy spit at me, then took off.

I took off too, but over in the south lane I saw a big American station wagon—an Olds or a Buick—wallowing through the traffic like an enormous boat with a broken rudder, so I turned and ran after it. "Cross the line, asshole!" I yelled. "Right up over the divider!" I was picking up speed. I'd sure as hell never run the bases that fast. "Smack somebody!" I yelled. "Right between the headlights! Every kid should grow up without a family!" But the wagon was gone.

I slowed down. I'd gotten kind of tired. I hung my head and tried to get my breath, and all of a sudden a car *had* jumped the divider and was headed right for me. It was a black and white VW, one of the square ones they have down here. When it got close I saw the two cops in it.

I blasted across the north lane, tires and brakes screeching all around me. I ran through that deep sand as hard as I could for the darkness near the water. I couldn't tell if what I heard was the surf ahead of me, the cops behind me, or the blood pounding in my head. When I got to the hard, wet sand I turned south and made for the rocks on the point down at the end of Leblon. The warts under my arms and on my inner thighs were starting to hurt. I picked up the pace. Maybe I'll rub a few of the fucking things off, I thought.

Before long I was hurting so bad under my arms and in my crotch I had to slow down and hold my arms out and run bow-legged. I turned around and ran backwards awhile. I couldn't see anything behind me but a little gray where the surf was foaming up and then the city lights back of the beach. I stopped and took off my shirt and felt real gingerly under my arms. My sides were all sticky. I held my fingers up to my face but I couldn't even see the fingers, let alone the blood I was afraid was on them. I touched one finger to my tongue. It was blood, all right. I held my arms out wide and turned a circle and let the ocean breeze dry the sweat a little. I felt myself calming down.

I'd just turned and started walking back towards Ipanema when a set of headlights appeared up the beach and started bouncing toward me. I turned and ran a few steps, realized that was stupid, and headed for the water. I staggered through the first couple of breakers and when the water was up to my knees I dove. That salt water stung the raw warts so bad I wanted to scream, but I was afraid the cops would hear me. Maybe they wouldn't have above the sound of the surf, I don't know. They were sweeping their spotlight back and forth from the water to high up on the beach. I ducked down when I heard the waves building, then popped up after they broke over me.

Soon the cops passed slowly in front of me and drove on down the beach. I crawled out on my hands and knees and lay in the sand getting my breath. Then I got up and kept walking south. I couldn't start home until later, when the streets cleared. I probably looked like a victim of some horrible accident, and I didn't want anyone calling an ambulance.

I walked to the rocks and climbed up high where I'd be out of sight if the cops came back and sat there awhile, leaning back against the smooth, cool stone and feeling ashamed of myself. I concentrated on the waves hammering away at the rocks, and soon the sound got into my head, and the rhythm of it, over and over, was soothing. The ocean beating on rock. It would beat just the same for any person, for eternity.

This is where the nutso part ended and the sorrowful part began.

If I hadn't been sort of hypnotized by the ocean, I would have heard their voices sooner. But as it was, a young guy and girl walked up near the rocks without me hearing them and began to make love in the sand so close to me I could hear the girl's little gasps between the breaking waves.

When the waves weren't crashing I heard them say things I couldn't understand but could feel with total fluency. I heard them kiss. I thought I heard the sound of him moving inside her, and I thought I could smell them. When they'd get too excited and too loud they'd shush each other. They held their orgasms till the waves hit.

I had a hard-on, and when I unzipped my jeans in the crash of a wave and held my warty cock in my warty hand, it was like the marriage of two ugly things. Way down deep inside me, as deep as where I'd believed I was beautiful, I understood that never again in my life would a girl want to make love with me.

When they were gone I climbed to a huge, flat rock and lay face-down on it. I spread my arms and legs to get as much of my skin on the cold, smooth surface of that stone as I could, and let myself cry until I exhausted my tear supply again.

The memory came to me of lying on the cold cement floor of the Northside Chevrolet garage when Dad would take me there with him on a Sunday night while he finished a job for Monday morning. And that made me remember how Dad had taught me to handle problems, how to get a job done. I thought of those days when he and Mom and Jesse were alive and we were all together, and thinking of that made me feel better. The ocean had turned from dead black to just the littlest bit of gray when I started home.

I washed the blood and sand off in the shower and slept till late Thursday afternoon. Then I got up, showered again, put on clean clothes, boiled some rice, and ate for the first time in close to three days. I listened to Mundial awhile, but then I turned off the radio and unpacked my stuff. As I was setting my books and my journal with my old compositions in it on the table I thought again of Dad. I found the composition I'd written about him and read it, then I read them all. Later, after midnight, I went out walking. I stayed on the back streets of Ipanema and Leblon, and I didn't get into any trouble.

When I got back about an hour and a half ago I sat down here to write and try to begin handling this. I want to get back home, be with Jen, finish school, and be happy. If I'm going to do any of those things, it means I've either got to get rid of the warts or learn to live as a wartman. Learning to live as a wartman is going to make being with Jen and being happy pretty difficult. So it looks like I concentrate on getting rid of the warts. How do I do that? I make an appointment with the Portos' dermatologist. Going through with that means I have to go out in the world, walk among normal-looking people. And that means I've got to have some courage. How do I get the courage? I have to believe it's worth the price in humiliation, then I make a commitment to myself and I walk out the door.

There's a problem with being courageous about this, and it's my inability to understand why it's happening to me. It's hard not to feel like I'm being singled out for punishment. I don't think I deserve it. I'm not quite twenty-one years old yet. I haven't had time to be a bad enough human being for these warts to be my justice. If Dad were alive, maybe he could tell me how to see it. But then he never talked to me much about stuff like justice or why things happen. Dad taught me how to fish and shoot and how to work and enjoy it—all good and important things to teach a kid, I think. But I see now that those things aren't enough.

I need advice. I need the inspiration that comes with listening to wisdom. I think that's why I always responded so well to coaches, and that's probably why I started reading so much after Mom and Dad were gone. I need somebody to tell me how to live with this.

Wind Rows

Composition I
Karl Russell
September 20, 1965
Topic: Things My Father Taught Me

My Dad taught me a lot of things in the fifteen years I knew him. Of course I don't remember the stuff from the first four or five years, but I'm sure it was the same kind of thing as later: how to fix what's broken. He showed me how to put a new tip on my fishpole and glue it and wrap it so it would stay. He showed me how to pull the wheel on my bike, take the core out of the valve, take the tire off the rim with tire irons instead of screwdrivers so I wouldn't puncture the tube, pump up the tube, spray it with water to find the leak, patch the hole, then remount the tire. He showed me how to cut a piece of glass for the storm door to replace the ones I'd break with various balls, and he showed me how to seal it up with glazing compound. The most important thing he taught me though was a general way of dealing with what needed to be done: my father taught me how to work.

My brother and I always had chores. Jesse had to put his toys in his toy box when he was three, for example. If he did, he got his allowance, which was "a big quarter." If he didn't, he got "a big spankin'," which was really just a swat. I had to take out the garbage and do the yard.

We had a big yard with pines and broadleaf tees, so I had a lot of needles and leaves to rake, and I hated it. One Saturday in late fall—I was eight or nine, I guess—I went out to rake the yard after Dad had told me for weeks to do it. The whole yard was covered, pine needles on the bottom, leaves over top of them, and the whole mess soaked from days of rain. I stood in the middle with my brown cotton gloves and my two rakes and my wheelbarrow, and I was in the deeeepest despair a guy can feel before he goes to junior high and reaches puberty and likes girls and needs to make the team and learns the true meaning of the word.

I was overwhelmed. I didn't even know how to begin. I started right where I stood. I raked a little circle clear, then I raked another little circle in another place, then I loaded a pile into the wheelbarrow and took it out back to the garden patch where we burnt our leaves and composted. When I got back to the front yard, Dad was standing with a rake in his hand in one of the circles of bare grass.

"I want to show you something, son," he said, handing me the other rake.

We walked to a corner of the yard and Dad started raking right at the corner of the flower bed. He raked back about six feet, then he started at the edge of the clear spot and raked back another six feet. He did that five or six times until he had a nice little square of clear grass.

"See that row of stuff I just raked up?" Dad asked.

"Yes," I said. The row of stuff was hard to miss.

"That's a wind row," Dad said. "The leaves and pine needles are bound up together. They're binding on each other, and when the wind comes it's gonna have a harder time blowing the stuff all over because of that. That's why it's called a wind row. And look at the straight line," Dad said. "A straight line is something a man can be proud of."

To be honest, I wasn't impressed. I raked the whole yard in wind rows, though, and the work did go easier. Even at that age I felt satisfaction in the straight rows of leaves and pine needles and the perfect squares of bare grass.

When I'd done half the yard and had a big pile of stuff in back, Dad came out with the kerosene can and soaked the pile down and lit it. After the kerosene burned off, that good smell of burning leaves began to rise up with the smoke. We stood by the fire taking a break. "A man just takes his time and goes about a job right," Dad said, "and he knows he's gonna get 'er done eventually. And because he does it right the first time, he knows he's not gonna have to do part of it again."

I wasn't all that impressed at the time. But I remember that day perfectly. It probably stuck so deep because it was always being reinforced.

After I got a little older, most of what Dad taught me to fix was some part of a car. But it was always the same lesson. Dad sat with me while I rebuilt my first carburetor. I had my two egg cartons there like he taught me, and I had my note pad. As I took the carburetor apart I put each group of parts in a numbered egg-hole, then I took the new parts from the kit and put the same group in the same numbered hole in the other carton. If something came off in a funny way, I'd make a note of it so I could put the new parts back the same way. If I ever got mad and started forcing something and ramming things around, Dad would grab me by the shoulders and tell me to take a deep breath and slow down, that if a guy was going to learn to fix things right, he had to learn patience.

I've kept trying to develop patience since then, and I think I've made some progress. Patience is a real hard quality to get hold of, though, and hard to refine. I remember one time when I was fifteen I lost my patience in a fairly spectacular way.

It was the spring before my folks and my brother got killed. I'd gotten Dad's pickup stuck in a muddy field near our house and burnt up the clutch trying to drive myself out. The clutch had been going for a long time, but since I was the one who got stuck and finally burnt it up, we decided it was my responsibility to put the new one in. We got the truck home and put it up on blocks one day, then the next evening I got my work lights all set up after baseball practice and was ready to go when Dad came home with the new clutch.

I liked a medium-hard job like that. It was a challenge, but yet you could do it by yourself because there wasn't a lot of heavy lifting, and you could get it done in a couple hours. I got down under there, dropped the driveline, jerked out the little three-speed transmission, disconnected the clutch linkage, pulled out the old clutch, and then for some reason had just a hell of a time after that. Maybe I was tired.

I began to get irritated and bang things around. Dad would check on me now and then, and when he heard me swear as I barked my knuckles I'd hear his voice from above me in the dark. "Have a little patience under there," he'd say. "A man can't fix anything right if he doesn't have a little patience."

I got everything back together finally. Clutch linkage hooked up, transmission back and the linkage connected, driveline back. And then I couldn't get it adjusted right. Dad got in and worked the pedal.

"Too much play," he'd say. "Tighten 'er up about a turn an' a half."

I'd tighten the adjuster, then I'd back off on it. I was starting to get sleepy and I had school the next day.

I backed off on the adjuster just a hair and Dad yelled down, "That'll do 'er!" I tightened the locknut and rolled out from under the truck and popped to my feet. I was looking down to see if I had all the tools in my hands when I took a long step that propelled me facefirst into Dad's big side mirror. It caught me right between the eyes. Dad said my hat flew off and both my feet lifted off the ground at the same time. It didn't quite knock me out, but tears came to my eyes and a line of blood ran down the bridge of my nose. I got up, grabbed Dad's big sheet-metal hammer out of the truck bed, and beat that mirror right off the side of his truck. Then I bent over with my hands on my knees, trying to clear my head and get my breath back. "I'll buy ya a new mirror," I said when I could speak.

"That's all right, son," Dad said. He was still laughing. He had been laughing from the time I kissed the mirror. "You put my clutch in for me. I'll buy the new mirror."

In spite of this concluding anecdote, my father actually did put me on the road to learning patience. And there's something else that goes along with the stuff he taught me. I doubt my father knew the word "symmetry"—he certainly never spoke it—and there's no way in the world he knew the word "aesthetic." But I believe he taught me the meaning of symmetry, and that creating it and appreciating it could be a beautiful thing in a person's life.

Queen of the Book Country

Composition I
Karl Russell
September 28, 1965
Topic: Things My Mother Taught Me

My mother loved reading, and she worked as a librarian. After I grew up a little I realized she'd been one of those lucky people who get paid for what they'd do for free. The library in Nine Mile Falls was and still is tiny—just the three rooms of an old brick train station the Northern Pacific Railroad gave the town at my mother's request— and when I was a kid I thought of it as a tiny country Mom was queen of. She told me she started reading to me before I was born and she taught me to read before I entered kindergarten, so I don't think I'm being visited by a spirit when I hear her voice clear as day sometimes while I'm reading. She didn't just teach me to read. She also introduced me to literature, and because of the way things have turned out in my life so far, that's become a real gift. I've got a couple practical reasons for feeling this way.

After Mom and Dad and my brother Jesse died and my world got real small for a while, I still had what Jesse would have called the "enormous big" world of literature. People from books were often more real to me than the real people I knew. I had Ulysses and Perseus and Hercules from mythology, George and Lennie from the Salinas Valley of California, Huck and Jim from the Mississippi River, a guy I thought was a lot like me named George Willard from Winesburg, Ohio, and a guy from New York named Holden Caulfield, who I hoped was nothing like me and who made me feel that compared to him I didn't have such a bad life. I had Yossarian from World War II, Sal Paradise and Dean Moriarty from the Beat generation, Hamlet from Denmark and Goofy, Donald Duck, Uncle Scrooge, and Gyro Gearloose from Disneyland. The thing about the world of literature is that it's truly infinite. Even if you were physically able to read all the books in the world, people would be writing others right behind you and there would always be a new book about a new character.

Religion—I should say Christianity, because that's the only religion I know anything about—never made much sense to me from the time I was about ten and Mom and Dad made me go to the Baptist church in Nine Mile Falls. They only went on Christmas and Easter, and I think the only reason they made me go was because they thought it was part of the training a kid should have growing up. It was the only church in town, and I could walk to it. I don't know if they'd have made me go if they'd had to drive me.

We learned about both the Old and New Testaments in Sunday school. I thought Jesus was fine, but God struck me as cruel, conceited, scary, and obnoxious. He was supposed to be our heavenly father, but if my earthly father had treated me like God treated people in the Old Testament I'd have run away from home. If God had been a person I wouldn't have liked Him, so I never saw why I should like Him, let alone *love* Him as a God.

I also thought a lot of the most religious people in the congregation were crazy. I had dreams about some of them. They were always talking about how evil they were and I was and we all were. But I didn't think I was evil. And my Mom and Dad yelled at each other about money sometimes, but you could just see by the way they treated me and Jesse that they weren't evil. I think our pastor was really insane. Anyone who'd looked into his face from as close as I was when he put me under the water to baptize me would have thought so too.

As I said, religion has never made much sense to me. But, like everyone else, I need to know the answers to a lot of questions about being alive on this earth. And I don't just need the answers. I also need to have the questions clarified. Literature does this, and I've never had a book threaten to send me to hell if I didn't believe what it said. I can think of an illustration of this point from our class:

> O, that this too too sullied flesh would melt,
> Thaw and resolve itself into a dew!

> Or that the Everlasting had not fix'd
> His canon 'gainst self-slaughter! O God! God!
> How weary, stale, flat and unprofitable
> Seem to me all the uses of this world!
> Fie on't! ah, fie! 'Tis an unweeded garden
> That grows to seed; things rank and gross in nature
> Possess it merely.

In this famous passage Hamlet makes it clear he's ready to give up on life. His father's dead and his mother has married his uncle. She's just told him to stop moping about his dad. "Do not for ever with thy vailed lids / Seek for thy noble father in the dust: / Thou know'st 'tis common. All that lives must die, / Passing through nature to eternity." So Hamlet wishes either that he could just melt away or that God hadn't made suicide against His law. Life seems pointless, and Hamlet doesn't see anything beautiful in the world.

There's a lot for me here. For one thing, it's comforting just to know someone else has felt like I have. Someone else has suffered loss and couldn't bounce right back—and this guy was a prince! I think it's good for people to see they're like other people in some ways. It's not good for a person to feel alone and freakish. So one of the Big Questions *Hamlet* clarifies for me is: How different am I from other people? That's not a very big Big Question, but I often wonder about it.

Then there's the stuff his mother said. Do we need to kick ourselves out of our grief after awhile? Is there a conclusion we need to come to about the eventual passing away of the people we love? And what about our own passing away? I know when Hamlet's mother tells him not to look in the dust for his father, she's simply telling him to lift his head up. But that line and this line—"All that lives must die,/ Passing through nature to eternity"—make me wonder: I wonder if people don't leave some of themselves around for a while after they die. I don't mean in nature, especially. Even now, almost four years after she died, I still feel the presence of my mother when I'm reading something I really like. And when I'm working on a car or on my motorcycle and I'm holding my patience and fixing it right, I feel the presence of my father. I'd like to think we could leave something of ourselves behind in the things we loved, if only for long enough to help the living people get over missing us. I'll abuse the words of

Ernest Hemingway here and say, Wouldn't it be pretty to think so?

Probably everyone has an enduring vision of their folks. A lot of times when I think of my mother, I see her in the same scene: she's about to her full term of pregnancy with my little brother, and she's in her big reading chair and I'm in my little reading chair beside her and she's reading to "us," meaning me and the baby that became Jesse. She's got the book propped up on her huge belly and she's sort of lost in dreams of the kind of people her children might become. She's reading from the *Stories from Greek Mythology* book, and this time she's reading about Daedalus.

I was fascinated by the Minotaur and the Labyrinth and worried about Daedalus and his little boy Icarus being imprisoned there. I was excited when Daedalus, who could fix things like my father could, made himself and Icarus wings so they could fly out of the Labyrinth and not get eaten up by the Minotaur. I don't remember being a bit surprised that Icarus was so excited about flying that he ignored his father's warning and flew too close to the sun.

Mom laid the book open upside down on her huge round belly and looked down at me. "And, Karl," she said, "do you know what happened to that little boy?"

"He got all burnt up!" I said.

"No," Mom said. "But the heat from the sun melted the wax that held his wings together. And his wings fell apart and he dropped through the sky and into the ocean. And that poor little boy never came up again."

Then she took the book off her belly and held her arms out for me and I climbed up and got in the big chair with her. She had one arm around me and the other arm on her belly like she was holding Jesse too. "My boy and my baby won't be like Icarus," she said. "They'll grow up to fly high, but they won't go too close to the sun."

It's hard to keep my spirits up. Every time I look at myself I feel stupid for doing anything but giving in. But I don't know how I'd go about giving in. I sure as fuck am not going to live my life in this condition, so not giving in means not living anymore. The only way I've ever thought of killing myself has been with a gun, and since I don't have a gun here and can't think of a way to get one, and since I'm not ready to think of other methods, that's an option I'm putting aside for now. But maybe I shouldn't. If a guy's going to face a problem, one of the things he's got to consider is what he should do if the problem turns out to be tougher than he is.

I called Dona Regina and told her I'd gotten sick and missed my appointment with her dermatologist and asked her for his number to reschedule. She wanted to come get me and take me. But I convinced her I was okay, that I'd just eaten something that didn't agree with me and the only doctor I needed was a dermatologist. She told me to quit eating in dirty little bars, and finally gave me the number. She also said Flavio would love to see me. That made me feel awful. I asked her to tell him I'd be over as soon as I got feeling better, and we'd collect more lizards.

The earliest I can get in to see the dermatologist is Wednesday afternoon. That's fine with me, because going outside in the daytime will take some psyching up for. The English-speaking lady was at the travel agency this morning, and she said my ticket was still good. I told her I'd have to wait a few days before I could decide when I wanted to leave.

I woke up this morning to a knocking at the door. I hollered and asked who it was, and thank God it was Dona Anna, because she had a key and I didn't have to get up to let her in. The second the knocking woke me I remembered I'd forgotten to put the rent back out for her.

I yelled that I was sick in bed, sorry I couldn't get up, and sorry I hadn't left her a note on the door with the rent money.

"Think nothing of it, Karl," Dona Anna said in that strong accent of hers—I don't know if it's German, Austrian, Polish, or what. "I know you don't hide from me," she said.

Oh, Jesus, I was thinking. Where did I leave the money? It was in the other room on the writing table. "As a matter of fact, I am hiding from you today, Dona Anna," I said. "I have a terrible rash and I'm afraid I might infect you. The doctor said he thinks I picked it up at the beach."

"In my lifetime, young man, I have been exposed to every contagion," Dona Anna said. "As terrible as your rash may be, I promise you, to me it will be dangerous like the freckles."

I heard her footsteps nearing the hallway to the bedroom. "It's just that I look so awful!" I said. "I'm embarrassed for anybody to see me."

"Nonsense," Dona Anna said. She was right outside the door.

"Please!" I said. There was no missing the desperation in my voice. "I'm an awful sight, Dona Anna. I left the rent money on the table with my books. Would you mind taking it?"

Her footsteps had stopped. "Of course I wouldn't mind, Karl," she said. "And perhaps you are right to be cautious. Perhaps there are horrors on Ipanema beach to which even this old soul may not be immune."

I wanted to talk to her. I wanted to know what she'd seen in the place where she got the number tattooed on her arm, what she'd learned about how to live when you think you might not want to live anymore but are afraid to die. But all I said was, "Thank you, Dona Anna."

"I thank you, Karl," Dona Anna replied. I heard her walking to the table. "I see you have the Bible here," she said. "And William Shakespeare." And then she quoted something, maybe it was a Jewish proverb: "'A wise man will hear and will increase learning. And a man of understanding shall attain unto wise counsels,'" she said. "You are a fine young man, Karl."

"At least I try to attain wise counsels," I replied.

"And you keep a clean home," Dona Anna said. She was at the door. "When your health is returned to you, this old lady's counsel is that you stay away from the beach." I promised her I would.

I heard the door close and latch.

I'm trying to live my life normally, so when I got up I started my normal routine, which means a shower. Running my hands over the warts, however, didn't turn out to be a positive way to start my waking hours. I haven't got a smooth square-inch of skin on my body, except my tongue. I got out of the shower feeling like the monster I appear. And I looked in the mirror and said to myself, Okay, you look hideous. All the more reason to be well groomed and dress sharp. So the first thing I do then is try to shave. I tried to fucking shave! I can't believe how stupid I am. I don't have a spot on my whole body, let alone on my face, where the head of a razor will lie flat. For a second I wanted to shave the fuckers off. But these warts are all a lot bigger than the ones I shaved off my wrist. God only knows what there'd be left of me if I tried it. And besides, I haven't got the guts.

I trimmed my hair with the scissors and put on clean clothes and felt a little better. I'm headed out for a walk now. I can't understand the news on the radio, so I'm going to look through the trash by the expensive apartments on the beach and see if I can find a *Time* magazine or a *Brazil Herald*.

Sunday, June 30, 1968, 1:00 p.m.

There's something about what's happening to me that I've got to face right now. Part of me thinks it's crazy, and part of me has known it was the truth since I was ten years old and looked down that alley back in Spokane and saw the wartman's face. It's real, real hard not to believe this isn't part of some plan. I've played with the idea before, teased myself with it, like peeking through my fingers at a monster movie. But I've got to stand toe-to-toe with it now. I've got to look it in the eye.

It's stupid to think God would single me out for anything. Anything! Good or bad! It's stupid, but I can't help thinking that's what He's done.

Since I was a kid going to Baptist Sunday school, I've always thought people who believed God had a plan for their lives were either nuts,

dumb as bricks, or incredibly conceited. I mean, it's a big universe—
why the hell would God fuck with me? If He's going to mess with
people on earth, it seems to me He'd mess with Johnson or Brezhnev
or Castro or the Vietcong or Sirhan Sirhan or Richard Speck. God
tortured and tormented Job in the Bible—or He let Satan do it—
because Job was supposedly "a perfect and an upright man." Job was
somebody. I'm just a fucking kid!

But it's hard not to think God took my parents and my little brother,
took my throwing arm and my baseball career, got me down here,
took my friend, gave me another friend, took her away and probably
got her beat to death, took away how I was starting to feel like a man,
and turned me into something I don't know if I could even show my
mother if she were alive to see me.

What's my sin? Is it the sin of pride? Have I got the tragic flaw
of "hubris"? I'd say thinking you might be able to play professional baseball if you worked hard and getting to feeling a little good-
looking to three women isn't what deserves to be called very fucking
prideful. If it's because I don't believe He's a good God or don't believe He even comes to earth at all, I'd say He should concentrate
on what people *do* and forget about what they believe. Take a look
in your big book, God, and see who has the most black marks after
his name: Is it me or Richard Speck? All old Rich did was stab the life
out of a dozen or so girls. How's Rich's complexion lately? He got
any warts?

Last night I was down at the end of Leblon going through the
barrels there lookng for something to read in English when I felt
someone's eyes on me. I looked up, and there was a little *favelado*
kid standing maybe ten feet away staring at me. When I turned around
his eyes got big and his whole body sort of tilted backwards. Then he
just froze like I was a Gorgon. I stood there for a second, then reached
out my arm and started to say something so he wouldn't be scared.
But he let out a yell and took off running.

I took off then too. I walked along the canal toward Gávea feeling
terrible that I'd scared the kid. I was thinking of the look on his face
and how he must have felt, and how the poor little fucker would
probably dream about it—and then it came to me: the same thing
had happened to me, the exact same fucking thing, on another continent and a decade before. And on almost the same day.

I got to thinking about all the things that had happened since I saw the wartman. There were the dreams about him, then the dreams about the atomic bomb falling and me dying alone without Mom and Dad and Jesse. And I thought of losing them and being alone because of a fucking drunk on the highway. And about hurting my arm and feeling alone and shitty, then finally really busting out of it this year when school got more fun, and I joined the fraternity and met Jen, and the goddamned dreams were coming again, and then the warts came. And about coming to Rio and being stuck here. I walked and walked and walked and wondered how all that stuff could come to pass coincidentally. And then I wondered, if it was cause and effect, what did I ever do to cause it?

I walked along the cobblestone streets up and down the hills in Gávea. The lights were off in all the houses and the trees blocked the streetlights all over the neighborhood so it was very dark and, for me, very peaceful and very beautiful. After a while I got to thinking that it didn't make any difference why I had warts. The thing that mattered was what I let the warts do to me inside. If I let them make me ugly all the way through to my spirit, then I was ugly. If I didn't, I wasn't. That would be my measure, I thought, as I walked through the beautiful darkness.

I began to feel Mom and Dad near me. The stars were blazing and three stars in the shape of a pyramid shone particularly bright up ahead of me over the mountain in the west. I smiled and shook my head. I didn't believe in supernatural experiences, and there I was having one. I thought of how Mom's and Dad's and Jesse's spirits had come to me as the dreams and the warts came. I knew they wanted to protect me. I ran my hand over my arm, and the warts were so tall and thick I got a few of them to mesh together and hold. Mom and Dad wanted to protect me—I could feel it—they just couldn't do much of a job from where they were.

I headed home by the beach and got to Ipanema just as the first blue began to show in the east. I felt Mom and Dad and Jesse with me all the way back to the apartment. I went right to bed and dreamed the dream where I fall from the cliff and scrape the warts off on the way down. This time the dream not only didn't scare me, it continued that comforted feeling. As I fell, I knew that when I landed I'd be home.

But I never hit the ground in the dream. I just fell and fell and fell. I heard the wind whistling and smelled the vegetation on the cliff and the breeze from the ocean and heard the sounds of the warts tearing. I felt them giving up their hold on me. I could feel them pulling way down deep inside me like the fucking things had their roots clear into my guts. But it was a good feeling when they tore away. It was like finally throwing up after you've been nauseated all day.

Sleeping and dreaming had been the best thing to happen to me in what felt like a long, long time. But waking up was bad. I looked ugly and I felt ugly and I was in a foreign country and the warts were growing. I'm as ugly a thing as anybody would ever care to see, and I'm afraid I haven't got the guts to be beautiful in my soul.

Wednesday, July 3, 1968, 11:00 a.m.

The janitor just slid my mail under the door, and I got a letter from Mac and a birthday card from Jen. She said if she were old enough she'd like to be the first person to buy me a drink now that I've reached the age of majority. If I left tonight I could make it home by the fifth. There would be a problem, though. We'd have to find a bar that served wartpeople.

What Jen could do is buy a small-business license and show me off on the street for a nickel a peek, a dime a gawk, fifteen cents a gander, and a quarter a gape. She could rent me out to people who had someone they wanted traumatized. She could donate me to Sunday school classes as living proof of what happens to masturbators, then we could deduct my fair-market value from our income tax as a charitable contribution. I may be ugly, but I ain't dumb! If I go back, I'll find the wartlady from the post office and take her with me. We could call our business "Rent a Wartperson."

Mac wrote from New York where Felicity's funeral was. He said he's staying there awhile, then going to Chicago with some S.D.S. people to demonstrate at the Democratic Party convention. I ought to form my own S.D.S. organization. The initials would stand for

Students for Dermatological Subversion. I could turn all the Young Republicans in the whole country into wartcreatures. Singlehandedly I could stop the war. "All right," I'd say to Congress. "You guys pull out of Vietnam, or it's Wartsville for every one a ya. Next election you guys'll be campaigning with gunnybags over your heads and holes cut out to talk through."

Mac says I wouldn't believe the "freaks" in the Village. He's talking about hippies, I think. I ought to write and tell him about the *Estação dos Mudados*, where there are some freaks *he* wouldn't believe.

I've decided I'll walk to Botafogo, where the dermatologist is. People are going to stare at me, but I'll be moving right on by them. On the bus I'd have to endure the stares, and the other passengers would have to endure the sight of me. I could take a taxi, but I might get in an accident and become disfigured. How could a person ever live with such a thing? (A little derm humor!!!) By foot is the way to make this trek. I ought to walk by the beach in my swimsuit and show those folks a body that would turn heads. I think, however, that walking the back streets is all I'm game for today.

So I'm off like a large bird, as Mom used to say. In my case, I guess I should say like a large toad.

Thursday, July 4, 1968, 3:20 a.m.

I knew the warts were growing. But walking to the dermatologist's office, I began to *feel* them grow. At first it was that itchy feeling like when a scab falls off and the new pink skin has the cut about sealed. But soon I could feel it *under* my skin as well as on top. It was inside, in the meat of me. It didn't hurt, but it was all over me. I felt it inside my toes, inside my cock. I felt it between my skull and my hair. I could feel points of pressure all over my head. I felt them on my cheeks and my jaw and in my eyes.

I began walking as fast as I could. It was all I could do to keep the panic from getting loose in me. By the time I'd gotten through Copacabana and into Botafogo, the armpits of my shirt were bloody from the warts rubbing and I could see the stain begin to grow high on the inseam of my jeans. I'd been self-conscious when I started out. Everyone turned to look at me, but most people turned away after a couple seconds. But when that feeling started spreading through me and I looked down at my forearms and could see the difference in the size of the warts just from when I left my apartment, I got so scared I didn't even think about the other people on the street.

The doctor's receptionist was an attractive girl about my age, and there was a mother and her teenaged daughter with about three pimples sitting in the waiting room. The receptionist tried to keep her mouth from twitching when she looked up at me and the other two picked up magazines and hid behind them after they took the first look at me, and their faces glazed over. My soul was shrinking so fast it felt like there was no way I could save it before it disappeared.

I told the receptionist my name, and she saw the blood and asked in perfect English if I was hurt. I said no, but asked her quietly if they had a room where I could wait for Dr. Bertão alone. She said of course and took me to a little room furnished like a bedroom in a home except for the examining table. After she left I walked to the mirror and looked at my face. The things had gone wild in the hour it had taken to get to the doctor's office. They'd advanced a stage in evolution. I wasn't a wartbaby anymore. I was an adult wartman. I'd reached my majority.

The sight of myself made me weak. I lay on the exam table and closed my eyes and folded my arms across my chest. That feeling of the wartroots running wild inside me was so strong I had the sensation I was moving on the table even though I knew I was lying still as I could.

In a half hour or so I heard voices speaking in Portuguese outside the door. I heard the receptionist say *"verrugas"* about six times, but that was all I picked up. Then I heard the door open. I was afraid to open my eyes because I didn't want to see how much more the warts had grown since I lay down. I heard the doctor's voice close above me. "You are Karl Russell?" he asked in English.

"Yes," I said. "And you're Dr. Bertão?"

"I am Dr. Bertão," he said. He asked me why my eyes were closed, and I told him the warts had grown so much while I walked there from Ipanema that I was afraid to look at them. I told him I could feel them growing.

I heard the sound of rubber gloves being stretched, then the squeaky sound as the doctor pulled them on. It reminded me of when the police had me. I could feel the warts on my butt. It was as if they were sending roots up my asshole like wartpolice on an anal search, and a shudder rippled from one end of me to the other.

"Are you in pain, Karl?" the doctor asked. I could feel his hands on me.

"No," I replied.

"And what is your age, Karl?" he asked.

"I'll be twenty-one tomorrow," I said.

"Karl," Dr. Bertão said, "I'd like you to sit up now so we can remove your shirt and look at this bleeding. Keep your eyes closed if you like, my boy."

I sat up and he helped me off with my T-shirt. "The blood's from the warts," I said. "When I swing my arms it rubs them raw."

He pushed me gently onto my back again. "And a physician in the United States told you these were warts?" he asked as he raised one of my arms.

"Not these," I said. "I got these after I was here. But at home I had some removed from my wrist and my back and some from my head. The doctor told me they were warts. He said the ones on my back were the biggest he'd ever seen."

"And this doctor was a specialist in dermatology?"

"I saw two specialists," I said. "Supposedly they were both hotshots."

"I see," he said. He placed my arms across my chest again. "Karl," he said, "I'm going to phone a colleague and I'd like you to rest just as you are until he arrives."

"Doctor," I said, "can you do anything for me?"

"We will certainly try, my boy," he said. I felt the cold rubber glove pat my hand. "First we must determine the nature of these growths. I don't believe they are warts," he said. "My colleague will examine you, then the two of us will put our heads together. Meanwhile I will take a tissue sample."

I kept my eyes closed. He opened a cupboard and I heard the clink of light metal. In my mind I could see the little stainless-steel dish, and it made me think of the Havermeyer brothers. I felt something cold touch my side, but I didn't feel any pain. Dr. Bertão said he'd send in a nurse to wash off the blood and give me something that would relax me. Then I heard the door close. I never got to see his face, and I regret it, because he'd been kind to me.

I lay there feeling the cool, grainy leather on my back. Actually I only felt it on the warts because there were so many of them and they'd grown so big they kept my back from touching. But still that coolness felt good as the sweat dried.

The nurses came in, and I kept my eyes closed. She spoke broken English, but she tried to be natural and cheerful and soothing as she washed under my arms and down my sides. The cool cloth felt wonderful and I thought I might drop off to sleep. My breathing got slow and regular and she slapped me lightly on my stomach and told me I cannot go falling to sleep without I am swallowing the pill. She helped me sit up, and I felt her gloved hand on my back. I kept my eyes closed. I figured if I didn't look at her I wouldn't have to see myself in her eyes. She pressed a pill into my palm and I put it in my mouth. She raised a glass to my lips and I drank water. Then I lay back down. She passed the cloth over my forehead once and said my friend would be there soon.

I sat up and opened my eyes. "My friend!" I said. "What friend?"

"Senhora Porto is telephone to come by here," she said. She was part Indian and reminded me of Leila.

I lay back down. "Thank you for phoning her," I said. But inside I was panicked. I couldn't let Dona Regina see me. I closed my eyes and breathed deeply and slowly until the nurse went out. Then I jumped up, put on my shirt, and peeked out the door. The hall was clear, so I made a run for it. I was through the waiting room and out the door headed for the stairs before the receptionist could get a word out.

I ran all the way home. Buy the time I got to Ipanema I was blood down to my knees. Traffic stopped and business ceased being transacted as I passed. When I turned the corner at Montenegro and Nascimento Silva the two cops watching the *favela* path looked like they might come after me. They probably thought I'd been set afire and put out with a golf shoe, and wanted to help me.

I got inside the apartment and locked the door. Then I stepped right into the shower. After I got my breath I undressed and tossed my bloody clothes in the bidet. I looked down between my legs, and the warts were still oozing blood. They did look like mushrooms—

MYSTERIOUS WAYS

or what was left of mushrooms after somebody'd raked the lawn. In the big ones you could see the tiny channels where the blood rose. I opened my legs and let the water wash me, then I watched the tiny channels fill with blood. I looked at my cock, and it didn't look like a cock at all anymore. It looked like a pale little cob of Indian corn. I sank down to the floor and laid my head against the tiled wall and cried and didn't try to hold back the tears.

I didn't have any feelings left in me. No more feeling of the warts growing, no more self-consciousness, no feeling but fatigue. I was so, so tired. I had a vision of myself just before I fell asleep. I saw myself lying in the shower the way I was, but it was a huge shower. It was huge and it was empty except for me lying in one corner. Something was falling down on me from the nozzles in the ceiling. But it wasn't water. It floated down like a cloud. And then I realized it was gas. And I breathed it in as deep as I could.

I slept in the shower until all the hot water was gone and the cold water woke me. As I toweled off I thought to myself that it was all over. I didn't know what I was going to do, but I did know it was over for me. I wasn't going home again, I wouldn't see Jen, I'd ridden my last ride on my father's Harley-Davidson on those little blacktop roads through the hills of the wheat country with that beautiful Harley exhaust note ringing in the blue twilight.

I knew finally that it was all gone. And my spirit was gone. The guy I'd been and the man I wanted to grow up to be were both gone.

I toweled off slowly and thought about it. I had been going to face the problem. I'd written up my little plan of action. What a fucking joke.

I was putting on my clothes when Dona Regina knocked at the door. "Karl," she said. "Karl, we talked to Dr. Bertão. We want to help you. He thinks he can help you, but you must allow yourself to be treated." She knocked some more. "Karl," she said, "are you in there, Karl?"

I sat down on the bed as quietly as I could. I heard Portuguese being spoken outside, then Senhor Porto spoke.

"Karl," he said, "we will stand with you through this illness. If you don't want to speak about it now, telephone us and we will come and take you to a private hospital where Dr. Bertão will treat you. Do not act out of impulse, Karl. You are not alone. Rest tonight. Telephone us in the morning and we will take you to the hospital."

They both wished me "*boa noite*," and then the apartment was quiet again. I lay back and thought about what Senhor Porto had said. How the fuck could anyone treat something that looked like me? And what if the warts grew again? Jesus Christ, I've got a wart—or whatever it is—on the inside of my elbow that's an inch tall and a couple inches around at the top. They can't be taken off. There wouldn't be anything left of me.

Senhor Porto was wrong about me not being alone. I'm alone, all right. I'm the worst bad dream anybody ever had. I can't even stand myself. You don't get any more alone than that.

I lay and watched the light leave the sky. I knew I had to make a decision. And then I heard a bony little fist rapping at the door.

"Karl," the tough old voice said. "Karl, it's Anna Schächter with soup and the good intention to pay a visit."

My first thought was that the Portos had gotten hold of Dona Anna somehow and they were all going to burst in with a net and capture me like Frank Buck capturing something for a zoo.

"Don't get up, young man," Dona Anna said. "I will use my key."

I dove under the bed. I heard the door close and her footsteps cross the wood floor, then hit the tiled floor of the kitchen. Maybe she was alone and did have soup. But then the footsteps were coming fast and fear jumped into my throat because I thought they had me. But there was only one set of old black shoes and skinny old ankles at the side of my bed. "Well," Dona Anna said aloud to herself, "I see the sick boy is well and gone."

The black shoes turned and had reached the bedroom doorway before I spoke. I'm just a coward. No guts to face people, but no guts to go it in silence either. "I'm here, Dona Anna," I said. "I'm under the bed."

"Karl?" she said. "Under the bed?"

"I didn't want you to see me," I said. "The rash got worse. But thank you for coming and for the soup," I said.

Her knees cracked as she knelt to the floor. Then I saw her gray head as she peered into the darkness where I ws. "Young man," she said, "you crawl out of there. You are the strangest American I have ever encountered."

Boy, I thought, you don't know the half of it.

I said I'd come out if she'd go in the other room. She kept looking in at me, but all she could see was my feet, which were right beside her. Thankfully, I'd put my socks on. Two pair, because running had torn up the warts on my feet so bad I couldn't get them to stop bleeding.

"Come out of there right now," she said as he got to her feet.

I waited till her footsteps hit the kitchen floor, then I rolled out. "I'm sorry, Dona Anna!" I yelled. Then I started to cry. I stood beside the doorway and blubbered and yelled out to her that I'd gone to a doctor, but that it had gotten worse in the little time it took me to walk to Botafogo and that the doctor didn't even know what it was and that they were going to put me in a hospital, but that I was so ugly and the condition was so far advanced I knew there was nothing they could do and that I just wanted to go home but I couldn't go home and I didn't really even have a home anyway and I hadn't had one for a long, long time and I was afraid.

"I am coming in there," Dona Anna said quietly. I heard her footsteps and hid under the covers. I heard her slide a chair across the floor, then I felt her hand on me through the sheet and blanket. "Karl," she said, "I want you to show me this rash of yours. I want you to give me your hand."

I was sobbing. I could barely speak. My voice wanted to say no, I couldn't do it. But my hand wanted to feel the touch of another person. I was sobbing and suffocating under the covers. My face was turned to the wall, so I opened an air hole and then I twisted my right arm behind me and pushed my hand out.

There was silence in the room for a few seconds, then two small, strong hands took my hand. After a few more seconds of silence, Dona Anna spoke. "You must never lose faith, Karl," she said. I could feel her fingers move between the warts into the smooth places left on the back of my hand.

"I don't have any faith to lose," I replied. "I never have had." It felt good to cry so hard, and the tone of her voice felt good inside my head.

"Then you must never lose hope," Dona Anna said. She kept her fingers moving slowly on the smooth skin she could find on my hand.

"You see it now, Dona Anna," I sobbed. "There's no hope. My hands look good compared to the rest of me."

"Yes, Karl," she said. "I see now why you have hidden from me. But as long as we are joined to the living, there is hope. There are many oppressions done to us in our lives, Karl. I myself knew a time when I found no comforter."

"You were in a concentration camp, weren't you?" I said.

"I was in one of the Nazi death camps for three years, Karl," she replied. "Yet here I sit with you now. I did not die, did I?"

I'd slowed down my crying a little. "No," I said. "You didn't die. But I can't live this way, Dona Anna." I started crying hard again.

"Who is it that has said you must live this way? I will find help for you. I know a wonderful doctor whom the Nazis also could not kill. I will bring him here tomorrow morning." She gave my hand a squeeze, then she released it. "Now I am going to bring your soup. I will wait in the other room while you eat."

"Thank you!" I yelled after her. I had already begun to smell the chicken soup, and the richness of the aroma made the air golden and glossy. I threw off the covers, but pulled them over my head again when I heard Dona Anna's footsteps.

"Eat, young man," she said. "To have faith or to have hope, we need our strength."

The soup tasted wonderful. It had big pieces of chicken and carrots and no bones, and it was wonderful. I could feel little bumps on my tongue that hadn't been there this morning. What's another few warts now? I said to myself. It was a big bowl of soup, but I was downing it fast. I made an effort to pace myself. "Dona Anna," I said, "can I ask you something about the camp?"

"Of course, Karl," she replied.

"How did you get through when you knew you had no comforter?"

"Karl, I reminded myself continually of the teachings of our sages that all things pass away and only God endures forever. I knew that I would pass or the camp would pass, but that one day it would all end. And I knew that although I seemed to suffer alone, God was judging me and had not abandoned me completely, but only as a father gives up his daughter to the world one day. The father and daughter are separated in many ways, yet they remain together in their hearts forever.

"It was not easy to maintain my faith, Karl," Dona Anna continued. "I despaired again and again. But God was with me in his way and

I was never alone. And I also was lucky, Karl. Somehow I remained healthy and able to work. And the Nazis would not kill the Jews who could work for them." And then her voice picked up. "And you too shall have good luck, young man! You too will survive your camp! My friend and I will help you."

"Thank you, Dona Anna," I said. "And thank you for sitting with me and bringing me soup and for holding my hand!" I started crying *again*. I knew that having Dona Anna as a landlady was the best luck I was going to get. I heard her voice by the bedroom doorway.

"Doctor Weissmandel and I will be here in the morning. Sleep tonight, Karl," she said quietly. "Know that you have friends who understand your suffering. Know that you are not alone."

"Thanks, Dona Anna," I said. "Good-bye. Thank you."

"Good night, Karl," Dona Anna said. I heard her lock the door behind her.

I know Dona Anna understands suffering. Maybe she even understands *my* suffering. But she doesn't understand this thing that's happening to me. I sure don't understand it. But I know I'm alone in it. I can only think of one place to be, and that's among people like me. It's another dream coming true. The only place I can go is to the *mudados*. They'll take me in. It won't matter to them if I'm ugly. And I've got money. I can pay them rent if I have to.

Dona Anna left about five hours ago. My bags are packed now and I'm ready to head out. I've got notes for Dona Anna and for the Portos to tape to the door.

Tuesday, July 9, 1968

I am a brother to dragons,
    and a companion to owls.
My skin is black upon me,
    and my bones are burned with heat.

Those are the words of Job, the Old Testament character notable for having been fucked by God and during the whole wild interlude not given even one tiny little kiss on the cheek.

A person might think being a brother to dragons is a bad deal, but I'm here in the flesh (in a manner of speaking) to say it's not so bad. Actually, I'm not a brother to dragons. I'm a brother to altered people, some natural freaks, and their friends and families. But I really am a companion to an owl, a tiny little *coruja* that lives in a crack in the wall above me here in my little corner of the *Estação*. I wouldn't be surprised if he were an altered owl. He's all bent up and he doesn't fly. He hops around the floor and walls eating (thank God) with his crooked beak the big black spiders to which I am also brother.

> I am a brother to freaks,
> and a companion to an owl and
> spiders.
> My skin is like a field of turnips upon me,
> and my bones feel invaded by tubers.

As incredible as it sounds to hear myself think it, as incredible as it looks to see myself write it, I am almost happy here. I had a few rocky days, but things are smoothing out (no pun intended). I have a board to write on, a brand-new kerosene lantern to read and write by, and I have new stuff to read because Emilio, the pinheaded guy who brought me the lantern, gets it for me for a slight fee. All this good stuff, plus I went through yesterday and today without feeling one quiver of self-consciousness.

These people couldn't give a shit what I look like. The wartlady I saw in the post office used to live with them. Wartpeople are old news around here. Emilio, who is twenty-two, short, and wiry, and always out to make a "cru" or two however he can, asked me if I was related to the wartlady. He smiled when he asked, so he might have been joking. He's smart and funny and he speaks fair English because of all the American and British tourists he hustles.

I answered him in English, whispering because a lot of these folks speak some English and this is definitely not the place for a newcomer to be making jokes about anyone's physical appearance. "Me related to her? Whaddaya mean, Emilio? That woman is ugly!" He laughed and slapped me on the shoulder. "A little wartperson humor," I said.

But as I mentioned, I wasn't exactly the Bob Hope of the *Estação dos Mudados* my first couple days. I got here around dawn Friday, limping bad on my bleeding wartfeet, my Converse All-Stars squishy with blood. I parted the vines that cover the entrance, but I didn't see any lights and I didn't hear any voices. No one was up yet and I didn't think having me be the first thing they saw in the morning would get us off to a good start. So I let the vines swing together and sat down on the cool stones a few feet away. I took off my tennies and looked at my feet. They looked like a dessert made of strawberries and miniature marshmallows. I was going to have to slit the sides of my shoes and cut the toes out like old people do.

It turns out, though, that I'm more comfortable without shoes. Except when the spiders crawl over my feet. And I've developed what I realize will be a permanent limp. I guess it's more of a hobble, since I do it with both feet. It's not because of running from Dr. Bertão's office or walking all the way here to Cosme Velho. It's just the nature of having warts all over your feet.

Anyway, my feet felt a lot better free of the shoes, and I stretched my legs out so my feet lay in a clump of tall grass wet and cool with dew. I laid my head back on my gym bag. I hadn't planned to sleep, just to rest until I heard someone awake in the *Estação*. But the second I closed my eyes I was gone.

I woke up in a fetal position on the stones. They weren't cool anymore, they were hot. It was mid-morning and I had that fat-headed feeling you get from waking up in the heat. Five of the *mudados* sat in a semicircle around me on the low stone wall: the white-haired man with no hands, his wife, the blind woman and the woman who leads her around, and the guy with the broken arms and legs I'd seen begging that night at the cemetery. Somebody had set him there on the wall in the sun. The others were talking together, not paying much attention to me, but this guy—his name is Adelino—was staring holes through me. I had the feeling he recognized me, but I don't think that's possible.

Professora Sofia saw I was awake and leaned over and whispered to the blind woman, Dona Gabriela, who turned her face toward me. Senhor Félix heard her and turned to me and pointed one of his stubs. The end has a thick, yellowed callus on it, just like a callus on a hand or foot. "Good morning," he said in English. I sat up as he introduced himself and the others in Portuguese.

All the people here aren't *mudados*. Professora Sofia and Senhor Félix's wife, Dona Amélia, are normal, and Dona Gabriela is only blind. It's Adelino and some of the others who stay inside most of the time who are the real "altered" people.

At least I can still stand and walk and hold a book to read and a pen to write. Actually, about all I can't do is go home and dance on *American Bandstand*, and that's just because my feet would hurt.

I told them I was an American and my name was Russ and it was a pleasure to meet them, *"muito prazer."* Senhor Félix said they understood why I was there, but couldn't imagine how I knew about them. I explained as best I could, leaving out references to the Portos and my visit there with Solono, in case any of them might want to reunite me with the normal world. Senhor Félix said it was an amazing coincidence that I would hear about them in the United States when I was well, become "sick" in Rio (it took him a while to find the word for what I had become), then seek them out and find them. Yes, I agreed, it had been a great coincidence.

"No," said Dona Gabriela. "It is God that has brought you to us."

I looked into her blind eyes. They looked normal to me except that they wandered a little as she kept her face perfectly on mine. *"Talvez, sim,"* I said. "Maybe so."

The fat little dwarf lady brought me out a coffee then. *"Um café para o senhor,"* she said, as she had before. Now, in the light and when I wasn't so scared, it was plain to see she was retarded.

She treated me exactly as she had when I was a normal-looking person. Senhor Félix introduced her as Natalina. I stood to shake hands, but she only bowed and held out her tray.

As I drank my coffee I asked if I could stay with them. I said I had some money and that I could work. I told them I couldn't beg—not because of pride, but because I didn't want people to see me. I really thought I'd blown it then, because *they* were people too. *"Não, não,"* I said. *"Desculpe."*

"We know what you mean," Senhor Félix said.

And then Adelino spoke, carefully, so I would understand. "We all have our pride," he said. "Nevertheless, some of us must beg to live." He looked down at his legs, bent nearly ninety degrees in the middle of his thighs, then at his arms, flopping and pointing behind him because of his broken shoulders and elbows. "Some of us were created to beg," he said, before he turned his pointed head and flattened face away.

"We were all created to fulfill God's will," is what I think Dona Gabriela said.

Senhor Félix told me they had plenty of room in the *Estação* for people who needed a home, and that they tried to have an equal amount of room in their hearts. He extended one of his handless arms toward the entrance and said in English, "After you." I picked up my stuff and led the little group to the entrance where Dona Amélia held back the vines and I crossed the threshold, scared as a newlywed.

The *Estação* was dark even in the middle of the day, but the good smell of beans cooking and the kerosene lanterns gave it a homey glow, especially so, I suppose, if your recent ancestors had lived in caves. The others went off to get ready for lunch, they said, and Senhor Félix took me deeper into what I could see in even that little light was a huge cavern. He told me they had bathroom facilities and a pool of fresh water to bathe in, and that they each put in a few cruzeiros every week for the good food Dona Amélia and the other women prepared. I gave him a hundred cruzeiros, and he told me that would be my contribution for the month. As we walked toward the source of the bean smell, I saw that some of the walls were tiled and some were still bare rock. Water dripped and moss grew deep and soft-looking on the rocks, and on the tile it looked like patches of green felt against the white.

The smell of fresh water moving through vegetation was the same smell as in my dreams of the place, and the sound of the dripping water was the same. The water drained into a long, narrow ditch that was obviously where the subway trains would have run. Five normal-looking naked little boys were playing in the water, and I began to wonder where the hell all the *mudados* were. The kids all got a good look at me, and none of them seemed surprised that such a creature would be walking the bank of their swimming hole.

We walked down the third set of stairs toward the bean smell, the light, and the voices, and when we turned a corner we were in the dining hall. The *mudados* were chowing down. It was like a summer camp for the inhabitants of nightmares. About fifty people were in line with their plates or already eating on the various wooden tables, rock ledges, or flat spots on the floor of the chamber. Twenty, maybe more, of the people were normal, or so close to normal you wouldn't notice what was wrong with them. You especially wouldn't notice because the rest of the crew had stopped your heart. From where we stood on the bottom step I saw a guy with webbed hands and skin like an alligator's. If he'd had slightly thicker lips, I'd have taken him for the Creature from the Black Lagoon. And one of the women spooning out beans and rice had the face of a pig—the leathery, hairy, snouted, pointy-eared face of a barnyard pig.

Then there was another lady who'd been terribly burned. She didn't have any hair and she wore a patch of red cloth over one eye. The other eye looked like it worked, but she only had half her nose and her lips were tight, red wrinkles around a hole in her face. Her skin had a shine to it like plastic. Her hands, drawn around her drinking cup, were like two big turkey feet. You wouldn't have been able to tell she was a woman except that the pretty yellow-and-white sundress she was wearing suggested it.

I didn't wonder long, because my attention was drawn to a kid— maybe he's a midget—who looks like a werewolf. The guy's a dead ringer for that little European prince with long blondish hair all over his face and the muzzle of a dog and pointed ears that you see in all the werewolf and human-curiosity books.

Professora Sofia introduced me to Emilio. He has an interesting look because of the shape of his head and his impish but strong little body. It's like his head was formed when protoplasm and molten bone were poured into an old alchemist's hat. It gives him a sort of comical, crafty air, like Merlin the Magician in *The Once and Future King*. I liked him right off, but he really won my heart when he shook hands with me and said in English, "Hi, man. How ya doin'?" You've got to love a Brazilian pinhead who greets an American wartman and puts him at ease like that.

Emilio and I ate our black beans and rice and tomato chunks in vinegar together, and I tried not to stare at the people. There are a lot of *mudados* here with their limbs broken like Adelino. He's the worst I've seen—most of these people can either walk or propel themselves on little creeper boards—and the youngest. Bone-busting must have been all the rage as a method of altering children back in the 1930s and 1940s. Then there's an old black man with a flattened head and a mouth like a duck's bill. He was sitting next to an old white lady whose nostrils had been stretched the full width of her face. They go out to her ears! Her nose is five or six inches across!

We were sitting near an Indian-looking guy in his fifties with the worst smallpox scars I've ever seen. He and I looked like a matched set of monstrosities. All my protrusions could fit right into his indentations, and we could present ourselves as a puzzle to educate the young about shapes and sizes. We could go to grade schools and the little kids could keep trying to fit us together until they got the right-sized warts on me plugged into the corresponding-sized craters in him.

Emilio saw me looking around and bent close. "When I feeling sorry for myself I look here at my neighbors, Roose," he whispered. He held his finger to his pointed head. "Then I give thanks to God that my *cabeça* handsome as it is."

I nodded. "You've got a good point, Emilio," I said. But he didn't get it.

After lunch Emilio showed me the vacant spaces and I chose my little nook here. Water drips down the rocks beside me and I like listening to it. It reminds me of fishing Marshall Creek back home, when I was a kid with skin as smooth as the eelgrass that waved in the water. Emilio told me he bought things for people for 10 percent of the total cost, and he asked if I needed anything. I told him what I wanted, gave him two hundred cru, and he said he'd bring back the receipts.

I laid my stuff down and sat there on the smooth rock in the dark and had a very large emotional collapse.

I remembered it was my birthday. All my birthdays as a kid popped and sparkled and boomed back to me like the fireworks we always saved to shoot until the fifth. I saw Mom and Dad so perfectly in my mind I started to cry because I couldn't jump inside my memories and run to them and have my life now be just a bad dream. I laid my head on my gym bag and covered my face and cried as hard as I could until I felt a spider on me that I couldn't shake off, and it was Dona Gabriela's hand on my shoulder.

I looked into her face. Professora Sofia stood behind her with a lantern. "What is wrong, Roose?" Dona Gabriela asked. "This must be a happy day for you because God has brought you to make a home with his children. Why are you crying?"

What could I say? I just put my head back down and cried more.

But Dona Gabriela shook my shoulder again. "What is wrong, our friend Roose?" she said with a sweetness that moved me.

Before I could answer Adelino boomed, "What is wrong? If you could see him, Dona Gabriela, you would know what is wrong." People were holding him on his wooden platform, I knew, but the way the light shone on him with the dark everywhere else, he looked like he was floating in the air. He was agitated, and his arms and legs bounced and flapped like tentacles. "If you could see us, Dona Gabriela, your question would be why are we all *not* in tears. You would ask why we are not in tears every day we live this curse you call the gift of life."

Adelino almost had me hypnotized. It was like the force of what he was saying was keeping him in the air. But Dona Gabriela spoke again and I looked into her eyes. "Why are you crying, Roose?" she asked again.

"*Hoje é meu aniversário,*" I said. I don't know why I told her, but I did. "Today's my birthday."

"Happy birthday, Roose," Professora Sofia said. She stepped closer with the light.

"Happy birthday, Roose," Dona Gabriela said. "Don't cry any more now."

I sat up then and we talked a little. I told them I was twenty-one, and Gabriela said she was thirty-five and Sofia said she was twenty-six. Emilio got back then. He had my lantern filled up, and I felt a lot better just having some light. I also had a *Brazil Herald*, a *Time*, and two school notebooks, one with a toucan on the front and the other with a giant sea turtle swimming across it. They felt like birthday presents even though I'd paid for them myself. Emilio gave me back my change and showed me the receipts and told me how much he'd taken for himself. "*Feliz aniversário,* man!" he said, as they all walked away.

I was into the *Herald* sports section reading about Denny McLain pitching a perfect game for seven innings against Cleveland when I heard a match strike and caught the flare out of the corner of my eye. I looked up to see Sofia lighting the candles on a birthday cake Emilio was holding. Standing with them were Gabriela, Senhor Félix, Dona Amélia, and, as far as I could tell, everyone in the whole *Estação* I'd seen that day. They sang a Brazilian song. There was so much kindness in those awful faces that I began to cry again.

They didn't mind me crying. When they finished singing we cut the cake and had a birthday party right there. We ate cake and drank fruit juice out of paper cups, and a good time was had by all. I met a lot of people. Shaking hands with the burned lady was like holding a warm rubber glove. And the old guy who looks like Donald Duck talks like him too.

Everybody faded off after a while, and I thanked each of them and shook hands again before they left. This time when I sat down in my corner alone, I was fine. I was even finer when I saw this funny little thing hop down the rocks beside me and gulp down the spider crawling across the piece of cake I'd been about to pick up and take to the garbage. I stood and held up my lantern and saw it was a strange little owl. I looked up "owl" in my dictionary and found it was "*coruja*." I was extremely pleased to have a spider-eating *coruja* for a neighbor.

My spirits went nowhere but up after that.

Friday, July 12, 1968, 6:30 a.m.

My days have been full since my last entry. I helped with dinner and the dishes Wednesday evening, then I sat and listened to a soccer game on the radio with a *mudado* guy and his normal wife and their two normal kids I'd swum with in the pool that afternoon. I didn't get two words of the soccer commentary, but it felt good to sit with them and see the kids and their dad get psyched about the game.

Emilio bought me a little pocket transistor with an ear plug. I haven't been very sleepy for some reason, and I listened to Mundial till about two this morning through the ear plug. I listened to the Beatles, the Stones, and Bob Dylan until I got so comfortable I sort of lost consciousness or something and began thinking I was back home in my old upstairs bedroom in the house in Nine Mile Falls listening to the radio when I was supposed to be asleep. I got up and walked outside then. It was a bright, starry night and I climbed the trail up the mountain and sat looking at Christ the Redeemer, who's just over on the next mountain top. A guy with a good arm could throw a rock and hit him. I couldn't help thinking it was sure too bad God didn't send him to die and save humanity from something practical like burns over 90 percent of your body or parents who sold you to people who broke your bones or being born with the face of a pig or having things growing all over you.

Christ is supposed to have died to save us from eternal damnation. I don't believe in eternal damnation. If you're going to save me, Jesus, save me from something here and now when I need it. Now's when I could use some clean, smooth skin, not when I'm just a spirit, a light in the sky, a good feeling like Mom and Dad. It's clear to me from the New Testament that Jesus really believed he was dying to save people. But what if when Jesus got to heaven He realized that His suffering and death were just more of God's whims, like letting Satan destroy Job's life or wiping out whole cities because He didn't like people fucking each other in the ass or turning guys' wives into salt? Jesus would have been one sad boy if that's what He discovered when He got to heaven.

I looked at Christ, then down at the city lights and the blur of the few car lights shooting along the beach. I wished I were back in Cheney driving on those little narrow blacktop roads to Jen's. I rubbed my thumb and forefinger together, and in spite of what I really felt—which was nothing but folding warttissue—in my mind I could feel the smooth old brass ignition key to the Ford.

I wonder if all people have this stupid, uncontrollable sort of optimism I have. It's an ability to be happy sometimes even in spite of what would seem fairly bleak circumstances. I mean, I'm almost blind in one eye now—I've got a wart spreading out over my eye like a big lily pad on a pond. And even on the occasions when I'm able to take a solid shit, it comes out like pinto beans through a colander because of all the warts around my asshole. I can't wipe myself and get clean. There are too many dirty nooks and crannies, too many shit-covered surfaces. I have to wash every time I take a shit if I want to stay clean. Which I do! But even so, I'm pretty happy at times. Emilio bought me some plastic and I folded it and stuffed it with leaves and grass and made a great bed. And I like the food here, and swimming in that cold, clear water with the kids was fun.

I don't understand how I can feel an ounce of happiness looking like I do and feeling as full of despair as I often feel. But even back when Mom and Dad and Jesse died, even then this happy feeling would rise up in me like helium and lift me off the ground until I began feeling guilty for not staying sad. In spite of all evidence to the contrary, something inside me will pop up and say everything's going to turn out all right. I'm not a totally stupid guy, but that seems to me a totally stupid feeling. But I can't control it. I can't keep it down.

I was walking back to the *Estação* when I saw Emilio slinking up the stairs like a pointy-headed ferret. "Hey, Emilio!" I said.

"*O meu Deus!*" Emilio yelped. "Man, Roose, you scare me, man. I think you the death squad here to clean up Rio of another 'marginal.'"

"Nope," I said. "It's just me out looking at our neighbor." I pointed my thumb up behind me where Christ's head shone above our mountaintop in the bright glow of His floodlight halo.

"Cristo," Emilio said. "Cristo is a good neighbor. He never play his radio loud. He make the good drum if you beat on him with a stick."

I laughed. We sat on the wall and looked down on Cosme Velho with its few lights and no traffic. It was quiet except for the insects and a siren far off. I asked Emilio if he ever wondered why his life had come out like it did.

"You mean my head, Roose?" he said.

I shrugged. I wished I hadn't brought up the subject.

"I am borned this way," he said. "But the answer is the same if some person make me like this after I am borned. The answer is it does not matter. I go to the city, get money, come home, make my *música*, go to the city again and get more money. I think about my *cabeça*, it only slow me down."

I looked out over the mountain at the stars.

"If you are wanting to talk of *os meios misteriosos*—the mysterious ways—" Emilio said, "talk with Senhor Félix. He was a priest."

"Senhor Félix was a priest!"

"He was Padre Félix," Emilio said. "And he had his hands. A long time he works in the *favelas*. He organize the *favelados* to vote, he and Dona Amélia—she is Sister Amélia then, and she is a nurse— they create the free hospital, they go in politics. The journals are saying he is *comunista*.

"When the government sweep all the *mudados* off the streets to make Rio more beautiful for the *turistas*, Padre Félix with the *mudados* and *favelados*, they make a big demonstration so the government makes a home for them. That night a death squad comes to the free hospital. They violate Sister Amélia—"

"They raped her?" I said.

"They are raping Sister Amélia, yes," Emilio said. "And they cutting off with big *facão*—with machete—the hands of Padre Félix. When he is well he brings Sister Amélia and the *mudados* here. When I come, he is Senhor Félix and she is Dona Amélia."

Emilio stood, wished me good night, advised me not to worry about the mysterious ways, and went in to bed.

God's Character as Illustrated
in the Book of Job

World Masterpieces
Karl Russell
May 21, 1968

The editors of the Dartmouth Bible say the theme of the Book of Job is "Why do the good suffer?" I don't want to disagree with a busload of eminent scholars, but I would submit that a more general statement of theme might be made, such as, Why do things happen as they do, why is life like it is?

Everyone would probably agree that religions exist to answer that question. We find God or we invent Him, and then He answers our question for us: life's like it is because human beings fell from grace and made it that way. Don't blame me! God says. All I did was make the rules—you guys broke 'em.

Although I've had a little Sunday school training, I'd never read the Book of Job before I took this class. Like most people in the Western world, I'd heard of Job as a mythic figure who got boils and endured them and other suffering. Sunday school and church tried to present God as both loving and lovable, but then we read a little in the Old Testament and I found out different. But I never read *anything* that makes God look as egomaniacal, cruel, and generally hateful as the Book of Job.

The portrait of God presented in the Book of Job is especially incriminating because it comes from God Himself. He wrote the book! I am not being facetious here. I learned in Sunday school in the First Baptist Church of Nine Mile Falls, Washington, that God wrote every word of the Holy Bible. The Book of Job should be bad news for God fans.

The God we see in Job has more negative human qualities than Job does. The first look we get at God shows Him as a smug braggart. All the sons of God have come together to present themselves before the Lord, and Satan's come too, from "going to and fro in the earth, and from walking up and down in it." And God says to Satan, "Hast thou considered my servant Job, that there is none like him in the earth, a perfect and an upright man, one that feareth God and escheweth evil?"

And Satan replies that it's easy for Job to be perfect and upright because God has "made a hedge about him, and about his house, and about all that he hath on every side. Put forth thine hand now, and touch all that he hath," Satan tells God, "and he will curse thee to thy face."

God is baiting Satan here! He's smugly tossing His servant Job into an arena where He and Satan are going to beat Job around and watch how he takes it. God says to Satan, "Behold, all that he hath is in thy power." Satan can do anything to Job but kill him.

So pretty soon the Sabeans steal all Job's oxen and asses and kill his ox- and ass-tenders. Fire falls out of heaven and burns up his sheep and shepherds. The Chaldeans steal his camels and kill his camel-tenders. A great wind from the wilderness smites the four corners of his eldest son's house and kills all Job's kids, who are having dinner there. Job's reaction to these terrible events is to pull out some of his hair, then shave his head and fall down on the ground and worship.

Job doesn't know it, of course, but we know it: this stuff didn't just happen. We have *evidence* that God allowed this to happen, that he *caused* it by taunting Satan. This is no God worth worshipping. It just astounds me that Christians are always saying there's some big mystery about the source of evil in the world. It should be clear from the Book of Job that at least some of the evil in the world comes from God.

"In all this Job sinned not, nor charged God foolishly."

So the sons of God get together with Him again and Satan is in attendance. And God says to Satan that Job still "holdeth fast to his integrity..." And He goes on to say something very important:

"...although thou movedst me against him..." God lies when He says Satan moved Him. Anyone can see that God was waving Job in front of Satan like a red flag in front of a bull. He admits Himself that He is responsible for Job's destruction, then He gloats over Job retaining his integrity.

When Satan smites Job with the infamous boils "from the soul of his foot unto his crown," Job's wife tells him, "Curse God, and die." But Job says, "What? shall we receive good at the hand of God, and shall we not receive evil?" Job knows God lays out the evil as well as the good.

Job certainly doesn't lose his integrity, but he does get mad. "Let the day perish wherein I was born," he says. "Why died I not from the womb? There the wicked cease from troubling, and there the weary be at rest." It's the idea of Death as a refuge from Life.

> Wherefore is light given to him that is in misery,
>   and life unto the bitter in soul;
>   Which long for death, but it cometh not;
>   and dig for it more than for hid treasures;
>   Which rejoice exceedingly, and are glad,
>   when they can find the grave?
> Why is light given to a man whose way is hid,
>   and whom God hath hedged in?

Job's friends come to comfort him, but he's covered with the boils to such a degree that they can't even recognize him. They have a very strange way of comforting him. The Dartmouth Bible calls their conversation a debate. I would say that Job's friends go into this battle of wits completely unarmed. Eliphaz the Temanite, for example, is a guy who has not been paying attention to the life going on around him. "Who ever perished, being innocent?" he asks Job, "or where were the righteous cut off? Even as I have seen, they that plow iniquity, and sow wickedness, reap the same. By the blast of God they perish, and by the breath of his nostrils are consumed." Let's forget about the big evil people who never perish by the blast of God— sackers of cities, for example—and let's consider infant mortality. Every baby or little kid who dies does so innocent.

Job begins his response by saying he wishes his friends had considered his grief and his calamity a little more seriously: "For the arrows of the Almighty are within me. But teach me," Job continues, "and I will hold my tongue. And cause me to understand wherein I have erred."

Job can't hold his tongue just yet, though, and he asks an important question. "Is there iniquity in my tongue?" he asks. "Cannot my taste discern perverse things?" Am I lyin'? Job asks. I don't think I'm lyin'. I'd know if I was.

Job agrees he must have sinned, but he can't understand why God has made him such a burden to himself. "Why dost thou not pardon my transgression, and take away mine iniquity?" Job asks.

Bildad the Shuhite answers, telling Job that he must have done something ghastly to the nth degree because God never perverts justice or judgment: "If thou were pure and upright: surely now he would awake for thee." Well, we *know* Job *is* pure and upright, because we overheard God tell Satan so. The Book of Job is proof that believers like Bildad and Eliphaz are being hoodwinked. The book tells us again and again that God's justice is a farce.

Job begins to consider the world a little differently now that suffering has changed his perspective. He doesn't see the justice in the world that he used to see. Here's the conclusion he comes to:

> He destroyeth the perfect and the wicked.
> If the scourge slay suddenly,
>   he will laugh at the trial of the innocent.
> The earth is given into the hand of the wicked.

Things are looking pretty dark to Job, but from what we know of God in this story, it's hard not to think Job is reading the situation right. In this case, at least, God has delivered Job's part of the earth into the hands of Satan.

I personally don't think things are this bad. I don't think the earth is necessarily in the hands of the wicked, but rather in the hands of the strong. I haven't seen any evidence that makes me think God favors the wicked or the good. Things aren't fair, of course. But I don't think God cares one way or the other. I think He just lets things run their course. The race, then, generally goes to the swift. And when, for some reason, the race goes to the less swift, it's that in this one instance the less swift had more courage.

Job pulls back a little after this blast and makes another good point.

Speaking directly to God, he says: "Thine hands have made me and fashioned me together round about; yet thou dost destroy me." What kind of father destroys his own children? Job's friend Zophar the Naamathite (suppose the guy's a New York Jets fan?) tells Job that God isn't giving him the punishment his sinfulness deserves. What's so interesting about this is the irony. The reader *knows* the truth because he saw God make the deal with Satan, so he sees these guys illustrating the falsity of their beliefs every time they open their mouths. Zophar ends his speech by telling Job to quit searching for God. Submitting to God is the way to find Him. "... prepare thine heart," he says, "and stretch out thine hand toward him." But Job doesn't want to submit. "I desire to reason with God," he says. "Though he slay me, yet will I trust him." What Job is trusting God to do, I think, is to have some respect for the humanity He gave him.

Good for Job! I say. How else are we supposed to find God, if not by following His trail through the world He made and drawing some conclusions about who He is from how He operates?

Eliphaz tells Job he's vain, Bildad wants him to shut up and quit insulting them, and Zophar the Naamathite reminds him that the triumph of wicked talkers is short. "Miserable comforters are ye all," Job says. He has more to say, and he asks them to listen carefully. We need to remember that Job is looking at the world in a new way now. I'll condense what he says:

> Wherefore do the wicked live,
>   become old, yea, are mighty in power?
> They spend their days in wealth,
>   and in a moment go down to the grave.
> One dieth in his full strength,
>   being wholly at ease and quiet.
> His breasts are full of milk,
>   and his bones are moistened with marrow.
> And another dieth in the bitterness of his soul,
>   and never eateth with pleasure.
> They shall lie down alike in the dust,
>   and the worms shall cover them.

Job's not going to desert God just because he's finally discovered how He really works. And he's not going to back down from belief in himself, either: "Till I die I will not remove mine integrity from me.

My righteousness I hold fast, and will not let it go: my heart shall not reproach me so long as I live."

Soon God Himself enters the debate. God's got quite a flair—He comes down in a whirlwind and speaks out of it. Maybe He's so ashamed of what He's done to Job, He can't look him in the eye. Maybe that's why He's hiding in a whirlwind. In any case, God's full of bluster and acts very offended that Job would dare to "darkeneth counsel by words without knowledge." He tries to impress Job with His work in geology, and He asks Job some pretty good questions, questions no one could answer yes to:

> Canst thou bind the sweet influences of Pleiades,
>   or loose the bands of Orion?
> Canst thou bring forth Mazzaroth in his season?
>   or canst thou guide Arcturus with his sons?
> Knowest thou the ordinances of heaven?
>   canst thou set the dominion thereof in the earth?

Well, of course Job can't do these things. No man could. Of course God is awesome in His power. But that doesn't excuse Him from being unjust in His exercise of that power on earth—among His own *children!*

Job buckles. God buffaloed him. "Behold, I am vile," Job says, "What shall I answer thee?" Job has lost his grip here. Just because he can't "loose the bands of Orion" doesn't mean he's vile. Somebody vile is someone who gives over his most righteous servant into the hands of Satan. That's what "vile" is.

God changes His tune entirely at this point. I think He's sorry and ashamed for what He did to Job. He should be. Here is where God calls a halt to the atrocity:

> Deck thyself now with majesty and excellency;
>   and array thyself with glory and beauty.
> Look on everyone that is proud, and bring him low;
>   and tread down the wicked in their place.

As I mentioned, the Book of Job is thought by many people to have a happy ending. I think it's a sad ending. Look how Job has been duped about God and about himself:

I have heard of thee by the hearing of the ear;
   but now mine eye seeth thee:
Wherefore I abhor myself, and repent
   in dust and ashes.

Job doesn't have anything to repent.

People think it's such a big deal that God restores Job with twice as much as he had before He took everything away. Job gets fourteen thousand sheep and six thousand camels and a thousand yoke of oxen and a thousand she-asses. And he gets seven sons and three daughters. Well, what about his children who were crushed when the wind from the wilderness levelled the house? Is Job supposed to forget those kids he loved who are never going to breathe the air with him again? God killed Job's kids! Hasn't anybody in Western civilization noticed that before? People you love who die can't ever be replaced.

I think the Book of Job shows us a man to admire and a God either to put at a distance from our lives or to actively hate. As for me? My purpose holds to admire my fellow human beings whom I judge worthy of admiration. People like Martin Luther King, Robert Kennedy, Job, Jackie Robinson, and my mom and dad.

Saturday, July 27, 1968

The time here has just been flying. "My days are swifter than a weaver's shuttle," Job said, and time's going by for me just that fast. I don't even keep track of the days anymore.

I've been thinking a lot about God, and I've read Job again. *King Lear* too. That made me think of Mac. If Mac hadn't broken his hand against Crookshank's head at initiation, he'd have been the one to drive Bolão to the airport. Bolão and Johnny would never have crossed paths, and Bolão would be alive. And if I'd never met Bolão, I wouldn't have come to Rio. If, if, if... A guy could build a whole different life on if's.

It's hard reading about Job without thinking God's got it in for me like that too. I certainly wasn't his most upright servant, though, back when the Buick station wagon blew out of the wilderness and collapsed the four corners of Dad's 'Vette. It's hard not to see that event starting a pattern that led me here. But I guess it started even before that, when I first saw the wartman.

It's funny: I go from being absolutely sure my life has been this big conspiracy to cause me pain, to laughing at myself for thinking so. Something's going on in my life, though; I have to admit I see and feel it. It's like a message I'm not receiving clearly. It came again three or four nights ago—days, I should say, because it came at sunrise.

One of the many differences between me and Job is that my friends treat me better.

Late on Friday night the *Estação* was about deserted. (Weekends are your heavy work times, when you count for your livelihood on the generosity of others. That's when people are out shopping, going to movies, getting an ice cream, and that's when they give money to beggars.) I'd read my *Time* and my *Brazil Herald*, found out Joe Frazier TKO'd Manuel Ramos in the fourth round last week, that our Marines finally all got out of Khe Sanh, that it looks like the Republicans are going to all vote for Richard Nixon at their convention, and I was tired of reading. I'd been reading the Old Testament and Shakespeare for days. I tried to sleep, but even though my new bed is as comfortable as a little nest, I haven't been sleeping well at all. I talked to the little *coruja* awhile as he sat clamped with his claws to my wrist pecking at the warts. He'll come to me like that as long as I keep my arm out of direct light. Put him in the light and he hops back up the wall to his hole. I know how he feels.

I tried listening to the radio, but I got to feeling sorry for myself thinking of all the kids back home driving around in their cars through the summer night listening to the same songs. I wondered how I was going to tell Jen I wasn't coming home. Then I got horny thinking about her and blew out the lantern.

You really have to be in need to beat off when you're a wartman. It's a real commitment. You rub the warts raw and they bleed. It's worth it to me, however, and it's the only way I can get to sleep. I fell asleep seeing and smelling and tasting and feeling on my lips—

in my mind, I mean—Jen's beautiful, sweet pussy that always kissed back as softly as a wet little mouth.

I woke to the scuffling of feet, the squeaky wheels of creeper boards, and the murmur of tired voices. The *mudados* cast grotesque shadows in the flickering yellow light of their lanterns. Some wobbled and talked like they were drunk. It was like watching all of sweet, sad humanity walk by me on its way to sleep. "*Cale-se!*" I heard someone say. "Quiet down. Roose sleeps here."

Adelino went past, carried on his platform by the young man and woman. His head lolled on his chest and his broken arms and legs bounced and quivered and in the dim light made you think he was wrapped in snakes.

I guess I dozed awhile. The next thing I remember was hearing Emilio's voice and opening my eyes in the near-total darkness. "Roose, man," Emilio was saying, "too bad you sleeping, man. We maybe drinking some *pinga* together and listening to Moon-dee-owwwww."

Emilio was drunk. In the thin line of light from the lamp down at the stairs I could see the bottle of clear liquid he was waving. "I'm awake, Emilio," I said. "Let's us drink some *pinga*." I lit my lantern, and Emilio cringed. As we were walking out he said, "I think these *verrugas* on you, they are more big now, Roose. You scare me when you come with the light."

I've noticed some of them are getting bigger. I've felt them growing like I did on the way to Dr. Bertão's. "Some of them are growing, all right," I said.

We parted the vines and stood under the great vault of stars. You couldn't hear a car, you couldn't hear a radio. I blew out the lamp and wondered what time it was. Emilio held his arm in front of my face. He had watches all the way up past his elbow. I laughed and read one of the luminous dials. "Four o'clock," I said. "You've been partying late, *o meio amigo*," I said.

Emilio handed me the bottle. "Oh, yes," he said. "I party with my friends in A Banda de Ipanema. We make a lot of samba tonight."

I told him I'd seen the Ipanema band, and I took a drink. The *pinga* burned my mouth, but when it hit my stomach it really ignited, like something you'd run in a double-A fueler at the drag strip. I coughed and the tears ran out the corner of my eyes. I had to move the big wart off my bad eye so the tears could get out.

We sat on the low stone wall. *"Pinga,"* Emilio said. "You are getting used to it. Don't worry, Roose. We listen to some *música*, we drink some *pinga*. Pretty soon you are getting used to it." He took his little transistor out of his pocket then, but as he brought it up it flew out of his hand. We heard it fall through the bushes in the dark below. *"Puta merda!"* Emilio said.

I told Emilio I'd hunt for his radio in the morning.

He took a big pull on the *pinga* bottle and told me he made *música* himself. "I am playing several of instruments," he said. He was kicking his heels against the wall. He seemed hypnotized by the twinkling lights of Cosme Velho below. "All Brazilians are musicians and make poems," he said. "Yes!" he shouted. "This is what we are doing! We are making ourselves *música*, by God!" He took a drink, handed me the bottle again, then spun off the wall, whipped through the vines, and was gone.

I took a pull on the bottle and began banging my heels against the rocks. The warts cushioned the blows like erasers on a bouquet of pencils.

When Emilio parted the vines a few minutes later, he was loaded down with musical instruments in a little net bag—a guitar and a little drum, a flute, and others I didn't know the names of. "Come, Roose," he said. "Bring your lantern and we walking up the mountain and making the *música*."

I lit the lamp again and we took the trail up the mountain. I stopped when we got to the grassy spot near the top, but Emilio told me we were going higher. I didn't know there was any higher place you could stand, but at the very top there was a little level spot where the dirt had been stamped hard and smooth. I blew out the lamp and set it down, because we could see pretty well in the light from Christ the Redeemer.

We were up even with Christ's outstretched arms. His fingers seemed so close, you felt like you could lean out over the edge a little way and touch Him. The view was spectacular, and I turned a circle. City lights surrounded us closely on three sides. Up close, on the fourth, the west side, it was all a deep black where the mountain dropped off to the forest below.

Emilio kept the guitar and flute and handed me the drum and one of those round, grooved pieces of wood with a smaller round piece to rasp across the grooves, and a whistle and a bell. "You do the *bateria*, Roose," he said. "You are making the percussion."

"You bet your shoes, man," I replied, taking another hit off the *pinga* bottle, which I'd been in charge of coming up the trail.

"Don't you say, 'You bet your boots,' Roose?" Emilio asked.

"Yeah," I replied, "normally you do."

Maybe all Brazilians really are musicians and poets. I didn't think I'd ever meet a better guitar player and singer than Bolão, but Emilio was better. Maybe it's the strange quality of his voice, or maybe it's his enthusiasm. He releases this music erupting from inside him and coming out through his fingers and his mouth and shaking him around like an earthquake.

After a while I quit rasping and tweeting and beating and banging and just listened. Then Emilio put down the guitar, shook his fingers, and reached for the bottle. A line of gray had begun to show on the eastern horizon behind him.

"If you can have anything in the world entire, Roose, what is it you are wanting?" Emilio asked. He was really out of it, because if you're possessed of your faculties you know the obvious answer to that question when you're asking a wartperson. If a wartperson could have anything in the world entire, he'd choose smooth skin.

"I don't know, man," I said. "How about you?"

"I am going to the States is my big wish," Emilio replied. "I have *uma tia*—"

"An aunt," I said.

"I have an aunt living in L.A.," he said. "And many brasileiro friends who are making the *música* there. If I am getting enough money, I am living with her in L.A. and making the *música* also."

You could make it, man, I thought. It must be a tough business, but you could make it. You're that good.

Emilio took something out of his back pocket. "See, Roose, I am having my passport all ready for going."

I opened the little green booklet. There he was in his passport photo. Dark coat, dark tie, his curly hair brushed perfectly all around his incredible head. Beneath the smiling face was the name in large black print, EMILIO HERMES JAGUARIBA. That same enthusiastic, hopeful smile was there as in real life. Everybody wants to go to the States. It's the promised land.

I handed Emilio back his passport. "I wish ya luck, Emilio," I said. "I've got a ticket to get back to the States, but I'm afraid I won't get to use it. Maybe I'll sell it to you cheap," I said.

Emilio handed me the bottle. "Roose," he said, "you my big friend."

"Great friend," I said. "You and I are great friends, Emilio."

"You are my great big friend, Roose," he said. "I play something for you. I play your request."

"Okay," I said. I asked if he knew any of the songs from *Orfeo Negro*.

"I am knowing all of thems," Emilio replied. He took one last pull on the bottle and flung it out into space. I followed the arc of the bottle, and that's when I noticed they'd turned off the floodlights around Christ the Redeemer. It had gotten light enough so you could see Him. He looked a lot farther away without the lights on Him. It was funny, though: Light coming from somewhere was shining on the top of His head and both of His hands, forming just the faintest pyramid in the gray dawn.

Emilio stood and held his guitar. He's such a little shrimp boat, I guess maybe I am his "big" friend. He walked as he played that song "A *Felicidade*" that Bolão had played so beautifully. Emilio played it differently, and a lot sadder. Maybe it was just a different version. I thought of the Eighth of May kegger, when Bolão was singing and Jen was standing between my legs, leaning back against my chest, holding my hands over her breasts, and I was translating the song in her ear. I could feel her big strong breasts in my hands, and on the backs of my hands I could feel her smooth palms.

"'*Tristeza não tem fim*,'" Emilio sang, "'*felicidade sim*.'" "'Sadness has no end, happiness does.'"

"'Happiness is like a drop of dew in the petal of a flower,'" he sang. "'It shines quietly, then it trembles lightly and falls like a tear of love.

"'Happiness is like a feather the wind carries off through the air. It flies so lightly, but it has a short life—it needs the wind to blow forever.

"The happiness of the poor seems like the big delusion of *Carnavál*. The people work a whole year for a minute of dreaming—to play a king or a pirate or a gardener. And everything's finished on Wednesday.

"'My happiness is sleeping in the eyes of my girl. It's like this night—passing, passing, looking for morning, speaking low. She wakes up cheerful as the day, giving me kisses of love.

"'*Tristeza não tem fim,*'" Emilio sang one last time, "'*felicidade sim.*'" "Sadness has no end, happiness does."

It moved me more than I'd been ready for, and I had to get up and walk around a little to clear my head.

Emilio was standing looking at the sun that had begun to crown, like a baby's head, breaking its way into the world. I hoped things would begin to happen better for him than they had so far. He turned then and began to play a happier song. It was the song Orfeo played to wake up the sun.

I started dancing like Bolão had taught me—my back straight, my ass in the air like I was impaled on a stalk of sugarcane. The sun had come up enough to turn the sky blue and the earth to all its natural colors. What a beautiful place the world is! I thought. What a beautiful place, in spite of everything! I danced all around our little level spot, and as Emilio finished I came to the western edge where the mountain dropped off into deep-green forest that ran for miles.

"Hey, Roose!" Emilio yelled from behind me. "Look out, man!" he said. "You are falling one long time before you land if you are falling from there!"

I looked over the edge. Yeah, I thought, it's a long way down. I knew this drop well. This was the cliff I fell from in my dreams.

Sunday afternoon, July 28, 1968

Emilio and I got drunk again last night. Everybody in the *Estação* got drunk and me especially. All day I've suffered, as well I deserve to suffer.

The evening started fine—it started beautifully, in fact—when I went down to where Agostinho and Jardelina stay to give their two boys Eastern Washington State College T-shirts. The shirts are way too big for five- and six-year-olds, of course, but I figured they could wear them for nightshirts, since it's colder and damper where they stay. The boys were all excited and wanted "Roose! Roose!" to stick around so they wouldn't have to go to sleep. Agostinho said they could stay up and teach me their bedtime song.

So Ubaldino and Inácio sat on their straw mat in their enormous new shirts and taught me their song. *"Pal-ma, pal-ma, pal-ma,"* they sang as they clapped their hands. Then, *"pé, pé, pé,"* they sang as they stamped their feet. Then, *"Roda, roda, roda,"* as they turned in a circle on their tiny little butts. Then they made crabs out of their hands and walked the crabs through the air until it was time for the crabs to turn into fish as they sang, *"Caranguejo peixe é!"* They sang the last part several times, and when they turned their crabs into fish on the final verse, they swam the fish over to attack me.

I guessed the fish were sharks or piranha from the way the kids were pummeling me. "It's the attack of the crab-fish people!" I yelled in English. "Socorro! Socorro!" "Help! Help!"

Agostinho and Jardelina yelled at the giggling kids and told them to behave, or they'd have to go to sleep right then. So the boys piled off me and went back to their sleep spots.

I then sang them the "Cadalina, Madalina" song, which comprises my entire musical legacy from Mom and Dad. It's the only camping song we ever sang—and a good thing for the forests of the Great Inland Northwest too, because the Russell family was not blessed musically. I sang the verses in Portuguese and made all the gestures I could think to make. "Cadalina, Madalina, Lukensteiner, Wallendiner," I sang. "Hogan, Logan, Bogan was her name."

Then I went through a verse in Portuguese. "She had two teeth in her mouth. One pointed north and the other pointed south." And I made a face and used my fingers for snaggle teeth. It cracked them up. "She had two hairs on her head. One was living and one was dead." Quite a few people had come to sit around us by then, so I taught them all the chorus. "Cadalina, Madalina, Lukensteiner, Wallendiner, Hogan, Logan, Bogan was her name," we all sang.

I finished up with a verse not inappropriate: "She had a lot of warts on her chest—and everywhere!" I added—"some just ugly and some grotesque." That brought the house down. And through the sizable crowd of sitters and standers strode Natalina serving coffee, followed by her helpers Senhor Félix, Dona Amélia, Dona Gabriela, and Professora Sofia.

Rafael, the little werewolf guy, asked me if that was a children's song in the States. I explained that it was a camping song. Then I explained about camping and about the state and national parks. Someone asked if every family in the States had a car, so I talked about families and the kind of job the father might have if he owned a certain make of car.

I told them the States was a great place because everybody had a lot of freedom to do pretty much what they wanted and that most people also had the money to do it, as long as they didn't want to do too much. I said I thought the people who lived in the small towns were the most free. I said, for example, that a guy like me in the States could go to college on a government loan and work a part-time job and have a buck in his pocket for enough gas to ride his motorcycle out on the little blacktop roads through the wheat fields around midnight when he'd finished studying. That he might ride slow and turn off his headlight so the night would be completely black all around him and he could see the stars better. Pretty soon he'd ride back to town, I said, probably never meeting another vehicle the whole ride. He'd pull into an all-night service station and put fifteen cents in the pop machine and get a bottle of pop and stand and talk to the attendant about baseball or motorcycles as they watched the bugs flying in the lights.

I was about to gag on my own nostalgia, but I couldn't stop. It was a good thing for us all that Emilio began to play a samba very lightly on his guitar. "They have a lot of excellent music in the States," Emilio said in Portuguese. "But I think they could also use some excellent Brazilian samba there." Then Rafael begn to hit his tiny coffee cup with his spoon. We were about to experience a samba eruption when Senhor Félix said we should take our party into the dining room so Ubaldino and Inácio could go to sleep.

When we got to the dining room, Emilio started right in on a song and everybody got with him, especially a teenaged guy named Raimundo, who'd had both his legs snipped off by a train as a kid when he fell asleep across the tracks.

Rafael, the little werewolf guy, had a drum, and rhythm was just pouring out of him as he pounded away. People were blowing whistles, knocking on wood blocks, ringing bells. One guy had about a six-foot bowed stick with a wire strung end to end, and he was thumping the wire and making sounds like a bass. The guy who carries Adelino was playing a tuba. I grabbed a fork from the table where I sat and started beating on my saucer, getting a bigger sound than you do with those little-bitty coffee spoons. I was hanging right in there with the samba beat. The Portuguese word for fork is *garfo*, and it's very difficult not to be transported into higher aesthetic realms when you're playing an instrument whose name sounds like one of the Marx Brothers.

Things reached an incredible pitch in a matter of minutes. Senhor Félix, no doubt "the samba priest" in his heyday, was drumming on the table with his wrist stumps. Jardelina was dancing with Agostinho, who'd been set on a table. Dona Amélia, Professora Sofia, and Natalina returned with bottles of *pinga*, which they poured into our coffee cups.

I looked around at all the dancing, singing, playing people. *Carnavál* is many months away but they talk about it all the time, the way kids in the States talk about Christmas. *Carnavál* is a big thing for Brazilians, and, like the song says, especially for the poor. They say the samba schools are already practicing, and I saw the Banda de Ipanema practicing myself.

That's when it came to me. We were a real band! We were A *Banda dos Mudados!* Why not? If Ipanema can have a band, why not the *Estação?*

I jumped up waving my arms. "Hold it!" I yelled. "Hold it! We're a band!" I yelled. "We're a real band just like A Banda de Ipanema!" I raised my empty cup. "I think we should be A Banda dos Mudados! And I think we should practice and march in the *Carnavál* parade!"

Everyone was silent, and all of a sudden I realized I had never heard a soul in the *Estação* utter the word *mudados*. Oh, Christ, I thought, as I looked from face to face. Out of the silence came a howl from back in the kitchen. Adelino was sitting on a table where someone had set him by the big cooking pots. "A Banda dos Mudados!" he shouted. "I will lead the march!" Then he started hitting the pot behind him with a big soup spoon.

Agostinho shouted it: "A Banda dos Mudados!" Senhor Félix raised both his stumps: "A Banda dos Mudados!" Dona Gabriela stood and started dancing with her arms in the air: "A Banda dos Mudados," she sang over and over. Then everyone was shouting it, and the music started again.

I had another idea. I jumped up, ran to my nook, grabbed all my EWSC shirts and ran back as fast as I could. "Hold it! Hold it!" I yelled again. "We've got uniforms!"

I gave everyone a shirt until my supply ran out. I took mine off and gave it to Dona Gabriela and helped her on with it. Since she was blind, she wouldn't know it had been mine and wouldn't think it might give her warts. People stopped dancing and put on their shirts, then they got right back into it again.

Dona Amélia, Professora Sofia, and Natalina danced around pouring everyone more *pinga*. We'd awakened all the kids in the *Estação* and they stood at the edge of the dining area looking at us like we'd gone nuts. But you could see they wanted to join in. Jardelina signaled her two boys to come on, and when they broke into a run the other kids followed. Inácio pushed Ubaldino out of the way and got to my lap first. And when Ubaldino bumped Dona Gabriela, she grabbed him up and started dancing. "I know how to make a little monkey dance!" she said. And Ubaldino broke into a big smile and began dancing in her arms.

We made music and danced and drank till all the kids fell asleep and began toppling off their chairs and people's laps onto the floor.

Natalina had coffee for us when we finished. We drank it, but mostly we passed the *pinga* bottle around. I was overflowing with all kinds of good feelings. I'd felt completely accepted all evening by everybody in the place. These people let their kids crawl all over me, they passed me their bottles to drink from, then took the bottles back and drank themselves. They *touch* me without batting an eye, even though I'm so ugly I can hardly stand touching myself.

I let all the feelings out. I told the guys how grateful I was to have found people like them. I told them about Bolão and his folks, about Dr. Bertão and Dona Anna and her doctor friend and how kind they'd all been to me, and how I'd run from them because I couldn't have faced the world where everyone was perfect and had perfect skin.

Natalina came up and put her fat, funny arm around my shoulder. I hadn't even noticed she was there. Emilio asked me to tell them more about the States, so I told them about Nine Mile Falls and Spokane, then about the Olympic Peninsula, Glacier Park, Yellowstone. We kept passing the bottle, including Natalina on each pass, until the bottle was empty. We said good night then, and shook hands all around. "Good night, Roose," said Emilio. "I am for sure going to the States now that you say these things. Maybe I not going to L.A. Maybe I going to a more small place where there is not so many brasileiros making the *música*."

I told him I thought that was an excellent idea, and we all parted company.

Except for me and Natalina. I'm so ashamed and embarrassed about this I can hardly bear even to write about it. My head lowers automatically when I think about it. I'd certainly had too much to drink and I was overflowing with loving feelings—which doesn't excuse anything! And Natalina had taken five or six belts of *pinga* herself—but Christ, she's retarded, for God's sake!

To make a short, sickening story even shorter, but no less sickening: Natalina reached up and put her arm around my waist and I reached down and set my hand on her shoulder and we walked to where she sleeps.

I can't go on! I can't even write about it, I make myself so sick in retrospect. At least we didn't make love. "Make love!" What a fucking joke! I don't care how bad off I am, how horny, how much I miss Jen. Natalina is a retarded dwarf! I nearly took advantage of a drunk, retarded, fat, sweet little dwarf who gets joy out of serving people coffee.

Anyway, in the middle of sloppy, *pinga*-breathed kisses, panting and humping, I was suddenly standing outside myself, looking down at the thing I'd become. It was flopped down there on the straw mat, grunting like a boar, about to fuck a retarded dwarf.

Natalina doesn't need to be ashamed. I doubt if anyone ever taught her to take pride in her behavior—other than her coffee-serving behavior. But I ought to be ashamed. I claim to want to think of myself as a straight-backed man.

I pulled myself together, got to my knees, gave Natalina a hug and told her "*boa noite,*" and that I was afraid I'd drunk too much and was about to be sick. She wanted to help me—God, what a sweet soul!—but I told her I needed to be sick alone.

And was I sick! Sick of myself, when I found half a bottle of *pinga*, and sick all over my body this morning, after sitting up outside most of the rest of the night drinking and looking all over the sky for three stars in a pyramid that might make me feel forgiven for being such as asshole. Forgiven and loved.

A few minutes ago, I got a house call from Doctor Duck. He's the old guy with the flattened head and broken jaw and lips enlarged and shaped like a duck's bill. He came walking slowly up the path with a lantern in one hand and a steaming pot of tea in the other. He set down his lantern and teapot and took an old blue metal cup out of the pocket of his old wool sport coat and poured tea for me. He and his wife had heard I was sick from the *festa* the night before, he said, and his wife, Dona Teresinha, had made me some herb tea. I knew right away his wife was the lady with the face-wide nose. I bet they hadn't heard I was sick, I bet they heard me barfing all the way down on their level.

I was already feeling a little better, since I'd made a promise to myself that I would never again allow myself to become so desperate and low. So Doctor Duck found me fairly receptive.

He said his name was Sebastião de Los Rios, that he'd been adopted by a good family when he was a boy in São Paulo and they'd sent him to all the best schools, including the Catholic College of Medicine. He speaks perfect English, but with quite an accent. He didn't graduate, because the other students ridiculed him, and with the help of the faculty ran him out. So he came to Rio, where he lived as a *mudado* and continued his medical studies. He asked me to come visit his library.

The upshot of it all was that he was pretty sure that the things growing on me weren't common warts. I didn't tell him I'd heard that speculation before. He asked if he might have a tissue sample to examine, and before he could get out his scalpel I pinched off a nice, fat wart with my fingernails and held it until he got out his little bit of newspaper. "Here, Doctor," I said. "There's plenty more where that came from."

Doctor Duck said he'd examine it and let me know his findings. He told me that there was a samba school coming to the *Estação* to dance, and that some of the people would also do *macumba*. He said I might think it strange for a man of science to say it, but he knew absolutely that many dermatological manifestations were of psychosomatic origin and could be cured by suggestion. I should have told him that was no big news to me, and that I knew a dermatologist back home who would love to meet him. He wanted to encourage me to allow him to tell the *macumbista* to prepare an exorcism rite for me. "Fine," I said. "I'll send out for a chicken. Just let me know when to cut its head off."

Doctor Duck put his hand on my leg and refilled my teacup. "That's the spirit, my boy," he said. "A chicken won't be necessary, but that's certainly the spirit."

Later

That thieving little fuck Emilio stole my plane ticket. I knew he did it. I'm glad I couldn't find his radio, and I would have pounded his pinhead flat if I'd been able to find him.

I was getting out a traveler's check to give him to cash for me, and while I was into my stuff I thought I'd see exactly how much the return ticket was worth. I looked all over for it. I took everything out of my bags and spread it over my bed. I pulled the bed out from the wall to see if the ticket had slipped behind. I got in a frenzy. The little *coruja* looked down at me like I was nuts.

To take a break and pull myself together I walked down to return Doctor Duck's teapot and cup. He showed me his library with a lot of pride. He and his wife have about thirty old mildewed books in English, French, Portuguese, German, and even one in Latin. That's a pretty nice library for folks who live in a cave.

Doctor Duck pointed out his old microscope and there was my wart—a slice of it, anyway—on a microscope slide. He told me he thought my warts were fibrous tumors. If that were the case, he said, the *macumba* would be of no help. He and Dona Teresinha told me about *macumba*, and how they'd seen miraculous cures. "Not miracles, mind you," the doctor said. "But amazing examples of the power of suggestion—faith, if you will," he said. Mostly, he said, the cured people had been victims of emotional trauma. They were mute or unable to use one of several physically perfect limbs.

"We have also seen what appear to be diseases of the skin vanish overnight," Dona Teresinha said in Portuguese. Then shyly but with pride she said she was a *macumbista*.

I pinched off a wart from the other side of my body. "Here, Doctor," I said, handing it to him. "Here's one from a different area. See what it tells you."

The old guy's face lit up as he held out his saucer and I dropped the wart in.

I turned the conversation to people in the *Estação*, and quickly got around to Emilio. They said he was a fine boy, that he never cheated the people he worked for. In the ten years they'd known him his big dream has always been to go to the States. "Has he shown you his passport?" Dona Teresinha asked. I told her he had.

I'd gone back to my place when Doctor Duck came hustling up the path. "Roose! Roose!" he said. "This tissue *is* different from the other. I haven't determined its nature, but perhaps I will be able to do so." He was going to say more, I think, but he noticed the cellophane tape I'd just put on to keep the wart out of my right eye. He moved close and peered at it.

"Take a look," I said. "I don't mind."

He lifted the tape and the wart fell over my eye. It felt kind of like a wet leaf. He held it in his fingers and felt its thickness—about a sixteenth of an inch. He tugged on it a little where it grows out of the skin at the end of my eyebrow. I could feel the pull deep inside my head. "I think we can trim this away for you without problem," Doctor Duck said.

"That would be fine," I replied. "I'd be very grateful, and I'd save money on tape."

Doctor Duck smiled and patted my shoulder. "That is the spirit, Roose," he said.

So we walked down to his place and I sat on a wooden stool beside the table where he had his microscope. Dona Teresinha cleaned the wart with a cloth dipped in alcohol, then she held another cloth lightly over my eye as the doctor went to work. I could feel him holding the leaf part of the wart away from its base with his cold tweezers, and I could feel his scalpel slice. I had no pain at all, but both Doctor Duck and Dona Teresinha let out yells. Then I felt the blood, and I swear I could feel the pumping deep in my head where the pressure had been when he tugged on the wart earlier.

Dona Teresinha kept the cloth over my eye, but she'd moved away so far she had to reach a full arm's length to do it. With my other eye I saw the line of blood across her faded cotton dress. It wasn't isolated spatters of blood, it was a heavy streak. Then in just a second blood broke over Doctor Duck's hand, then the cloth was soaked and the Doctor told Dona Teresinha to run get another. I still didn't feel any pain, just the pumping feeling deep in my head.

"We are encountering something very strange here, Roose," Doctor Duck said. "These should not bleed as they do."

"*Muito misterioso,*" I said.

"Yes, my boy," the Doctor replied. "Very mysterious. That's the spirit."

Blood was all over my face and running down my T-shirt. Dona Teresinha came with a towel and started mopping. I could tell she was a little shaken, so I spoke as calmly as I could through the towel. "The ones I pull off with my fingers hardly bleed at all," I said.

"That's so," grunted Doctor Duck as he applied a great deal of pressure to the area of my right eyebrow. "So we must assume we have encountered already three different manifestations of this growth."

I could feel his big thumb pressing on the wart stump. I was beginning to get weak. It had begun to take a lot of effort just to keep my good eye open. The inside of my head was pounding like surf.

"Don't worry, my boy," Doctor Duck said. "We will soon have this stopped."

The old guy was strong. It felt like he was about to punch his thumb through my skull. He walked me to a ledge where he made me lie down as he kept the pressure on.

Dona Teresinha washed my face and neck with another towel, a wet one, and in a minute or two the doctor pulled his thumb away. All I felt was relief from the pressure. In a few seconds I felt a big, soft pad go over my eye, then hands held my head up as other hands wrapped strips of cloth around my head to hold the pad.

"There you are, Roose," Doctor Duck said. "It's nearly stopped bleeding. We will keep it tightly wrapped a little longer."

"I'm blind!" I whined.

They both laughed, and I felt fingers spreading the cloth strips so I could see a little out of my good eye.

"Thank you, Doctor! Thank you, Nurse!" I said. "You've restored my sight."

They laughed again. Poor Doctor Duck—his sportcoat and shirt were soaked in blood, his face was bloody, his old rimless glasses looked like they'd been fashionably tinted a deep, rich red. They pulled up chairs and talked to me until the weak, dizzy feeling went away and I sat up. They invited me to be their guest at the big *feijoada* dinner for the samba school Friday night. All that means is I'll sit with them. But what else have they got to give except their kindness and graciousness? I accepted the invitation and thanked them for trying to help me. Dona Teresinha said she'd get me a white robe for the *macumba* ceremony.

I headed back to my place then, saying I wanted to change my shirt before supper, which was certainly true. But what I wanted to do first was search Emilio's stuff while everyone was eating. And that's exactly what I did.

I checked to see he was nowhere around, then, with my lantern low, I went through everything he owns—everything he didn't have with him at the time. Just because I couldn't find the ticket doesn't mean he didn't steal it, though. He's probably got it with him. He's probably got the cash for it by now.

Going through his stuff made me feel funny. I'm still going to thump him good when I find him and get my ticket back—or my money. But it made me almost warm up to him again to see the great care he takes of all his instruments, and the photos of people I guess are his folks (the woman in the photo is a pinhead too) and the pictures and magazine articles on the States in his scrapbook.

It's after midnight and the little crud isn't back yet. I'd think he was already on a plane if all his instruments weren't still here.

I've got to write fast. There's an awful lot left to tell and not much time left to tell it.

A couple days ago Emilio came back to the *Estação*. He'd been gone a few days, so I'd cooled down, and I'd also begun to miss him. I followed him down the path and caught up just as he lit his lamp. Someone else had wanted to beat the little guy around and had, in fact, done quite a job of it. Both his eyes were puffy, his cheek was purple, and his lip was split. He said he'd had a few cru, and some guys beat him up and took the money. He said it happened to him all the time. He was acting real funny, and wouldn't look at me.

"Emilio," I said, "there's something I need to ask you."

He turned and looked me in the eye. "What, Roose?" he said. He seemed ready to cry.

I asked him if he took the ticket. "Oh, no, Roose," he said. "I am not taking your ticket." He was all agitated, and I felt bad for asking. "I am never doing such a thing," he said.

I felt like shit immediately. Emilio turned away again. I told him I was sorry I'd suspected him and that I'd leave him alone, but I was out of stuff to read and he could make a run later if he felt like it. I asked him to visit me when he got ready to see his friends again.

He avoided me until tonight, when the samba school came and we got the band together. Jesus, what a night!

I ate *feijoada* with Doctor Duck and Dona Teresinha, Agostinho, Jardelina, and the boys. And as we were all sitting down together, I realized I wanted things to stay as they were. I had a real life here with the *mudados*. It wasn't playing Triple-A ball for the Spokane Indians and being on the five o'clock sports news twice a month, but it was a life.

After dinner the samba school people got into their costumes while we all cleared the dining area. They are black as crude petroleum, and nearly all the ones who danced were beautiful and physically perfect as cut diamonds. The fat ladies dancing and clapping and singing on the sidelines were the *macumbistas*.

All the dancers and the band wore gold costumes covered with gold sequins. The band had pants and vests and the male dancers wore just the gold pants. The featured female dancers wore tiny, tiny bikini bottoms and gold-sequined flowers over their nipples, and the regular crew only slightly bigger bottoms and tiny regular bikini tops. The people are so richly black that when the music got going and everybody got all sweaty, their skin glistened as brightly in the light from the kerosene lamps as their sequinned costumes.

We played and played, and eventually everybody, including the kids, joined in the dancing. Little Natalina waddled through the crowd pouring *pinga*. I didn't feel much like drinking, so I just blew my little chrome whistle and rapped on my woodblock and watched people.

I was having a fine time, but I couldn't enjoy it like the others did. I came down a little when I realized this, thinking how different I was from these people in spite of our similarities, and yet how close I felt to some of them. Even with the darker warttops that are all I have for a complexion now, I'm still fifteen shades whiter than anyone else, and it made me feel lifeless in comparison.

By midnight, when the fat ladies—and Dona Teresinha too— reappeared in their long white dresses and white head-wrappings, the samba school began putting away their instruments. All of us from the *Estação* yelled and danced as we finished. "A Banda dos Mudados!" we all shouted. "A Banda dos Mudados! We march tomorrow!"

Emilio and I were standing together, jumping up and down. He was holding his guitar in the air, shaking it, and all of a sudden I noticed something flapping in the hole of the guitar. I grabbed the guitar and brought it close. Terror crossed Emilio's face. I saw that what I was thinking was true: the piece of paper was my plane ticket.

Things began happening fast, and out of either my or Emilio's control. It wasn't that I was drunk—I just lost my temper. I guess it was because it made me feel like a fool to think how close I'd been feeling to Emilio just a few seconds before. "You thieving little cocksucker!" I yelled in English. "You lying, thieving little asshole!" I held up the ticket in one hand and the guitar in the other. "*Ladrão!*" I yelled as I waved the ticket. "*Ladrão!*" "Thief! Thief!"

All of us from the *Estação* were crowded around, and the guys from the samba school and half the women began pressing in, probably hoping to see a fight. People got to pushing and shoving. Adelino went ass-over-teakettle off his table.

I was *not* going to hit Emilio with the guitar. I wasn't going to do anything with the guitar. But hands were grabbing for it and I was pulling on it, and it came down on Emilio's head. Anyone can imagine what a head like Emilio's would do to the thin rosewood back of a classical guitar. The poor guitar looked like it had been rammed by a torpedo. And Emilio's head was cut a little.

My anger turned to sorrow in a flash. I'd known since I first saw him play on the mountain that playing his guitar was how he made himself beautiful.

Senhor Félix had worked his way to us by then. "Who is this thief?" he asked.

Now here is where someone who sees this whole thing differently than I do is going to say I made my mistake. I do not believe, however, it was a mistake. I slipped the ticket in my back pocket and didn't say a word about it. Maybe I should have gone to Senhor Félix before, the minute I realized it had been stolen. Anyway, it doesn't matter now. Instead, I apologized and explained that I'd wanted to play Emilio's guitar and tried to take it from him. Emilio rubbed his head, grabbed his bashed-in guitar, and pushed off through the crowd. Finally Senhor Félix, Dona Amélia, and one of the *macumbistas* I'd recognized as Betinha's mother quelled the disturbance.

Dona Teresinha grabbed me by one arm and Doctor Duck took the other as we joined a procession led by the *macumbistas*. Dona Teresinha and the good Doctor Duck—what a loving pair. She's *so* ugly, the poor, sweet lady. I know I'm no one to talk, but at least I don't have a nose the size, shape, and nearly the color of a hefty eggplant.

As the procession headed down to a lower level I bent my head and asked Dona Teresinha what to expect. She said the *macumbistas* would pray for us to be delivered from our pain. "Someone may receive the saint. One of the saints enters the body of the devoted. Sometimes the devoted speaks the heavenly language."

Oh, my God, I thought. This is going to be worse than dunk day at the Baptist church back in Nine Mile Falls.

I thought about Betinha's mother as we walked. Her sister's probably here too, then, I said to myself. She's a *macumbista* too. I got thinking about Betinha, then right away about Jen, and my spirits began sinking lower and lower.

We were deeper into the mountain than I'd ever been. Some people carried those big white candles, others carried armloads of flowers, bowls of rice, and—I was not surprised—a few white chickens and one black rooster, and by the candlelight you could see that none of this part of the *Estação* had been finished at all. Water dripped down the walls, and that smell of rich vegetation—as if the roots of the forest grew through the walls—was thicker here than anywhere. And then I stopped myself—not than anywhere, I thought. Not thicker than in my dreams.

We walked carefully down a series of ledges and stopped where the cave floor flattened out. It wasn't easy to see in the candlelight, and I was glad the doctor had trimmed up my eye for me. The fattest of the *macumbistas* moved out in front. She was smoking a big cigar nearly as black as her skin.It looked like strips of tobacco braided into a thick tobacco rope. She began giving directions. The guys in white with the big drums walked up front to one side and the thinner women in white moved to the other side and stood like a chorus. Maybe it was the cigar in her mouth, but I couldn't understand a word the macumbista was saying. It didn't even sound to me like Portuguese.

The drums began then. It was a little like samba, but minus the joy. People put their candles and rice on ledges in the rock wall and along its base and spread their flowers around.

It got awfully dark back where we were standing. Three of the other big *macumbistas*, one of whom was Betinha's mother, also smoking cigars, joined the leader, who had begun to sway and chant and smoke the hell out of her cigar. She'd also begun to drool. Tobacco juice was running out the corners of her mouth. Soon her eyes rolled back. All four women were swaying and chanting and puffing on those cigars like there was no tomorrow.

Everybody around me began to sway and chant, so I did too. I turned to look for a friendly face, but everything was hidden in the dark. I heard all this breathing in along with the chanting and over the sound of the drums, and then I thought of the dream: the cave, the feel of swaying shapes all around me, their breathing, the darkness, the smell of being in the ground. I snapped back toward the light like I was spring-loaded.

The four *macumbistas* were puffing on their cigars and swaying and drooling, and then the leader yelled out something and women from the chorus broke out of line and headed for the crowd. One of them was Dona Teresinha—she's so short I hadn't spotted her among the other women—and she came for me. When we moved out into the clear area with the others who'd been brought forward, she tugged my shoulders down and put a white robe over my head. The drums got louder and the *macumbistas* swayed more wildly and raised their voices into a song.

I was starting to want out of there bad. The cigar smoke was burning my eyes and about to gag me, and I was scared. Mostly, though, I began to feel ashamed. Okay, so these people were devout about this crazy shit. I wasn't. Why had I stooped again to something such a big part of me was ashamed of? In a tiny place way deep inside me I'd hoped that acting like an asshole in front of God and other people acting like assholes would make me normal again.

I shook my head to get the hood off my face a little so I could see again. And what I saw made me skip a breath. Betinha stood across from me in the semicircle. At least, I thought it was Betinha. It looked like Betinha with all the life squeezed out of her. I took a quick look around and saw that all of us in the hooded robes had some physical problem. Except the girl who looked like Betinha. She was perfect physically, but there was a vacant look in her eyes and her skin had no luster.

I was at one end of the semicircle and the girl who looked like Betinha was at the other. Now some life had grown in her vacant eyes, and they were fixed on me. The main *macumbista* swayed up to Betinha, puffing on her cigar and sort of barking her song. Yipping and barking—that's what it sounded like. She blew smoke in Betinha's face.

The *macumbista* dusted Betinha with a white powder and barked at her in the language I couldn't understand. Then she slapped her lightly on both cheeks, threw her head back and howled, then slapped again. Tremors began to run through Betinha's face. Her eyes twitched, her jaw twitched. The *macumbista* let out a yip of triumph and danced back to a sort of altar where the candles and rice and flowers were.

She and the other three began to gesture at Betinha and to yip and bark for her to come to them. But Betinha—and I still wasn't sure it was Betinha—started walking toward me.

She didn't walk normally. Something was wrong with her. She didn't have any grace. But she'd begun to sweat and her skin had taken on a glow in that flickering yellow light. And the closer she got to me, the more she looked like Betinha as I'd known her. Her eyes were locked into mine and boring deep.

The *macumbistas* danced forward and surrounded us both. By then Betinha was standing about a foot from me. Her eyes fluttered a bit, then you could tell she was looking at my face. It was like her eyes made this little survey of my features—what my features might have been if they'd been visible. Then she began to shriek.

The *macumbistas* thought that was great. They yipped and barked right along with the shrieking. I didn't think it was great, though. I'd had it with *macumba* and I'd about had it with my whole ugly, sorry self. I just wanted to get the fuck out of there.

Then the girl stopped screaming and sort of wilted. Her legs buckled and I moved to catch her. But Betinha's mother beat me to it. A clear liquid brimmed over the girl's lower lip and began to flow down her chin. A gold *figa* on a gold chain flopped out the neck of her robe. It was Betinha after all.

I don't know if it was anger or shame or shock or sorrow, but tears burst from my eyes like a storm had blown up inside my head, and I let out a shriek myself and was out of there and headed up those rock ledges like the glue-footed tall toad I'm sure I appeared to be. I ran out of the *Estação* and kept running up the mountain. It was a starry night and you could see okay. But I wasn't watching where I put my feet, and I ran all the way to the very top. I really abused my feet doing it, but where I'm going I hear you don't use your feet much. People just fly around on silken wings playing their harps, occasionally making landings on the streets of gold to take a little drink from the milk and honey flowing in the gilded gutters. That's a joke! A little spirit-person humor!

My robe was flapping so loud when I crested the grade and ran out onto the packed dirt that I didn't hear Emilio singing and playing his bashed-in guitar. And he'd been playing and singing so loud he hadn't heard me huffing and flapping up the trail. He did hear me when I burst into the clearing, however. And he saw me too—a great white-winged creature in full flight come to sweep him off to the dark place where thieves were punished and pinheads forbidden to raise their voices in song. He let out a scream of fright that should have made Christ the Redeemer pull those outstretched arms of His in to cover His ears. I let out a whoop and fell backwards.

Emilio was on his knees, trying to work his way behind a rock. I whipped back the hood and stepped toward him. "Emilio," I said, "it's me, man. It's Roose." That scared him worse. I was real and I'd come to take him to the place where thieves were punished.

Like I said, there was plenty of starlight, so with the light from the stars and from the floodlights on Christ across the way it was bright as day up there. I looked down at little Emilio hiding behind his guitar and then I focused on the head-sized, jagged hole in its back. Every sorrow I'd ever felt in my whole twenty-one years swooped down like a flock of heavy birds and landed all over me. The weight of it put me on the ground. And that's where I stayed, crying just as hard as my body could cry, until I felt Emilio's hand on my shoulder and heard his voice break through the sobs thundering in my ears.

"Roose, man," he said. "You are getting your ticket back to you. What is wrong, Roose?"

"I'm okay, Emilio," I said. And I was. Things had come to me while I was crying. I understood that peace was very close if I'd only take the step and reach for it. I got to one knee and wiped my eyes with that stupid robe. Then I stood up, pulled it off, and walked to the edge of the cliff.

"Roose, no!" Emilio yelled.

I laughed and turned. "I'm not jumpin', Emilio," I said. "I'm just gettin' rid of this piece-a-shit robe." I flung it out and watched it flutter through the light, then descend into the darkness like a ghost. I pulled the beat-up plane ticket out of my pocket and walked over to Emilio and held it out. "Take this, please, Emilio," I said. "I'm sorry I made such a fuss and I'm sorry about your guitar. I want to be your great big friend again."

But Emilio didn't take the ticket. He slumped to the ground and threw his head back against the rock. He kept his head turned like he couldn't bear to look at me. "I do a terrible thing, Roose," he said.

"No, man. It's all right," I said. "I want you to have the ticket."

"I do a terrible thing," Emilio said. "I tell Senhor Félix I think you are going crazy—"

"Shit, man," I said. "You're right. I am crazy. I'm nuttier than an oven fulla banana bread."

"No," he said. "I tell a lie. I tell him about those people who want to help you. I say to him I think you maybe suicide yourself unless we are getting these people to save you."

"Oh," I said. I slumped down beside him. I wasn't really too bothered by it, just deflated a little from the good feeling the crying had left me with.

"I was afraid you tell Senhor Félix I thief the ticket," Emilio said. "And then all the *mudados*, they are making me leave the *Estação*."

I grabbed his chin and turned his face toward me. "Emilio," I said. "It's all right. I'm not mad at you. It's time I left the *Estação* anyway." I let go of his chin and he hung his head. I was thinking fast.

"I take the ticket and all my monies I am saving to get my exit visa and to give a little to the people for changing the ticket to my name," Emilio said. "But nobody is changing it or giving me money and taking it. Then I see some guys I am knowing downtown and they are knocking me and taking all my monies."

"Emilio," I said, "I'll exchange my ticket for one in your name. But I want you to do something for me too. Okay?"

"I am doing it, Roose," Emilio said. "You my tall friend and I am doing it for you." He told me Senhor Félix had gone to talk to the Portos while I was doing the *macumba* and that their plan was to be there when the band quit marching tomorrow and take me to a hospital where I'd have the best care.

I asked Emilio to tell Senhor Félix the two of us would go together to the little bar in Cosme Velho where the band was going to meet and that he'd keep a close watch on me so I didn't freak out before the Portos showed up. I told him I had a lot to do before I could leave and asked him to stall them the best he could after the band marched and they realized I wasn't there.

"Roose," Emilio said, "I do it all. You are betting your shoes on it."

Then I took off back down the mountain. I was psyched and getting more psyched every step I took down the path. I knew I was doing the right thing, and I know it now.

I got back to my nook, lit my lamp, and turned it low. Then I leaned back against my mossy rock wall to think a little more before I started doing things.

Later, when the *Estação* was black and soundless, I got up and went softly down to where Emilio slept. He too had his lamp burning low and was looking through his scrapbook at stuff about the States. I startled him because he was so absorbed.

"Roose," he said, "I am wanting to talk to you. You are waiting for these friends of you at the *Estação* tomorrow, or you are going somewhere your own self?"

I sat down beside him. I wanted to trust him and I wanted to feel close to another human being. "Emilio," I said, "I won't be here when they come for me. I'll be with my parents and my little brother by then."

Emilio looked down and bit his lip. "When you come to the *Estação* Senhor Félix is telling me your family are died," he said. "I am thinking this is where you are going." He lifted his head and looked at me. "I am understanding, Roose," he said. "I am having a lot of *saudade* for you—I am missing you. But I tell the people you are gone to your home."

I told Emilio I'd miss him, too, then I gave him the note with the address and phone number of the fraternity house and Gordon Crookshank's name. I'd written my signature so he could copy it on the titles of the Ford, the trailer, and the Harley-Davidson, which I was giving him. I told him I'd written Crooks he was coming and to please help him with the titles and whatever stuff of mine he wanted. I said I had some money I was giving him, but I wouldn't have it till I got back from town. I'd put it inside my journal along with his plane ticket.

He nodded his head up and down. His eyes had gotten about the size of Ford hubcaps.

I told Emilio the journal would be on top of the mountain, hidden by the rock he'd tried to hide behind earlier in the night. I asked him please to keep the journal with him, to hold on to it a few years until he was a famous musician, and then he could see it got published after his biography was a best-seller. I was mostly kidding, I guess. But I would like people to know about my life, especially the end of it, which I'm going to be proud of.

"I am doing it, Roose," Emilio said as he shook my hand. "I promise it."

I've been writing about a thousand miles a minute here, and I just ran out to the entrance and saw the sun's been up awhile already. It's time to get cleaned up and head for town.

Later

I'm back. I'm up on the mountain now, and it's a beautiful day. Just me, Christ the Redeemer, the beautiful land, and the clear blue sky. All the members of A Banda dos Mudados are probably starting down the hill about now. All except me.

I got dressed in my best duds, put the *figa* Betinha gave me around my neck, shouldered my leather bag, and took a taxi to the Copacabana Palace, where I exchanged my ticket for one in the name of Emilio Hermes Jaguariba at their travel agency.

I felt good riding through the streets. People who caught sight of me stared, and the poor driver kept crossing himself and mumbling to the pictures of saints stuck to his dash, but I only nodded and smiled at the people whose eyes met mine. I was proud of myself, and felt my back getting straighter all the time. My parents didn't raise me to live a life like this. Sure, a man has to endure. But how much? I have a choice here.

We all know what's right to do, I thought, as I rode through the noisy, crowded streets. It's just that we can't very often muster up the courage to do it. I knew what I was doing was right, and by the time I'd walked through the hotel lobby my back was straight as backs get.

I told both the lady at the travel agency and the lady at the *cambio* please not to be alarmed by my appearance. I said I wasn't a "monstro," just an ordinary young man with a temporary skin condition.

I mailed a letter to Jen from the hotel. I told her I was going into the interior to seek my fortune and couldn't say when I'd be back. I asked her to always remember I'd loved her in case I got ate by a snake or something and never returned.

On the way back to the *Estação* in another taxi, I got to wondering how much it would hurt and how tough it would be to do. I got scared that maybe I didn't really have the guts. But I'm okay now that I'm up here. And the sun's shining off Christ's head and His fists, making three points of light in a pyramid. I'll be beautiful there no matter what I look like. And I'll be home with Mom and Dad and Jesse.

It won't be hard. I've done it a lot of times in dreams. So what if it hurts for a few seconds. That's nothing compared to how my whole life hurts now all the time. It'll be a snap. Easy as falling off a mountain.